HE FELT AS IF HE WERE ... ANIMALS....

Someone reached out and ran a hand along his back, tugging at his jacket. "Nice suit."

Andy practically jumped down the next three stairs.

"Hey, suit," a hoarse female voice drawled. "Aren't you afraid of being out here all by yourself?"

Andy concentrated on reaching the bottom of the frozen escalator. A gray-bearded man dressed in a worn U.S. Army uniform stepped into Andy's way as he neared the bottom. "Where you going, suit?" the soldier asked.

"Home." Andy heard his voice quaver.

"You sure? You think you're safe? Let me tell you, suit. Nobody's safe."

Andy took a deep breath and brushed past the soldier.

"Run away, little suit," someone called out from behind him. "Run home to your safe corp sell-out...."

SHADOWRUN

JUST COMPENSATION

Robert N. Charrette

A ROC BOOK

ROC
Published by the Penguin Group
Penguin Books USA Inc., 375 Hudson Street,
New York, New York 10014, U.S.A.
Penguin Books Ltd, 27 Wrights Lane,
London W8 5TZ, England
Penguin Books Australia Ltd, Ringwood,
Victoria, Australia
Penguin Books Canada Ltd, 10 Alcorn Avenue,
Toronto, Ontario, Canada M4V 3B2
Penguin Books (N.Z.) Ltd, 182–190 Wairau Road,
Auckland 10, New Zealand

Penguin Books Ltd, Registered Offices:
Harmondsworth, Middlesex, England

First published by Roc, an imprint of Dutton Signet,
a division of Penguin Books USA Inc.

First Printing, January, 1996
10 9 8 7 6 5 4 3 2 1

Series Editor: Donna Ippolito
Cover: Jim Thitsen

 REGISTERED TRADEMARK—MARCA REGISTRADA

For the cast and crew of one of the strangest road shows it's ever been my pleasure to know, the Fredonian Air and Space Administration. Long may you fly.

NORTH

TSIMSHIAN • ATHABASKAN COUNCIL • ALGONKIAN-MANITOU COUNCIL

Vancouver Island • Vancouver • Edmonton • Saskatoon

Pacific Ocean • Seattle • Calgary • SALISH-SHIDHE COUNCIL • Regina • Winnipeg

Pomona • Salem • Spokane • Helena • Butte • SIOUX NATION • Bismarck • Fargo • Duluth

TIR TAIRNGIRE • Boise • Idaho Falls • Billings • Sheridan • Rapid City • Minneapolis • St. Paul

Eureka • Reno • Salt Lake City • Provo • Cheyenne • Sioux Falls • Des Moines

San Francisco • CALIFORNIA FREE STATE • UTE NATION • Boulder • Denver • Omaha • Kansas City

Bakersfield • Las Vegas • Colorado Springs • Topeka

Santa Barbara • PUEBLO CORPORATE COUNCIL • Pueblo • Wichita

Los Angeles • Phoenix • Santa Fe • Albuquerque • Amarillo • Tulsa • Oklahoma City • Little Rock

San Diego • Yuma • CONFEDERATED AMERICAN STATES (C.A.S.)

Tucson • El Paso • Roswell • San Angelo • Ft. Worth • Dallas • Shreveport

Pacific Ocean • Chihuahua • San Antonio • Austin • Houston

Culiacan • AZTLAN • Monterrey • Corpus Christi

La Paz • Durango • Ciudad Victoria

AMERICA

FEDERAL DISTRICT

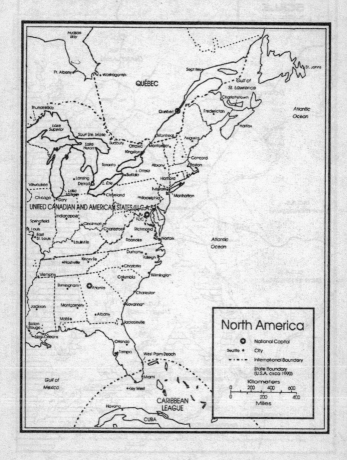

Hudson Bay

Ft. Albany • Waskaganish

QUÉBEC

Sept Iles

St. Johns

Gulf of St. Lawrence

Charlottetown

Thunder Bay

Quebec

Fredericton

Atlantic Ocean

Halifax

Lake Superior

Sault Ste. Marie

Montreal

Augusta

Sudbury

Ottawa

Montpelier

Lake Huron

Kingston

Concord

Toronto

Albany

Boston

L. Ontario

Milwaukee

Lansing

Buffalo

Hartford

Detroit

L. Erie

Lake Michigan

New York

Chicago

Gary

Cleveland

Manhattan

Philadelphia

UNITED CANADIAN AND AMERICAN STATES (U.C.A.S.)

Springfield

Indianapolis

W.D.C.

St. Louis

Cincinnati

Charleston

Richmond

East St. Louis

Louisville

Roanoke

Norfolk

Atlantic Ocean

Durham

Nashville

Knoxville

Raleigh

Memphis

Charlotte

Columbia

Wilmington

Birmingham

Atlanta

Jackson

Montgomery

Albany

Charleston

Savannah

Baton Rouge

Mobile

Jacksonville

New Orleans

Orlando

Tampa

West Palm Beach

Gulf of Mexico

Miami

Key West

CARIBBEAN LEAGUE

Havana

CUBA

North America

⊕ National Capital

Seattle • City

–·–·– International Boundary

········· State Boundary (U.S.A. circa 1990)

Kilometers

0   200   400   600

0   200   400

Miles

FEDERAL DISTRICT
OF COLUMBIA

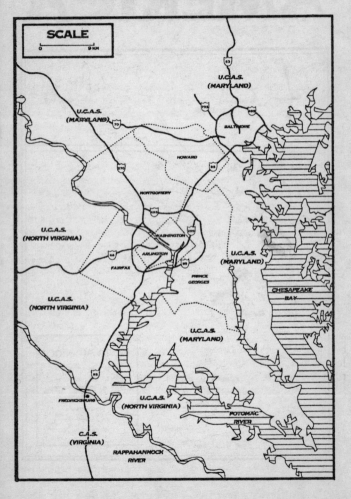

THE COMPENSATION ARMY

The occupation of the Federal District of Columbia by the so-called Compensation Expedition Force, or Compensation Army, begins its third month today. These homeless and forgotten "soldiers in the army of justice" have come to the Federal District to dramatize their long-ignored demands. The Army has come not to fight, but to lobby, to march, to form picket lines, and to insist that the compensation owed them be paid—and paid immediately.

Most of these soldiers are not warriors; they are just ordinary people who believe they have been taken advantage of. The first to arrive in FDC were folk who had actually endured displacement from what are now the Native American Nations. These unfortunates were ousted from their homes and lands nearly forty years ago, when the old United States ceded most of its western states to the emerging and magically triumphant Native American Nations. Following the Treaty of Denver in 2018, the federal government promised compensation to the refugees. With the end of the old U.S.A. in 2035, the government of the new United Canadian and American States restricted those promises to all persons who originally resided in old U.S. lands north of the 38th parallel, leaving the Confederate American States to care for the rest. Both U.S. successor governments have denied restitution to any persons displaced from the now Free State of California.

Today's Comp Army is more than a few old men and women. Every day new "soldiers" arrive in the District—friends, relatives, dependents, and sympathizers of those already here. The scattered tents and shanties have become a low-tech sprawl coating the FDC like a mold. Conditions in these makeshift communities are bad and growing worse. The federal government issues promises, claiming that it is addressing the issue. Yet no real relief appears under way, and the mood among the Comp Army grows bleaker and more desperate.<<<<<

1

Andy was a shadowrunner.

All his friends knew. He liked the way they looked impressed when he told them about his adventures. Except for Biddy Blackwell. Nothing much impressed Biddy.

This run was going to be one of the good ones; he could tell already from the way the meet was going. Mr. Johnson—not his real name, of course—was laying it out with just enough vagueness that Andy knew the story was pretty straight. When the details got real specific, it meant the scam was on. Andy took in everything the Johnson gave them, filing it on his headware.

The Johnson said he represented a consortium of small businessmen trying to make it in the Anacostia Barrens, the worst turf in the DeeCee sprawl. Brave souls—if they existed. Problem was, the Barrens were hotter than usual. The Halfies, top go-gang in the area, were rampaging. The go-gangers were thumping places up and down the Anacostia Barrens, everything from chop shops to clinics. The police were looking the other way—standard—and the locals were terrified—also standard. Word was that somebody had stirred up the Halfies. Mr. Johnson wanted protection. He also wanted to know who was really responsible—and why they were doing it.

Johnsons were never what they said they were, but Andy took the run anyway. Being used to duplicity from employers, he retreated to his Appaloosa and set the autopilot to drive so that he could do other things.

The fixer from whom he'd gotten the Ferrari Appaloosa had said it was "surplus," which for such a high-demand vehicle meant it was hot. It was hot all right, and not just because it had been liberated from some military somewhere. Sheena the Appaloosa was the fastest armored vehicle on wheels. Street word said that wiz rigger Willie Williams swore by Appaloosas for high-threat runs, and now Andy understood why. The Appaloosa, with the custom shell that made Sheena look like a workhorse delivery truck rather than the thoroughbred predator she was, had cost him just about all the cred he'd racked up from his last three runs. But she was worth it. Jacked into Sheena's board, Andy could fight a small war or outrace just about any corp or FedPol pursuit car. Sheena was *meltdown* hot.

But he didn't need the Appaloosa's combat capabilities just now. No amount of real-world firepower meant drek in the Matrix; cyberspace had its own rules. But Andy was hot there, too. He started with turtle stuff, priming a herd of gophers and unleashing them on the media and public records. While they were hunting, Andy jacked and did a little direct prospecting in the FedPol database. He slipped past the outer IC shell with an ease and sleaze that would have impressed even FastJack. Not that cracking it was hard; the police department computers handled too much data to put it all behind serious IC, and the Intrusion Countermeasures protecting the incoming reports and complaints were light, little more than speed bumps for deckers of Andy's or FastJack's skills. Andy collected copies of every file on Halfie activities, dumped them into his bag, and flew back to his couch aboard Sheena to do a sort where he'd be safe from prying eyes or inadvertent discovery. Andy didn't like chance encounters in the Matrix; too much trouble and no reasonable expectation of gain.

Secure in the womb of the Appaloosa, he dumped his loot into a sorter. As the gophers came back, he added their finds. Monitoring the returns, he tweaked the search parameters as likely threads starting shaping up. The Johnson came back as a cipher—like *that* was a surprise?—so Andy looked for connections among the Halfies' targets. Mr. Johnson's interests should show up there. All Andy had to do was recognize them.

There were chopshops on the target list, and that didn't fit with the Halfies' interests. Street word said that they controlled most of the shops in the Barrens. Why hit your own income sources? As a cover, maybe. There was no doubt the Halfies were spreading their good cheer around, but they seemed to be thumping some targets harder than others. How bad were the chopshops hit? Not bad at all. The cover theory was starting to look good.

So who was taking it on the chin the hardest? A quick sort

by level of damage turned up a list that had a lot of free clinics and doc-in-a-boxes on it. Real nest-fouling stuff to trash the local medical care, and not like the territorial Halfies at all. A closer look showed that the go-gangers' choice of clinics wasn't random; for example, not a single DocWagon operation had been thumped. Andy scented a clue and popped into the Matrix to run down a few leads. He came back with the connection he was looking for: all the wrecked clinics were either sponsored by or ran programs funded by Biotechnics, the genengineering and pharmaceutical multinational. A quick check of media databases showed no similar rash of attacks on Biotechnics clinics in any other cities.

What made the Anacostia clinics different? Andy bet that Mr. Johnson, or his bosses, knew. A direct Matrix run against Biotechnics was contraindicated just yet, so Andy picked a thumped clinic at random and went after its files, looking for anything unusual. He found records for three test programs. A second clinic's records only held one match: a drug treatment pilot program for something called Azadone, trademark still pending. It was a conclusion-jump, but Andy felt sure that Azadone was at the heart of Mr. Johnson's concerns. He'd check it out later.

Right now, Sheena was beeping that they'd nearly reached their destination. That was fine by Andy. He switched jacks and took over Sheena's control. This run wasn't going to be solved with just a little Matrix decking. They never were. That also was fine by him; he liked a good mix of action. It was time to move on to the next step. He nosed the Appaloosa into the first available parking spot after crossing Maple Avenue.

"Take care of yourself, Sheena," he told the Appaloosa as he dismounted, activating her anti-theft routines. Fairfax wasn't the worst of the districts that made up the DeeCee sprawl, but this wasn't the best part of Fairfax. Even if you didn't know that from previous experience the way Andy did, you could see it in the broken streetlights, graffiti-covered walls, and boarded-over storefronts.

The night outside the Appaloosa held no secrets from him, because his eyes were Telestrian Cyberdyne 48's, built under license from Zeiss. Not the latest model, but then cybereye technology hadn't advanced much in the past ten years. The 48's weren't fully featured either; they didn't have the full thermal imaging package, just ambient light amplification.

But that was more than enough to pierce the gloom of Old Courthouse Road and note each and every one of the derelicts and streetrats huddling in the doorways and skulking in the alleys. All locals he'd seen before; they would know his rep and wouldn't bother him.

His team was waiting for him at Eskimo Nell's, their usual watering hole and gathering place. There were just two today, Buckhead and Feather; he didn't figure he'd need more. Buckhead was muscle, simple but not cheap. The ork was very, very good at what he did, but all of his personality was in his cyberware and his guns. Feather was an elf and a mage, and her style of dress was more suited to *Runner Babes* than to real shadowrunning, but what she wore—or rather, didn't wear—didn't affect her performance, so what was there to say? Besides, Andy enjoyed looking at her.

"Hoi, Boss. Whuzzappening?" It was Buckhead's standard opening line.

Andy dove right in and told them about the job he'd gotten them, and about his theory that the clinics were the focus of the violence. "We're reactive protection, but we're also supposed to find out who's behind it."

"What makes Johnson think dat all the thumpin' ain't just boys 'n girls out ta have fun?"

"You can't think that the patients and staff at the clinics are having fun," Feather said.

"We need to make a move," Andy said. He wasn't in the mood for sitting around and hashing out the possibilities. He and his runners needed a connection, and their best bet lay with the Halfies. Who would know better than the go-gangers why they were thumping their way through the Barrens? "I think we should go have a chat with some Halfies."

"I know one of their squats," Feather said, surprising Andy.

He knew she had a lot of street connections, but he hadn't figured on her knowing much about go-gangs. He was quite happy to be wrong. "Let's roll, then."

Following Feather's directions, Andy piloted the Appaloosa across the river and out into the fringes of the Anacostia Barrens. He drove slowly, as much because of the road conditions as the need to recon. They scouted the old poured-concrete building that Feather led them to, and determined that some of the go-gangers were home; it was still early for them to be out raising hell. The place was solidly built, probably why the gangers laired there. Whatever it had once been, it sported a pair of vehicle doors on one side. The only human door was on that side, too. Andy decided on the direct approach, and put Sheena's nose through the flimsy corrugated plastic of the left garage door. The building wall would cover their left flank.

Once they'd crashed through the door, Buckhead exploded from the Appaloosa with a whoop. Feather was quieter, but no less eager. Arcane energy raised her hair in a crackly static halo that would be a fright to see coming at you. Andy almost felt sorry for the scrambling Halfies—at least one of whom had been caught literally with his pants down.

Having used Sheena to crack open the Halfies' squat, Andy was willing to let Buckhead and Feather take care of the gangers. Combat just wasn't his thing. He got no jolt from it like some people did. He'd step in if he had to, but he didn't think that would be necessary. He had a good team and the opposition this early in the run wasn't likely to be anything they couldn't handle.

"We need a talker," Andy reminded his team over the commlink. There was no acknowledgment, but when the ruckus died down, Buckhead and Feather returned with one of the gangers.

"We could turn him over to the badges," Feather suggested. She had a tendency to offer the law-abiding solution. Andy figured it was just so he'd know there was one. "The FedPols will be happy to see him. Of course, if he tells us what we want to know ..."

"I ain't talking," the Halfie said. The black pigmentation on the upper half of his face almost hid his frown of determination.

"I can make him talk," Buckhead said. The ork slid his paired chrome spurs in and out of their wrist sheaths to demonstrate the method he intended to employ. It was nasty, but it might get them fast results. Life in the shadows wasn't nice.

"Do it," Andy said, "but try and keep him quiet."

The Halfie had known he was living dangerous when he took money to go thumping innocents.

Buckhead grinned and led the Halfie away. In an elapsed time of twenty minutes, exactly, he came back with an address. The address supposedly belonged to a middleman.

Andy and the team paid the guy a visit, and he proved to

be surprisingly reasonable. For a fee—that Andy would list as an expense when he billed Mr. Johnson—the fixer confirmed the Halfie's story about a simple violence-for-hire gig. The fixer couldn't confirm the power behind the job in spite of Andy's offer to double the fee, which lent credibility to the man's claim. Yet for another fee, the fixer offered them a cryptic clue. "Wanna see who's casting shadow? Drive up Wisconsin and drop anchor six south of the cathedral."

They followed the directions.

Andy remembered the building as being the offices of Micronetics, a Saeder-Krupp subsidiary, but a throbbing neon sign proclaimed it the property of Vilanni Corp. Whenever he hit a switch like this, he reminded himself of just how fast things changed in the corp world. More often than not, today's hot corner was tomorrow's washed-up loser.

The Vilanni name wasn't new to him. He'd crossed paths with them before, and he knew the corp was about as slimy as they came. Andy didn't think them above trashing clinics just to ruin a competitor's market test. The thought of ruining test markets reminded him of Vinton and the Hanging File run. The sort of thing going down in the Barrens was just Vinton's style.

But Andy's hunch and a fixer's hint that Vilanni was behind everything wouldn't be enough for his employer. Andy needed to come up with a convincing connection. There was also the little matter of determining *why* Vilanni was involved. No Johnson was ever satisfied without knowing why he'd been targeted.

Word about their hit against the Halfies would be filtering up the food chain. There would be no better time for a fast run against the Vilanni mainframe. Andy went a dozen blocks down Wisconsin and onto one of the quiet, narrow side streets of Georgetown before parking the Appaloosa and jacking in.

The Vilanni mainframe showed as a black monolith in the Matrix. It was a tough nut, but Andy knew better than to come at it head on. He tried something new, running a side program to jigger things a bit. With effortless precision he focused in on a small section of the monolith, narrowing his perception until pits on the black surface grew to pocks, then holes, and finally tunnels. He'd used one of those tunnels before, a back door set by a renegade Vilanni programmer.

Since he'd used it in the Hanging File run, the entry should have been locked and sealed, but he was pleased to see that the tinkering he'd done had worked. The door remained operable. Inside, he zoomed to Vinton's private space and started nosing around the Vilanni exec's files. It wasn't long before he struck paydata: a list of clinics, Biotechnics clinics.

While he was nosing through the list, a time-date stamp clicked next to one of the names. That was the cue for the file to activate a slave routine. Andy scoped the program. Somewhere in Vilanni HQ, a call was being made. Andy slapped a tag on it just before the connection broke. He kept digging while waiting for the tag to come back. He still hadn't managed to find anything juicy by the time it returned, trailing a string of connections that were more than enough to cut out a tag that lacked the advantage of getting on board at the start. The final destination of the call was in the Anacostia Barrens, and all the tag's message-backfeed feature held was the address of the clinic and a time-date stamp—the same as the one on the list. Andy had discovered the time and place of the next thump.

It was decision time. Did he cut short his run against the Vilanni mainframe and lead his team in an intercept of the thump about to go down, or did he stay in the system to take advantage of his penetration and go after incriminating evidence that would put an end to all the thumps? If he pulled out, the system would be tougher to crack when he got back—but if he didn't, people would be hurt, maybe killed. Then again, more would be hurt and killed if he didn't get what he needed out of the Vilanni mainframe, and he might not get this good a chance again.

The datastore's walls shimmered and a crystalline spider oozed through—Vilanni IC had found him. First things first. He engaged his Claw Hand attack program. The battle against the IC was short and sharp, but the outcome was never in doubt. Maybe FastJack could have taken the spider down quicker. Maybe.

But the spider was just the first of Vilanni's defenses. There would be worse soon.

FLASH!

Cyberspace around him winked from its normal image to a negative version.

Sooner than soon.

FLASH!

Frag! Not now! Clearly, he'd lost track of time. There was nothing else Andy could do now but bail. He'd be hosed if he didn't get out.

He hit Save. He'd pick up his adventure later. Feather and Buckhead would wait for him. They always did. Vilanni would wait too. It wasn't like they were real-world.

The real world had its own imperatives. And right now was one of those. No more games. Time to go to work.

>>>>>NEWSNET DOWNLINK
  —[05:10:31/8-14-55]

NORTH VIRGINIA STATEHOOD CONTROVERSY

A new bill apportioning voting districts in the former North Virginia counties of Fairfax, Alexandria, and Arlington is moving through the North Virginia General Assembly. The legislation is an undisguised challenge to the constitutionality of 2024's Federal Capital District Act, by which the UCAS government annexed those counties, removing them from North Virginia's jurisdiction.

Commented State Senator Wendell North (Arch-PW): "Like all of this bill's sponsors, I am gratified by the strong support the Senate has shown in its swift passage of our bill. We have every confidence that the measure will pass with an equally overwhelming margin in the House of Delegates. UCAS made a mistake thirty years ago. The people of this region have had time to see where their interest lies and, believe me, the people are ready to act. We have a lot of good folk here in North Virginia; people who know their minds, know their hearts, and know where their loyalty belongs. You'll all be seeing that soon enough."

COMP ARMY UPDATE

Senators Gorchakov (Dem-MN) and Drinkwater (Lib-ME) introduced a bill today calling for the immediate payment of all overdue displacement compensation. [*Crossref Finan-*

cials: CAU.] To the cheers of assembled Comp Army soldiers, Drinkwater made the announcement from an improvised podium. "There is no question about it," he said. "We must pay this debt of honor."

Reactions on the Hill have been mixed. Speaker of the House Betty Jo Pritchard (Rep-ONT) led the opposition. In a public statement made today, she said:

"As I stated when the first of these 'marchers' showed up on the Capitol steps, with our country running a fifty-billion-dollar deficit annually, I don't see how responsible legislators can justify any measures designed for the special benefit of only one segment of the population. It makes no practical sense."<<<<<

2

Major Tom Rocquette poked his head out the commander's hatch of the Ranger command car to scan the urban landscape with his unaided eyes. His vision was blurred by fatigue, and he considered taking another wideawake. Could he afford any further degradation of his reflexes? More importantly, could he afford a microsleep during which he'd miss something important? Unwilling to disgrace his new leaves, he dug a tab out of his kit and popped it. He had to stay alert. His unit had already gotten caught once by relying solely on their helmets' augmentation visors; he wasn't about to let that happen again.

From the east came the sound of weapons fire. That should be Santiago's task force. He wished he knew what was happening over there, but the battalion recon drones weren't feeding anything to his tac computer; they hadn't for more than twelve hours. Olivetti, in command of the battalion's tele-operated assets, had nothing but excuses every time Tom called for data or support. This time Tom didn't even bother.

At least something in Olivetti's command was still functioning. Half a block away, the sprawled-starfish shape of a Steel Lynx wheeled drone squatted in the street, temporarily halted in overwatch while First Team advanced. This drone and its controller, call sign Gold Autumn, had proven themselves the best tele-operated unit in Tom's task force, and it was the only one still running. The drone's turret swiveled slightly, adjusting its angle of fire to clear the troops it was supporting. Or was there more to it?

Tom opened the link to the task force's rigger command vehicle. "Gold Autumn, this is Gold Count. Are you reading targets? Over."

"Negative, Gold Count. Area scans clear. Over."

"Affirm. Stay sharp. Gold Count out." He didn't want to be surprised again.

"Major?" It was Captain Vahn, his second in command. "We gonna go help Santiago's team?"

"We haven't been asked," Tom said.

Vahn didn't look happy with the answer. Tom wasn't happy either. It wasn't easy going on with your job when your buddies had found a hot zone, but they were on a search-and-destroy sweep and if they abandoned their job to make like the cavalry and help Santiago's team, they might be opening themselves and everybody else up to a strike by the hostiles. The brass knew what was going on; they would know if Santiago needed help. You had to trust them; it was part of being on the team.

Right now *his* team needed his attention.

First Team was moving forward past a building that belched smoke from every orifice. The roiling black clouds obscured the upper stories of most of the structures ahead of them. Dangerous. Unaided eyes couldn't pierce that gloom; he'd have to hope that the troops' augmented vision would spot any danger from that quarter. He concentrated on the street level.

It was good that he did. He spotted a flicker of movement in the rubbled building along which First Team's right flank moved. The team was on point and almost on top of whatever it was.

"Point Team, halt!"

The scramble to cover started immediately and was completed quickly. Although he could locate all of them on his tac comp, only one soldier remained visible from Tom's position. Even the Steel Lynx had scuttled sideways and found some rubble to shelter against. They were good troops. Tom wished he could take the credit for honing them so well, but they hadn't been under his command long enough for that;

he was happy enough to have them. Later, he would send a thank-you note to their former commander.

Unfortunately more troops had gone to ground nearer the suspicious movement than made him comfortable, but nothing jumped out to get them.

"What's going on, Major?" Sergeant Omenski asked.

Tom hadn't seen anything he could characterize as a threat, but he felt uneasy. He'd seen movement, hadn't he? He hoped it wasn't wideawake-induced paranoia. Still, caution was better than stupidity. "You picking up anything ahead and to your right?"

After a moment to confer with his Team, Omenski was back on the line. "We don't see anything."

Had he been wrong? The gathering dusk and drifting smoke made it hard to be sure. He realized that the firing from Santiago's position had stopped. It was very quiet. He didn't like that. It had gotten quiet just before they were jumped the last time. "Watch your front, Sergeant. Special attention to your one through three. Stand by."

"Understood." Omenski's tone made it clear he disagreed with his commander's order to stop the advance for no apparent reason.

No *apparent* reason.

Tom slipped back inside the command car, ignoring the questioning expression of his commo chief. He wanted to talk to the man reclining, eyes closed, on the couch set against the armored outer wall. Tom tapped rhythmically on his arm. When the man opened his eyes, Tom asked, "You got anything, Hooter?"

Hooter was the nickname of Lieutenant Carolstan, the task force's magician. The small man had picked up the sobriquet because he wore thick-lensed glasses that made his large eyes, peering from within dark rings, look even larger than they were. The image had reminded someone of an owl. It didn't help that Carolstan had a steady, unblinking stare. Those glasses marked Carolstan for what he was, even more obviously than his radiant sword insignia. The man had significant myopia, a defect that could be permanently and invisibly corrected with a minor implant, but he wouldn't allow it. Like most mages, the refused any implants that would threaten the psychic integrity of his body. The Army wouldn't permit contact lenses, so glasses it was, and "Hooter" was the result.

Carolstan, also like most magicians, didn't much care for the nickname the troopers hung on him. "The name's Carolstan, Major."

Tom didn't care. Troops didn't much like magic or magicians. Such animosity—though fear played a part, too—was why they coined demeaning nicknames. Years of working with the specialists of the Army's Thaumaturgic Corps had taught Tom that there were magicians who deserved both animosity and fear; Tom hadn't worked with Hooter long enough to know if he was one of them. One thing was certain: troops especially didn't like people—magicians *or* officers—who let them down. "It's Dogmeat if you're not doing your job."

Hooter pursed his lips, drawing his face down into an expression that suited his nickname. "I have nothing to report from the astral."

"Go take another look. Pay attention to the building anchoring First Team's right flank."

Instead of going back to his command station, Tom crawled up into the command car's turret. He wanted to get his own eyeballs back on the terrain while Hooter did his astral recon. Whatever he'd seen wasn't visible now. He kept searching anyway.

He routed his tac feed to that station, so that from time to time he could glance down at the turret's bank of monitors. No sense losing touch. One displayed the positions of his men, each marked with a blue symbol; no red showed. Neither did the input relayed from the troops' helmets or the M-6 Ranger's own sensors indicate the presence of any hostiles. Yet something still made Tom hesitate to resume the advance.

Another display showed the interior of the command car, where the magician lay still as a dead man while he did his arcane scout. Hooter was taking longer than he should, but he showed no signs of distress. Maybe he was just being thorough. Tom wished he knew the magician better, so that he could make a better informed guess about why he might be taking so long. Finally Hooter stirred, indicating that he was coming out of his trance.

Tom was on him at once. "Well? What did you see?"

The magician's eyes shifted into focus. "There is nothing to be seen."

"Then it's all clear?"

"You have my report," Hooter said brusquely. Mages were notoriously touchy about people questioning their competence. Apparently Tom had insulted this one.

Tom had more important things to do than nursemaid Hooter's ego. The task force still had a mission. He returned his attention to the street just in time to see a half-dozen squat green shapes emerge from the ruins. The hostiles were little more than silhouettes with the raw, rough-hewn shape of trolls, but shorter and broader. The trollish hostiles moved fast—very fast—bounding in among First Team's position. Small-arms fire erupted as the Team recognized their danger. One of the green things went down, but the rest surged forward.

"Active magic," Hooter announced. He had popped up in the commander's hatch.

"So get active yourself and try to knock down some of those things," Tom told him.

"Don't expect much," Hooter snapped back, but he did start to mumble a spell.

Tom didn't have time to figure out what Hooter was trying. A larger shape, orange this time but still vaguely humanoid and no better defined, rose from the rubble and lumbered forward. The orange hostile stormed past First Team and headed straight for Second Team's position. No one in Second Team fired at it.

Why hadn't the team opened up on the thing?

Questions later; now, they needed help. "Gold Count to Gold Autumn, shift support to Second Team."

The drone's rigger didn't reply, but the Steel Lynx rolled out from behind cover, its turret swiveling to bring its weapons to bear on the hulking target. The drone scooted into the monster's path. Rolling backwards down the street in front of the hostile, the Lynx opened up. The stream of fire appeared to hit the target, but to no effect.

Some kind of displacement illusion?

Tom swiveled the turret's minigun around to bear. He depressed the firing stud. The gun rumbled as a fiery stream of tracer poured out, raking the air to one side of the monster. Slight aim shift, then the other. No visible effect. *Hell with that!* Tom shifted his aim and speared the thing. The orange hulk staggered, but didn't stop.

The smaller green hostiles rampaged through First Team's position. On Tom's tac comp, blue lights started flashing everywhere as one of the hostiles reached his troops. One by one, the blue lights winked out. First Team was being annihilated.

Tom called for help. "Gold Count to Tin Leader!"

"This is Tin Leader." Olivetti's voice was calm, almost detached. "We're a bit busy here."

"Olivetti!" he screamed over the tac commo. "We've been jumped. Get your fragging mechanical birds down here!"

"Wilco," replied the rigger commander.

Tom could only hope that Olivetti was telling the truth. It wouldn't be the first time he had promised support he didn't have.

What they really needed were a few Yellowjacket light choppers, or even one Destrier close-support ship, but Tom's Special Resources battalion hadn't been assigned any heavy aerial assets. All the task force had was their share of the battalion's integral rigger company with its MCT-Nissan Shadowhawk rotor drones. The Shadowhawks were lightweight, but his mission briefing had said that those assigned to support this mission would be armed with antipersonnel weapons.

Could their opposition be considered personnel? The orange and green shapes looked humanoid, barely, but they acted more like relentless killing machines. They sure as hell didn't go down like men.

An unnaturally loud hornet-buzz announced the arrival of Olivetti's drones. A pair went by the command car, too fast for Tom to get a good look at them, but the tac comp flashed stats on them. Both Shadowhawks packed miniguns, rotary tri-barrels like that on the command car, which could spit out a stream of lead that would cut a man into bits.

The orange monstrosity advanced through the drones' fire without stopping. Its outer edges flickered a little. It was taking some effect from the weight of fire pouring down on it. The thing sought cover. But it wasn't stopped; the drones' firepower only made it take a longer route to Second Team's position. That was all.

That was *wrong*. Nothing living should be able to withstand such a volume of fire.

The orange hostile disappeared from Tom's line of fire as it continued its approach to Second Team's position. The thing was almost on top of the troops and they still weren't firing in their own defense. Tac comp showed them all unwounded. So why weren't they firing? Tom knew they were better trained than their performance was showing. Second Team's nonreaction was wrong too. No one responded to his calls on the team's frequency. Wrong, wrong, wrong.

"The scenario's screwed up. What the hell's going on here, Hooter?"

Hooter raised an eyebrow. "You know the rules, Major. Stick to the scenario. You want to discuss context or simulation parameters, you save it for debrief."

Tom gave the mage his best junior-officer-frying glare, but Hooter didn't wither. The magician knew something he wasn't telling Tom. Like most mages, he was probably looking out for his own hoop and couldn't be bothered worrying about his teammates. Didn't he understand that the team came first? If the team didn't win, nobody won. But here the little fragger was, keeping secrets and standing on the rules.

"All right then. By the rules. Give me a situation evaluation, *Lieutenant* Carolstan. What is the magical threat?"

"The details are obscured, but as I said, there's active magic. Can't you feel it?"

"I'm not the one supposed to be a mage."

"Look at the hostile."

Hooter pointed to where the Shadowhawks buzzed around, hovering and picking their shots. The orange hostile continued to move through the rubble, rarely exposing itself for long, and the drones didn't get off many shots. Always, inexorably, the hostile moved closer to Second Team's position.

The rubble through which the hostile was moving was bad going for the Steel Lynx. Tom ordered the drone back to support what was left of First Team. He also ordered his driver to take the command car in closer to the fight. He needed clearer fire lanes to support Second Team. The M-6 Ranger command car wasn't a panzer or even a tank, but it was the heaviest piece of equipment the task force had left. Concrete grinding under its wheels, the armored command car moved forward.

As they approached the hostile playing hide-and-seek among the rubble, Tom began to feel something. There was a strangeness that radiated from the monster, something that touched deep wells of loathing in Tom's soul and woke the small animal spirit in him. That spirit cried out and urged him to run away from the thing stalking ever closer, to hide and cower, to do anything but confront it. Now he understood what had happened to Second Team. Magic-induced fear was suppressing them. He'd been annoyed by the hostile before, but now he hated it for what it had done to his men and was trying to do to him.

"Counter the thing's spell," he ordered Hooter.

The mage aborted the spell he'd been constructing. "I thought you wanted me to attack the hostiles?"

"Are you questioning orders, Lieutenant? In combat? You know what the *rules* say about that."

"No questions," Hooter said sullenly. "Sir."

"Then earn your fragging specialist bonus! Protect Second Team!"

Hooter shrank back from him, but he started a new spell.

Whatever else was happening around them, the feelings Tom was getting from the hostile were very real. And they were growing stronger, weakening the walls of anger he threw up to steel himself. He feared he might succumb to the waves of overpowering dread emanating from the hostile. Second Team had already fallen victim. If he did, too, the task force was doomed. He ordered his driver to halt.

The thought of this single, cheating, orange fragger beating his task force was like gasoline on the fire of his anger. Tom aimed the Ranger's minigun toward where he guessed the hostile would appear next. That orange bastard wasn't going to beat him! He was about to order his driver to advance again when the thing appeared at the edge of an alley. Tom's thumbs came down and his weapon roared.

Tom roared with it. Somewhere deep down he knew he was losing it, but he didn't care. The days of butting through the urban wilderness and wiring himself with wide-awakes had pared away the insulation and left him a little raw. That was the enemy out there in his sights. *His* enemy. And he wasn't going to let it win!

The orange monster flickered.

Tom didn't know why, and he didn't care. He kept firing. The heat from his weapon's barrel washed back over him.

Someone in Second Team started to fire. Then a grenade crumped next to the hostile. Though sporadic, the new attacks caused the orange monster to stumble. The team seemed to take heart at that. More troops brought their weapons to bear. Tom shouted encouragement to them and continued to rip at the thing.

Their orange enemy seemed to shrink a little. Tom roared his triumph, seemingly louder than the sustained coughing roar of his weapon.

The humanoid shape froze in mid-stride, then faded, revealing the drone beneath: a Steel Lynx variant. The drone folded away its sensor-projector array and relaxed its legs, sprawling into its breed's characteristic star-shaped relax pose. Its job in this war game was done.

Tom's tac comp was flashing a message from battalion headquarters.

"All units:

        Game terminated.

        Hold position until verified by an umpire.

        Stand down.

All officers:

        Debrief 1830."

The same message would be showing on tac comps, datascreens, and helmet visors all over the unit. Tom slumped down in his commander's seat and stared at the screen. The battle, never real, was over. The very real exhaustion of three days of field exercise asserted itself, threatening to overwhelm Tom's chemically reinforced awareness. It seemed that every one of his bones ached with weariness. Tired as Tom was, his men would be no less weary; he had to get them squared away before he could let go. Part of him was happy the exercise was over, but part of him was annoyed. It hadn't been exactly fair. He held onto that annoyance, using the anger to keep him going.

What in one Christian hell, seven Buddhist hells, and an uncountable number of unpleasant afterlives did the designers of this scenario think the troops were going to be fighting?

>>>>>WFDC FEED COVERAGE
 -[18:22:11/8-14-55]
REPORTER: DERRY DALE [DALE-365]
UPLINK SITE: FREDERICKSBURG, NORTH VIRGINIA

Dale: "Governor Jefferson, what do you say now that State Senator North's challenge to the Federal Capital District Act of 2024 has cleared the state senate?"

Jefferson: "The honorable senator has his views. I have mine. I'm sure that Congress and the Supreme Court will have their own. I can't stop the senator from setting up this challenge; that's his right, indeed it is the right of any honest citizen. But I am the duly elected governor of North Virginia, and as long as North Virginia remains a part of the UCAS, I'll be here in Fredericksburg doing my job."

Dale: "Do you attach any significance to the margin of passage?"

Jefferson: "The margin isn't the whole story in politics, as we all know. I think you might find that support isn't as strong as the good senator would like you to believe."

Dale: "Eighty percent in favor seems pretty strong to me."

Jefferson: "Derry, you and I both know that not every senator votes his conscience every time a bill goes through. The story's not told till we get to the end."

[*Cut to courthouse steps; Dale standing alone. Inset: Teresa Lee (Rep), Regional Commissioner of Fairfax District, FDC*]

Dale: "There are those both north and south of the Potomac who question the Governor's evaluation of the situation. To some, the scent of unrest and dissatisfaction is in the air. Commissioner Theresa Lee, had this to say: 'Governor Jefferson is out of touch with the hearts and minds of the people. The area between the Potomac and Rappahannock Rivers has always been a unique and coherent region. Arbitrary lines on a map can't change that. Those of us who live here know what North Virginia is, and where it belongs.' "<<<<<

3

Russ Sanchez was waiting for Andy at the entrance to the Track. Russ was Andy's mentor, which wasn't as stuffy as it sounded; Russ was an okay guy. The Track was the virtual arena where Telestrian Cyberdyne tested its new models, or rather their virtual analogs.

"Running a little long, Mr. Walker?" Russ asked.

Anybody else would have said "running late," but the odd syntax wasn't a mistake. Not with Russ. Andy had long suspected that Russ knew what was behind Andy's tendency to tardiness, but it wasn't something they talked about. So Andy said, "I got a little preoccupied. I'll go late tonight if it's a problem."

The computer resources Andy used for his runs weren't exactly his to use. If he and Russ talked about Andy's virtual pastimes directly, Russ would be obligated to ask after details of access and allocation, and Andy would feel obligated to give them. Which would have put another, different obligation on Russ—that of having to report Andy for theft of Telestrian's computer resources. Neither of them wanted that, so they never talked about Andy's adventures.

Russ's implicit condoning of Andy's irregular activities was only one of the things Andy liked about Russ. Although Russ was officially Andy's boss, he was more like a friend. Russ wasn't as stuffed as the other Telestrian managers. He was an all right guy, not the corp stereotype at all. In a lot of ways, Russ was the father Andy had grown up without.

Andy's biological father was Matthew "Cruncher" Walker. Cruncher had worked security for Telestrian East, Cyberdyne's parent company, but he hadn't been just a shuffle-along prowl guard. Telestrian didn't demonstrate the prejudice of Cruncher's previous employer, the sanctimonious and hypocritical UCAS government. The fact that Matthew Walker was an ork wasn't a problem at the big T. Telestrian's bosses knew that the bottom line was performance, and they rewarded whatever metatype delivered. Cruncher had been a site supervisor with numerous commendations and bonus citations. He'd been on his way up in the Telestrian security force. It had taken death in the line of duty to stop Cruncher.

Unfortunately, Andy didn't remember much about his father. The dust-up in which Cruncher died had happened when Andy was three. Andy knew what Cruncher looked like, and he remembered the strong, rasping grip of his father's hardened hands and the fierceness of his hugs. There were other memories too; but they were more vague, less pleasant, so he didn't try very hard to remember those. When it came right down to it, though, he had no real grasp on his father as a person, and all the pictures and recordings Andy's mother had kept, even the stories she'd told him, didn't tell him near enough about the person Cruncher had been.

With Cruncher's death, the family had become corporate pensioners. Telestrian East administered the estate and the not inconsiderable loss benefits. The big T ensured that Andy and his sisters got a good education. Telestrian had also arranged slots for his mother and his sisters. His mother Shayla currently worked as a senior receptionist for the Internal Marketing bullpen. Two of his sisters had slots in the admin pool and the third, Asa—who everyone knew was the smart one—was working an advanced study program-internship for a bigwig at Telestrian's home office in Tir Tairngire.

Even Andy had grown into the family business, as it were. Though he was still attending classes two days a week, working toward his advanced studies certificate, he held down a slot within Telestrian Cyberdyne as a test driver. When younger he'd worked with the teams developing entertainment simulators. What he was doing now was familiar stuff, not surprising since he'd been playtesting for the corp since he was a kid, since even before Telestrian had funded his datajack. These days he was getting more real development work and that was exciting. It felt good to be a contributing member of the corporate family.

But even a paternal, caring corporation wasn't a real father. Russ wasn't either, but he was as close as Andy was likely to come. Maybe that was why Russ's approval was so important to him.

It was an approval he was likely to lose if he didn't stop daydreaming.

As usual, Russ was one step ahead of him.

"Welcome back," Russ said. "Shall I go over the brief again or did you record?"

Fortunately, by force of habit, Andy *had* set to record. He liked being able to see if the postbrief matched the prebrief, which it didn't always do, especially when someone other than Russ handled the session. Russ's briefing was stored in his hardware memory. "I've got it," he said.

"Good. I wouldn't want to think I was *totally* wasting my time." With a wave of Russ's hand the entrance dissolved, and he and Andy were standing in the open. Bright sunlight flooded down all around them. "You ready to get down to work?"

Andy was still taking in the scenery. Today the Track was configured for a badlands setting, with lots of mesas and buttes, and not a road in sight. The land forms were low res, sketchy shapes with minimal modeling and bland, flat surface modeling. There were no clouds in the sky. All of which suggested that the Track's resources were focused on vehicle parameters and full-feedback monitoring. Andy knew that meant he'd be rigging one of the newer models. Real work today.

"Montjoy?" he asked. The Montjoy Project was Telestrian Cyberdyne's latest foray into cybernetic vehicle-control systems. It was cutting-edge stuff, and very, very secret. Andy had test-driven early versions of the vehicle. Partials, to be sure, but an honor nonetheless.

"It's not like you earned it," Russ said. "But you're right."

Two dark shapes winked into existence beside them. The Montjoy vehicles were sleek and tapered, reminiscent of broad-headed sharks without dorsal fins. Thrust-vectoring nozzles made slight bulges at strategic points along the vehicle's surface. The canopy over the cockpit was blanked this time. For this run the Montjoys would be relying purely on their sensor suites. Andy's name hung in the air above one of the vehicles, the dark letters beckoning him forward. He took a slow tour around the Montjoy, admiring its looks.

"I know a dozen test drivers who'd kill you if they thought it would let them take your place," Russ said.

"But they didn't have my test scores, did they?" Russ had

once let it slip that Andy had shown an early aptitude in cybernetic control, with higher scores than anyone in his age group. Andy liked to think about it as his special edge. Andy quoted the corp's motto, "At Telestrian we go with the best."

Russ shook his head. "Let's just say they didn't have your availability."

Andy let Russ's ego-checking comment roll past him. He didn't really care about the reasons. What mattered was that he was here and going to rig the Montjoy. But there were two vehicles, and the other had no name over it.

He looked at Russ. "You're rigging today, too?"

"We'll be playing tag, remember?" Russ gave a theatrical sigh. "I suppose you've also forgotten that if you get more than five hundred meters off the deck, you get tagged out. Triple A or something like that. In any case, you lose the run and make certain engineers very unhappy. Got it?"

Andy didn't remember, but he supposed the details had been in the brief. Those details were important or Russ wouldn't have mentioned them again, so he said, "Got it."

"Okay, in you go."

Andy's viewpoint shifted. He was no longer standing on the open field of the Track. Instead he was sitting, reclining actually, in the cockpit of the Montjoy testbed. The Montjoy vehicle wasn't real, and he wasn't really in its cockpit, but it was awfully hard to tell.

Russ had told him that back in the previous century, manufacturers had actually had to build physical prototypes to test their designs. Andy found it hard to imagine building something before you knew whether it would work or not. Physical manufacturing was a lot more costly than computer time, making such a venture a big investment gamble. Even if the design was mostly good, any unanticipated flaw could result in expensive retooling before production could start. Manufacturers were a lot smarter these days; they'd learned that it was a waste of good money to build something just to see if it worked.

Still, there was a certain allure to such a way of doing business. It must have been terribly exciting to strap yourself into a vehicle, not knowing if it would work, but completely assured that you were betting your life that it would. Medical tech was pretty primitive in those days. You couldn't count on the docs rebuilding you if something got hosed and you cracked up.

Andy had no worries about dying on the Track. If he wiped on the Track, he wouldn't get hurt, not physically anyway. Mistakes still had their costs, in computer time to determine whether a crash was due to vehicle design or operator error, but either way the techs just reset and he could take the vehicle out again. He *would* take a hit on his evaluation, though, and that would hurt his chance of doing this kind of work all the time after graduation.

He ran his hand over the smooth surface of the Montjoy's control banks. The surface would extrude whatever buttons or toggles were needed for positive touch interface control. So slick. His fingers rimmed the chrome surface of the dataport. So sleek. The Montjoy was the most sophisticated vehicle he'd ever test-driven. Much tougher to master than any of the panzers or LAVs he rigged in his shadowrun simulations. But then, the Montjoy was better than any of those.

"You asleep in there?" Russ's voice came over the cockpit speakers.

"Just orienting."

"Oh? Well, tag, you're it."

Time to go to work. Cocking his wrist, Andy willed the emergence of the dataspike.

The docs weren't ready to do the replacement on his real-world hand and install one. They said they were waiting for his bone-growth rate to slow a little. But it must be getting close. Last week they'd had him in for some preliminary work. His arm had almost immediately started to itch fiercely, and it still did. Psychosomatic, they'd told him when he called in, worried. Not an uncommon reaction, they said, nothing to worry about. He really couldn't feel the nanobots laying the circuitry under his skin. No one could do that.

In the Matrix that didn't matter. Andy's persona icon, the visual image that would represent him in cyberspace, was whatever he told it to be, and in this regard he told it to be what he would one day be. Here he had the sharpest, chilliest interface going. He snugged the spike into its receptacle and the Montjoy came alive for him. Its sensors became his eyes, its engine his heart. Man as machine. Glorious! The power was incredible. Eat your systemic fluid pumps out, street samurai!

He looked around. The other Montjoy was gone. No heat trail, which was something of a cheat. Russ's vehicle must have been computer-teleported to some other location on the Track. They would be playing hide-and-seek as well as tag.

"Sooner done, sooner done," Russ liked to say. Andy agreed. He revved his turbines to optimal and leapt into the sky.

His confidence proved to be overconfidence. Andy lost all four of the morning's matches. Hardly the performance he'd wanted to turn in, but flying the Montjoy *was* tricky.

After the lunch break, Russ reviewed his performance with him, pointing out the weak spots. Andy did better in the afternoon, but it wasn't until the fourth run that he managed a clean tag on Russ. The success made Andy eager for another chance. Russ was hesitant—it was pretty late in the day—but finally caved to Andy's insistence. Sure that he'd tag Russ easily this time, Andy watched Russ's Montjoy disappear among the buttes while he waited for his "go" signal. To Andy's annoyance, the controllers gave Russ a good long lead. The heat trail was too cold to be useful by the time Andy got permission to launch.

Andy headed straight to a spot he'd noticed in the last run. It had looked like the perfect ambush spot, and he was sure Russ had seen it too. Russ might not be there, but at least it was a place to start the hunt. And if Russ *was* there, Andy figured he could get the jump on him by coming in with cannons blazing. Which was exactly what he did—to no effect. Russ wasn't there.

Russ *had* been there, though. The air was contaminated with fresh exhaust. Andy went on looking. For a long time. He was beginning to wonder if Russ had left and turned the run into a flying exercise when he spotted the other Montjoy. It was backing from the blind canyon where Russ had caught Andy on the second run of the day. Andy put a shot across Russ's rear just to say hello.

Russ vectored down and his Montjoy shot up like a rocket, right out of the path of Andy's second burst. There were still a few tricks left in the old master. Russ's Montjoy scraped belly dropping behind a ridge and out of sight. Andy throttled up and went after him.

The ride was wild. They screamed past rockfaces and hurtled over the broken terrain at far greater speeds than Andy would have dared in a real-world machine. The human mind could guide a terrain-following program only so fast. They pushed the envelope, weaving among the buttes almost too fast for even the powerful Montjoy engines to keep inertia from smearing them on a rockface. Andy hadn't expected Russ to jam things so hard, but he wasn't going to complain. The only thing better than what they were doing would be to rig one of these babies over such a course for real. Andy was having the time of his life.

Until Russ pulled a maneuver Andy hadn't seen before, and ended up behind him as they roared into a broad river canyon. Cannon shells raked across the sky in front of Andy. The bursts buffeted his Montjoy, taking the flight briefly out of his control. The Montjoy's brief loss of supervision probably saved him; the course change being just enough to slip him free from Russ's targeting projections. None of the shells caught him.

Andy knew a clue when he got one. He vectored thrust every which way and skittered across the sky, staying one jink ahead of Russ's cannon shells. But he couldn't shake Russ, and the canyon walls were narrowing. Andy was running out of room to dodge. The only open space was the sky. Andy shunted power to aft thrust to surge ahead, pulling his nose up as he did. He sent the Montjoy up into a loop that with luck would put him behind his pursuer. His speed was high—a legacy of the burst he'd used to get the jump on Russ. He could put only so much push on the airframe to fight the inertia. For the next few seconds he might as well have been flying a missile.

The Montjoy arced higher, nosing for the sun. Andy brought his nose up more, as much as he dared. The loop would be wide, almost too wide. He watched the altimeter rise. He was cutting it close. He tucked the Montjoy tighter as it approached the zenith of its path. Buzzers warned of the threshold. He fought to cinch the loop tighter. Instruments blurred as he grayed. Too tight? He fought the simulated G's, barely maintaining consciousness. The buzzers vibrated through his bones. Slowly, slowly the Montjoy leveled off, showing its belly to the sun. He'd made it! By a handful of centimeters, if the altimeter was to be believed. If he'd been flying belly down, the Montjoy's tail would have clipped the barrier and he'd have scratched.

He could see the other craft following him up into the sky. The other Montjoy didn't have his speed, which meant it could loop in tighter. Andy jinked, anticipating that Russ would apply cross-vector thrust to mutate the maneuver. He found himself shifting through empty air. Russ hadn't shunted—instead he continued the loop as if he were running a fixed-wing. Russ had to know that he'd go through the barrier. Why would he try such a maneuver?

Russ wouldn't.

The anomalies suddenly made sense. Someone other than Russ was in control of the other Montjoy. Before Andy could wonder at the why or how of it, the other Montjoy hit 500 meters and popped out of existence.

"Frag it! We're too late," someone shouted outside Andy's cockpit. The voice had to have come from the real world. Trouble. Real trouble.

Andy's vision blanked as dump shock slammed him. Someone had engaged the manual override on his console capsule. He was cut off, unable to warn the controllers of the breech in building security. Hissing hydraulics announced the impending opening of the hatch. He barely got his eyes shut in time to avoid the invading glare of the ready room lights.

Blinking his aching eyes against the dazzle, he saw four people in the room: a troll who nearly filled the space by himself, an ork whose eyes reflected chrome highlights, a scruffy-looking norm, and—the only female—a small Asian woman with white hair. They wore white coveralls slung with various belts and bags, all except the woman who wore hardly anything at all. Despite the bad viewing angles, Andy could make out the shoulder patches on the coveralls. They said Telestrian Cyberdyne Maintenance. They lied. This was no maintenance crew. It couldn't be. Had they been real, all four would have worn coveralls. There was only one thing this crew could be. Shadowrunners.

"Let's geek the little piece of drek," the ork said.

>>>>>LIVE FEED WFDC
  -[22:04:06/8-14-55]
REPORTER: TAYLOR WEINGARTNER [WEIN-324]
UPLINK SITE: ALEXANDRIA DISTRICT, FDC

Weingartner: "It's another hot August night here in the nation's capital. I'm talking to you from the fringes of the ever-growing shanty camp of the Compensation Army. You saw me here last month when I told you how bad the camp's sanitary conditions were. As the heat wave has continued, things have gotten worse. The miasma of suffering clings everywhere. But amid all the squalor, something new is moving.

"You see them here and there, moving in small groups. They're carrying food and medical supplies. They stop to help an ailing marcher. They settle a dispute. Who are they? The government doesn't know.

"Look at them on their errands of mercy. You can spot them easily. They all wear neon-blue berets and matching armbands. It's a uniform of sorts. Clearly they're organized. Do you want to know who they are? I know I do. Let's go find out."

[*Viewpoint shift: over Weingartner's shoulder. Short, stocky woman wearing blue beret comes into frame. She ignores camera until Weingartner speaks.*]

Weingartner: "You, ma'am. Yes, you. Would you mind pausing for a moment? Can you tell us about the beret you're wearing? What does it mean?"

Dwarven woman: "I'm kinda busy."

Weingartner: "Just a moment, ma'am. The country is watching and wants to know about you. Can you tell us who you are?"

Dwarven woman [*into camera*]: "My name's not important, but you want to know who I am? I'm somebody who knows we've got to care. [*Touches beret.*] We're the Conscience of the Country, and we care. We are mothers and fathers, sisters and brothers, children even. We are elves and orks, trolls and dwarfs, any metatype you can imagine. And we believe in justice.

"Now I gotta go. Got work to do."<<<<<

4

When Captain Olivetti, last of the officers to give his private debrief, returned to the group outside the Tactical Operations Center, the talk had gotten around to catching up on careers. Tom Rocquette had served or schooled with most of the battalion's officers and as yet he'd had little time to renew acquaintances. He hadn't been at Fort Schwartzkopf for more than ten hours—and he'd slept six of those—before planning for the exercise had begun. That had been three days ago. He'd only received his promotion four days ago. It had come with his assignment and immediate transfer orders.

Tom hooked a thumb under his collar tab to emphasize the dull black-enameled leaves pinned there. "I was supposed to get a furlough along with this. Instead I got transferred here from Denver, and out on this raggedy-ass boondoggle. Sorry you guys got me dumped on you like that."

"We don't mind, Major," Vahn said. It was an appropriate comment for a second in command, but Vahn sounded like he really meant it.

"Call me Tom when it's informal, okay? Goes for all of you. As to minding, *I* do." An operational command was something he'd longed for, a rare and jealously sought slot in the UCAS army, but—"I was looking forward to that time off."

"Machine Rocquette wanting time off?" Olivetti sounded incredulous. "Machine" was a nickname Tom had picked up in his last year at the Point; supposedly it referred to his machine-like dedication. It hadn't been dedication driving him back then, but Olivetti didn't know that. "You're worse than my lamest reality-impaired rigger. What would you do with a furlough?"

"I'd sleep for a week," Tom admitted.

"I know *I'd* head for bed," Santiago said. "But I don't know how much *sleep* I'd get."

"Really, Santi? I can't think of anything else you might be capable of doing," Vahn commented.

Santiago's reply was cut off by the call for the officers to assemble in the TOC for the general debrief. The ragged, tired group shuffled under the camouflage netting strung between the command vehicles, and found places among the workstations and commo sets. The general and his staff, all with eyes as red-rimmed as any trooper's, were already in place.

Contrary to Tom's expectations, general debrief did not allow a forum for explaining the anomalies of the field exercise. The general and his staff weren't interested in hearing Tom's complaints about the umpires' unfairness in scoring kills by making the green and orange hostiles super strong. In fact, the brass weren't interested in hearing *any* of their officers' complaints. All they wanted to know was why decisions had been made and how they'd been implemented. Every gripe about the skewed scenario was shot down as it started. The general's reaction wasn't S.O.P. Sure, it was within the regs for the general just to take input, but he wasn't being fair. He also wouldn't answer any of their questions. The lack of output didn't go down well with the exhausted, frustrated men who'd been out on the maneuver. Tempers flared, but the brass just stood behind their stone wall and took it. Debriefs were supposed to be give and take. Not S.O.P. at all. The only good thing to come out of the one-sided debrief was an early dismissal to barracks.

By chance or design, all of the officers of Tom's battalion decided to exit the TOC between the same two vehicles. The rigger commander Olivetti picked the same path. Tom recognized the pattern; there would be an informal debrief before this crowd actually hit the sack. It didn't take long to get started.

"What kind of drek was *that*?" Santiago's voice was loud enough to carry back into the TOC where the general and his staff remained, but the look on the captain's face suggested he didn't care. When Santiago got angry about something, everybody knew about it. "We don't know squat more than we did before we went out. Nothing added to nothing is still nothing. *Less* than nothing, considering the drek the umps were pulling out there."

"Hey, hey, Santi. Chill it, eh? The exercise is oh-ver." Vahn clapped his arm around his friend's shoulder, urging him to a quicker step away from the TOC. Vahn whispered in Santiago's ear, "Store it till we get back to barracks, eh?"

Vahn and Santiago were same-year graduates from the Point. Tom remembered hazing them. He also remembered that Vahn had spent a lot of time cleaning up after his quarrelsome buddy. It looked as though Vahn was still trying to watch out for his friend and cover up his impolitic excesses. Mistakes made during an exercise weren't supposed to reflect badly on an officer, but mistakes made in conduct *concerning* the exercise were another matter. Having made it clear that they didn't want to hear complaints, the brass wouldn't take kindly to Santiago's mouthing off while still in earshot. Vahn, as usual, was more concerned about the future than his buddy.

Santiago wasn't ready to listen. "What the frag happen to the Informed Army? Tell me that! How the hell are you supposed to make an informed decision without information? Did I miss something? When did we become the old Red Commie Army?"

"We most assuredly are not," said a voice that made Tom feel sudden pity for Santiago.

" 'Ten-hut!" Tom called belatedly.

The surprised group went to stiff attention. Most of the others looked surprised and a little nervous like Vahn. Clearly he wasn't the only one to have missed Colonel Malinovsky's approach. Santiago had the sense to look a little guilty.

Malinovsky was their regimental commander. The colonel came from a career military family with a history of service going back over a century. Most of his ancestors had served in the old Soviet army and its immediate successors. Like many fleeing the turmoil in end-of-century chaos, the Malinovsky family had been buffeted in the EuroWars of the early thirties. They had finally found a home in the West, where they built new careers, proving themselves intensely loyal to their new country. Some, like the Colonel, were sensitive about their past.

But Colonel Malinovsky didn't seem to be interested in Santiago. He addressed Tom directly.

"At ease, Major Rocquette." The colonel's stiffness didn't

allow more than the most minute relaxation. "You lost almost half your task force in that last encounter, Rocquette."

Tom was aware of how poorly they'd done.

"Anything to say about that?"

"I've nothing to add to the download or the debrief, Colonel."

Malinovsky's cold gray eyes stared into Tom's. Tom couldn't read anything in those blank steel walls. Slowly the colonel nodded.

"I am impressed," he said. "You did a damn good job out there, Rocquette. If the rest of the task forces going through this scenario do as well, we'll have a chance at winning this one."

Good job? Sure, relative to the other teams, Tom's troops had weathered the frag-up well enough. But *well* enough wasn't *good* enough. The job had been far from good.

Whatever Tom thought of the exercise's results, clearly the colonel had a higher opinion. Malinovsky had broken ranks with the rest of the brass to come out and talk to them. If he was willing to go that far, maybe he'd go further.

"You know, Colonel, we'd all feel a lot better if we knew what the exercise was about. Just what *is* going on?"

"You shouldn't be asking that question and you know it," Malinovsky said.

"There are times you still have to ask," Tom said.

Malinovsky nodded. "I *will* tell you that we're operating under security conditions. At this time, you all have no need to know the reasons."

"There hasn't been an announcement," Olivetti said.

"It's going out now," Malinovsky told him.

"It's not because of what's happening in Washington, is it?" Tom asked.

"If it were something to do with that nonsense, I couldn't tell you."

That was an answer in itself, and they all knew it. So if the threat wasn't the mobs infesting Washington, what was it? Where was it? The UCAS was at peace with all its neighbors.

"Then the exercise wasn't just a psych test?" Captain Hayne asked.

Hayne had commanded the task force that had been wiped out in the first encounter, and hadn't been shy about complaining about the unfairness of the scenario. Tom hadn't considered that the whole skewed testing, and stone-wall response to the officers' reactions, might have been designed to see how they would take it. Such a theory could explain a lot.

"Not *just*," the colonel said. "The threat is real, gentlemen. That's all I'm allowed to say. For now, forget it, and get yourselves some rest. You've earned it."

The colonel headed back into the TOC, leaving Tom and the others to head for their rides.

"Not *just*, he says." Hayne was still primed for bitching. "That has to be part of it too. Sure, that's it! The whole thing, even the colonel's nicey-nice, is part of the psych. They're messing with our heads, guys. I might have known. Should have known it when we got jumped after a negative scout. They were gunning for me. What a crock!"

It sounded like Hayne was edging into a paranoiac episode from too much wideawake. He needed to be calmed down. "Everybody got jumped after a negative scout," Tom pointed out. "The umpires said that the OpFor's ambushes were legit."

"The ambushes were crocks," Hayne insisted. "Nothing hides from astral recon that well."

Tom had encountered a few things, but none of them fit the rest of the profile of the OpFor they had fought. "I don't think the hostiles really *were* hidden," Tom said. "I think Hooter saw them."

"Your upload said the astral was clear," Vahn said with a hint of accusation.

"That's what Hooter said," Tom told him. "I just relayed it."

"If Hooter saw those things before they attacked, why didn't he say anything?" Olivetti asked. "More 'I can't talk about that' drek?"

"Fragging with our minds," said Hayne.

"Hell, Hooter's a mage," Santiago said. "Maybe he just wanted to see us ordinary folk get our heads handed to us so he could make some flashy play in the end game to show off."

"Hooter's a stuck-up fragger, but he's a team player when it comes to going along with the other hoodoo boys," Vahn said. "Furlann probably dictated Hooter's scout reports to him."

Furlann?

"Rita Furlann?" Tom asked.

"The one and only Ice Heart," Vahn said. "She's head of the magical OpFor field team here."

Tom had worked with Furlann in Denver. Besides being an excellent field mage, she was an expert on exotic magics and the psychological applications and effects of hermetics. Tom was beginning to see.

The UCAS Army had excellent virtual training facilities, and Fort Schwartzkopf here in the Midwest had the Army's best, which meant the best in the world. There were a lot of reasons why the Army made extensive use of those facilities, among them lower cost than real-world training, better security, and less wear and tear on equipment and terrain. It had been decades since any battalion-sized field exercises had been conducted, but now the joint chiefs had authorized these expensive war games. Why?

"It's the magic angle," Tom concluded. "It's gotta be."

"How's that?" Olivetti asked.

"Those are a major's leaves you're wearing, aren't they?" Tom asked. "Everybody knows that physical response to magical effects doesn't model well in cyberspace. Look at the OpFor we were facing. Most of the tactical problems in the exercise were oriented toward defeating magical whatevers. We hardly saw mundane opposition."

"So you think that whoever the threat is supposed to be they can hide from both magical *and* tech recon?" Olivetti asked. "I don't think I like that idea much."

"It *was* part of the scenario," Tom said. He didn't like the idea either.

"You don't think the injuns are working up another Ghost Dance, do you?" Hayne asked.

If he was feeling paranoid about that possibility, he was justified. The U.S. military's complete helplessness against the magical assets of the emerging Native American Nations still rankled. The subsequent loss of large chunks of territory and the break-up of the old United States remained an unhealed wound in many quarters. There were scars deeper than Vietnam on the UCAS body politic and on the country's military. It would take something on the order of a Desert Storm for a payback.

"I'd like another crack at them injuns," Santiago said.

That wasn't the right answer. "The NAN haven't had the unity to do anything that magically heavy for more than a decade. Even if the OpFor were supposed to be NAN, why was the setting urban? Except in the Southwest, there aren't a lot of cities left in NAN territories, and none of the boundary nations are in shape to invade. I just came from Denver. There's a lot of shadow stuff out there, but nothing seriously military. Believe me, I know—the Indian nations are in no shape to invade."

"Hey, Tom, you worked with Captain Furlann out in Denver, didn't you?" Vahn asked.

"Once or twice."

"She'd have a need to know what was going on. Maybe she'll spill to you." Vahn raised a conspiratorial eyebrow.

"I haven't got any special relationship with her," Tom said.

"But I'd bet you'd like to," Santiago said, miming ample handfuls before his chest. "Bet old Ice Heart knows some *real* tricks in the sack. The heartbreakers always do."

"Yeah," Vahn agreed. "Bet she can shrivel your rod with a glance. And without magic. You're hopeless, Santi." Turning back to Tom, he said, "Seriously, though. The two of you shared a difficult duty station. Can't you play on that?"

"Yeah, yeah." Santiago's turn to agree. "Comrades in arms—and, oh, what arms—shared dangers, old times, and all that."

"She and I did *one* tour on the response team. I was pushing papers most of the time." Tom couldn't tell them about the Arsenal incident even if he'd wanted to; the compulsion that had been laid on him took care of that.

"So pull rank on her. You're a major now."

Rank had never bothered Furlann much, and somehow he doubted that the transfer to Fort Schwartzkopf had changed her. But they were right to think that if anybody would know what magical threat was being represented in the exercise, the commander of magical OpFor was the one. She might be willing to tell them now that they'd been through the exercise. Tom thought it worth a try.

They all agreed that he would have a better chance without a squad of guys at his back, so Tom headed for the special compound that served as a barracks cum laboratory for the Fort's mages. The place had the best security on base, magical and otherwise. Unfortunately, the precautions were not taken just to protect the mages from outside dangers; some in the military did not approve of mages in uniform. It was well known that a sleeping mage was, more often than any other time, a defenseless mage, one with few defenses to detect or stop a fragmentation grenade. The result was that the mages lived in isolation. Tom didn't think it was the best policy, but he had to concede that it was a reasonable precaution on the Army's part until more of the population's prejudice could be rooted out.

He had almost reached the main gate when a convoy of staff cars pulled up beside it. The people who debarked were a wild mix of heights, weights, and builds, but almost all were norms. Tom only saw three elves and a dwarf; no goblin metatypes and no exotics. A good half of the crew were over or under the weight and height limits imposed on ordinary troopers. The combination of details told him that these were the Fort's mages. Tom had no problem picking out Furlann from among them. Her auburn hair was long and flying loose, not regulation, but that was something else mages got away with. Getting closer, he saw that she still made BDUs look better than they had any right to. Tom didn't disagree with Santiago's attitude about Furlann's desirability, just the captain's expression of it. She was making directly for the gate.

"Captain Furlann!" he called

She turned, saw him, and stopped to wait. Her expression showed neither surprise nor welcome. Such coolness had earned her the nickname Ice Heart. Her wide green eyes were calm and collected, though their color was made more startlingly bright by the dark smudges of exhaustion beneath them. Even rag-ass tired she looked good.

"Major," she said as he reached her. "I'd heard you'd been assigned here."

"I got in just in time for the recent party."

She looked at him with reserved expectancy.

"I just heard you were here," he said awkwardly. "It's been a while since Denver. I thought maybe we could stop at the officer's mess. Get a drink, some food, talk a bit. You know, unwind after the exercise."

She raised one eyebrow, and almost smiled. "Why, Major Rocquette, I didn't think you had it in you. I'm afraid I'll have to pass. It's been a long few days. All I really want right now is some sleep. You need some too, I'd say."

She was right, of course, but exhaustion made him single-minded, too. "You *are* head of magical OpFor?"

"That's right." Any thawing he'd seen in Ice Heart was gone.

"Well, there are some things about the exercise that are bothering me."

"I'm sorry to hear that."

"I thought maybe you could help me out by explaining a few details."

"You thought wrong."

"Look, I'm not asking for secrets. All I need to know is whether the OpFor represented a reasonable threat. Were we dealing with potential hostiles, or was it rigged as a psych test?"

"I can't talk about any of that."

"Can't or won't?"

"Tenacity can be a virtue." She gave him a cold half smile. "You know better than to ask about this stuff. That's not how the game is played."

"There's more than a game going on here," he said, suddenly annoyed at her cavalier response. "The exercise was dangerous. We had people really get hurt out there. There's got to be a good reason for it."

"Oh, there is," she said. "Just hope you get good at what you're doing. You'll need to be."

She left him standing there and joined the last of her colleagues passing through the gate into the secure compound.

>>>>>LOCAL FEED WFDC
 -[20:18:06/8-14-55]
WFDC NEWS ANCHOR: SHIMMER GRACE [GRAC-A303]
UPLINK SITE: BETHESDA STUDIO, FDC

Grace: "Well, thank you, Taylor. What about that, friends? Conscience of the Country, eh? I guess they must have a special grace from above. Conscience for the *whole* country? I'm not sure I like them being *my* conscience. [*Query cam angle*] What about you?"

[Audience response: 57% negative]

Grace: "Well, it is a little scary, isn't it? But I bet I know somebody who isn't afraid of doing *her* conscience. Cynthia Locke is Chief of Police for the Federal Capital District, and she is ready to uplink with us. Live! *[Screen inset: Locke]* "Chief Locke, what do you know about the Conscience of the Country?"

Locke: "Would you care to rephrase the question, Shimmer?"

Grace: "Surely. Let's take a limited view. We honest citizens of the District have a veritable army of the displaced and the potentially troublesome camped in our front yard. I know *I'm* worried. Do you think President Steele is acting effectively in this crisis?"

Locke: "The White House isn't my beat. I'm just a cop, after all."

Grace: "A cop, eh? And your beat *is* FDC. How will a *cop* deal with the Comp Army?"

Locke: "Within the law. The Compensation demonstrators need to know that violence will not, repeat, will *not*, be tolerated. Violence can be exciting and terribly attractive, but it is not the solution to problems." *[Cut screen inset]*

Grace: "As Chief Locke says, violence can be terrible. But you know, sometimes you have to take a hard line. For instance, if you were threatened on the street or someone entered your home uninvited, you would do whatever was necessary to stop the threat. *[Query cam angle]* Wouldn't you?"

[Audience response: 78% positive]<<<<<

5

"We haven't much time," the Asian woman said. She sat on the rail of the catwalk encircling the console cockpit, looking undisturbed by her own pronouncement, but her words served to make the others nervous, especially the ork.

"That's why we need to geek him quick," he said.

Andy couldn't tell if the chrome shields over the ork's eyes were implants or paste-ons, but the twin blades of gleaming metal that slid from beneath his sleeve were real cyberware; there was no tell-tale bulge of a strap-on unit under his sleeve. This ork was a real street samurai. The needle points projected twenty centimeters past the ork's wrist and were perfectly spaced to pierce Andy's eyes dead center.

Placing his palm in front of the spurs' deadly points, the norm runner said, "We didn't come here to make noise."

"All he'll make is a nerdy bleat," the ork said. "Won't you, sheep?"

"Don't hurt me," Andy pleaded.

Andy's connections with real shadowrunning went no further than lurking on the shadownet. He'd *heard* about a lot of real shadowrunners, but he'd never actually *met* any. Now that he had, he was quite sure he wasn't one of them. His fantasies of being a runner seemed very far away and very, very foolish.

"Nobody's going to hurt you, kid," the norm said.

"That's right," the ork agreed, snapping his blades in and out of their forearm sheath so quickly that Andy wasn't entirely sure they'd moved. "Be over so fast you won't feel a thing."

"Wait a minnit, wait a minnit." The troll cocked his head to the side, as if he were listening to something. After a moment he said, "Yates is okay, but he's locked out of the research banks. He won't be driving the loot home."

"Drek. We're hosed." The ork didn't sounded surprised. "And it's all because of this little piece of corp drek."

"Dump it," the norm said. "We knew we were taking a chance when Yates found the back door. We'll just have to go back to the plan."

"They're coming," the woman said.

"Then we're going," the norm said.

The woman did a backflip off the rail and disappeared from sight. The norm and the troll looked at each other and shrugged.

"Just one more piece of business," the ork said, cocking his arm back.

Andy's eyes were riveted to the twin points of the ork samurai's spurs. He saw his sight, his very life balanced on those needles. He waited, sweat trickling down his sides, hoping he wouldn't shame himself by wetting his pants. He'd never thought he'd die this way. Hell, he'd never really thought he would die. It wasn't the sort of thing he thought about at all.

But the spurs came no closer.

Finding himself still breathing, Andy forced himself to widen his focus and saw the norm's hand wrapped around the ork's wrist. The two men were glaring at each other. The troll looked on passively, apparently content to let his fellow runners settle their differences between themselves. For the moment, the "they" who were "coming" were forgotten.

"He'll squeal," said the ork.

"That's no reason to kill him," said the norm.

"Good enough for me."

"Not for me. Think about this, you leave him dead, they'll know we've been here. We take him with us, and all they've got is an empty locked room. Taking him with us will give us some slack."

"Marksman's right," the troll said.

"Nobody asked you, Rags," the ork snapped. His eyes never left the norm's. The norm, whose name was apparently Marksman, stared right back at him. Andy would never have been able to stare down the samurai, but this Marksman guy clearly had chutzpah. The ork wasn't ready to give up. "You let him live, he'll squeal. Put the corpcops on us for sure. I ain't got no interest in watching my hoop twenty-four a day."

"No!" Andy shook his head vigorously. "I won't tell anybody."

The ork rolled his eyes. "Oh, and *that's* chiptruth."

"Hurry!" called the woman's voice from below.

"We got no time for this," Marksman said. "Rags, get the kid moving."

Rags did as he was told, hustling Andy toward a break in the railing near the nose of the cockpit console. From there a ladder ran down into the shadowy recesses beneath the cockpit entry level. Andy had never been down there before. The drivers didn't go down there; it was tech territory.

Behind him he heard Marksman say, "We'll take care of the kid later."

"Later," the ork agreed.

Rags laid his immense trollish hand on Andy's shoulder and propelled him toward the ladder. Andy barely managed to get a grip on the handrail, before he took the fastest way down. The troll crowded close, and Andy had to scramble to stay ahead of Rags's descending bulk and avoid getting stepped on.

Below the catwalk level the air was warmer with the heat radiating from the pipes and vents and motors around him. The space wasn't small, but it was claustrophobically cramped by the support struts and gimbal mounts interwoven with hydraulics and other simulation enhancers.

Virtuality could do a lot, especially with simsense tracks on the circuits, but some effects were still best simulated by manipulating the user's physical environment. Telestrian did a lot of simulation testing, and that testing demanded a lot of variable environments. That was what this down-below was all about. The console chambers had been built to accommodate such testing and make it as realistic as possible. Some of this machinery was responsible for Andy actually feeling the G forces in the Montjoy simulation. In a way, dirty and smelly and noisy as it was, it was fascinating.

But he didn't have time to be fascinated. The troll urged Andy on, emphasizing his words with piledriver blows to Andy's kidneys. Rags didn't sound mad, but those shoves hurt. Andy had the horrible feeling that the troll was being gentle. Trolls were inhumanly strong, and Rags was bigger than average for his metatype. Maybe he didn't know his own strength? Andy shivered despite the heat bathing him. Was the troll strong enough to tear a person limb from limb? Would Andy find out the hard way?

Not being in complete control of his forward motion—thanks to Rags—Andy caromed into the hardware surrounding him. He yelped from the pain, then he found out what real pain was when Rags cuffed him.

"Keep quiet," the troll said menacingly.

Andy did his best, but Rags kept giving Andy shoves that sent him into the hard and often scaldingly hot hardware. Andy managed to stifle the noise, but he couldn't keep himself from crying.

Even without Rags's help, Andy banged his head and barked his shins as they progressed through the tightly packed maze of machines. It wasn't fair. The troll didn't seem to have half Andy's trouble negotiating the twisting course.

With one last shove, Rags propelled Andy through an open doorway in one of the walls. Which one, Andy couldn't be sure; he had lost all sense of direction during the trip through the machinery. Rags followed him through, crowding him up against the cool wall of what appeared to be a maintenance corridor. Marksman and the ork were right behind Rags. The norm spun just inside the entrance and ran a card through the maglock. The door hissed shut.

There was another ork waiting in the maintenance tunnel. He wore Telestrian coveralls like the others. Though lacking the obvious chrome of the first ork, he still didn't look like a Telestrian employee; there was something feral about him that was quite unlike the orks Andy knew. This one didn't belong in the corporate world.

"Who de frag is dis?" the ork asked, clearly unhappy to see Andy.

"Baggage," the first ork said, shoving Andy toward the other. "And it's your job to see he don't get us into trouble, Beatty."

Beatty looked to Marksman, who nodded.

"Don't get hungry," the ork samurai said.

"You mean I don't get ta eat him here?" Beatty looked disappointed as he ran a finger along one of his tusks. "Shamgar, you never let me have any fun."

"Fun's for later," Shamgar said.

Andy thought he saw the samurai's spurs snap out briefly. The light wasn't good in the tunnel. Maybe he was mistaken?

"Right now, we're back to the original plan," Marksman said.

"I tought Yates had a short cut," Beatty said.

"The geek here changed the road map," Shamgar told him.

Beatty looked annoyed. And hungry.

"I'm sorry," Andy stammered. "I didn't mean to cause you any trouble. I mean, I didn't even kno—"

"Just shut up," Shamgar growled.

Andy shut up.

"Things aren't so bad," Marksman said. Andy wasn't sure if Marksman was talking to him or to the other runners, but what followed was definitely for the runners. "We head for our original target and get Yates his connection. We'll have time if we get moving."

"He gonna see everyting we do. He seen all our faces already," Beatty complained, pointing at Andy.

"Kit will take care of him," Marksman said.

"Oh, yeah." Beatty sounded embarrassed, the way you do

when you remember something you shouldn't have forgotten.

Kit? Who was Kit? And what was Kit going to do to him?

"She ain't the answer to everything," Shamgar said.

"Don't be so sure," Marksman said.

Kit must be the Asian woman. Andy still wondered what she was supposed to do to him. He hoped it would be better than being torn apart by a troll or eaten by a feral ork.

The trip through the maintenance corridor wasn't as hard on Andy's body as the one through the down-below of the cockpit room, but his nerves didn't take it any easier. These runners were desperate people. They didn't want him along. Some of them didn't even want him *alive*. What if Telestrian security discovered them? Andy wasn't really much of a hostage. There would be a firefight for sure. The idea didn't sound as appealing in reality as it always had on his virtual runs.

Despite his misgivings, they reached the runners' destination without encountering anyone. The door before them was marked "Industrial Robotics Design Center." Marksman stood at the maglock, readying his card.

"You don't want to do that," Andy said.

Marksman looked at him questioningly. "Why not?"

"The Design Center's main computer system was scheduled to be down for maintenance tonight." The news had been posted on the morning update. The designers would be gone, but the corporation's *real* maintenance techs would be hard at work on the other side of the door. If the runners barged in on the Telestrian work team, they would have more hostages. Or worse—if somebody on either side panicked, Shamgar might get his way and there'd be corpses, maybe Andy's among them.

"You want an inside connection to the Telestrian net, right? I know another place where you can hook in. There won't be anybody there."

"That so?" Marksman asked.

Andy nodded solemnly. It was. At least he'd take them where no one else would get hurt.

Unfortunately, the runners didn't believe him. Marksman swiped the card through the reader. The door hissed open on a dark and deserted room.

The Design Center was dark, uninhabited.

"We're the scheduled fix-it team," Marksman said.

The runners moved inside swiftly. Shamgar went to the other door, a sentry. Beatty remained in the tech corridor as he had done before. Rags selected one of the cyberdeck stations and dragged a black box out of his satchel. Opening a side panel, he revealed a cradle into which he put the workstation's phone handset. He jacked the cyberdeck into the box, leaned over his apparatus, and whispered, "Yates?"

"Good link," the box said.

"Make it fast, Yates," Marksman said.

"Lightning is slow," the box said. "I'm gone."

Almost a minute passed before the box began to curse.

"Problem?" Marksman asked anxiously.

"This place is iced in heavy." Ice, slang for IC or Intrusion Countermeasures, was defensive programming. The nastiest forms could fry a decker's synapses. "Frag it to hell, I'm locked! I—"

Their decker had clearly run into serious trouble. One by one the runners turned to look at Andy. He could see it in their faces, especially Shamgar's—they were blaming him for trapping their decker.

>>>>>LIVE FEED COVERAGE
 −[22:54:55/8-14-55]
REPORTER: TAYLOR WEINGARTNER [WEIN-324]
UPLINK SITE: ARLINGTON DISTRICT, FDC

Weingartner: "As you can see behind me, all is not peaceful here among the tents of the Compensation Army. Moments ago a scuffle broke out between police and some of the demonstrators. I'm not sure what this sudden violence was about, but it was serious. The blue-beret woman I spoke to earlier tonight has been carried away on an improvised stretcher. That woman claimed to be on an errand of mercy; now it seems that the quality of mercy hereabouts is somewhat strained.

"What a minute. Christian Randolph, self-proclaimed general of the Comp Army, has just arrived on the scene.

"Mr. Randolph, Mr. Randolph!"

Randolph: "Yes?"

Weingartner: "Taylor Weingartner, WFDC. Tell me, sir. A woman who earlier this evening identified herself as a member of Conscience of the Country was injured at the heart of the scuffle. Do you think this fight has anything to do with your blue-beret soldiers?"

Randolph: "My blue berets? What are you talking about?"

Weingartner: "Are you denying that the Conscience of the Country is connected to your Comp Army?"

Randolph: "Without knowing exactly what you're talking about, all I can say is that I came here to DeeCee to see justice done. I have nothing but open arms for anyone of a like mind. If the people you're talking about are here for that reason, if they are due compensation, then they are by definition a part of our Army."

Weingartner: "So you condone the violence they appear to have instigated."

Randolph: "You know that's not what the Army's about. We do not now, nor will we ever, resort to violence to achieve our just demands."<<<<<

6

"Yates is in trouble. Ice has got a hook on him." Rags sounded worried.

"Tell him to cut and run if he needs to," Marksman said.

"I told you the geek hosed us," Shamgar said. "We oughta cut and run ourselves."

"Yates isn't down yet," Marksman said.

"The ice is black." Rags's morose expression was growing bleaker.

From Andy's excursions into the shadownet, he'd heard that Telestrian used black ice, the kind that could kill an unauthorized decker. He hadn't really believed it. So much of what passed back and forth on the net was just noise. But the troll sounded sure. And if he was right—

Andy didn't mind playing with black ice in his shadowrunning fantasies, but the real thing not only scared him, it made him angry. He'd never understood how a corporation—or anybody, for that matter—could justify using that kind of deadly force just because somebody was trespassing on their cyberturf.

If Yates was tangling with black ice, his synapses could be frying. So why were the runners standing around debating? Their decker was in trouble in the Matrix. Didn't they know how fast things moved in the cyberspace? Yates could already *be* fried.

"Aren't you going to help him?"

"Nothing we can do, kid," Marksman said. "None of us are deckers."

"I've decked," Andy said. Had he really said that?

"Are you saying that you want to help?" Marksman sounded a little surprised and a lot suspicious.

"He'll jack in and squeal," Shamgar said. "We'll be wearing corpcops before his butt has a chance to warm the chair."

"No I won't," Andy said. Leastwise not until he was sure Yates was safe from any black ice. And by then Andy would be in the Telestrian net, and there wouldn't be anything the runners could do to stop him from alerting security.

"Yates needs help," Rags said.

"I know, I know," Marksman said.

"You can't just let him fry," Andy said. "I mean, I don't have a lot of experience, but I might be able to do something. I could at least try."

"Get us *all* fried," Shamgar said.

"What about Yates?" Rags asked.

"He knew the risk," Shamgar said.

"That's not very loyal," Andy said.

"What the frag would you know about loyalty, geek?" Shamgar snapped.

Andy thought the ork was going to jump him, but Rags shifted, shielding Andy with his bulk. The troll was looking at something behind Andy.

"Can we trust him?"

"Trust him," the woman said. Andy hadn't seen Kit come back, but when he turned his head she was sitting on one of the workstations, long pale legs tucked underneath her. She smiled at him, but her eyes were distant.

"You sure, Kit?" Marksman asked.

"He wears the corporate brand, but he does not show the corporate heart." She shrugged. "Life is never utterly sure. Is that not part of life's charm?"

"All right, kid. We'll give you a chance," Marksman said. Shamgar growled, but Marksman ignored him. "You cross us, Shamgar gets you. You call corp security in on us, there'll be nothing they can do fast enough to stop Shamgar from shredding you. You don't strike me as ready to give your life for Telestrian Cyberdyne. You've got too much ahead of you. Don't you, kid?"

Andy nodded, because it was easier to agree. He was really getting tired of the way Marksman called him "kid," but now wasn't the time to complain.

"You think you can help Yates, you do it," Marksman said. "Just remember, we'll be watching. Anything goes bad, Rags will know. Understand?"

Andy wasn't sure he believed that, but he said, "I understand."

While Rags set up a link with his black box, Andy sat down at one of the workstations, settling himself in the recliner. He slid the cover back from the keyboard and input suite. Light glinted cold and wan on the datacord plug as he pulled the connection from its housing.

This was real shadowrunning stuff, not some virtuality imitation. He was about to go decking against black ice. Hadn't he always dreamed of living the life of a shadowrunner?

Well, no, not always. He remembered when he'd first become fascinated by the idea. He'd just taken a dare and decked into the shadownet. There he'd heard of "famous" runners like Sam Verner, the Seattle-based runner rumored to be the first since Howling Coyote to raise and control the power of the Great Ghost Dance. The freedom and power the runners enjoyed had seemed seductive.

When Andy learned that Verner too had started as a corporate geek, he'd been inspired. If Verner had broken free of the corporate world and become a shadowrunner, Andy was sure he was capable of doing the same. For a month or so afterwards, he'd worn leathers, fringed like he saw in the West Coast fashion fac-files, and had gotten really deep into the shaman stuff. Trance drum chips, fetishes, meditation chips, dream catchers, Indian legend chips. He'd even gotten himself a Narcoject pistol like the one Verner was supposed to carry. It wasn't a real Narcoject—he couldn't afford the carry permit, but his corporate affiliation did let him possess a non-functional replica—but the logo-inscribed butt sticking out of a genuine Nauga-leather fast-draw holster added a real frosty touch to his look.

When he wasn't strutting his stuff down at the Landover Mall or the Telestrian Plaza Dome, he'd spent hours alone in his room, running the chips and opening himself to the universe, waiting for the spirit visions. He never did have any. All he'd gotten was a lot of grief from his older sisters. He'd been so embarrassed that he'd given up the vision quest thing and gone back to his studies, but less than a month later he'd started his virtual running.

And now, sitting at the cyberdeck workstation he'd chosen, he wasn't playing a game anymore.

It was a magic moment, though not the sort a shaman like Verner did. Andy's magic was the metaphorical magic of technomancy. His early test scores showed that. If he had a totem spirit, it had to be the Ghost in the Machine. The magic of rigging, where a man became one with his machine, was Andy's path to enlightenment and the wonder of decking, where anything you thought could be real. Virtually real, anyway.

Almost as real as the ork breathing down his neck. Andy snugged the cord home into his datajack and poised his hands over the input surface. The moment of truth. He stabbed a finger down on the Engage button, made a fast trip through the identification protocols, accessed his own Matrix management files, launched his persona program, and—

A shining exoskeletal man-shaped robot, identical to the ultimate form of *Exterminator T-2050,* stood beneath the electron skies. The machine terror wore only a dark leather jacket whose back glowed with a great red neon "C" and a smaller blue neon superscript "3." Passing data pulses splashed light against the exterminator's chrome skull as its red-lit ocular units scanned the cyberspace horizon.

Andy suppressed the ominous music that accompanied each move the exterminator made. Despite his icon's appearance, he was no killer decker. This was no pretend foray into the Matrix; here and now, the audio conceit seemed foolish. Besides, it used processing power he might need.

He felt a tug and understood it to be directions, fed in through Rags's black box. Andy went with the flow, moving through the Matrix sky on boot jets of flame like an armored superhero. The landscape below him changed from the normal black void and scattered lights of system icons, connected by pulsing data streams, to a deep violet. The lights retained their characteristic shapes, but the icons were dimmed, as if they were wrapped in some protective, translucent fabric. Letters began to appear in the air before him, scrolling along into words: "Your clearance is inadequate. You stand in danger of violating a Telestrian Cyberdyne secure matrix zone. Desist. If you do not, your intrusion will be met with deadly force. You have been warned."

Andy launched his best sleaze routine and hoped. He was a user in the Telestrian system and his legitimate codes gave him a leg up that an outside decker wouldn't have. But was it enough?

It seemed so. Nothing came to gobble him up.

Urged forward, Andy focused on a datastore. That was his destination. He eased through the gate and was confronted by a battle in progress. A Telestrian executive icon struggled with a figure in golden armor with the Telestrian logo etched into the breastplate. From Rags's feed, Andy knew that the exec wasn't legit, but simply Yates's disguise. Until now Andy had never seen anything like the knight icon, which looked like something out of *The Legend of Excalibur,* but he knew that it *was* Telestrian and it was an intrusion countermeasure. Just being in the same Matrix location with it, he could feel the program's power—the full mainframe, he guessed, which meant that there was a *lot* of computer behind it.

The knight icon had an open-faced helmet and the visage that showed in the opening looked carved of the darkest onyx, black as night, black as the blackest ice. Yates and the knight were locked hand-to-hand, and it looked as if the knight was beginning to overpower the decker. Hoping he wasn't being really stupid, Andy materialized his exterminator's multi-phase pulse rifle and pumped plasma into the knight.

Andy's attack program didn't even make the knight icon flicker, but it did cause the knight to turn its dark face in his direction. The knight's baleful eyes promised destruction. Andy felt very, very stupid.

But apparently the distraction was all Yates needed. The decker surged against the knight, throwing it off balance.

Then he struck, in a series of martial arts moves that blurred his icon. Andy didn't quite see what happened, but one second the knight was a threat and the next, it was staggering back, its armor disarticulating. The shed pieces, along with whatever they might have contained, shriveled into floating shreds of ash. Last to go was the knight's head, which seemed to be trying to say something as it crinkled and shrank.

"Tough bastard." Yates turned to Andy and looked him up and down. "Thanks, stranger."

"Null perspiration," Andy lied. The thought of going against the black ice had most certainly made him sweat. Not that he would notice or feel it here in the Matrix.

"Hey, you're running a Telestrian ID. Who the hell are you, and why the hell did you help me against that ice?"

Andy couldn't take his eyes off the flaking remains of the knight. "The knight. It really was black ice, wasn't it?"

"Blacker than a corp auditor's heart. You didn't answer my questions."

"Sorry. My handle's C-Cubed."

That's what the C³ on the jacket was all about, but Andy wasn't about to tell this decker or anyone else what it stood for. Nobody *really* had to know it stood for Cruncher's Cybernetic Cub, a tag his sister Asa had stuck him with while setting Andy up for his first foray into the Matrix. She'd locked the handle in on his terminal, and by the time Andy had learned enough to break the lock, he'd gotten used to the tag. His rep in the Matrix might not be great, but he didn't really want to start all over again under a new name.

"That's one, but it don't cover why."

"Your friends sent me. Rags helped me find you."

"Yeah? Well, okay. Thanks again, Cee."

Yates stuck out a hand and Andy reached out automatically to grasp it. He felt a shock on contact and the Matrix blurred for a nanosecond. Andy hadn't experienced direct contact in the Matrix before; the buzz that the physical sensation put in his head surprised him a little. Yates smiled, pumping the exterminator's multi-digit manipulator with a firm and controlling grip.

"I haven't glommed what I came for yet. Since Rags and the crew sent you, you probably want to help me prowl around."

He really didn't. Saving someone from black ice was one

thing, helping with a data theft was another. "I don't know what you're looking for."

"Yeah, well, I can't say I know exactly either, but I'll know it when I see it. But I think maybe you might shorten the search. Your codes say you're a test driver, right?"

"Yeah."

"Want to show me where you launch from?"

"I guess." Andy showed him. He knew he shouldn't, but it seemed the right thing to do at the moment. Yates wasn't such a bad guy, and Andy had always liked showing off. He opened the ready room for the test drivers, although he was a little embarrassed by the old-fashioned ambiance of the iconographic representation. The place was supposed to look like a mid-twentieth-century fighter squadron's headquarters, or so Russ said. The filing cabinets were awfully low-tech imagery to impress a cutting-edge decker like Yates. Still, the Montjoy files seemed to impress him. Yates pulled and perused a few, dropping several into a briefcase that appeared and floated at his side. He came to Andy's control file and looked up.

"Say, you're the one who was flying the other prototype, aren't you?"

Realizing that Yates had to be the stranger he'd been chasing during his Montjoy test run, Andy said, "Yeah."

"Not bad flying, Cee."

The praise gave Andy a thrill. And why not? Yates was a real shadowrunning decker, and a good one, yet Andy had managed to impress him. It was no small feat. He managed to stammer out "Thanks."

Yates prowled around the virtual room some more, poking into every datastore. It took him a while, but he didn't waste any time either. More than once he added files to his briefcase. Andy knew he ought to protest the theft. In fact, he started to several times, but each time he did his persona program started to glitch; by the time he got it under control, the urgency to act had passed.

"Time to go," Yates said. "Don't worry, Cee. I wiped the tracks your entry codes left."

That was when the full weight of what was happening hit Andy. It was *his* codes that had gotten them in, *his* codes that would be linked with the data theft. Telestrian would see *him* as the thief.

That was also when the black-faced knight in golden armor materialized in front of them.

This knight had more ornate and more complicated armor than the first. The knight stretched a gauntleted hand toward Andy, a seemingly pointless move from where he stood more than an arm's length away. But as the armored fist moved, a flaming sword appeared, reaching out for the exterminator's cranium-torso flexor junction. Andy was too slow to dodge.

But Yates interposed a shield, catching the sword and causing sparks to fly. Andy staggered back and the knight engaged Yates. It was an effective defense, the sword splashed flame as it jammed against the shield. But Andy could see that it wouldn't last forever. The knight's attack was developing a series of spidery cracks in the shield icon that represented Yates's defense.

Andy didn't know what he could do. His attack program hadn't fazed the other ice, what good would it be against this one?

Yates parried the knight's next attack—but while he did, he shoved his briefcase toward Andy. Without thinking, Andy took it.

"Get out of here, Cee."

"What about you?"

Yates's answer was preempted as the knight slammed his sword into Yates's shield with a fury that destroyed any hope of holding out against the onslaught. Between blows Yates shouted, "Go! I'll cover."

"But what about you?"

"No way I'm gonna stay and play with this any longer than I have to. Go!" The knight landed another attack, causing Yates to grunt. Pieces fragmented from Yates's shield and flew away, burning.

"Drek, don't be a tortoise."

Yates snatched the briefcase back and used it to slug Andy in the head. The shock felt physical. Cyberspace started to strobe around Andy, disorienting him. He struggled, trying to stabilize his Matrix connection, but there didn't seem to be anything he could do. He was caught, his Matrix presence unfocused.

Helpless, he watched as the knight swung again and shattered Yates's shield into a billion shards of fire. The sword swept in and sliced clean through the false Telestrian exec's shoulder. Arm separated from body and was no more. Yates screamed as black fire ignited along the wound and rose to consume him.

The knight turned to look at Andy, stepped toward him, raised the sword. There was nothing Andy could do. He was frozen as the virtuality around him flickered. His mind was flickering, too. Then he was gone but not gone, whirling away from the black ice knight and lying, panting, in the console chair. He was out, and not out, all at once. Away from the virtual ready room, yet still standing beneath the electron skies; spiraling away from the secret places through open cyberspace among streaks and stars of data, yet blinking meat eyes at the faces of a troll and a man. Out of the Matrix and falling back down into his sweat-plastered, limp body, yet already there, although simultaneously standing, frozen, watching the knight raise his sword of fire. The duality tore at his mind and overwhelmed him.

The next thing his senses recorded was the troll saying, "Yates is gone."

Andy's awareness crawled back, and with the understanding that he had experienced dump shock for the first time. Yates must have held some kind of control over Andy's Matrix presence. He hadn't known another decker could do that, but somehow Yates had cut him loose from the Matrix and sent his persona program crashing home. Andy didn't understand, but he was glad he hadn't had to face the black ice alone.

"He got the stuff?" Shamgar asked.

"He gave it to me," Andy heard himself say.

That was a stupid thing to say, even if it was true! But dump shock was supposed to do that to you: make you stupid and slow. It was supposed to pass, too. Andy hoped so. He felt like drek.

"There's nothing on the deck," Rags said.

Shamgar cursed long and hard.

"Our new ally has headware," Kit said.

"Could Yates have dumped it there?" Marksman said.

"Maybe. I haven't got the tools to find out here," Rags said.

"And we haven't got the time," Kit added.

"Then somebody's going for a ride," Marksman said. "He's too shaky to make time. You'll have to carry him, Rags."

Andy tried to object as the troll heaved him out of the console couch. His stomach hit the troll's hard bony shoulder and knocked the air out of him. He didn't even feel them pull the datajack free.

>>>>>NEWSNET DOWNLINK
  -[6:22:14/8-15-55]

COMP ARMY: REACTION FROM THE HILL AND THE WHITE HOUSE

While Federal District Police and Compensation Marchers clashed in yet another shouting match outside, President Steele spoke from the White House today. "I want to assure you all that everything possible is being done to ensure that each and every member of the so-called Compensation Army receives his or her just and proper compensation," he said. "I know the country is with me on this."

Congressional leaders agree. Speaker of the House, Betty Jo Pritchard (Rep-ONT), on a scheduled trip to her home in Toronto, Ontario, holds the hard line. "Lawlessness and disorderly conduct are not conducive to justice," she commented. "No one is denying the justice of the compensation claims, but the approach being taken by Randolph and his Compensation thugs is criminal. The UCAS government does not, cannot, and will not support criminals."

Meanwhile, the Gorchakov-Drinkwater Immediate Compensation Bill remains in committee and Christian Randolph, spokesman for the Compensation Expedition Force, is not happy. "Delay is what they really want," Randolph said. "They're expecting us to fade away. Well, I'm here to tell them that I'm an old soldier, and this old soldier is not going to fade away. Old soldiers know how to fight. We're all Americans here, and we all know that Americans don't like to start fights. But we're not afraid to finish them. Back us into a corner and you'll see what I mean."

When asked to speculate on whether Randolph was now threatening violent confrontations between the government and the Marchers despite his previous anti-violence stand, Cynthia Locke, Federal Capital Chief of Police would only reply, "No comment."<<<<<

7

Ten hours wasn't enough to wipe the sludge of the field exercise from his brain, but nature couldn't be denied and Tom woke up. Instead of drowsing back off, he found his mind racing across the events of the last week, from the sudden transfer orders through the war game and on to the dismal debrief. All the secrecy bothered him too much to go back to sleep. And his small room was too stifling, not just from the day's rising heat. The walls were too constricting.

The kitchen at the officers' mess hall was between breakfast and lunch, leaving the Nuke 'Em self-service section as the only food source. Tom knew how to deal with that. He went right past the dismal Protein Pick-ups, Breakfast Burritos, Easy Eggs, and Scrambled Starters to the drinks section and filled the biggest cup he could find with black soykaf. The cup he'd chosen wasn't rated for hot liquids, so it slagged, and Tom barely avoided being scalded. Still half unconscious, he observed blearily. He found another cup, hot-rated this time, and filled it. Caffeine wasn't supposed to chill the effects of too many wide-awakes, but it had gotten him through his share of mornings after.

The hall wasn't crowded, and he didn't see anyone he knew. Just as well; acquaintances would have demanded acknowledgment. He didn't feel like making new friends yet, either; so he looked for a table as far away from people as he could get. Spotting one in a nook near the empty buffet station, he headed that way, targeting the seat that would give him the best view of the hall's big screen. From the snatches he heard as he walked, there was a news program on—weather just now, but they'd likely follow with at least the headlines. He'd missed several days of what was going on in the world and needed catching up.

He got situated and tried focusing his bleary eyes on the screen. The map graphic was mostly obscured by a guy standing in front of it and doing a weatherman's dance with lots of arm-waving, finger-pointing, and hand-sweeping. Pointless antics, Tom thought. The whole country was caught in a stagnant hot spell. You didn't need to be prescient to predict more hot and humid annoyance.

It took Tom longer than it should have to realize that the guy on the screen wasn't a meteorologist and the map wasn't a weather map. The guy was Johnny Lessee, the talk show star, and the map was of the Federal District. Lessee was doing his Comp Army Forecast routine again. Tom was annoyed. The long, drawn-out joke on which way the wind was blowing had gotten old in its first week of July when the first marchers, not yet an army, had arrived in Washington. But for some reason Lessee was clinging to the shtick, dragging the undead routine through July and into August. Tom wondered if Lessee's writers were among the marchers, leaving the star short of material.

Still, Lessee, or more likely his people, had the good sense to keep their graphics current. Or did they? Certainly the map didn't match what Tom remembered, but could it be true that the tent city that had begun in the Tidal Basin parks had really grown so huge? Lessee's map showed the camp to have spread across the river into Arlington and up the Mall as well, lapping at the centers of government power like a tide.

Had he misread Colonel Molinovsky's hint last night?

Using the table's console, Tom tapped in a vote to change the screen to a real news program. Nothing changed; so the computer's tally of the diners' preferences must still favor Lessee. Having learned to take what he could get, he sucked down a draught of throat-searing coffee and tapped on the sound feed for his table. Lessee's voice came through loud and raucous.

"So that's the long and short of it, folks. Not to put *too* fine a point on it, the unmoving mass of hot air sitting atop the Hill is still having *no effect* on the situation. A smaller but no *less* turbulent mass sandwiched between Pennsylvania and Executive Avenues has begun to rotate in concert with the larger air currents around it. Though *this* should come as no surprise to all you veteran weather watchers out there. The way the wind is—"

Tom cut the sound. He'd forgotten how annoying Lessee's voice was, and he knew he didn't need the fatuous liberal's opinions.

"Wouldn't surprise me if Steele up and joined the fragging marchers. Guy's a wimp."

Tom turned to see Olivetti standing beside him. The rigger's teeth shone in a broad smile. Olivetti gestured with his free hand, the flesh one.

"Mind if I join you?"

Tom did; Olivetti wasn't the sort he preferred to associate with. But there were times when it was politic to be polite. "It's a free country."

"Not all of it," Olivetti replied.

"We're not the West without the West." As Tom gave the traditional reply he raised his cup, and Olivetti brought his to meet it. The shock of contact slopped some of Tom's soykaf onto Olivetti's hand. The dark liquid beaded and ran in rivulets across the shiny chrome.

"Sorry," Tom said automatically.

"Not like it matters, man," Olivetti said taking a seat. "Unless they've gone back to draining waste battery acids into the coffee urns." He put his cup down and flicked his wrist, shedding the last of the droplets. "Tactile sensors cut out at discomfort levels and all they leave behind are digital updates, informative but not painful. Wouldn't want to lose a hand and not know about it, eh?"

In Tom's view losing a hand completely was preferable to replacing it with such an obviously mechanical substitute. Not exactly the current opinion in some circles—circles in which, it appeared, Olivetti ran. It wasn't wise to have the commander of your support drones believing that you thought him some kind of perverted freak, even if you did. Tom wasn't as sure as he once had been that cyber-replacement was a perversion—there were medical necessities, after all—but he still wasn't comfortable around people who'd had it done voluntarily. He suspected that Olivetti's enhancements weren't medically necessary, but he gave the man the benefit of the doubt.

"Can't sleep either?" he asked, hoping to get onto a more comfortable subject.

"Sleep is for meat," Olivetti said, not helping at all.

"Yeah, well, you need what you need." Tom nodded toward the screen. "Interested in a change of subject?"

Olivetti glanced at the screen, frowned, and swept his gaze across the hall. When his chrome replacement eyes came back to Tom, the rigger said, "Can't have much support. What did you punch for?"

"NewsNet."

"Good choice."

Olivetti cocked his wrist inward. A data spike snicked out above his knuckles. He slipped the spike into the table's terminal and the picture changed; his vote had pushed the tally over the threshold. The news program was reporting on a speech President Steele had made to the Businesspersons' Council for the Advancement of Science.

"Steele." Olivetti shook his head and made a rude sound. "He's just lucky that Adams went belly up. Otherwise our dear commander-in-chief wouldn't be sitting in the oval office sucking from the great corporate teat. It's not like any thinking beings would have voted the geek in."

"Funny, I would have guessed you for a Technocrat."

The cold chrome eyes regarded him for a long moment before Olivetti said, "You've been hanging with the hoodoo squad too long. I've been a registered Techno Republic policlubber since the beginning back in '32." Olivetti tapped finger to eyeball; metal clicked against metal. "Chrome covers the future. Be plated or belated, your choice. The future's already begun."

Tom didn't want to discuss techno philosophy either. "Steele had a pretty high approval rating in the last poll I read."

"Polls are worth the paper they're printed on, and they're all electronic. Besides, Steele being a fragging Technocrat the e-polls are going to do nothing *but* favor him. Now I'm as forward-looking as the next guy, but these Technocratic bozos? Sure as there's a God in the Machine, they're gonna slot the country up worse than ever. They were 'crats long before they were techno, and like all good 'crats they can't find their backsides without a road map and a guide. Drek, they can't even get a decision to crap out of committee. And I'm not the only one who thinks that way, let me tell you."

Tom didn't need Olivetti to tell him; he'd had his ears filled with anti-Technocrat sentiment at the Point, and overfilled in Denver. Most of it came from just the sort of people you'd expect: rednecks, displacees, Humanis sympathizers, the hoodoo crew, metas, and just about everyone not sporting chrome. When the same sentiment started coming from converts to the cyber revolution like Olivetti, the feelings had to be everywhere. Tom hadn't been keeping up on Technocrat doctrine, but he wondered if what had once been the most rational branch of the Democratic Party hadn't gone a little glitched once it got out on its own.

Steele might be a Technocrat, and he might even be as slotted up as Olivetti implied, but he was still the President, and that still meant something to Tom. Olivetti's ravings reminded Tom of some whispers he'd heard back in Denver, sourceless rumors about factions who found the president unsuitable, factions who might be interested in doing something about it. Were the whispers more than empty air?

"Steel's still commander-in-chief," Tom said, just to see how Olivetti would take it.

"Yeah? We'll be getting a new one in '56. Maybe sooner if Steele gets his butt gobbled up by those squatters on his doorstep."

Not by a secret conspiracy? "You mean the Comp Army?"

Olivetti nodded. "Bunch of dangerous malcontents. Ought to be hosed out of town like vermin. If they won't go peaceably, they can go feet first far as I'm concerned. World'll be better off without the beggars."

Sounded to Tom like somebody's Final Solution, or the Humanis Policlub's Contract for a Better, Stronger America. "Pretty harsh."

"Harsh world," Olivetti said sharply. "A *man* works for a living. He don't go begging." He rapped on the table with his chrome fist. "No matter what it costs him, eh?"

"They're only asking for what's owed them."

"Yeah? So *they* say. But you know what? I think there's a deeper truth here. One they don't want to hear. It's real plain and easy to see, but folks who got their hands out, going 'Gimme, gimme!' don't see nothing but 'what's owed them.' Vermin! We'd still have the West if those old time cream-centers hadn't folded. What they got to cry about, eh? They walked out on what they had, nice and peaceable. But, hey, since they're all good little children, why don't you go pat them on their heads and send them all home? Be good to see them all straightened out just fine."

Despite Olivetti's deadpan delivery, Tom assumed the remark was a joke. He had to; otherwise he'd have to consider spitting on the man. Besides—"I'm not headed that way any time soon. Got my leave denied in the morning posting."

"Ain't so. The grandson of old General Rock ain't going

to be sitting around nowhere warming chairs," Olivetti announced. "Ain't gonna happen. Priv-il-edges of rank and that drek."

Tom wanted to tell Olivetti to shut up, but he said, "Any privileges are my grandfather's, not mine."

"Who you slotting, man? Just *remind* them a little bit who you are. That's all you got to do. Drop the name, man. All there is to it. You'll be on the next flight out, you'll see."

Tom had a fistful of Olivetti's fatigues. "I don't need a rebuilt man telling me how to run my career. I've earned everything I've gotten in this army."

"Don't mean nothing, man." Olivetti's voice was up an octave. "Don't mean nothing. Nobody never said you ain't chill. Chill, man."

Tom didn't remember kicking his chair back and standing, but he obviously had. He let go of the rigger's uniform and eased back from the table. Sheepishly he recovered his chair and sat in it. He reached for his soykaf, but the cup was gone. Olivetti's cup was still on the table, spinning slowly in a widening, black puddle

"It's the wide-awakes," Tom said.

"Yeah, man. The wide-awakes. That's it." He smiled placatingly. "We just watch the news now."

"Yeah, sure."

"Yeah, man. Real chill."

But Tom noticed that Olivetti kept glancing at him throughout the rest of the NewsNet 'cast.

>>>>>NEWSNET DOWNLINK
 —[06:36:43/8-15-55]

POLICY CHANGES IN WASHINGTON
After weeks of concern over the growing unrest in the nation's capital, an alliance of extranational corporations with business interests in the Federal District took concrete steps today, announcing a "closed border" policy. Under the policy, effective at noon today, only persons affiliated with one

of the allied corporations will be allowed access to any of the holdings or properties of that corporation. These entrance restrictions will effectively close such attractions as Telestrian Plaza Mall, the Saeder-Krupp Museum of Air and Space Technology, and the Renraku Conservatory and Arboretum.

Stephen Osborne, president of Telestrian Industries East and chairman of the Alliance of Concerned Corporate Citizens, dismissed concerns about the impact of the new policy on business in Washington and put the policy in a sympathetic light.

In a prepared statement, he said: "Though we are in effect standing on our corporate rights of extraterritoriality, our actions in this matter should not be taken as an indictment of the police forces here in Washington. We of the ACCC have nothing but admiration for the men and women who daily put their lives on the line to protect the good, honest citizens of Washington. Those good folk are operating under constraints that make their jobs extremely difficult, especially given current staffing levels. But the ACCC cannot stand idly by while members of our corporate families are in danger.

"When a government cannot ensure peace and prosperity to its people, action must be taken. Current conditions in Washington are such that sane people must exercise caution. And so we of the ACCC are opting to exercise caution. We are doing what we can to ensure the safety of all members of our corporate families. Once the current crisis is behind us, we believe we can look forward to a day when all citizens can find greater prosperity in a more congenial atmosphere that is better suited to business. May that day come soon."<<<<<

8

The pavement beneath Andy was cool, but the surface at his back had already started to warm in the raw morning light. The division of temperatures across his body was as sharp as the building shadow crossing him. He hadn't been sitting, propped against the concrete wall, for long. *That* much he remembered, even if he didn't remember how he'd gotten here—wherever *here* was. There was a buzz in his head, rattling his nerves. The sun had hurt his eyes in his first, brief attempt to orient himself, and he hadn't seen anything useful before shutting them again. He wasn't quite ready to try again. He could smell that this wasn't a nice place, and the restive skitterings he could hear told him it wasn't the sort of place where he should spend much time. He ought to get his muzzy thoughts together and get on with things.

The feather-light touch of probing fingers told him he'd waited too long.

Flailing arms and legs, he tried to simultaneously brush away whoever was accosting him and get to his feet so he could run. His assailant, a scruffy streetrat, fell away from Andy as he stood, apparently as frightened as Andy.

"Should have checked," squealed the streetrat in a shrill voice. "Should have *checked*! I told you we should have checked."

Andy looked around frantically, afraid the groper had friends. But there was only the one streetrat, and he stood between Andy and the alley's mouth. The man was short and thin, and his clothes were a collection of rags so ratty that Andy wasn't sure how many layers the man wore, let alone what the garments had once been. He was festooned with bits of bone, and tufts of gray and black feathers, and small bits of sparkling things all tied with cord and thong. Some even hung from his greasy dreadlocks. Fetishes, Andy realized. The man rattled as he waved his arms to deny his attempt to roll Andy.

"No harm, no harm," he squeaked.

It was Andy's own plea. Trying to crank down his own fear reaction, he said nothing. If no violence was forthcoming, that was fine by him—it wasn't like he was armed and ready. His head hurt, but the droning buzz appeared to be a fault in the feedback loop monitoring the prelim work for his replacement eyes. His headware wasn't fritzed, but as cyber mods went, headware wasn't useful in a fight, fully operational or not. Even if he'd had combat cyberware, Andy wouldn't have known how to use it. So he watched the streetrat watching him, and wondered what he would do if the scruffy little man decided to attack him after all. It was possible. The man's beady eyes were fastened on Andy, and his expression was avid beneath the grime of homeless life.

"You've been made strange," the streetrat said.

Strange was what this scuz was.

"A shadow is cast over you," the streetrat said. "Yes, a shadow. Clouding your mind it is. A strange spell that I do not know, and strong. Harmonious, though. A shaman maybe, but one I do not know."

Spell? Shaman? Could the streetrat's talismans be real? If the scrawny little man was a real magicker, Andy was out of his depth. Who was he kidding? Andy was out of his depth no matter *what* the streetrat might be.

"Who could it be?" the maybe magicker asked. "Who, who? Who did this to you?"

Andy realized he didn't know. Neither name nor face came to mind when he thought about it. Vaguely, but only vaguely, he remembered that the spellcaster was a woman. The sweet tones of her voice were his clearest recollections, but he couldn't remember what she'd said. Still, he knew she'd been in his home, at the Telestrian East complex, and that she hadn't belonged there. Neither she nor her friends had belonged there.

Her friends? There had been others with her, but he couldn't remember their faces or names either. Shadowrunners. He wasn't even sure how many there had been. It scared him not to be able to remember. What else had she done to his mind? He was sure something had been taken from him. He remembered a machine and a troll. Or was it an ork? Someone had jacked something into his head.

"Wandering in body as well as mind. Far from turf." While Andy's mind had wandered, the streetrat had shuffled close. Grimy fingers plucked at Andy's lapel, tugging at his corporate affiliation pin. "You are lost, yes?"

Andy felt that way, but somehow it didn't seem safe to admit it to this scuzzy specimen of streetlife, magicker or not. He'd at least be able to locate himself physically wherever the shadowrunners had dumped him; all he had to do was find a telecom. But mentally? That depended on what the sorceress had done to him. Which was what? It didn't seem to be much; he just couldn't remember any details about the shadowrunners. Was that so bad?

"Lost now, but not forever," the streetrat said. "With others you run. Blood bonds and magic. Strong magician by your side. Could be you've met who you should. Perhaps a good morning this is, if a hungry one."

Crazy words. How much did this creepy guy know? Had he seen the shadowrunners dump Andy? Did he know them? "Blood bonds?" "Magic?" "Met who you should?" It all sounded more than a little crazy. "What are you talking about?"

"A karma," he said, nodding eagerly. "I can taste it. Yes, a karma you have."

Yeah, right. If Andy had a karma, it was getting skinned alive by both his mother and Russ. What the hell did this ratty little guy know about karma? "Are you supposed to be some kind of soothsayer?"

"Soothsaying? Bunk, junk, and nonsense for simpletons and fools. Me? I am a shaman. My totem is strong in these parts."

A shaman? The guy looked like a homeless derelict. "If you're a shaman, what's your totem?"

"Mother never teach you manners?" the self-proclaimed shaman said indignantly.

"Sorry. I didn't realize it was so personal."

"Personal, yes. Very personal. Ultimately personal. What else would it be?" The shaman gave a snort. He ran a grubby hand beneath his nose, inspected the result, and wiped his hand on his sleeve. "Forgiven already. I know better than to run counter to karma. Learned my lesson long ago, I did. Go with the flow, say I. Dig in claws and take the ride. Karma can't be denied. Okay, say I. Find a hold and cling. There'll be scraps aplenty for all at the end."

"I really think I ought to be going."

"Okay." The streetrat stepped out of the alley and onto the deserted sidewalk. "Where to?"

Andy edged his way to the sidewalk while the opportunity presented itself. "I'm going home. I don't know about you."

"Call me SpellMan, one word, capital M."

"Nice to meet you, SpellMan. Glad we had the opportunity to talk." Andy backed away as he talked. "I'm sure you have a lot of shaman stuff to do, so why don't you get to it, and I'll just be running along."

Andy spun, ready to make his words literal, when SpellMan called out, "Gonna need nuyen for Metro, Andrew Walker."

Andy froze when the shaman called his name. He looked back over his shoulder. SpellMan was holding up a credstick. Andy's? The casing was in Telestrian colors and it had the Cyberdyne crest. The shaman scuttled forward and, to Andy's surprise, handed him the credstick. It was Andy's.

"Nice new deposit." SpellMan smiled, revealing sharp, discolored teeth. "Very nice. Very fresh. Plenty to treat a friend to food."

Andy thumbed the credstick's recognition pad and dialed up his balance. His account showed substantially higher than it had been. Not only hadn't the shadowrunners robbed him, but they'd left him with more money than he'd had before he met them. Maybe they weren't as bad as they'd seemed.

"How'd you know about the deposit?"

The shaman winked. "Survival skills."

Without a reader and authorization codes, the credstick wasn't supposed to respond to anyone but Andy. "You've got a reader tucked among those fetishes, don't you?"

"You were in a hurry." SpellMan hooked an arm around Andy's and tugged to get him started. "Let's go. Where we going, by the way?"

Andy shrugged his arm free, but started walking. This part of the city seemed deserted, and he saw from a street sign that they were in Southwest, on the corner of C and Third Street. They couldn't be too far from The Mall. That big cross street ahead had to be Independence. At least he hoped so—Independence bounded The Mall. He wanted to get away from these seemingly dead office buildings and their rattling, deficient mechanical systems. They didn't offer any succor from this weirdboy streetrat, but people would. There would be more people around the museums and monuments; a crowd, or even one police officer, would offer Andy a chance to scrape loose of the dirty shaman.

The street *was* Independence. The vehicle traffic was non-existent, so they crossed right away. Unfortunately the pedestrian traffic was light, and all the people looked more like SpellMan than Andy. He hadn't realized how few people would be downtown so early on a Sunday. It wouldn't be as easy as he thought to lose SpellMan. Andy's eyes fell on the Saeder-Krupp Museum of Air & Space Technology. It was too early for the museum to be open, but its presence reminded him of other things. He smiled, envisioning the Metro entrance about half a kilometer past it. SpellMan had given Andy back the means to use the transportation system. Andy doubted that SpellMan had a System Identification

Number, and the SINless weren't welcome on public transportation. The Metro would be Andy's way not only out of the downtown, but out of SpellMan's reach as well. Eager, he started walking faster.

Andy didn't get half a block before SpellMan tugged at his sleeve, bringing him up short. "Wait. Will you not acknowledge this monument to a dominant force in shaping your past?"

Andy was puzzled. "What kind of a question is that?"

"A curious one."

"I'll say."

They stood beside the Block, a two-story rectilinear solid of smoky gray material that filled most of the block next to the Air & Space Museum. The dark, tumbled-down shape of a rubbled building resided in the center of the Block, but it was hard to see—the substance of the Block was barely translucent. The only decoration on the Block was a band of light-colored, raised lettering affixed to the surface about three meters up. The words were in Latin, which Andy didn't read, but he'd heard they said something about memory and the promise of justice. The Block was a monument, all right, but a weird sort. Andy had never paid much attention to it. Why did SpellMan think he had any connection to it?

"What's it got to do with me?"

"You don't see?"

Andy looked at the Block. He'd seen it before, of course. How could anyone visiting The Mall miss it? But it had never meant anything to him. The Block didn't look any different to him now except for the odd array of things nestled against it. Andy saw piles of clothing, household and personal goods, pieces of furniture and vehicles, boxes and bundles with indeterminate contents, jars filled with what looked like dirt, and even envelopes and papers weighted down with rocks and chunks of concrete. To judge by its battered, rusted, or burned condition, some of the stuff was junk; but much was in apparently excellent condition. It was amazing all that stuff sat undisturbed. SINless derelicts like SpellMan could make use of the clothes, if nothing else.

"I'm surprised you haven't picked yourself up a new set of clothes," Andy remarked.

"I am not so foolish as to disturb the gifts of memory," SpellMan said.

"Gifts? From whom?"

"Those who remember. They used to do the same at the Wall."

The Wall was a part of the Vietnam Veterans Memorial. Andy remembered reading about how people used to bring mementos of their lost loved ones and leave them at the wall. He'd never heard of anyone doing that sort of thing here. When did it start, and why?

"This used to be a museum, didn't it?"

"That, and more. It was a place built to honor those people who were here before the Europeans came. It was built in the Fifth World and was not, it seems, meant to be a part of the Sixth World. A mistake, you think?"

"I guess."

"But on the part of which World?"

SpellMan grabbed Andy's arm and, with surprising strength, dragged him nearer the Block.

"Touch it."

The shaman spoke in such a commanding tone that Andy could do nothing but obey. Half expecting some sort of jolt when his fingers touched the surface, Andy felt nothing more than the cold hardness of the Block's face. It was just some kind of superhard plastic, smooth and slick.

"Spirits were raised here," SpellMan said. "Terrible things. Some say they sleep here still, waiting. I've never seen them, but it could be so, it could be. Wisely, the mundanes feared what had been done here. Their response was crass, crude, rude, but effective." He rapped his knuckles against the Block. "This mass of dead stuff seals the womb and makes a tomb."

"People are buried in there?"

SpellMan nodded. "I hear the ghosts cry in the night. They cried last night, mourning their loss, and our loss, but they are hedged in by anger and hate and can do nothing." SpellMan dug under his rags and pulled out a piece of chalk. He swiped it across the surface of the Block, but the mark he made faded nearly as fast as he made it. "A magic that is not magic. A legacy of the makers, that none should defile the purity of their hate. It is their shame, and our shame."

SpellMan knelt and tenderly lifted one of the abandoned offerings. Unwrapping the checkered cloth, he revealed an ornate buckle that looked as if it might actually be silver. "Yet it is defiled, in a way that such as they cannot understand. For in the heart of hate there is often love. Love binds too, and can lead us, blinkered, on the path to the future. We walk, we talk, we play games, but the future comes for us and will not be denied. We fight it sometimes, proving that we are fools. Happy fools sometimes, ignorant fools always." He rewrapped the buckle and placed it gently back against the Block. "The dead mass that seals this place only *promises* the death of the struggle. It does nothing to make it happen."

Andy had thought the shaman strange before this performance, now he was sure the man was definitely weirded around the bend. He looked down the street to where the sign of the Metro entrance beckoned.

"Look, I got to go now."

"Not your path."

"Yeah, well, there are people going to be wondering where I got to." Andy started straight toward the Metro. The entry system would scrape the shaman off his back.

The shaman sighed, and followed. As soon as they stepped into the street, the shaman's mood became lighter. He chatted almost casually.

"City's not a place for the natural world," SpellMan said, "not a place for most with my orientation. Shamans are rare here and most of us bond with the creatures man has corrupted. But not me. You don't pick your totem, you know, it picks you, because you are already one with it. Makes you think twice about those bonded to corrupted totems, doesn't it? What *has* Man wrought? But I'm here to tell you that Man has no hold on my totem. We get along without, nay, despite his interference. Prosper, we do. And we will. You can prosper, too. Not hard, really. Gotta know who your chummers are, gotta know the grease and the greed, and how to play them both for yourself. Find the cracks and hide in 'em."

Hiding sounded like a good idea to Andy right now. He found SpellMan's good-natured advice as bewildering as his mystic pronouncements. In some ways, the seedy little shaman was more unnerving than shadowrunners who threatened your life. Andy wondered how he could ever have wanted to be a shaman. Shamans weren't all like SpellMan, were they? Sam Verner wasn't. Or was he? Verner was a shadowrunner, too, and the shadowrunners Andy had met hadn't been like those he'd dreamed about; he remembered *that* much about them.

The Metro stop and freedom from the babbling shaman were little more than a block away, just a little past the gallery and garden compound of the Smithsonian Castle. Andy walked a little faster, but when they reached the corner of the Freer Gallery, he stopped, stunned to see the source of the buzzing sound he'd been hearing since he awoke in the city had a source. He'd thought that it was some kind of mechanical noise pollution, the rattle of heavy-duty ventilators perhaps. Now, through the gap between walls and buildings at Twelfth Street, he saw the source of the sound.

People! Thousands of people crowded the western end of The Mall. There was movement everywhere. But this was no ordinary crowd—there were tents and makeshift buildings on The Mall, and these people were clearly living in them. What was going on?

He took a few steps around the corner, fascinated. Tents, and shacks of cardboard and plastic, and scavenged sheet metal huts covered the western end of The Mall. A cluster of grimy white canvas spread up the shallow rise of the monument grounds, looking like dirty snow humped against the base of the Washington Monument. Who knew how much further the improvised slum extended? It was as if the sleaziest neighborhood of the Barrens had been dumped into the middle of Washington. It was unbelievable—but the noise and smells and sights were real!

Twelfth Street seemed to be some kind of boundary. The police had set up barriers on the east side, and officers in light torso armor and helmets patrolled the makeshift fence. The dark shape of a Citymaster riot control vehicle sat in the middle of the grass like some kind of guard beast. Finding an officer had been one of Andy's hopes, but this wasn't what he'd had in mind.

"What's going on? Who are these people?" Andy wondered aloud.

"Too wrapped in your corporate cocoon you are, not to know that they were here," SpellMan said. "They are gift givers, wanderers, beggars, dreamers, thieves, idealists, rabble-rousers, honest people, the homeless, and the hopeless. Like most people, some are more than one of the above. Most want justice, a few fear it, and some are just looking for a handout. Perhaps there are as many reasons to

be here as there are bodies camped upon the green and huddled in the crevices of the concrete. It would not be surprising."

Andy felt as though he were looking through a window at
an alien world. He'd been intending to use his usual entrance to the Metro, the one on the Mall, but it lay just
within the fringes of the tent city. So many scuzzy people
packed so tightly together scared him, and he was a little
afraid to go near that entrance.

There was another entrance across Independence. It
wouldn't put him on the end of the platform he preferred,
but that seemed a petty point at the moment. He crossed
without looking for vehicles, hitting the entrance well of the
station almost at a run. The escalator wasn't running, but
that wasn't unusual. He was down a half-dozen stairs before
he realized that the entry well wasn't empty.

There were people here, too, as cramped and crowded in
the confines of the entry as their lookalikes out among the
tents and shanties. The mass stirred as Andy burst among
them. Bloodshot eyes stared from beneath bundles of blan-
kets. Haggard faces turned to him. They had been here for
some time; the entry smelled like a sewer.

But the Metro, and his way out of downtown, lay beyond
them. Muttering apologies to those he disturbed, Andy
started working his way down the frozen escalator. He didn't
meet anyone's eyes; that's what you did, the safe course.

Halfway down, he realized that SpellMan had evaporated.
Though Andy had wanted to get free of the shaman, he was
suddenly spooked by being abandoned. The shaman had
been weird, but he'd at least been friendly. Most of the eyes
on Andy were indifferent, but some—many—were hostile.
He felt as if he were among wild animals.

Someone reached out and ran a hand along his back, tugging at his jacket. "Nice suit."

Andy practically jumped down the next three stairs.

"Hey, suit," a hoarse female voice drawled. "Ain't you
afraid of being out here all by yourself?"

Andy concentrated on reaching the bottom of the escalator.

A lump tucked into a corner unfolded into a gray-bearded
man as Andy neared the bottom of the escalator. The man
was dressed in a worn, old US Army uniform, but his hair
was pulled back in a very non-military ponytail. He stepped

into Andy's way. Though Andy was relieved not to see any weapons on the man, the old soldier's physical bulk offered its own threat. Andy was intimidated and feared he was showing it.

"Where you going, suit?" the soldier asked in a raspy voice.

"Home." Andy heard his voice quiver.

"You sure? Maybe the gov'mint gone and gave it away while you were out partying last night. They good at that. You think about that, suit? You think you're safe? Let me tell you, suit. Ain't nobody safe."

Andy didn't feel safe at all. "I don't want any trouble."

The soldier laughed mockingly. He laughed until he started to cough a cough that was deep and raw. The man doubled over. Andy felt sorry for the old soldier's obvious pain, but he knew an opportunity when he saw one. He took a deep breath and brushed past the soldier, avoiding the hand that groped out to stop him.

"Run away, little suit," someone called out from behind Andy. "Run home to your safe corp sell-out."

Andy did run, all the way to the turnstiles. To the jeers of the crowd in the stairwell, he fumbled his credstick into the slot. The reader was slow and Andy urged it on with whispered pleas for speed. He didn't really breathe again until he was on the other side of the barrier. The station attendant in her kiosk stared at him with incurious, uninvolved eyes as he slumped against the wall and panted.

The Mall hadn't been like this the last time he'd been down here. It had changed, turned strange.

>>>>>NEWSNET FILES
WFDC DOWNLINK OPTIONS

CONFEDERATES RATTLING SABERS?
COMMENTARY
Synop: The Senate of the Confederated American States has pledged support to all North American and Caribbean political entities holding coincident interests with CAS. Political analysis expert Sandra Coulson comments on implications of the seemingly innocuous wording of the Confederated States Senate.
    Last update: [14:07:38/8-14-55]

COMPENSATION ARMY UPDATE BACKGROUND
Synop: Recent events involving Compensation Army.
    Last update: [17:00:00/8-15-55]

POLICE MOVE AGAINST MARCHERS COVERAGE
Synop: Police disperse Comp Army demonstrators gathering for vigil at the Block. Minimal violence.
    Last update: [02:23:30/8-15-55]

POLICY CHANGES IN WASHINGTON COVERAGE
Synop: The Alliance of Concerned Corporate Citizens announces "border closing" due to weeks of growing unrest in the nation's capital. Statement from ACCC head Stephen Osborne of Telestrian East.
    Last update: [06:36:43/8-15-55]

RANKS OF THE COMPENSATION ARMY GROW
SIDEBAR
Synop: Street interviews with local citizens, marchers, and SINless on the Conscience of the Country [*Crossref "Consies"*], the newest element of the Comp Army. Upbeat tone.

Last update: [07:26:03/8-16-55]
[*continued next screen*]<<<<<

9

All through his Metro ride home, Andy couldn't help thinking about what SpellMan had said. Despite denying that he
was a soothsayer, SpellMan had acted like one and said that
Andy had a karma. The idea of having a destiny—of being
important—made Andy feel good. He *wanted* to believe he
had a karma.

But karma could be bad as well as good.

What if Andy's karma was *bad*? What if last night's mis-
adventure with the shadowrunners was the start of a down-
hill slide? What if his position with Telestrian Cyberdyne
was compromised? What if they wouldn't let him test-drive
anymore? There were a lot of what-ifs. Like, what if
SpellMan wasn't a shaman at all, but just a crazy streetrat?

Andy felt like he had to talk to someone about what had
happened to him. His friends from class were out, and so
were his on-line chummers; he didn't dare let any of them
know there'd been a data theft from Telestrian. His mother?
Could he tell her what had happened to him? What about his
sisters? Why not? They were his family, weren't they? If
they wouldn't help him get this mess straightened out, who
would? Maybe he should get in touch with Genifer; his half-
sister wasn't connected with the big T, and she would have
a different perspective. Of course, to do that he'd have to
call the General's house, and he hated doing that.

He could try Russ. Russ always listened to Andy's problems. But *could* he try Russ? Russ had disappeared from the
test drive when Yates had taken over the Montjoy prototype,
and Andy didn't know what had happened to him. Russ
probably hadn't suffered anything worse than dump shock,
but Andy didn't know. He was worried about his friend. He
found he was also worried about how Russ would react to
Andy's cooperating with the runners—*if* that was what he'd
done. Starting with their interruption of the test drive, everything was still hazy. Whether Andy had helped the runners
or not, it certainly would look that way since he'd left with

them. For all that he was an atypical suit, Russ was a loyal
company man, and would feel obliged to report Andy. Talking with Russ would have to wait until Andy had assessed
the situation. He'd start by talking with his family.

Still, he brooded on the possibilities all the way to the
Telestrian complex, in through the lobby doors, past security, and up the elevator that would take him to residential
floors.

The apartment's doorplate said that his mother Shayla was
home. Andy remembered that she was on shift rotation; she
had the day off today, so he'd have his chance to tell her
right off. He found her snuggled up in front of the family
room telecom with her latest "friend," an ork named Chunk
Gonsalvo. Andy didn't know Chunk's real first name; he
usually didn't bother learning stuff like that till a guy had
been around for at least a month. There was a small phalanx
of beer bottles on the table next to the couch; that, along
with the early hour and the rumpled state of his clothes, said
that Chunk had spent the night.

"Hi," Andy said as he entered the room. He was nervous
about starting, having half-convinced himself that he should
just keep quiet about the whole thing. His mother didn't
make it easier.

"Where you been?" Shayla's voice was already keyed to
call-on-carpet mode.

Since her clothes were as rumpled as Chunk's, he guessed
she must have spent the night waiting for him to return from
work. Her vigil hadn't left her in a good mood, and if she
felt any relief at seeing him safely returned, she hid it well
under sharp-tongued anger. Andy hoped she'd be more understanding once he'd explained what had happened. But
how did he start? "Well—"

"Aw, leave the kid alone, Shayla. A guy's embarrassed to
talk about things like that in front of his mom." Chunk
winked at Andy. He'd been trying to get on Andy's good
side since the first time he'd overnighted. "When ya gets
lucky, ya gets lucky, eh, Andy? Go grab yourself some sack.
No, no, don't say nothing. I been there, so's I know ya need
it. Shayla will log ya in sick if ya want."

"I will not," Shayla said.

"Don't worry about it," Andy said. "I'll be going in." He
couldn't afford not to go in to the Track today. If he didn't,
it would look suspicious, and he didn't want to look suspi-

cious; that was one of the things he'd figured out on the ride home. "Mom, I want to tell you about what happened last night. I ran into some trouble with some shadowrunners—"

"Shadowrunners!" Shayla rolled her eyes. "If you're going in to work, you haven't got time to waste with another of your gaming stories. Look at you! You look like you slept in your clothes. You'll change and put on something clean before you leave this apartment. I won't have people thinking my son is a slum derelict."

"But this isn't—"

"No buts! Go change or you'll be late."

"But—"

"What did I just say?"

"Listen to yer mom, Andy," Chunk advised.

Andy glared at them. So much for Chunk getting on his good side. Shayla *wasn't* right, and no amount of motherly bluster would change that. He could see he wasn't going to get any sympathy here. He decided to try his sisters.

The hour being what it was, Cyndie and Lola were getting ready to go into work. The girls were in their usual whirlwind of preparations—*they* had no intention of letting anyone think Shayla Walker's girls were slum derelicts. They also had no time to listen to Andy. Like Shayla, they thought Andy was trying to tell them another story about virtual adventures, and they wouldn't give him the chance to say otherwise.

Too bad Asa was away. *She* would understand. *She* would listen. He could call her, but that would leave a record, and he wasn't sure he wanted to do that. What if he was connected to the shadowrunners' theft?

Somewhere in the back of his mind, there was an assurance that he was unconnected to what the shadowrunners had done.

But if that wasn't true? What if someone linked Andy to the theft? Andy was a Telestrian dependent, for God's sake! How could the big T *not* track him down if they thought he'd fragged them by helping the runners? Calling Asa would connect her to this mess, and corporations like Telestrian believed in group responsibility. What might a corp that used black ice to protect its data do to the family of a data thief?

Telestrian using black ice? Where had *that* thought come

from? He'd never seen any evidence of any such thing, or had he?

His memories had been messed with; *that* was certain. He knew the runners had taken his memories of who they were and what they had done. How much more had he lost?

Anger flared in him as he thought about what they'd done to him. What gave them the right to go messing with his head, tromping around in his brain and deciding what he could keep and what he couldn't? He was a person, God damn it! They'd used him and thrown him away, like a worthless piece of unrecyclable junk.

But then why shouldn't they? What had Andy, duty-bound Telestrian employee that he was, done to stop them? What had he been *able* to do? He'd been worthless to the company. The shadowrunners had only demonstrated his worthlessness.

Maybe he didn't want to tell anybody about what had happened, after all.

He showered and changed, all the while wondering if there was a point to getting ready for work. Did he really have a job to go back to? Did it matter? He knew how to find out the answer to the first question—all he had to do was go in for his assignment. Upon leaving the apartment, he found it strangely hard to walk through the corridors of the Cyberdyne branch of the complex, but he made himself do it.

The Track was quiet when he got there, and Russ wasn't waiting to meet him. No one was. Andy tried the ready room. Russ wasn't there; no substitute either. Nonstandard, but not the first time such a thing had happened. Andy saw from the big board that Montjoy was running today, but there was no drive scheduled for him. He called up the work assignments and found he'd been assigned to desk work.

Did the Telestrian honchos know? But if they did, wouldn't they just drag him down to security for questioning? The fact that they weren't hauling him away must mean he hadn't been connected to the shadowrun. Maybe the run hadn't even been discovered yet. Had the runners been that good? Part of him hoped they were. If no one knew they had struck, no one would know how worthless Andy had been.

But he knew, and that knowledge didn't do much for his picture of himself.

The desk work he'd been assigned was inconsequential busywork. He hadn't had such drek dumped on him in over a year. It was a status demotion; it had to be. Well, it suited him, because he'd earned it. Andy jacked in and spent most of the morning poking desultorily at the assigned data manipulations while he brooded over what had happened. Yesterday he'd been a happy wageslave, happy enough to scoff at the term. He'd had a bright future, but that seemed gone now. The shadowrunners had done this to him. They'd taken his future away from him. And for what?

He couldn't even remember.

And they'd done *that* to him as well.

His anger at his losses swelled to overcome his frustration, embarrassment, and self-loathing. Just what *had* the runners done to his head? He felt sure they'd done more than just wipe his memories, though of course he couldn't imagine what. He wanted to know. He *needed* to know. He might not be able to investigate his own wetware, but he *could* check out the cyberware installed in his head. And that was just what he *would* do.

He might be agitated and worried, but he wasn't entirely stupid. He set a special subroutine loose in his work files; the system would look busy now, so there'd be no more pointless busywork dumped on him.

Beneath the mask of phantom busy-working, he called up his best diagnostics and sicced them on his headware. When all systems came up nominal, he looked for anything out of place, anything he hadn't put there. Nothing. Still, something seemed wrong. He checked again and again, almost obsessively, watching for hidden things, until he found something: a file swollen bigger than it should have been, an executable file. And not just any file, but his headware's main resource file—the heart and soul of his internal systems.

The cyberterminal he was using had the resources and Andy used them ruthlessly to flay open the corrupted file and spread its entrails for inspection. In among the expected system routines he found a pigback, a program designed to operate along with and within another. Upon examination, it looked to be an association reinforcer or a mood modifier. Whatever it was, it had minor simsense functionality. He forced a code read onto the pigback and learned that it was an associational reinforcer designed to give him warm fuzzies whenever Telestrian Cyberdyne was mentioned or brought up on an internal file.

He doubted that the runners had put *that* in his head. He was shocked to find that shadowrunning data thieves weren't the first to have messed with his head. The pigback was so deeply embedded that it could only have been installed along with his headware's basic operating system, which led to an inescapable conclusion: Telestrian had authorized it.

He shredded the pigback, slicing its code into component parts and purging each with a savage glee. After finishing the destruction, he felt drained, and a little embarrassed. When thought about calmly, the pigback wasn't such a bad thing. It wasn't like it had been a coercive program—it had only been a persuader. Was it any worse than the association reinforcers in blipvert advertising?

All this time, he'd thought he liked belonging to the Telestrian family because *he* liked belonging to it. Well, he *had*, actually. He hadn't gotten the headware until he was fifteen, so he hadn't been living with the pigback associator before that. Why had Telestrian doctored the headware programming? Didn't they trust him to like the corporation without it?

Trust seemed to be a big issue all of a sudden. The runners hadn't trusted him. Apparently, the big T didn't either. Who the hell could *he* trust?

The busy work that he'd been set could be a manifestation of the trust issue. What if the Telestrian honchos *suspected* he'd been a part of the datasteal but didn't *know*? What if they were keeping him away from anything important while they investigated? They might—who was he kidding?—they *would* want to keep things quiet. A publicized data theft could cost a corp mega-nuyen in the stock market.

Too much speculation. Too much unknown. He had to *know* where he stood.

He would start with his own corporate personnel file. Everyone had direct access to their own files through their System Identification Numbers, but Andy didn't think direct access would get him anything. If he were under suspicion, there wouldn't be anything in his file to alert him—nothing he could access directly, anyway. Going in through another Telestrian access code would offer him the chance to see whether other members of the corporation were being warned about him. Fortunately, he had a TAC other than his own: Russ's, cadged almost two years ago from an unintentionally active terminal in the ready room. At the time, Andy had thought he might someday want to see what his boss was saying about him, but he hadn't had the nerve to use it until now. Today seemed to be the day to try it.

He accessed using the TAC and nothing jumped him. Encouraged, Andy called up his file. He found no alerts and nothing he could reasonably call cautionary notes—until he took advantage of Russ's access and did a review of his file's background structure and found a watchdog alarm and a tag-along with a relay tracer stuck to the file's access gate. The watchdog would tell whoever had set it that someone had accessed the file, and the tag-along would be set to follow the trespasser wherever he went in the Matrix after that, letting the relay tracer ship out bulletins on his activity whenever convenient. It was the Matrix equivalent of a "tail," commonly used by security operations that wanted to observe somebody's Matrix activities. Observing the placement of the programs, Andy decided they didn't belong to Telestrian matrix security; security's watchdogs would be embedded in the file rather than tacked on.

If Telestrian security hadn't set this trap, who had? The runners? That didn't make sense; what did they care about him now? Some rival to the runners, hoping to access them through Andy? That made only marginally more sense. Whoever had set the watchdog must think Andy knew something. Considering the holes in his memory, the joke was on them.

But it might not be. He was unaware of anything that might be important enough for shadow action, but he might not understand the importance of something he knew. He understood how "the biz" could work. Nobody would take his word that he was ignorant. If whoever wanted to tail him were serious—and he had every reason to believe they were—they could decide to use his family to persuade him to cooperate. Unfortunately, there was no way for him to cooperate—but would they believe that? Unlikely. And even if he did babble everything he knew, what *did* he know? Nothing. Certainly not enough to please whoever was after him. They would lean on his family. He couldn't let that happen. He couldn't let his mother and sisters be hurt.

So what *could* he do?

He studied the watchdog and tag-along. The sophistication of the stuff on his file suggested that he would be out-matched going head-to-head with whatever decker had done the work. Though he was a good enough decker, rigging was Andy's talent. Even with more time and better hardware than he had available, he might not be able to get into any-thing the decker had protected. Chasing down and identify-ing his hunters wasn't an option, and waiting for them to come calling wasn't bright.

Every corner he turned revealed something new to worry him. He felt more than a little out of his depth.

He could go to Telestrian security. They'd be very happy to get their hands on someone who'd penetrated the big T matrix. But unfortunately, having been used by the runners, Andy fit that description, too. Not an option.

Too bad he didn't have Buckhead and Feather to turn to, but this was no virtual adventure. Adventures were supposed to be fun, not scary. This was real.

And scary.

Andy the shadowrunner would have plotted a course of action in a microsecond and executed the plan regardless of consequences, but the real-world Andy couldn't do that. He dithered, unsure how to find a safe course. Finally he real-ized he was wrong to look for a safe course, because there weren't any. He wished he could ask Andy the shadow-runner for a better solution, but make-believe answers couldn't solve real problems.

Maybe his virtual shadowrunning had an answer for him after all. He'd played enough games to understand some of the rules of shadow business, and though he knew that the mirror of virtuality wasn't a true one, he also knew that the basic principles of strategy applied in or out of the Ma-trix. As if in a dream, he saw a way out.

After examining the idea and looking for weaknesses, he decided it had a chance. It was drastic, but it could make sure his family wouldn't get dragged into the quagmire de-veloping around him. Making it happen would take a lot of work and would stretch his skills to the limit, but he figured he could do it if his nerve held out.

Taking advantage of Russ's code, Andy set out to do some serious decking. It was three in the morning before he was finished.

He didn't have a lot of time left. The fake ID he'd constructed using Russ's TAC would get wiped out in the morning system update, which was just two hours away.

He headed back to the apartment. It was still, and he did nothing to disturb the silence. His mother wasn't waiting up for him this time; a simple call to the Location Centrex would have told her that Andy was still safe within the Telestrian East complex and on an extended work shift. But he wasn't safe. None of them were, nor would they be unless his plan worked.

From his room he gathered the belongings he thought would be useful. There wasn't much, which was fine, because he couldn't carry much without looking suspicious. He selected clothes he thought would hold up well and help him blend in. Of all the stuff he was taking, the most important items were his Sony CTY-370 cyberdeck and his tool kit. They filled most of his bag, so he really didn't have any choice but to travel light. Lastly he took the Narcoject replica and some of the talismans he'd bought during his Verner phase. The gun wasn't real, but it looked like it might be, and the talismans—who really knew?

Despite what he'd told his sisters, he hadn't trashed the talismans; saving them had been a whim, and maybe that fancy would pay off. They were supposed to be protections from spells and malign spirits. He'd been assured they were real when he'd bought them, but he was a mundane—how could he tell? They might be real; and if they were, they'd help. Lord knew he needed all the help he could get.

After all, if things went as expected, he'd be dead within the hour.

>>>>>NEWSNET DEEP BACKGROUND FILE
GOBLINIZATION

The thirtieth of April 2021 was a day unparalleled in recorded history. Today that date is known worldwide as Goblinization Day. Despite the growing movement on the part of certain minorities to have the date declared a holiday, it is not a date remembered fondly by those whose lives were thrown into turmoil. For on that day millions of ordinary people *changed* and became something different. *Homo sapiens* has not meant the same thing since.

Although estimates vary, it is generally conceded that at least ten percent of the human population of our planet underwent metamorphosis on that single day, with a further twenty percent beginning more prolonged somatic transformations. We have come to refer to the Changed variants as metatypes. Most of the Changed became what are commonly called "orks" (*H. sapiens robustus*), and the second most common metatype (*H. sapiens ingentis*) is often called a "troll." But there have been a bewildering variety of Changed, ranging from those who remain almost indistinguishable from basic human stock to those about whom it is hard to see anything human. Despite striking physical differences, research has shown that the common metatypes, while breeding true within a metatype, remain capable of breding with *H. sapiens sapiens,* thereby maintaining all the variety within the scientific definition of a species.

In 2021, the new magical age was only a decade old, and much that we take for granted today was new or even unknown. The Change was dreadful and awesome, and could not but inspire panic. Terror infected homes, businesses, schools, and the streets. Families were torn apart, sometimes literally, by the mobs or deranged victims of the Change. Anguish and fear ruled the day. Now, a generation later, all that has changed—>>>>>FILE INTERRUPT: "Bullshit sayeth the oppressed."—Trogs Über Norms<<<<<

10

The orders for Tom's leave came through on 19 August, nearly three weeks after he should have gotten them. Tom was happy to see them until he noticed they were marked "hardship due to death of family member." He was sure it was his grandfather until he read the accompanying e-mail from his sister Genifer. The old warhorse was alive and kicking. In fact, it had been his influence, with Genifer pulling the strings, that had gotten Tom's leave approved. It wasn't the way Tom had wanted to get his leave, but with the orders cut, he didn't see much point in kicking up a fuss.

The deceased was Andy Walker, his half-brother and youngest of their four half-siblings. Tom wasn't looking forward to the inevitable social occasions connected with the funeral; he'd never been involved with that part of the "family." Such contact as he'd had with that "side" had always come through Genifer's machinations.

He and his sister had often fought about her attempts to make a family out of all of Matthew Walker's children; she complaining about his lack of sympathy and love, and he countering with her lack of sense and family pride. The bouts never solved anything. She kept trying, he kept dodging. She remained unwilling to believe that Tom had no interest in the affairs of their father's second family, or that he wanted no part of anything to do with the bastard who had sired them.

He was using tickets Genifer had arranged, riding a Can-American commuter flight into Balt-Wash Airport. Like the leave, the pre-paid tickets were a fait accompli. Genifer's style. She knew he would have preferred a military transport into Andrews, just as she knew he wouldn't arrange the military flight anyway and pocket the price of the tickets. They knew each other too well, which was why he was sure she'd be waiting when he deplaned.

Which she was.

He spotted her among the clump of folk standing outside the security barrier. He couldn't miss that hair. She had the same raven hair he did, though she wore it a lot longer, and she still had the frosted streak she'd adopted during her rebellious period after their mother had died. The sight awoke memories.

Genifer had been a holy terror the first year after their mother's death on the Night of Rage in '39. They'd been living with their grandparents, as they had since their father had deserted the family. But with Mom gone things changed. Despairing of Genifer's avowed intention to dump school and go live on the streets as soon as she was fully legal, Gram had spent a lot of time predicting that Genifer would be the death of her. Gramps had just nodded quietly through the storms, though he had once privately confided to Tom that he thought Genifer was just taking their mother's death a bit too hard. Gramps didn't much care for hysteria in the family women. "Genifer has some of her father's blood," the old man had said. "And blood will tell." But the General had been wrong—not about their parentage, of course, but about its necessary result. Neither Genifer nor Tom had ever shown their father's blood, remaining unChanged, normal people.

The Change was something Tom had spent years fearing. His father had goblinized into an ork, and it had damn near killed his mother. The Change *had* destroyed his parents' marriage. Fortunately Tom's grandparents had taken in his mother and her children, and Tom had a good family to grow up in—no thanks to Matthew Walker, his father. The drunken ork had shown up on Tom's eleventh birthday, shattering Tom's belief that his father was dead. For Tom it had been the beginning of eleven years of nightmares as he waited to goblinize. It wasn't until he was a year older than Matthew had been when it happened to him that Tom was sure he was safe from that fate. He thanked God for it every day in the almost decade and a half since. He still didn't like orks—or his father.

But old nightmares weren't suitable for a fine, hot, summer day. He watched Genifer's face light up as she spotted him. He put on a smile for her.

"Hello, Tommy."

The childhood diminutive was something he let her get away with. She hated any diminutive form of her name, so Tom only used one when he wanted to get her angry. This wasn't the time or place for that.

"Long time, Genifer."

"Too long, Tom."

She seemed hesitant and unsure; he decided they needed an ice-breaker. "You're looking good—for an older sister, I mean."

"What would you know about it, soldier boy?" she asked, picking up on his bantering tone. "I hear your kind thinks anything with the right equipment looks good."

"You've been listening to the wrong people. I've got some discrimination, you know. Can't you see the uniform?"

"I see it."

"Yeah? Then how'd you mistake me for Navy?"

She frowned mock anger at him and tried to slug his shoulder. He slipped her punch and wrapped her in a bear hug. She hugged him back. Despite his joking, she did look good, and he was glad she'd come to meet him. Maybe he *had* stayed away too long.

"Where's the General?" he asked as they walked through the terminal. He'd hoped their grandfather would be with her.

"You know him," Genifer said with a theatrical roll of her eyes. "He wouldn't come into the terminal. He's waiting with the car."

"Orbiting the terminal?"

She nodded. "Wouldn't do to pay those usurious rates for parking. Are all army men crazy about spending money, or is it just Rocquettes?"

"Probably everyone. Too many years of budget cuts. Pinching pennies gets to be a habit." He shrugged. "You didn't have to buy the tickets."

"Didn't I? Would you have come otherwise, Major Frugal Soldier?"

"Soldiers, frugal or otherwise, don't pass up leave."

"But they don't like going to funerals, either. I needed the insurance that you'd come here, instead of heading for some trashy Club Carib resort to chase elven bimbos."

"You know I wouldn't even think of that," he said, turning to follow the passage of a young elf moving in the other direction along the concourse. Genifer punched him in the shoulder. In fact, women, elven or otherwise, had held little attraction for him since Winona died. Eleven years, and he still didn't feel ready, which neither surprised not upset him. But he knew how to pretend, which is what he'd just done, in order to keep Genifer off his back on the issue. Someday he'd be ready for another relationship; just not yet.

"Gramps will be waiting and wondering where we are," Tom said to get her thinking about other things.

If not wondering, Gramps was at least waiting. The vintage Mitsubishi Gallant, the Rocquette family's fancy transportation for the past fifteen years, was pulled over at the end of the passenger pickup area. A bit older, a bit more battered and shopworn, but still running; just like its owner. He sat behind the wheel, his white hair quite a bit thinner than Tom remembered. His grandfather must have been watching in the rear view mirror, because he got out of the car and waved as soon as Tom and Genifer hit the sidewalk. As they approached, he drew himself up into a salute. Even without the salute, the casual clothes would have failed to disguise the General's military bearing. Tom halted and snapped back a salute of his own.

"Welcome home, Major Rocquette," the General said with a smile.

"Been too long, General." Tom's doubt of that vanished. If *was* good to see the General, good to be home.

While they shook hands, the General said, "Good to have you home, Tom. Haven't see nearly enough of you these past few years."

"You know what the life's like, General."

"Yes, I do."

They locked eyes for a moment. They both knew that Tom's excuses were just that; but the General was too big a man to say anything about it, and Tom wasn't ready to. He changed the subject.

"How's Gram?"

"Cranky." The General winked. "But no more than usual, for which the Lord be thanked. She's anxious to see her only grandson."

"Then let's get going," Tom said, stepping between the General and the driver's door. "I'll drive."

The General shook his head in resignation. "Getting you your slot at the Point was the last thing you let me do for you."

"And I wouldn't have allowed that, if I'd known," Tom said, not for the first time.

"You can have the front, Gramps," Genifer said, tugging open the rear passenger door.

They made good time out to Columbia and the Rocquette house. Gramps filled the time telling Tom about his latest woodworking projects. It wasn't a subject that much interested Tom, but he was willing to listen for the old man's sake. Genifer called ahead, and Gram had tea and cookies ready when they arrived. Tom was expecting to have the evening to relax, but before the tea was cold, Genifer brought the conversation back around to the funeral and insisted that Tom go with her to the last night of the viewing. He argued that attendance at the funeral was sufficient, given the relationship, but Genifer was having none of that.

"Andy was our brother," she insisted.

He tried looking to his grandparents for support, but they stayed prudently neutral. "Up to you, Tom," his grandfather said, which meant he wasn't willing to cross Genifer on this one. Ultimately Tom decided he wasn't either, but he drew the line at wearing a suit instead of his uniform. He was, after all, what he was.

Genifer, fearful of the turmoil downtown, insisted on taking a vehicle rather than Metro. Metro would have put them right into the Telestrian enclave, and the passes Shayla had arranged would have gotten them in from the station as easily as from a public parking garage. But Genifer wouldn't listen to his argument that the classic Gallant would stick out as a target for anyone looking for the "haves." Convinced that if trouble spread, it would spread over public transportation, she thought the danger less to go by car than by rail. Again, Tom gave in. It wasn't that big a concession, since he really wasn't expecting trouble either way; he just didn't like driving in the city any more.

On the way in, he realized he didn't know anything of the circumstances of Andy's death. He figured he ought to know the basics, if only to avoid embarrassing himself.

"Your note didn't say what happened to Andy."

"It was an accident. Apparently he was working late in some sort of experimental simulator. The techs had all gone home and something started to go wrong. Since Andy was in the Matrix working on a virtuality simulation, he didn't know what was happening in the real world, and a bug had cut out the warning circuits. There was an explosion and a fire. He didn't have a chance. Lola says that if they hadn't known from the computer records that Andy was in the simulator, they wouldn't have been able to identify him. The body was incinerated to ash."

"It'll be closed coffin, then, I guess. A pile of ash isn't much to look at. Oh, well, it's not like I would have recognized him."

"Don't be insensitive."

He'd thought he was being practical.

Tom really didn't remember what Andy looked like. It had been a few years since he'd seen him, and Andy had been just a kid them. He would have changed a lot, possibly even Changed—but Tom was pretty sure Genifer would have told him if that had been the case. "What I meant was that Andy was—what?—ten or eleven last time I saw him. He hadn't even hit puberty."

Genifer had a recent picture, of course. When their drunken father had smashed his way back into their life,

Genifer had been pleased to see him and to make the acquaintance of their half-siblings. Even after their father had been killed, she'd kept up ties that Tom would rather have seen dissolved. Since the car's dogbrain was handling the highway driving, Tom couldn't avoid looking at the picture she dug out of her purse. He made what he hoped were proper half-brotherly noises of approval. They were good enough to satisfy Genifer. Unfortunately she took the feigned interest as real, and spent the rest of the trip detailing the kid's boring corporate and school career. She was still going when they left the car and walked to the gateway of the Telestrian East Family Enclave, where the viewing was being held at the public facilities center.

Corporate security was tight at the enclave's entrance; Genifer had to insist on a family relationship to get past the guards. The gateway guards were armored and packing more than a basic load. Tom wondered if there was something to Genifer's concerns after all. He'd heard the stuff on the news about near riotous scuffles between police and those "gimme" beggars of the Comp Army, but he'd put all the fear talk down to media hype. Now he wasn't so sure. Corps didn't spook as easily as your average vid junkie. He reconsidered the garage he'd chosen and decided it was safe enough—he hadn't seen anything out of the ordinary on the streets they'd traveled. He did resolve to leave as soon as possible. No point tempting fate.

Their escort to the public facilities center wasn't standard. Genifer seemed to take it as a courtesy, but Tom had seen this sort of thing before and knew it for what it was: Security's unwillingness to let non-employees roam freely. Something had definitely put a bug up Telestrian's hoop.

The room set aside for the viewing was small and crowded. Tom's first scan didn't turn up anybody without a Telestrian employee badge. He recognized Shayla Walker and guessed that the two nearly identical young woman nearby were two of Andy's three sisters. He'd never been able to tell the triplets apart. He wondered where the third one was. If *she* didn't have to be here, *he* surely didn't.

Genifer started to drag him toward the group. Tom balked, noting the hulking ork with a possessive arm around Shayla's waist.

"Who's that?"

Genifer didn't have to ask whom Tom meant. "Shayla's

friend. His name is Ricky Gonsalvo. Everyone calls him Chunk."

"He's an *ork*."

"Now, Tom—"

"It's not that I have anything against them ..." Tom said automatically.

"Except when they're in the family. Can we just be polite tonight?"

Tom didn't say anything more. If he did, they'd be into another round of a very old fight. Whatever he thought of Shayla's taste in boyfriends, this wasn't the place to make a scene.

He said hello, extended his condolences, went through the introductions, and edged away from the conversation as soon as he could. There was a refreshment bar set up in one corner. There being nothing serious available, Tom acquired a tall glass of mineral water. Without intending to, he also acquired a conversational partner.

"Hi! I'm Josh Barnaby," said the scrawny desk geek in the ill-fitting suit. The Telestrian badge confirmed the name and said that Barnaby worked for Cyberdyne in something called Software Revisions. "I worked with Andy. You must be his brother."

"Half-brother."

"Oh, yeah. Okay. I knew that. The one in the army."

Tom hoped the software only needed obvious revision. He *was* wearing his uniform.

Barnaby didn't seem to notice Tom's less than warm reception of his conversational gambit, but he had noticed something else. "I couldn't help seeing your reaction when you came into the room. Do you know Mr. Gonsalvo?"

"Never met him before tonight."

"Don't like orks much, do you?"

"They're people, just like anybody else," Tom said, giving the answer he'd learned to give.

"You'll pardon me if I say you handle the popularly approved line with something less than conviction."

Tom gave Barnaby a suspicious glance. "Just what sort of a conversation do you think we're having, Mr. Barnaby?"

"A friendly one, I'd hoped. After all, humanity is found among humans, isn't it?"

So that was it. Tom knew the slogan from his days with Humanis, before he'd learned of their real agenda and their connections to the terrorist group Alamos 2000. He still sympathized with the attitudes, but just couldn't go along with their chosen path of expression. "That was a long time ago. I'm an army officer now."

"The military doesn't restrict membership in policlubs."

True enough; this was America, after all. "But it does discourage public association of the uniform with any political organization. As they say, a soldier serves his country, not his country's politicians."

"And they tell the truth by my lights, sir," Barnaby said earnestly. "Every patriot knows the country comes first. Things will not always be as they are now."

"I don't think we're having this conversation, Mr. Barnaby."

"But I thought—"

"Think again."

Genifer arrived at Tom's side as Barnaby faded into the press. "Who was that, Tom?"

"Someone who hasn't learned to live with the times. And speaking of time, have we put in enough here?"

She looked him over, searching his face for something. Whatever she found prompted her agreement. "All right. We can go."

They did.

>>>>>NEWSNET INFOMERCIAL FILE
TELESTRIAN CYBERDYNE [COURTESY-TEL INDUS.]
NORTH VIRGINIA FOCUS FILE [REC: 8-21-55]

TELESTRIAN CYBERDYNE: THE ADVENTURE OF THE FUTURE

Navigated your car around town recently? Spent hours balancing your household budget? Found any part of your home at less than optimal temperature? Of course not. At least not if you have the benefit of cybernetic control systems or computer aids from Telestrian Cyberdyne.

You know us, you trust us, and we're glad you do. There's more to us than you know, and we're helping you in lots of ways. Just because we don't touch you directly, doesn't mean we're not there, or that we're not helping. For example, much of what you own and cherish was built on robotic assembly lines guided by Telestrian Cyberdyne systems. In uncounted ways we've made your life easier, and we're only just getting started.

But the past isn't what we're about. Under Stephen Osborne's leadership, we've broken away from the undistinguished pack of computer and robotic suppliers, into the realm of the leaders in innovation. We're stepping out and making our place in the world, with everything from interfaces for everyday appliances, to Governor Saul Jefferson's personal schedule manager, to important electronic systems for CAS's top-of-the-line Stonewall main battle tank. Other companies may be one step from the future, but at Telestrian Cyberdyne, we're already programming it.<<<<<

11

Andy didn't have to worry where death's sting was—he'd found it. All around him. He'd known that life outside the corporate enclave was rougher and dirtier and noisier and less orderly than he'd been used to, but he hadn't realized just how much *more* it was of all of those things. But he was a shadow now, and this was his life. And if it didn't match his fantasies of what such a life would be like, he'd just have to get used to it.

Had faking his death been the right decision? There were advantages to being "dead." After all, who would bother to hunt down a dead man?

But he was a dead man with an agenda. He stared at the walls of what was now his home and tried to decide if he was ready to get on with it. The walls, with their blistered and peeling paint and unidentifiable, multi-hued stains, were disheartening. Just like almost everything since his "death."

He'd taken this one-room in the Green Tree Hill Apartments, a run-down, sleazebag motel that offered monthly rates. The ad for the apartment had sounded far better than the reality had turned out, but it was better than the rest Andy had checked out. Some of those hadn't even had locks on the doors. He'd taken it because he needed somewhere to slump, and he needed to conserve his cash, especially after dumping so much for upgrades to the Sony.

Even though Andy had paid extra for all the security features that Green Tree Hill offered, he didn't feel safe. How could he, when he didn't trust those features? He was sure half of them were nothing more than fake security operation labels and hot air on the part of the landlord, and half of the rest were inoperative. The door and window locks worked; he'd found that out the first night when someone had tried to break in. He'd pressed the PanicButton to no effect, which was how he knew *that* system didn't work, but fortunately the prowler hadn't been able to defeat the door's physical locks and had gone on to easier pickings. The incident had left Andy feeling vulnerable. What if the prowler had been a troll who wanted in? The locks wouldn't have slowed down a marauder of that strength.

If Andy was going to survive in the shadows, he'd need contacts; runners *always* had contacts. But being afraid to go outside wasn't the way to make connections.

Or friends.

For the first time in his life Andy was out on his own, *really* out on his own. He had no one to turn to: no friends, no family, no colleagues, not even a boss or teacher. He hadn't realized how fast a person could get lonely. He wanted to talk to someone—just talk was all—without worrying whether that someone was assessing him as a target for a mugging or a sexual assault—which left out all the other residents he'd seen so far in the Green Tree Hill Apartments. Maybe if he knew some of them better, he wouldn't think they were eyeing him as easy meat. But he didn't know any of them. He didn't know anyone on the street. Everyone he knew was corp. If he tried to talk with anyone he *did* know, his secret would be shot, and everything he'd done would be for nothing.

Which it would be anyway, if he didn't make some connections.

It was time to stop putting it off, time to jack in and take a shot. Andy had always been more comfortable meeting people in the Matrix. It made sense as a place to start.

His choice as a first stop was Nell's Basement, an address

he'd picked up while lurking on the shadownet. Supposedly the place was connected to Eskimo Nell's, the rumored runner hangout that was his base in his virtual fantasies. He figured the virtuality bar would be mostly full of wannabes like himself, but he hoped there might be a scout or two looking for new talent. He couldn't expect a direct connection to runners; the addresses of the places where the real runners hung weren't modemed around where anybody could gander them. If they were published anywhere, it would be in Shadowland, the real runners' net, but Andy didn't have a way into that place. For now, he'd have to try what he could. If he got real lucky, maybe someone at Nell's could hook him into Shadowland.

He switched on the Sony and ran diagnostics on his additions. The console was a real cyberdeck now—not a powerful one, but better than the off-the-shelf console it had been. *Real* deckers didn't use off-the-shelf, because there wasn't enough edge, and edge was what kept you alive in the shadows.

Hoping that nothing would disturb his meat body during his trip, he jacked in.

Decking into Nell's Basement was easy. The ice was light and pure white, though tricky enough that some skill was needed. Andy had more than enough to breeze in.

The virtual bar was full of persona icons, some at the bar, most at the tables. By far the majority of the images were chrome metahumans with bits of clothing or jewelry, or markings of neon, to make them distinctive. There were a fair number of cartoon characters and classic blocky dawnage icons. A few patrons opted for animated inanimate objects like walking toasters and more obscure things. Not all of the crowd were deckers, some were hitchers. Andy could tell the difference when he looked close enough. The hitchers didn't have quite the same resolution, and sometimes he could spot a faint line linking one to its gateway decker.

Nell's Basement was furnished in shades of gray. Even the icons passing beneath the scattered overhead spots remained colorless under the light. Something in the virtuality architecture, Andy guessed, an ambiance thing. Andy looked around for a table with an open-conversation light, but didn't see any. There were more tables set back in the gloom, but it was hard to see very far. He'd have to wander a bit.

He hadn't gotten three virtual meters before he found a leg stretched out in his way. At least he assumed it was a leg. There were no joints or bulges in the spike of constrained liquid, but it did join to the hip of an icon that looked like a man made of rippling cartoon lightning bolts. The icon's head was a smooth-mapped human face with glowing eyes. The eyes were staring straight at Andy. So were the eyes of the other icons around the table.

"Hoi, chummers, looky here," the lightning-man said. "It's somebody wants to be the Arnold man and ain't clued to where they left the texture maps." To Andy, "You gots too much mem to spend on icon, newbie. You slumming or just plain stupid?"

It was a provocative question. A runner would give a chill answer, so Andy said, "Neither."

"Oooh. That so?" The glowing eyes narrowed to rectangular slits. "My handle's Zagfoot. Maybe you heard of me."

"No," Andy replied honestly.

"So you *are* stupid," Zagfoot said.

"Leave him be, Zagfoot," said a wolf-ork hybrid so close to the original *Castle Lowengrim* game icon that a circle-R floated in the air over it.

"When did you go wuss, Wolfie?" Zagfoot shot back.

With Zagfoot's attention diverted, Andy started to step around the road block, saying, "I'm not looking for trouble, Zagfoot."

The next instant he was slamming face first into the floor. The simsense circuits on his deck made him feel it as though it were real. Andy hadn't fallen over his feet; Zagfoot had "tripped" him. The decker sneered at him.

"That's Mr. Zagfoot to you, newbie. Too bad you ain't looking for trouble, 'cause you found it."

Andy tried to get up, but the Exterminator's motor functions were locked. Zagfoot laughed at Andy's struggles. "Watch this," the decker said.

Photorealistic lightnings chewed at Andy's icon, pitting and discoloring the Exterminator where Zagfoot's attack program gnawed at Andy's graphic interface. Andy's simsense connection translated the attacks as painful electric shocks. His meat fingers flew over his deck's keyboard as he tried to find a way to escape. Zagfoot's lock held and the Exterminator's shiny surface corroded further.

Andy's torment abruptly ceased, leaving him limp and

disoriented. For a moment he thought he was in dump shock, but then he realized his vision was grayed because he was still in Nell's Basement. He knew he hadn't done anything to break the relentless press of his tormentor's programs. Thankful for the respite, he could only stare as Zagfoot now writhed under attack from someone. The lightning-man froze, looking more than ever like a cartoon, and popped out of existence. On that cue, a small ebon boy in a glittering silver cloak stepped into the nearest spotlight and said, "Verily, there must be more suitable quarry afoot in the Matrix tonight."

There was general murmuring of agreement as icons turned away or simply left. Several used a name as they addressed apologies or salutations to the new arrival. Andy had heard the name whispered on the shadownet, but he couldn't believe he'd heard correctly. *The Dodger.* The fact that the icon before him was showing in full black demonstrated that this decker was capable of overriding Nell's ambiance. But it couldn't be the Dodger, could it? Not Verner's decker, not here! First, such a legendary decker wouldn't be slumming in a place like Nell's Basement. Second, such a wiz runner wouldn't have any reason to be concerned for Andy. Third, well, third, it just *couldn't* be. How could a decker with the Dodger's rep have so unimposing an icon?

"Are you really the Dodger?"

" 'Tis a name to which I answer," the ebon boy replied as he took a seat at the now-vacant table over which Zagfoot had presided. "Pray, sir, take a seat and tell me how you are called."

"Cee-three," Andy said, pleased he'd remembered to use the variant on his usual Cee-cubed as he he'd intended. He took the seat across the table from the Dodger. He didn't want to seem too familiar.

The ebon boy's lips quirked into a curious half-smile. "Last name P-O, by some chance?"

"No," Andy replied. Had he made a mistake? Was there another Cee-three? "Why?"

"Have no care for my remark. 'Tis but a jocular reference and of no consequence." The ebon boy regarded Andy for a moment before speaking again. " 'Tis passing strange that you are known by but a letter and a number? Such things are no names, certainly not for free folk such as you and I; thus we must dismiss the number out of hand, good sir. C, you have said? As in the gleaming cyberman all studded with cylinders that you appear to be? Nay, trouble not to answer, for 'tis none of my business. However, it is, I must assume, my honor to make your acquaintance, Master Cylinder." The glittering cloak whirled with a flourish as the ebon boy bowed. "You are, I would venture to say, somewhat new to these digital domains. As you have learned, that ruffian Zagfoot likes no better prey."

Andy denied he was a newbie, but he knew the Dodger wouldn't believe him.

"You show spirit to jest, but 'tis only a jest. Plain truth is not so easily hidden, for though he is a lout, Churl Zagfoot was correct. 'Tis plain to see that for a deck as leaky as yours, you have invested far too heavily in your icon. The error of a novice. You would be well advised to make some adjustments ere next you venture forth."

Andy would do that. "Do you have any other advice for me?"

"I? I never give advice." The ebon boy smiled, showing gleaming, midnight teeth. "Not without remuneration, that is. Free advice is treated with the respect given all that comes at no cost."

"I'd be willing to pay for good advice from someone who really knows his way around," Andy said, doubting he could offer enough to pay for such a famous decker's time.

"Truly?"

"Yeah. Some."

" 'Tis said that a true knight aids the downtrodden for virtue's sake and the simple sake of the needy unfortunate. Alas, 'tis my misfortune that you see me not as a true knight. 'Tis, mayhap, my greater misfortune that you see truth." A pause. The ebon boy's expression grew serious. "You said you had funds."

Andy produced a virtual credstick, previously limited to half his available funds. He hoped it would be enough to persuade the Dodger to help him. He thought about adding more—the Dodger's help could be invaluable—but he decided to do so just after setting the credstick on the table. It was too late then to snatch it back; it would be too unchill.

Jet fingers caressed Andy's credstick for a moment, then retreated. The Dodger sat quietly for so long that Andy feared his meager offering had offended him.

"How curious," the ebon boy said softly. "You are Telestrian."

"How do you know that?" Andy blurted out.

"Technomancy," said the ebon boy with a negligent wave of a hand. " 'Tis true then?"

"Ex-Telestrian," Andy said. When the Dodger made no reply, he added, "Chiptruth. I don't work for anybody. But I'd like to. If you get my meaning."

"You will work for no one while you retain ties to Telestrian."

"I told you. I'm history with the corp. I'm a free agent."

" 'Twould make me happier 'twere true."

"I don't know how I could prove it to you."

"Can you not?"

Andy really didn't know how. "No, I can't."

"Will you not offer me an open portal to their secrets? You are so recently come from their employ, surely your codes and protocols have not all faded. Such an offer would be worth far more than this." The ebon boy rolled the credstick at Andy.

Andy hadn't even thought of making such an offer. He could have. Though his legitimate codes and accesses would have been trashed as soon as his "death" was logged, he'd left himself a few back doors. He could still get into the system. "If that's the price of your help, maybe we can arrange something. But I won't help you steal anything from them."

The ebon boy inclined his head slightly. "I see. You shall open the door and stand aside while I alone enter to loot and pillage."

"Something like that."

" 'Tis an arrangement with which I have a passing familiarity. And in return you only ask advice? A small, inconsequential price. Pray tell, what sort of advice do you seek?"

It sounded as if the Dodger was going to help him. This trip to Nell's Basement was turning out far better than Andy could have hoped.

"I want to meet some people," Andy said. "The kind of people I'll need to know, to survive on the street and to get into the biz. You know, the kind of people you'd be willing to work with."

"Perhaps those very same folk with whom I associate?"

"That'd be wiz! If you'd be willing. I mean, I don't want

to take any biz from you, but, geez, to get an in with the Dodger's connections. Who would have thought?"

"Who, indeed. And nothing else?"

Andy couldn't believe how accommodating the Dodger was being.

"Well . . ." There was something else praying on his mind. He wasn't sure he'd been completely successful in wiping out his tracks. If someone discovered that he'd faked his death—

"If you could help me make sure I'm a shadow."

The ebon boy gave him a toothy smile. "There are many ways of ensuring that."

Didn't Andy know it! "I think I covered all the bases, but someone put a watch on me before I cut out. I don't know who, but I want to. I want to make sure they don't have anything to use on me. And I'd like to know why they were looking and what they found."

"All laudable goals." From beneath his cloak, the ebon boy produced a chromium ferret. "This is a hunter program. It is very good at tracing connections, if somewhat short-lived, and is primed to bite the hand that tampers with it. One must preserve one's secrets, as I am sure you understand. I can set this fine beast to find any files associated with yourself, including trails left by your hunters, if you provide the proper source codes. Will that be sufficient?"

"Sounds great." Andy reached across the table to take the ferret, but the ebon boy didn't offer it.

"The codes are necessary to prime it."

"Right." Andy handed across a virtual facsimile of his old corporate identification tag.

In the Dodger's hand, it transmogrified into something that looked like cat food. He fed it to the ferret, placed the beast on the table, and patted its rump. It humped across the table to Andy. "The ferret is yours to use before the morrow's dawn."

"Wiz!" Andy gathered in the ferret, popping open a panel in the Exterminator's central chassis to provide the beast a home. "What about the connections?"

"First, show me your magic portal."

That seemed fair. The Dodger had already helped him, now it was Andy's turn to hold up some of the bargain. They departed Nell's Basement and flew across the Matrix to the Telestrian system. The Cyberdyne branch was a molten gold oak tree, hanging root and branch in the electron sky. Andy leading, they ducked below the roots and wove in among the tangled mess. When he found the right point—his second safest way back in—Andy showed the back door to the Dodger. The ebon boy stopped to examine the doorway.

"Nice work."

The compliment from the Dodger caught him off-guard. To be praised by one of the greatest legends of the Matrix was high praise indeed! Maybe Andy did have a future as a runner.

But he clearly had a lot to learn. The Dodger was spending a long time at the doorway. Andy had expected him to duck in and be on his way, doing whatever he was intending to do in the Telestrian system.

"What are you doing?" Andy asked.

"Taking precautions," the Dodger answered amicably. "Something a wise man does often, Master Cylinder."

"That sounds like free advice."

"Does it? How could it be advice from me, if 'tis free?" The ebon boy finished his examination, but he made no move to enter the Telestrian system.

"Aren't you going in?" Andy asked.

"Nay, I think not. Mayhap some other time." The ebon boy stepped away from the door. "One last thing, Master Cylinder. The place at which you enter our mutual hallucination. It is safe?"

"It's the best I can do right now. I paid extra for the security options."

"Paid? With your fine corporate credit, no doubt."

Andy wasn't *that* stupid. "No. It was some other money." The money the runners had left him.

"So happily resident on your credstick?"

"Yeah."

"Ah, poor naive Master Cylinder. Such a formidable appearance and so frail a real presence. Electronic cash is electronic cash, but electrons have tails most plain to those with the eyes to see." The ebon boy produced a white card and placed it in the Exterminator's multi-digit manipulator. "Accept this address for a relatively honest money changer. Tell him you seek a beginner's work and mention the Dodger."

With that the ebon boy swirled his cloak, becoming a spinning pillar of flashing silver. The column dissolved into a glittering swirl of stars, and as the stars spread and faded, his voice offered a last, unremunerated piece of advice. "And, pray, find a better place to stay."

With the Dodger gone, Andy wasn't sure what to do next. He had come to the Telestrian system and opened the back door, expecting to see the Dodger vanish inside; but instead the Dodger had just vanished. So here he was, the door was open, and the Dodger had said that the ferret program had a limited life span. What better time? It wasn't like he had a date to be somewhere. Andy slipped into the Telestrian system and unleashed the ferret.

The ferret led him to a number of files with his name on them. Concerned about being an unauthorized user on the system, Andy copied the files he hadn't seen before, intending to read them later. Copying was less intrusive than trashing or swiping the data; either of those options would leave far more obvious footprints, and this was a covert run. Everything went wiz, until the ferret came up with a security breach file. Discovering that Telestrian was associating him with a security breach gave Andy pause. A cursory look told him it wasn't going to be easy to open, so he copped a copy and went on. The ferret, now on another trail, plowed nose first into the armored legs of a black-faced golden knight. Andy didn't hesitate; he turned tail and ran, leaving the ferret to take the first attack of the black ice.

Panting in his squalid little room, he stared down at the datacord in his hand. His head ached and his vision was blurred, vibrant colored spots swirling around the edges. He'd gotten away.

Of course, he'd crashed the run and left without closing his back door. He'd never be able to use *that* one again. Neither had he gathered everything about himself in the system; the ferret had been caught while still hunting, but right now he didn't care. What was important was that he'd escaped the black ice and would live to try again another day.

If he dared.

Andy was too keyed up to sleep, and the light coming through the window showed that morning had come. He tried the contact the Dodger had left him, but couldn't get a meet set up for another day. He spent a restless day cruising through the data he'd taken, looking for something—anything—that offered a way to understand what had happened to him. When he discovered that the watcher set on his file was supposed to deliver to a military data-drop, he understood that there was too much he didn't know. He needed more data, but he wasn't ready to go hunting it until he felt more secure. That night he got a little more sleep, but only a little.

In the morning he set out for his meet, glad to be heading toward something definite. Dealing with the fixer turned out to be no big deal, especially once Andy mentioned the Dodger. Even so, the transaction cost more than he'd have been able to afford if the Dodger had taken the money Andy had offered him, but to Andy's surprise the Dodger hadn't touched the cash offering. All of the famous decker's help had come free; despite his protests, the Dodger had turned out to be a true knight.

Andy was feeling pretty good about his prospects when he left the meet. The fixer had taken Andy's credstick and given him a handful of new ones, certified, and another one set up under a false SIN, his new identity. He could ride the Metro again, which would be a far better way to get back to his slump than the crowded, stinking, un-air-conditioned bus he'd taken to this part of DeeCee. Best of all, the fixer had said he might have some work. Andy would have to check back in day or two.

With the tension of the meet gone, Andy discovered he was very hungry. He started wandering, looking for some-place to get a meal. He didn't know the area well and the first few streets he tried weren't commercial enough, just residences and a few converted office suites. Looking down the next street, he saw a promising possibility in what was obviously a mixed-use building. The building was mostly offices, to be sure, but the street level had big windows for shops. The place looked large enough to support a deli, or at least a Stuffer Shack. Stomach-driven, he plowed toward the building and right into some suit coming out of the alley.

"Drek, kid! Watch where you're going," the man said.

Andy started an automatic apology and stammered to a stop. *Kid?* Andy's brain did a sidestep. He knew this guy. Or did he? The man's face wasn't familiar, and his suit was nothing special, just a cheap off-rack thing. Nothing flashy in his accessories. The buzz-side cut of his hair was equally unremarkable, but the face was of a rugged mold that should have been hard to forget. Yet Andy had forgotten it.

Forgotten it?

Hooting laughter echoing in the street grabbed Andy's at-

tention. A couple of blocks away and heading toward him
were a half-dozen orks, jostling each other and having a
good time. They were unimportant. Andy turned his attention back to the puzzle in front of him and found that the
guy had walked away and was nearly in the building.

"Hey, wait a minute," Andy called.

The man stopped, hand on the pull bar of the main door.
"Do I know you, kid?"

Kid. Yeah. Andy had heard that dismissive tone before. A
name popped into his head: Marksman. "Yeah. Yeah, you
do. Telestrian Cyberdyne. Last week. We met in a very small
room. What's the matter, Marksman, didn't think I'd remember?"

The man stared at him without a change in expression.
Andy couldn't tell whether he'd scored or not.

"Name's Markowitz, not Marksman, and I haven't got a
clue to what you're talking about, kid. Now buzz. If I were
you, I'd want to be off the streets before things got too un-
healthy."

The man turned his back on Andy and walked into the
building. Andy stared stupidly after him, wondering if he'd
been right or if his mind was just playing tricks on him. He
didn't even realize he was in trouble till the first ork grabbed
his arm. He'd only begun to struggle when they dragged him
into the alley.

>>>>>WNVA FEED COVERAGE

 — [12:10:18/8-22-55]

REPORTER: KATHERINE KRISTIN KAYE [KAYE-328]

UPLINK SITE: FREDERICKSBURG, NORTH VIRGINIA

Kaye: "We're here in Fredericksburg at the Heritage Festival
and having a wonderful time. But there's an edge to the
mood of some folks here celebrating today. Yesterday, as
you undoubtedly know, State Senator Wendell North introduced a bill calling for a referendum on the secession of

North Virginia from the UCAS. The bill passed the Senate on introduction and will come before the House of Delegates tomorrow. It seems clear what the politicians think. We wanted to hear from the public. So we're asking them what they think."

Well-dressed father with two children: "I think the treatment North Virginia gets at the hands of Washington is disgraceful. Atlanta couldn't possibly be worse. So, yes, I think it's a good idea."

Ork concessionaire: "Secession? Yeah, I guess I'm for it. I mean, why not? What's Washington done for us lately?"

Tourist from Richmond: "What North and the State Senate have done is, of course, illegal under the Constitution of the UCAS, although not under that of CAS. They obviously think they're already under CAS law. They're going to find out differently, I think."

Dwarf woman: "I'm a corporate citizen. None of this affects me."

Two teenagers wearing look-alike cyberchrome fashions: "I didn't hear about it." "You sure it's not a hoax? Like, I think it ought to be a hoax." "Sounds like one to me. I mean, really."

Man in "It's a human thing" T-shirt: "Secession wasn't a good idea in 1861, nor in 2034. It's not a good idea now. North don't like being a part of our country, he can fragging well move!"

Woman in gray képi: "Wahoo is what I say, and about time. I hear the Confederate States has got two armored divisions just over the border in Virginia. Well, come on up, boys. You're long overdue. The south shall rise again!"<<<<<

12

The funeral went almost as painlessly as Tom could have hoped. There was a decent turnout, including a pair of stiff executive types making the formal corporate condolence call—though the way they hung back most of the time reminded Tom of security officers rather than social callers. Barnaby showed up, but he didn't make any attempt to talk to Tom, which was fine. Even the third sister, Asa, had made it in sometime during the night. She stood with her siblings and cried through the whole thing, the three of them looking like sobbing crows in their funereal black suits. Minor differences in their suits made it possible to tell them apart, but Tom still couldn't put the right name to the right woman, as he proved while the crowd was breaking up. There was a reception planned after the service at the cemetery, but Tom had played on Genifer's safety concerns to convince her to skip it. They'd done their duty.

"Andy was a good kid," Shayla said by way of a goodbye.

Tom supposed she was right. He didn't have much memory of the kid. What he did have fit the eulogizing reverend's description of a bright and eager kid who was a bit of a nerd. Not so bad, Tom guessed. He'd been young and annoying once himself. And when all was said and done, Andy wasn't to be faulted for his father's sins. Certainly not by Tom; blaming the son for the father's failings was a position Tom couldn't afford to buy into. If anything, there was less of Matthew Walker in Andy than there was in Tom.

Genifer didn't say much on the ride home, but it wasn't pique over his wanting to skip the reception. She was just being contemplative. Tom was quiet too. It seemed right. When they got back to their grandparents' house, she announced she had a billion things to do and disappeared off to the telecom to take care of them.

With the morning's obligation completed, Tom took advantage of the rest of the day to laze like a slug. He spent his time racked, or staring bemusedly at what the cable had to offer. He studiously avoided anything that smacked of news or commentary. Gram's dinner was an exercise in overeating. Since she'd made most of his childhood favorites, he had to have seconds of everything. In the evening after dinner, he helped the General clean and oil his gun collection. Those venerable weapons were the first Tom had ever been allowed to touch, and cleaning them had become a ritual with him and his grandfather. They sat and worked, the smell of well-oiled steel and the faint tang of old powder filling his nose and bringing an echo of older, simpler times. The calmness that had been a part of those sessions came back to him.

When the last gun was put away, all the oils sealed in their containers, the rags disposed of, and the cabinet locked, the General said, "You know, I made a few calls for Genifer."

"I don't hold it against you, sir. I know how she can be."

"That's not what I meant, Tom." The General's face wore a worried frown. "When I made those calls, I got to talking with some old cronies. There was an undercurrent in much of what they said. I get the sense that there's a lot of unrest in the officer corps. Much worse than when I retired. You're the man in the field, as it were. You feeling any of that current?"

"I was just a shavetail when you mustered out, General, so I don't think I can make a comparison, but I'd have to say you're right—there are unhappy people in uniform. There are a lot of folks who don't have much respect for our commander-in-chief."

"Wouldn't be the first time."

"Maybe not, but I've heard some people talk about not following orders if he gave them. That's serious."

"But are they serious enough to do something about it?"

"Hard to say, sir. I think some of them might be."

"Anyone talk to you about it?"

"Not directly, although I've had a few hypotheticals tossed my way."

"And?"

"And I hope they didn't take my response, or rather lack of it, badly. Politics isn't a soldier's business, even if you do have to do a certain amount of it within the service. You taught me that, sir."

"I don't have a lot of students in active service."

"So I've noticed, sir."

The General leaned back in his chair and gave a weary sigh. "Seems to me that our armed services are foundering more than a bit. You don't have to be an old warhorse like me to see. Things just haven't been the same since the Air Force lost most of their strategic assets, and the Navy lost the Marines to the Confederate States and got itself mostly confined to one ocean and the Lakes. Our own branch has fared better, but not well. We're an awfully long way from the superpower we were at the close of the last century. Could be that the country has taken to the closer-to-home view, maybe a bit too much. We're still bigger and more powerful than England was when the sun never set on her empire."

"Empire, sir? Except for commercial empires, that sort of world died a long time ago."

"There are those who would tell you what goes around comes around."

Was Tom talking to one of "those"? It wasn't the sort of thing he was used to hearing from the General.

"Tom, you're looking at me as if I'd grown a second head. Which, I suppose, gives me the answer I've been fishing for. My apologies if I've offended, but you've fallen in with bad company before."

"Ancient history, sir. From the days of my headstrong youth."

"Your bullheadedness is hardly ancient history. Just ask Genifer."

"That's as may be, but whatever else I am, sir, I'm loyal to my country."

"I'm glad to hear it, Tom. Very glad. Glad to hear that you're thinking too. That's important." The General paused for a moment, indicating a shift in focus. "You're in General Osmolska's Special Resource Command. What do you think of the cyberization strategy?"

"As you say, sir, I *am* in General Osmolska's command. By request, as you know."

"So you're in favor of the whole thing?"

"General Osmolska considers any discussion that does not repeat the version of policy the General has espoused to be political, and I've already given you my opinion on political statements, sir." The General raised his chin at that, so Tom added quickly, "With all due respect, sir."

"You haven't become the old Russki's puppet, have you?"

"No, sir. But a good officer is loyal to his superior."

"Well, near as I can tell you haven't been loyal enough to sign up for his Augmented Soldier Program. I don't see so much as a datajack."

"That's correct, sir. Non-invasive aids still enable this soldier to do his job." Which was as close as Tom could come to saying he considered Osmolska's Augmented Soldier Program a mistake. The psychological issues of returning a soldier to civilian life had always been a problem; adding a physical component would only make it worse. The least problem would be determining how you disarm a soldier with built-in weapons when it came time to discharge the guy.

"You ran a combat rigger platoon out in Denver, didn't you?"

"Officially we were a combat unit, but we did border patrol and smuggling suppression. Nothing I'd call combat."

"And all your troops had datajacks. Officers, too?"

"Datajacks are pretty common, sir." Most people thought no more about getting one than they did of getting their eyesight corrected. Tom had taken a lot of ribbing from his noncoms over the fact that he wasn't able to jack in the way they could.

"A jack's the first foot in the door," the General said. "I know I sound like a fossil, but a man is what he is. You know, the tele-operation revolution was already underway in my time, creeping into just about every support branch you can name. Let me tell you, it's not the answer. All that rigger stuff is worse than ICBMs, in its own way. Dehumanizing, that's what it is. What's war without the human element? This augmentation stuff is worse still. It makes the dehumanization personal. I can't see why it's being pushed."

"President Steele backs it."

"Steele the Technocrat." The General shook his head sadly. "He wants smaller, more efficient forces and sees high-tech, low-body-count forces as the solution. He's forgetting the people again. Typical Technocrat. At least President Adams, Democrat though he was, understood that we need men and women in the services. Thank God Steele has been too indecisive to cancel Adams's recruitment policies and reduce the manpower establishment. I suppose he thinks keeping the slots open makes him look like a humanitarian."

Tom had heard that manpower cuts were coming, but with the General getting up a head of steam, this wasn't the time to mention it. "General, you've got more experience than I do with how an autocratic army lives in a democratic state. Do you think people would be taking matters any better if Steele had been elected directly?"

President Steele had come to office when President Adams died of a stroke the day after his second inauguration. There had been whispers of foul play, as might as expected, but nothing had stuck.

The General thought about it only briefly. "Maybe, but I doubt it. A Technocrat is a Technocrat. And he could have made a better move than appointing Booth as his vice president. Booth's another Technocrat, for God's sake. Steele got his vice presidency running on a coalition ticket. Adams knew what he was doing, marrying the Democrats with the Technocrats. You'd think Steele would have noticed, having served a full term with him. I'd have thought Steele had enough sense to realize he still needs that coalition, but I guess he's got the standard Technocrat blind spot about people's needs. Must be why he's let this Comp Army thing rot on his doorstep."

Their talk shifted away from the real Army and on to the so-called Compensation Army. The rag-tag horde of beggars infesting the Federal District was not Army business, and was therefore something about which Tom could freely express his opinions. He did, and so did his grandfather. Tom was surprised to find his own attitude more harsh than the General's with regard to the former servicemen involved in the protest. The general had some sympathy for them because of shared service in the Dissolution Campaigns, as the General referred to the military and paramilitary operations surrounding the break-up of the old United States. Tom still didn't think the service of such veterans was a reason to dismiss their civil disobedience. The talk, drifting only occasionally into argument, went late into the night and on into the morning. They'd been apart so long that neither man seemed willing to pass up the chance to catch up. Tom had just noticed that they'd been hearing birdsong for some time, when the telecom's beep joined the morning chorus.

The general furrowed his brow. "That's not our line's normal beep. Who the hell would be decking into our line this time of day?"

"No one," Tom said, getting up to answer. "That's my contact tone."

Tom logged on and took receipt of the on-line orders. Reading them as they came out of encryption, he cursed. So much for his leave.

"What's the trouble?" the General asked, looking over Tom's shoulder.

Technically Tom's orders were for his eyes only, but the General had held clearances Tom wouldn't see for another decade. He was no security risk. Still, Tom blanked the screen before turning away from it. "No details. It's a general issue call-up. All on-leave personnel are being recalled to duty stations. My personal tag says I have to report to

Fort Meade and await first available transport back to my unit."

"This is a war-footing call. The women aren't going to like this."

"Who *is*? If I pack out now, I can be gone before they wake up."

"If this really is trouble, they definitely won't like you sneaking out. The call gave you till noon," the General pointed out.

So he had seen the screen. "I don't want to be late."

"What *you* don't want to do is face Genifer and your grandmother and tell them you're going off into danger."

The accusation stung all the more for being true. "All right, so I don't want to deal with it."

"Don't feel bad, Tom." The General's tone was sympathetic now that Tom had owned up. "I wouldn't want to either. But if you're planning on coming home again, I'd advise you to try. I've been there, and it's better if they get to see you off."

Tom knew the General was right, but he went to do his packing. The chore was short, but he dallied over it long enough for him to know that he ought to delay a little longer—at least until the women were awake. Though he'd decided to say a proper goodbye, he found himself curiously reluctant to open the conversation once he'd sat down to breakfast with Gram and Genifer.

Breakfast was quiet, and from the way Gram kept asking if there was anything Tom wanted, Tom guessed the General had told her. But she was a trooper; she wasn't going to say anything until Tom brought it up. He asked her to sit down along with the rest of them, and repeated what he'd told the General of his orders. Genifer was the first to speak.

"So you have no idea what these orders are all about?"

He had a few ideas, but it wasn't his place to bring them up. The training he'd been doing was top secret, need-to-know. As far as he could reasonably assume, none of his family needed to know. Besides, he wasn't sure, and if he told them how dangerous he thought the duty was going to be, they'd be even more worried. They were already worried enough.

"Is there time for you to go to church with us?" Gram asked.

"If we go to the mid-morning service," he replied. He'd have to leave from the church.

Genifer, looking past Tom and out the window, stiffened a little. "There's an Army mupper coming up the drive."

Everyone turned to look as the military-issue GMC Multi-Purpose Utility Vehicle rolled to a stop. Rita Furlann was behind the wheel. As she got out, Tom saw that she wore civilian clothes under her black, armored Thaumaturgic Command duster. The coat's long tails mostly covered the holster she wore in violation of peacetime uniform regs. The General went out to greet her.

"I'm here for Major Rocquette," she said, looking past him to smile at Tom where he stood in the doorway. "Morning, Major."

"What are you doing here, Furlann?" Tom asked

"Picking you up."

He assumed that. "I meant that I hadn't expected to see you until I got back to Schwartzkopf."

"Surprise. Even Ice Hearts have families and friends to visit on leave." She tossed her head to settle her long hair back from her shoulders. "When the balloon went up, I got word that you were in the area and was told to pick you up. You ready to roll?"

"Just need to grab my bag."

And make the last goodbyes. Gram promised prayers, Genifer demanded e-mail as soon as he could find a station, and the General shook his hand silently. Furlann watched it all with her usual detachment. She slipped into the mupper while he was tossing his duffel into the back, then had the vehicle rolling even before he had the door closed. When they hit the street, he asked, "You know what's going on?"

"Here or in Chicago?"

"Chicago?"

"Haven't seen the news, eh?"

"No," Tom admitted.

"Really ought to stay up on things, even on leave. You'll get a briefing. Right now, all you get to know is that for the moment we're on the same course. Things are getting choppy downtown, and we've got an Osprey III vectoring on us even as we speak. We meet the bird soon as we can and take to the air. It'll be a whole lot faster than slugging along the road."

"I don't rate that sort of transport."

"No, but I do. You just happen to have the combined advantages of a fortuitous location and being headed for the same landing zone."

>>>>>LIVE FEED COVERAGE
  —[05:34:51/8-23-55]
REPORTER: SUZIE CHIANG [CHIA-704]
UPLINK SITE: ELGIN, IL

Chiang: "This is Suzie Chiang of WCHI coming to you courtesy of WLGN because I cannot get to my studio. I cannot even *contact* my studio. Powerful jamming signals emanating from somewhere near O'Hare Airport are blanketing the broadcast frequencies and all standard communications satellites links to the city are offline. We are still searching for alternate data routes.

"What is clear is that something terrible has happened in Chicago. Federal and National Guard troops are mobilized and are cordoning off the city, stopping everyone headed in or out. Those attempting to flee the city are being detained or turned back. Private security troops belonging to the Ares Macrotechnology subsidiary, Knight Errant Security, are everywhere, working hand in glove with the military.

"The authorities are silent. The Governor's office has no comment at this time. *What* is going on? The troops aren't talking. Rumors of an outbreak of VITAS plague are rampant. One city escapee told me of a new goblinization taking place in the heart of Chicago. Whatever is going on in the Windy City, we are not meant to know. Link by link, the city is being isolated.

"The public has a right to know. That is why my team and I are going in. We believe we have a way to break the illegal communications blackout, so we're going to get past the armored vehicles and soldiers in order to bring you the story. The next time you hear from me, I will be 'casting direct from Chicago, bringing you the truth."<<<<<

13

Andy hit the wall with his shoulder first but not exclusively. Blood oozed as his cheek slammed against the rough concrete. The impact sloshed his brain in his skull.

Something brushed his hip. Dazed, he turned to see one of the ork kids holding his Narcoject replica. Three more orks lurked behind the first, and two others stood sentry at the mouth of the alley. They were all teen-aged, but even adolescent orks were bigger and beefier than most fully grown norms. Several wore face paint or tattoos in geometric shapes—some sort of gang affiliation mark? Andy was afraid so. There were parts of DeeCee where gangs ran wild. He hadn't realized this area of Arlington was one of them. His mistake. His very bad mistake.

"Ooh, ooh. He's seen us. Whaddever will we do?" The ork pointed the pistol at Andy and smiled. It wasn't a pleasant smile, and the dark line of decay separating the ork's yellowing tusks from his bright pink gum line only made it worse.

"Johnson says, 'Don't get caught,' " said the one with an oversized left eye. The ork had a burgundy star painted atop the orbit, as if to emphasize his asymmetry.

"But we already gots caught. Whuddever shall we do?" asked Bad Teeth in mock distress.

"Johnson says, 'Clean up any messes you make,' " responded Star Eye.

"I like makin' messes," said the lone female. Her hair was cut as buzz-short as the others and her face was as harsh and hard, but her mammalian heritage showed her sex. She pumped her fists up and down in Andy's face, letting him see the words "Pucker up" tattooed on each. "Kiss de boyz and make dem cry."

She made a grab at Andy's crotch. He deflected it clumsily. She backhanded him across the face and he went down into the stinking refuse littering the alley, his deck skittering out of his hands. Then she kicked him in the gut, and he vomited, as much from the garbage in his face as from the blow.

"Ain't nice ta refuse a lady," Pucker Up told him.

All the orks laughed.

"Johnson says, 'Don't play around,'" Star Eye admonished her.

"Ain't playin' around," Pucker Up said. "I'm a real, loyal, lovin', ork gal. I jus' live ta give all my attention ta my pale, smooth, sweetface wuss of a breeder suitboy. I be a one-guy kind of gal. I ain't no thankless, scummy, thieving scuz who don't know when she got it good. I be little Miz Faithful. Don't play aroun' at all. He be de stupid, damfool one don't understan' loyalty."

She emphasized every adjective with a kick at Andy. He tried to curl up and protect his vital spots, but every time she found something he'd failed to cover. He lay sobbing when she stopped, each breath wracking him with pain. His tears streaked runnels on his filth-covered face. He whimpered as she went through his clothing, taking what she wanted. He felt her strip him of his carry-bag, heard the crack of his cyberdeck's casing as she dropped it carelessly to the ground. She took her feel of him as well. He couldn't stop her.

All the orks Andy had met growing up were people, just like everybody else. But these, these were animals. Not just animals, predators . . . and he had become their prey.

Somewhere far away, one of the orks grunted in confusion. Andy forced his eyes open. Bad Teeth was looking down at the Narcoject and frowning in puzzlement. The ork hefted the gun and shook his head. Mashing the magazine release with his thumb, he ejected the cartridge. When he saw that it was no more than a solid block of plastic, he snorted.

"Dis ain't no tough-gut wannabe. Johnson been playing us for funnies. Dis here breeder, he ain't nothing but pure corp fluff," Bad Teeth said disdainfully. He tossed the fake magazine to his companions.

Each examined it in turn, snorted or guffawed, and tossed it to the next. By the time the last one caught it, all the orks were hooting in derision. Bad Teeth squatted down and stuck his face into Andy's. The ork's breath was fouler than his body odor, and Andy nearly lost it again. He tried to turn his face away, but the ork wrapped a meaty paw around his jaw and wrenched his head back around. "Whatchu doing out in de real world, fluff?"

"Johnson says, 'Don't talk to the meat,' " Star Eye said warningly.

"Dis don't add," Bad Teeth told him. "Maybe be healthy ta know why."

"Healthier to do it and be done," Star Eye said.

"You ain't da boss, is ya?" Bad Teeth spoke to Star Eye, but he poked Andy with a finger. The next words were meant for him. "Listen. We talk ta dis breeder, maybe he tells us something we wanna hear, maybe he don't become part of the garbage."

"Johnson won't like it," Star Eye said.

"Johnson's got a lot of 'don't need ta know' for us. Well, dis is a 'don't need ta know' for Johnson. It's free enterprise. Got it?"

"I don't know. Bad business, crossin' Johnson," Pucker Up said, leering at Andy. "Less fun too."

They argued. Andy knew he should be thinking about escaping, but all he could think about was how much he hurt. When they stopped arguing they'd hurt him some more. Maybe kill him. He didn't want to die lying in a pile of trash.

A hissing from the alley mouth shut down the argument. Bad Teeth stomped down to see what his sentries had spotted. Beyond the whispering orks, people, mostly street people, flowed by on the sidewalk, hurrying away from something. The orks wouldn't let any of them into the alley, cuffing away any who were persistent. The rest of the gang joined Bad Teeth at the alley mouth. They started a new argument. It was low-voiced and Andy couldn't follow it.

This was Andy's chance, but he hurt too much to crawl away.

The orks broke from the alley mouth like jackals before a lion. They swarmed past where Andy lay, but one stopped. Pucker Up stood over him. A knife gleamed in her hand.

"No more time ta play, suitboy," she said.

Andy expected to feel the knife, but instead he felt a rain of tiny fragments of concrete as thunder echoed in the alley. A gun. Pucker Up cursed and was gone. Someone stood at the alley mouth, someone big and bulky with a swollen, oversize head. Andy's vision was blurred. A troll? Too small. For a second Andy's vision cleared. Not a troll, but a soldier in combat armor. The soldier fired another burst to hurry the fleeing orks, chipping more concrete from the building walls.

"Hey, Sarge," the soldier shouted, looking back down the street. "Looks like them tuskers were having themselves some fun."

With a rattle and whir a massive vehicle rolled to a stop athwart the alley mouth. Someone was standing in the topside hatch. He wore body armor and helmet like the first soldier.

"Citizen?" the rider asked.

"Dunno, Sarge."

"Well, go check him out."

The soldier advanced cautiously down the alley, looking past Andy, watching for the return of the orks. Andy tried to thank the soldier for rescuing him, but only produced a wheeze that startled the soldier, who pointed his weapon at Andy. Andy decided not to try to talk or to move at all. Nervous people with guns were dangerous. He'd gotten a reprieve from death, and he wasn't going to throw it away.

The soldier eased up his rifle, apparently satisfied that Andy wasn't about to attack him. He knelt beside Andy and conducted a quick, one-handed search of his clothes. The soldier cursed when he got blood and vomit on his hands, and wiped it off on Andy's pants leg. Finished, he straightened up.

"Well?" the sergeant asked. "Is he a citizen?"

"Maybe. He's got a datajack, but he looks more like street trash. Ain't got no ID. Tuskers probably took it."

"Give me the serial number on the jack."

The soldier squatted down and used the butt of his rifle to turn Andy's head to the light. He still had to bend close and squint to read out the code on the chrome lip of the datajack. The sergeant disappeared into his vehicle, reappearing almost a minute later.

"Jack's registered to a dead suit," he said. "That guy look dead to you?"

"Not yet."

"Tech database says he's got a jack that ain't his, so he's an illegal. Damn, those black docs move fast. Suit's only cold a few days and already his hardware's on the street."

"This guy needs a doc, Sarge."

"Found one on his own to get his hot jack planted in his

skull, didn't he? Come on back, Espinoza. We've got other things to do."

"What about this guy?"

"We ain't the cops. Leave him be."

The engine on the armored vehicle revved and it started to roll. Espinoza hesitated for a moment, then trotted after it.

More vehicles rolled past the alley. Soldiers moved along with them. None of them had time for a battered kid in an alley. Too bad he wasn't a citizen. Andy *had* been a citizen, until he'd arranged otherwise for himself.

He had to do something. He really didn't want to die lying among the refuse. But he hurt so much. It even hurt to breathe.

Sometime after the soldiers had passed, he forced himself to his feet in a swirl of gray and a blaze of pain. He collapsed after trying to pick up his deck, and then three times more before he made it to the mouth of the alley.

The street wasn't deserted, but it might as well have been. None of the passersby moved to help him; most didn't even look at him. He tried to ask for help, but only a rasping croak came out. Pucker Up had gotten a kick in to his throat.

He knew he wouldn't be able to get far. The building holding him up had office space, maybe a doctor. He dragged himself to its door and forced his eyes to focus on the sign listing the tenants. No doctors. No hope. Or was there? Among the second-floor listings was "Harry Markowitz Corp., Investigations." Markowitz. Marksman. Andy had done something for him once, hadn't he? He'd help. He had to.

When he found himself in the stairwell on the second floor landing, he didn't remember deciding to take the stairs. The climb had taken almost the last of his strength. He needed the wall to hold him up as he shuffled down the corridor. He reached Markowitz's doorjamb exhausted. He was sure something was leaking inside his belly. He would die if he didn't get help. This really was his last chance.

He couldn't make his fingers grip the doorknob. All he could do was slap the rebellious hand against the frosted plastic pane. It was a poor excuse for a knock. He left a smear of gore across "Investigations."

The way his blood was pounding in his ears, Andy couldn't hear very well, but he thought he heard someone say something. It might have been "come in," but if it was,

Andy wasn't going to be able to comply. It was all he could do to slap the door again. The last of his strength gave out and he slumped against the door. The frosted pane was cool against his abraded cheek.

Then his world tumbled as someone opened the door. Losing his support, Andy collapsed over the threshold. He hit the floor like a Goo-Child doll.

Someone leapt over his sprawled body. Markowitz. The man threw himself against the door frame, drawing a short-barreled automatic from a shoulder holster. He peered cautiously into the corridor, first toward the stairs up which Andy had come, then back the other way.

Andy felt the brush of fur against his cheek. Something grabbed the collar of his shirt and tugged, pulling him all the way into the office. The angle of the pull was too low to be a human—unless the person was on the floor with Andy and the tug was too steady for that. And the fur? Some kind of dog? What did it matter, he hurt too much. He shut his eyes, wishing the pain would stop.

"Just the kid," Markowitz said. Andy heard the door close. Claws clicked softly against the floor as the animal ran away. Markowitz's footsteps came closer. His voice came from above.

"Shit, kid, you're bleeding on my floor."

Sorry. I didn't mean to. I'll just die now.

"Great. He can't even talk." Markowitz sighed exasperatedly. "Why'd you have to come here, kid?"

"Shush, Harry," a soft feminine voice said. Bare feet slapped softly on the floor, coming closer. A whiff of something floral floated by Andy's nostrils. So out of place. He opened his eyes and saw a beautiful Asian face before him, expression concerned. The woman had a classic, ageless winsomeness that clashed with her white hair. The contrast triggered a memory. Andy matched voice and face with the memory: this was Kit. Andy focused on her dark eyes. He knew those eyes, but he couldn't remember from where. Her delicate fingers lifted Andy's eyelids one at a time. Her expression grew sad. "He is damaged."

"I can see that. I still want to know why he came here?"

"You said he recognized you."

"*You* said he wouldn't be able to."

She shrugged. "And you never make mistakes? We must do something. He needs help."

"Who doesn't? Haven't we got enough troubles right now? We can dump him at the hospital on our way out."

"He may not last that long," Kit said gravely. "We touched his life. Now he touches ours. Instant karma, *neh?*"

"Are you going to do something for him?"

"I will try."

"Just do the minimal to get him on his feet and out of here. You don't need to waste your strength on a street stupid like him. He's a complication we don't need right now. In fact, we might be better off if he stops breathing."

"Harry, you don't mean that."

"Don't be so sure. Look, I'm going back on the horn to Cog and see if he can scare us up a sub. The kid don't show improvement by the time I'm done, we dump him. Okay?"

There was more argument, but Andy faded out. It seemed too unimportant. Besides, when everything was dark, the pain wasn't so bad. He dreamed he was a kid again, running in green fields the like of which he'd never played in. He had a fluffy-tailed white dog with him. A bitch. She loved him and would wash his face for him if he gave her half a chance. All she wanted to do was play, and her barking called him to play with her, urging him out of the dark.

Out of the dream.

His mind was clear. He remembered Kit and Marksman now. Yates, Rags, and Shamgar the ork samurai, too. There were two other runners, another ork and a female norm rigger, but he didn't have names for them. He remembered the runners bursting in on him. The rescue of Yates, and his subsequent clash with the lethal ice. The flight through the maintenance corridors of the Telestrian complex. The machine Rags had used to suck Andy's headware dry of the stuff Yates had crammed in there. The ride downtown that had ended with Andy staring into Kit's deep, deep eyes. The cloud coming down, and his subsequent dumping. He remembered it all.

He lay on a bed. Not his own. The bedclothes carried a hint of floral scent. The room, when he looked at it, wasn't feminine at all. But Kit was there.

"You are feeling better?" she asked.

"I'm feeling like drek, but at least I don't feel like I'm dead. You did something to me."

She looked down, like a modest girl. "You are lucky."

"I believe it. Thank you."

"Our karmas are linked now, Andrew."

Andy understood that he owed her a lot. He'd repay her. How, he didn't know yet.

"Who beat you so badly?" she asked.

Answering her questions would barely cover interest on what he owed. "A gang of ork kids. They pulled me into the alley outside. I think they were going to kill me."

"They came very close. Did they have a reason?"

"Do the street scum need a reason these days?" asked Markowitz. He was standing in the doorway of the room. Behind Markowitz, Andy could see the office in which he'd collapsed. This was Markowitz's place, which meant that Kit was—something to Markowitz that Andy didn't want to think about.

"Well, kid. *Did* they have a reason?" Markowitz asked.

"One of them kept saying 'Johnson says,' " Andy told him. "I think someone hired them."

"You know who?"

"No."

"Why?"

"No."

"How about how they knew to hit you here?"

"No idea."

"Great." Markowitz rolled his eyes. "You're trouble, kid, and I don't want any part of it."

"It's not his fault, Harry," Kit said.

Markowitz shook his head. "Sure. Of course not. It never is."

He left the room and Kit said, "Don't let him bother you. He is not so rough as he makes out."

"I want to know as much as he does," Andy told her.

"We'll find out," she assured him. "First things first."

Andy could hear Markowitz start a telecom call in the other room. Before long Markowitz was yelling at whoever was on the other end.

"I ain't got any time, and you know it. If you're trying to hold me up for a premium, it won't work. There are other people who can take my business." A pause, then calmer. "Yeah, yeah. I know."

The rest of the conversation went on in lower tones that Andy couldn't catch. Kit kept looking toward the other room, as if she were still listening. Andy didn't understand what was going on, but he'd obviously fallen into their lives while they were in the middle of something.

"What's the problem?" he asked.

Kit looked at him, but didn't speak right away. "Harry has arranged to transport certain medical supplies across the border from the Confederated States. Those supplies have a limited period of usefulness. If they are not delivered to the distribution point tonight, they will be worthless. People will die without them." Kit looked distressed by the prospect.

"I don't understand. Why can't you make the run?"

"Sammy Locksley, our driver, is not to be found. It is unlike her. She knew the importance of tonight's run. Harry is afraid something has happened to her. It makes him . . . unhappy. That is why he is so harsh with you. Usually he is more kindly to our guests."

"I could help."

She smiled indulgently. "The car is special, a rigger model."

"I'm a rigger." He would have said so even if he hadn't had any experience. He wanted to do something to repay a part of his debt. And he wanted to make Kit happy. "I could drive it."

"Really?"

"Really."

Her expression brightened, warming Andy with the sun of her smile.

Markowitz came back into the room. "We better hope we don't run into trouble, Kit. Cog hasn't got anybody on tap. I'll have to drive."

"How can you?" Kit asked. "You always tell Sammy you are no rigger."

"I'm not, but the datajack will let me supervise the autopilot. Won't do us any good if the drek hits the fan, so you better hope we're lucky. Know any good-luck spells?"

"Several, but they all have unfortunate side effects when focused for the benefit of the caster or those dear to her. We may have another answer. Andrew is a rigger."

"Yeah?" Markowitz eyed Andy suspiciously. "How convenient. I've been thinking about the convenience of today's events. How do I know you're not a stalking horse for Telestrian?"

Andy wasn't stalking anything. "I suppose you don't, but

I'm not working for them anymore. I helped Yates, remember?"

"Yates didn't exactly survive your help. Remember?"

Andy wasn't going to let Markowitz lay that guilt on him; he had enough of his own. "It was the black ice that got him. Yates was the one who decided I couldn't help him against the ice. He dumped me out of the Matrix, remember? Besides, do you think I'd let myself be nearly killed just to gull you?"

Markowitz looked as though he were considering that very possibility.

"He really was seriously injured, Harry," Kit said.

"You and Kit helped me, and this will give me a chance to return the favor."

"You think you can pay a life-debt with a turn at the wheel?"

"No, but I have to start someplace."

"Let him help, Harry."

Kit's plea thawed Markowitz's frosty expression, by a degree. "You got any experience with a Cougar-6200 rigger interface?" he asked.

"I ought to," Andy said. "I was one of the drivers in the beta test."

"We need a rigger," Kit reminded Markowitz.

"No pay," Markowitz said.

"Okay."

"You're crazy, kid," Markowitz said. "But maybe it's karma that you're here. I've got a lot more questions for you, and no time to ask them, and I don't really have a good place to stash you till after the run, so I'll give you a chance." He tossed Andy a bracelet. "Here, put this on."

Andy tried it on. The catch latched and an LED indicator came to life, spelling out "Armed."

"What the hell is this?"

"Insurance," Markowitz said. "If I'm not around to feed it the delay code every hour or so, you'll be short a hand."

"Harry!" Kit sounded appalled.

"You shush," he told her. "We can't afford to take chances. You know that. Now put on your coat, it's time to go."

>>>>>NEWSNET DOWNLINK
   -[12:06:49/8-23-55]

HIGH-LEVEL MEETINGS AT WHITE HOUSE

There was turmoil in the White House this morning as unscheduled visitors arrived. Arriving separately and within moments of each other, delegations from the elven nations of Tir Tairngire and Tir na nÓg converged on the White House with demands for an immediate meeting. The delegates, whom the presidential press secretary will only describe as "extremely high ranking," were admitted at once and are still meeting with President Steele after nearly five hours. Though no statement or explanation has been issued, the rumored topic of concern to the visitors from the reclusive elven nations is the growing crisis in Chicago. At a time when the people of the UCAS are being told very little about what is happening in one of their country's greatest cities, the public can only wonder what interests these foreign powers have in the country's internal affairs.

Reliable sources within the White House report that the meeting was interrupted an hour ago by a telecom call from the notorious dragon Lofwyr. Persistent rumors that Lofwyr has offered some sort of "final solution" to the problems in Chicago have been called "nonsense and exaggeration" by the presidential press secretary Lee Atwhiler.

In a clearly related action, General Lewis Draeger, Chairman of the Joint Chiefs, held a brief press conference at noon today to issue a prepared statement confirming that the entire UCAS military is on alert. In the brief question-and-answer session that followed, General Draeger refused to confirm or deny that the threat was strictly internal, although he did issue what he called "a warning to troublemakers" that the UCAS was "more than prepared to defend *all* of its interests."<<<<<

14

Tom watched Andrews Air Force Base slide by beneath the
Osprey. The craft didn't change its flight path, or shift to
vertical flight mode. He pointed out the window as the last
runway slipped from sight. "I thought that was where we
were going."

Furlann put her head back and closed her eyes. "You
thought wrong."

Apparently he thought wrong to think he could trust her,
too. "What's going on? We have orders to report there for
transport by twelve hundred hours."

"Doesn't matter."

"It matters to me. I've got orders."

"The orders have been modified."

Nobody had told him. "No, they haven't."

Furlann sighed. "Ease off, Walker. You'll get straightened
out when we land. Relax, enjoy the flight."

Relax and enjoy? He was being forced AWOL. He considered going up to the cockpit and ordering the pilot to turn
around and head for Andrews, but decided it probably
wouldn't get him very far. If the pilot didn't have orders
from higher up, it would come down to the pilot choosing
between Tom and Furlann. The mage would win that contest, in spite of her lower rank. He'd watched it happen before. People just didn't like to go against a mage.

What was Furlann dragging him into? Clearly she was
operating according to someone's plan. He hoped it wasn't
one of her whacked magical snipe hunts. This wasn't the
time. Whatever it was, she knew more about it than she was
telling. He'd hated it in Denver when she'd withheld information. Secrecy was a habit with her, a habit Tom hadn't
grown to like over time.

"I think you owe me some answers."

"When we land, Walker," she said, speaking as if to an
annoying child wanting to know when they were going to arrive. "When we land."

Waiting until they landed seemed to be his only option
short of violence, so he waited.

"Coming in on Fort Belvoir now," the pilot announced over the intercom, just before the Osprey shuddered as the pivot-mounted engines on its stub wings began their rotation up into vertical flight mode. They descended below tree level. Through the windows on Furlann's side, Tom caught glimpses of a huge geodesic dome and an array of antennae.

Furlann was up and moving before the pilot cut the engines. "Come on, Walker. You're with me until you're told otherwise."

Her attitude overstepped the latitude given officers in the Thaumaturgic Corps. Tom wasn't sure how much longer he was going to go along with it. She had better be right about a change in orders, otherwise he was well and truly fragged. There wouldn't be enough time to make it to Andrews before 1200 hours. Mage or not, she was going to boil in the same water he did if she landed him in the pot.

To judge from the activity around them, they had landed in the midst of a kicked-over anthill. Tom scoped the bustle. He recognized the antennae going up, the array of consoles winking to life under canvas stretched between armored vehicles, and the armed guards whose still alertness was a striking counterpoint to the frenzied activity of the other soldiers swarming though the area.

"This is a combat headquarters," Tom said as they walked toward what appeared to be the focus of the tumult. He ran his hand along the gray-shaded side of a Tactical Operations Center van. This was field command stuff, enough to serve a division, maybe even a corps.

"You were expecting me to be taking you to a rec hall dance, maybe?" Furlann asked sarcastically.

"I was *expecting* transportation back to Schwartzkopf," he reminded her.

"You may get your trip yet, but we're here to see General Trahn," Furlann said.

Tom halted, stunned. Trahn was one of the only officers who'd come out of the Dissolution Campaigns with a decent record and a clean reputation. Word had it he was the fastest-rising star in the Army, in line for the Joint Chiefs. "Trahn? Why? Any why does he want to see me now? I've got a responsibility to—"

"You're here at my order, Major."

Tom snapped to attention as he saw the stars on the collar of the man who had stepped out of the TOC van. He didn't need to read the name tag to recognize Trahn; the general had often been pictured in *Stars and Stripes*.

For a moment the tableau held. Trahn had that smooth-skinned, exotic Eurasion look that showed few signs of age. He might have been thirty or he might have been sixty. With his rank and position, he had to be closer to the latter. That smoothness gave him a killer poker face; Tom couldn't tell the man's mood. The general might be annoyed at the ink-still-wet major who could have been considered to have questioned his authority, or he might not.

"Is there a problem?" Trahn asked.

"No problem, sir! Just a little confused."

Trahn finally returned Tom's salute. "Confusion I understand. We've got entirely too much of it right now. I'm glad you could get here so quickly, Major."

"Nothing to it," Furlann said.

Trahn ignored her, drawing Tom with him back into the TOC van. "You're Matt Walker's kid, aren't you? I served with your father back in '17. Good man, before he Changed."

"If you say so, General. I didn't know him before."

One of General Trahn's staff officers interrupted the awkward moment, stomping up the ramp with a raft of questions. The information she wanted was the general's preferences on technical set-up, but her questions offered Tom no clue as to what was going on. Having given his answers and sent the officer on her way, the general turned again to Tom.

"As I was saying, Captain Furlann tells me you've got a knack with Special Resources. With this op being put together on the fly, I haven't got a lot of SR assets, and it's a real mixed bag. My regular SR officer was at Schwartzkopf when Chicago blew, and he got co-opted. I need somebody to ride herd on my SR assets and pull them into shape. You that man?"

"I thought I'd be heading back to my unit."

"Your unit's already in the thick of it up in Chicago," the general confided. "No way to get you in there now."

Already in? "I don't understand, sir. Why wasn't I recalled before they went in?"

"I wasn't consulted, Major. The trouble in Chicago uncorked faster than anyone expected, and we're all still adapting. You're not the only officer caught away from his station. For the moment people are filling in wherever they are. We're all improvising and not worrying a lot about the niceties. For me, you happened to be in the right place at the right time, and I intend to take advantage of it. With the Chicago operation drawing so heavily on available assets, I'm short-handed here, and I need to get as many good officers locked down as I can."

It would be wonderful to work with an officer like Trahn, but—"I really ought to be with my troops, sir."

Trahn frowned. "I think it's more important that we put you to work here, Major. I'd have thought you would understand.

"We have to deal with this mess our esteemed President has let fester to the point of needing surgery. Chicago's bad, but it's only a symptom of broader problems. One more officer there wouldn't make a difference. If we tried to dump you out to Chicago, hook you up with your unit, and make that team change horses in mid-op, we wouldn't be doing them any favor. You can help them by working here. You don't want to see their butts in the air because the home front collapses, do you?"

"No, sir."

Dropping the frown, Trahn said, "Captain Furlann also tells me you're the one who set the standard on Green Twilight." Green Twilight was the code name for the training exercises developed from Tom's first nightmare exercise at Fort Schwartzkopf. "If you trained those people, they'll be okay. And if they can't do it without you, you didn't do your job right, which I am assured you did. They'll do fine. Haven't you any faith?"

Faith he had. Worry, too.

Trahn kept steamrollering. "Your performance at Schwartzkopf tells me you have a flair for the field as well as organization. Since I'm running short, I need double-threats if I can get them. I want you to advise me on special ops and I want to give you tactical charge of the SR unit once you get it laid out."

Both staff and field work? Trahn *must* be running short. It would be a hell of a job, but it would be a chance to shine, and right under Trahn's nose. Having his approval wouldn't do Tom's career anything but good. But why the sell job, and not just a transfer order? He asked.

"I need people who *want* to be here," Trahn replied. "The

current crisis is a fire brigade kind of thing. It may be a flashpoint for worse things. If it is, good people in the right places will make all the difference to the survival of this country, and life as we know it. I've been told that you've got the right stuff."

"I hope so, sir."

"Hope?"

"I mean, yes, sir!"

"All right, then." Trahn stuck out his hand for Tom to shake. "Welcome aboard. Just remember, I expect one hundred percent plus."

"I won't disappoint you, sir." Tom hoped it was true.

Trahn led him out of the van and performed quick introductions to his staff officers and left Tom in charge of Colonel Jemal Jordan, his J2. The intel officer filled Tom in on their basic mission: to stand ready in case the violence in the city escalated.

"And how likely is that?" Tom asked, thinking maybe he should insist on Chicago after all. He'd had his fill of police back-up work in Denver.

Jordan countered with his own question. "Are you a betting man, Rocquette?"

"Sometimes."

"Well, if someone offers you a hundred to one for you to bet against escalation"—Jordan flashed a smile full of brilliant teeth—"don't."

The colonel found Tom a station, cleared access codes for him, and left him to do his job. While Tom was sorting out just what he had to work with, a bevy of corp types arrived. Tom noted that most wore Telestrian corp affiliation pins, but he spotted Fuchi, Ares Macrotechnology, Shiawase, Oracular Systems, and Geistco as well. "Representatives from the Alliance of Concerned Corporate Citizens," an aide announced.

Trahn abandoned the mission briefing that Jordan was giving him. He marched out to meet the suits near the ramp of one of the TOC vans.

"Shall we step inside, gentlemen?" Trahn asked, offering his personal caravan. There were no introductions; Trahn must have met with the suits before. Tom wondered just who they were that the general should drop what he was doing to chat with them.

Their apparent spokesman, a whip-thin elf with his ash-blond hair in a non-corp-standard trash cut, shook his head slightly, smiling the while. "We would prefer to remain outside. Our concerns are public, but some expressions of those concerns might be better done in privacy. Perhaps we should speak over there in the shade of the trees where some little breeze, if it is to be, will find us. You need have no concern over privilege. My staff can provide all the privacy we will need."

The general agreed and walked off to the trees with the suits. As they moved, the whole group seemed to go a little out of focus. Tom blinked. No, the trees beyond them were still clear. Only an area around the people was blurred. Tom's eyes were fine; it had to be magic. Presumably the spells were muffling sound as well.

That one or more of the elf's staff were magickers was not unusual. In general, the corps were far better supplied with magickers than the government, including the military. Usually payscale won out over patriotism.

Colonel Jordan stepped into his line of sight. The intel officer looked right at Tom. "Got your unit organized already?"

"No, sir."

"Then you have work to do. You haven't got time to spare if you're planning to deliver a report to the general on schedule."

Jordan was right. Tom had no time to worry about whatever was concerning the local suits; he had a job to do. He dove into the details. He didn't realize that Trahn had returned to the TOC until he heard the general's voice.

"All right, folks. Listen up. As of now, we are operational."

Colonel Jordan added, "All report timetables are advanced to half an hour from now, when there will be a full staff briefing."

"In the meantime, I don't intend to sit still," Trahn said. "We're rolling with contingency plan Baker. Jemal, while you're setting up the commanders' conference line, get me a secure link to the President." Trahn's eyes swept over the officers, techs, and clerks in the TOC. "Time to earn our pay, people. Get to work."

Tom did. He didn't know yet what plan Baker was, but if it had involved Special Resources, he would have been told. As it was, he could scope the scan at the briefing. Till then, he had plenty to occupy him, since the only Special Resources available were individuals and a few experimental units at Belvoir for testing. All the standing units had gone to Chicago. Organizing a coherent and combat-capable unit was going to be a challenge; doing it in half an hour was going to be impossible.

```
>>>>>LOCAL FEED WFDC
  -[06:17:05/8-24-55]
WFDC NEWS ANCHOR: SHIMMER GRACE [GRAC-A303]
UPLINK SITE: BETHESDA STUDIO, FDC
```

Grace: "I've just been told that our ace techs here at the studio *did* indeed capture the override we just experienced. *I'm* still not sure what to make of it. What about *you*? How about we see it again?"[*Query cam angle*]

[*Audience response: 91% positive*]

"All right then, techboys, let's get to it!" [*Replay inset*]

Weingartner: "This is Taylor Weingartner speaking to you from the steps of the Lincoln Memorial, proud symbol of America's commitment to justice and equality. Tonight began as just another night of hustling and scavenging for members of the Comp Army, but it is no longer. Yesterday's rumors of UCAS troops marching on the city are now reality, but while fears of violent confrontation with the military are abating, tension between marchers and police has skyrocketed. All evening we've been witnessing minor scuffles between police and angry marchers. Tension is running high. Now, we seem to have reached a critical point. Even as I speak, something is happening among the tents and shanties—

[*Static fuzz dissolve: woman in extreme closeup*]: "We call ourselves the Compensation Army, and it's time the slugs and liars of Washington learned why. Peaceful discourse has achieved nothing. We have come to demand our just compensation! We will not take silence and lies for answers. We want action! If we don't get it from the corporate puppet politicians, we'll take it ourselves. President Steele, you hold the future in your hands."[*Static fuzz: feed return; cut to studio*]

Grace: "Wow! What do you make of that? As you can see, the unnamed speaker was wearing the blue beret of the Conscience of the Country sect of the Comp Army. Looks like the Consies *have* had a hidden agenda all along. Are we looking at trouble here in old DeeCee? [*Query cam angle*]

[*Audience response: 83% positive*]<<<<<

15

The Concordia slammed hard, scraping bottom, as Andy swerved her onto the grassy verge. He was sure they'd left something of the car behind. But there were some things it was good to leave behind. Over the external mikes came the sound of machine gun fire chewing the pavement where they had been. The chopping throb of the Yellowjacket attack helicopter's rotors thundered overhead.

The synth view on the monitor showed the Yellowjacket banking hard to come around for another pass. Andy goosed the Concordia, and the car's engine raced faster, the Cougar-6200 interface revving Andy's heart and pumping up his adrenaline. Such was the link a rigger shared with his machine. But fear was damping Andy's usual high-performance high. It would take more than gas and adrenaline to get away from the hunter. This Concordia was armed, but she was strictly a streetfighter; she didn't carry ground-to-air weaponry.

If it had been *his* Concordia—

But wishes were as good as fishes right now. They Y-J passed overhead, trying to line up again to blast them as Andy put the Concordia back on the pavement; she wasn't built for going cross-country at their current speed and the last excursion had hurt her. The road was snaking and Andy was hugging the edges and swerving erratically, doing his best not to offer the Y-J pilot a decent firing run. The Yellowjacket banked away, the chopper grabbing sky to prepare for another run. Andy had managed to avoid giving the

Y-J pilot any shots on that pass. He was relieved. Real rigging wasn't as easy as virtual rigging.

He tweaked the interface to bump up the air conditioning. He'd been sweating so much, he was starting to stink.

"Nav update shows the Roosevelt Bridge still closed," Markowitz said. It had been their chosen crossing. Markowitz's voice was so calm he might have been commenting on rush-hour traffic as he griped, "Hell of long time to clear out a traffic accident."

"Then how the frag are we supposed to get across the river!"

Andy wanted to know, and soon. They were running out of road. So far the trees shading the northwestern part of the George Washington Parkway had been offering them some cover. That would be gone once they hit Arlington—in about a minute. The Roosevelt Bridge offered the fastest route across the Potomac, and if they didn't take it, they'd have to go further south; and if they went further south, they'd be running over some seriously open ground near Arlington Cemetery. They'd be easy meat for the Yellowjacket.

Which was back. Nerves stretched, Andy sought cover. Not enough. He swerved. The Y-J stuck to them. It fired. Andy swerved again. Slugs hammered the starboard rear quarter-panel, but the Concordia's armor didn't care.

Unfortunately, at least one slug caught the right rear tire. Feedback stung Andy's right leg as he fought to keep the Concordia from fishtailing. It hurt like hell, but it wasn't crippling. The ReFlate system kicked in, foaming the tire. Response came back up. They'd be running a while yet as long as the Y-J's pilot didn't improve his aim.

"What about Key Bridge?" Markowitz asked.

"Not with him so close on our tail." Andy was having trouble finding enough air to breathe and talk at the same time. "Besides, if we made it across, we'd get snarled in Georgetown."

"Okay, okay. Cut into Rosslyn."

"Streets will slow us down."

"Won't help him either."

Andy did as Markowitz suggested. Working the streets and dodging the Yellowjacket didn't leave time to find a route. "Come on," he urged Markowitz. "Give me a vector."

"Cut back north on Military and head for Chain Bridge," Markowitz said. Andy's map shifted, highlighting Markowitz's suggested route. "Should give us enough cover to lose him."

"We'll be slower on the other side," Andy pointed out.

"At least the bridge is open to traffic. Latest update shows nothing else crossing the river is."

Andy couldn't argue, but he had another thought. "The Y-J pilot will know that. It's a lot less important than the other bridges. What's to keep him from splattering us?"

"Nothing but timing. We've got to cross when he isn't looking. So lose him already."

"Whatever happened to shadowrunners staying in the shadows?" Andy asked.

"Don't ask me, kid. I'm not flying that bird."

Andy tried to hide while the Y-J pilot sought. He'd played such games in virtual runs, but this was no game, as the lingering pain in his leg reminded him. Fortunately for them, the pilot seemed more reluctant to fire at them in the residential areas through which they moved. A trash fire near the Glebe Road overpass offered them their break. Hitting it at a moment when the Yellowjacket had overflown them, Andy halted them under cover, right at the edge of the blaze, and bled the Concordia's heat into the flames. Their IR signature blurred into the fire's. Finally judging it safe, he edged the Concordia out and sent the radar looking for the copter. He found it patrolling over the Potomac, scuttling back and forth between bridges, trying to make sure it would be wherever they attempted to cross.

Andy timed it to blast across Chain Bridge while the chopper was moving south, then continued up away from the river and into the placid, tree-shaded residential zone around MacArthur. The radar didn't yelp that the Yellowjacket was zeroing in on them. Andy relaxed. He was tooling down Loughboro Road when he learned that he wasn't the foxy one—the Yellowjacket pounced, coming around a building and showing on radar no sooner than on visual.

The Y-J pilot *had* spotted them, pretended that he hadn't, then used buildings as cover to close in. Tired as Andy was, exhaustion was no excuse for being stupid. No excuse was good enough. This wasn't a game, and a need for an excuse meant a need to dodge bullets. Only there was nowhere to go as the Yellowjacket started its attack run.

The pilot had learned his lessons, directing his slugs at the Concordia's vulnerable tires. A torrent of lead clawed away tread, sidewall, and foam. The car tilted, started to skid. Andy fought it, but between the sim pain and the loss of control there wasn't anything he could do. The crash bags blossomed.

The Concordia slued sideways and tipped, covering half a block on her side before a light post caught her fender. She spun around hard and crashed into a building. Andy felt like the little ball in an aerosol can that someone was trying to shake loose. The Concordia tipped back down onto her wheels and rocked to a stop. Like wannabe shrouds, the air bags deflated and draped Andy and Markowitz. The riders had survived, but the Concordia was dead. The interface was down, the windows dark, and the stink of burnt rubber and burning plastics fouled the air in the car. Andy coughed in the increasing smoke.

"You okay, kid?" Markowitz asked.

Battered, bruised, burned, dizzy from the ride and sudden disconnect from the Cougar-6200, and starting to asphyxiate. Oh, yeah, he was fine.

"Kid?"

"I'll live." Andy pulled the useless datacord from his jack. "What now?"

Markowitz squirmed around and hauled something from one of the racks in the back seat area: a rifle thing with a huge-bored barrel.

"What's that?"

"Capture gun. Used to use it for putting a net over unnatural animals. Iron banding on spun polycarbonate mesh, with silver-plated spikes at the junctions. Makes all sorts of things unhappy. The silver part's not going to have much effect on *this* unnatural animal, though." Markowitz cracked the door, letting in the outside air. It didn't make the inside any cooler, but it did let out some of the smoke. "Stay put."

Markowitz slipped on a pair of augmentation specs as he slid out of his seat to crouch under the cover of the gull-wing door.

The Yellowjacket was coming back. To confirm his kill, no doubt. Andy could tell from the sound that the pilot had cut in the stealth baffles. Why not? He didn't need speed anymore.

Andy started fiddling with the Concordia's manual controls, trying to get the windows to polarize so he could see something. He succeeded just in time to see the helicopter finish its approach and shift to hover. A block away, the Yellowjacket hung in the air like a giant metallic dragonfly waiting to pounce. The ball turret under its chin swiveled, the machine barrel snouting about as if sniffing for prey.

The Yellowjacket shunted sideways as if the pilot was trying to get an angle for a look through the Concordia's open door. Markowitz gave him something to see, taking a step out and shouldering his weapon.

Suicide.

But Markowitz had timed his move; the Yellowjacket's turret was pointed away from him. As it started to rotate toward him, Markowitz fired. Not waiting to see the results of his shot, he dove back into the Concordia. Slugs chewed up pavement and spanged against the car's armor, but none caught the audacious Markowitz.

Sprawled across the seat, Markowitz could not see whether he had shot true, but Andy had a front row seat. The canister that the rifle fired peeled away, releasing the net to spread as it flew. The pilot tried to sideslip and avoid the projectile. He managed to shift the fuselage clear, but the net engulfed the whirling disks of the craft's rotors. The blades whipped the mesh around themselves, wrapping it down to their hub. The chopper's engine screamed as it fought to do its job against the binding. Smoke began to pour from vents and the Yellowjacket tilted. Rotors frozen, it dropped from the sky like a stone. The nose hit first, splintering the canopy. The shock of impact jarred the rotors free. One blade swept into the sidewalk, crumpling and dying. The Yellowjacket bucked and flipped onto its back for a final crash into the street. A torrent of flame-lit smoke billowed out through the smashed canopy. Within seconds the dead craft was engulfed in flames.

"You took it down." Andy was astonished and knew he sounded it.

"You think my street name was just empty hype?"

He hadn't really thought that Marksman might actually *be* a marksman.

Andy hoped the pilot had died in the crash. Andy had died his apparent death in a cockpit fire; he didn't wish the real thing on anyone. "Did you have to kill him?"

"Like he didn't ask for it? He was trying to kill *us,* remember?" Markowitz hauled the freezer case out of the back of the car. "Come on, kid, we can't hang around here."

Andy had to crawl out of the passenger door, then crawled back again to snag his deck. He'd backed up the info files to his headware, but he'd need the hardware if he was going to do anything about decrypting the stuff, and the deck was all he had to do that. He'd almost lost the Sony to the ork gang when they took it from him, but he'd been lucky. After Kit had healed him and he had enough functioning brain cells to remember that Pucker Up had dropped the deck, he'd gone back to look for it and—to his amazement—had found it still lying in the alley. Too weak to carry it, he too had been forced to leave it behind. But when he went back for it, somehow it was still there. He couldn't count on the same luck if he left it here in the car.

By the time Andy was done, Markowitz had cracked the locks on the freezer case, extracted the box of drugs, and was slipping individual receptacles into his pockets. He seemed oblivious to the eyes watching from the houses and the edges of buildings.

"Good thing we haven't got far to go. This stuff won't last long in the heat without refrigeration." He walked back to the Concordia and ran a hand along a row of bullet scars. With a sigh, he tossed something into the back seat. As they walked away, fire blossomed in the interior of the Concordia.

"She was a good old beast," Markowitz said. "I'll miss her. We'll probably wish we still had her before this run is over."

Markowitz walked past the downed Yellowjacket without a word. Half a block later, he bent down and picked something up, again without a word. Andy trailed along behind him. What was the point of words anyway? He looked back at the two burning vehicles. This wasn't virtuality. You never smelled the virtual bad guys roasting.

Despite Markowitz's misgivings they made the transfer of the drugs without any more problems. The medicine had made it, and lives would be saved. Kit would be pleased. What they had done had helped. Did it balance against the life of the man Markowitz had killed? The helicopter pilot *had* been trying to kill them. Markowitz had just defended them.

It was so much easier killing the virtual bad guys. Andy could still smell the stink of the burning copter.

"Don't think about it too much," Markowitz said.

"What—"

"It's better that way. Trust me." He took Andy's arm and led him away from the meet site. "Come on, kid. I know an all-night shop not far from here. You'll feel better if you get something to hold your stomach down. Or something for it to toss up, if that's the way you're going to be."

The all-night shop was an All Hours, a dark, quiet little place, that combined a convenience store with a sit-down food service area. They were the only customers at the tables. Markowitz made a selection at the counters and put something down in front of Andy. Andy didn't even look at the plate, but he did wrap his hands around the cup of steaming soykaf. His hands felt cold despite the sultry night. Markowitz didn't bother with his food either. Instead, he took something out of his pocket and began turning it over and over in his hands. Despite his mood, Andy was curious.

"What's that?"

"A chunk of the bird that tried to scrag us." Markowitz continued turning the debris over and over in his hands. After a while he stopped and scrubbed at a section with his thumb. Angling the piece against the light, he squinted at it. "This is military issue. We got problems with the *army*."

"Don't be ridiculous. Lots of surplus and hijacked stuff gets to the street. This is just a coincidence."

"Believing in coincidence can get you dead."

"So can seeing conspiracies were there aren't any."

"I'm here to tell you, kid, you can't afford *not* to see conspiracies. Better you suspect the mess you're in runs deeper than it does, than to think you're jumping into shallow water and end up over your head. That Yellowjacket was current service. If it wasn't, the serial number I found on this piece of scrap would have been laser-cut away."

"So it's current service. Must have been the border patrol. We *were* smuggling." But the Concordia's threat database didn't list Yellowjackets with the border patrol; Andy had checked when the chopper first showed on radar.

"You can do better than that, kid."

"Okay. The border patrol can call on military assets under certain circumstances to interdict the drug and chip trade. We were carrying drugs."

"Not that kind of drugs."

"All right then. If there's a conspiracy, what's the connection?"

"We can start with the Johnson who hired my team for the run against Telestrian. He must have been Army."

"He told you that and you believed him?"

"What he told us was nothing, but he smelled military to me. I didn't think a lot about it at the time; a lot of ex-military work for the corps as part of the I-do-yours-you-do-mine symbiosis. The connections were in front of me and I didn't see them. Geez, I must be getting slow."

"Didn't you check him out?"

"Of course we did," Markowitz snapped. "We took what he fed us, looked him over, snooped a bit, and what we came up with was Fuchi. Made sense, I thought. Fuchi had a business interest in what Telestrian was doing, and if the Montjoy Project was as cutting-edge as Johnson claimed, Fuchi would want a jump on it. I thought the scam made sense, but something about it itched Yates. He looked harder and when he couldn't find anything, he looked at the frame it came in. He said our Johnson used military-issue hardware for all his decking. Like an idiot, I didn't think it was such a big deal. Like you said, the military is enough of a sieve that you see their hardware on the street all the time.

"But when you see *too* much of their stuff in one place, especially a full range of stuff, you're seeing *them*. Why? Because most shadow operators use the stuff they've got, because that's what they're used to and that's what they trust. Why shouldn't they? It's not like they expect to get caught. I should have seen it sooner, but better later than postmortem. There's entirely too much Army in this mess, and it stinks."

"But why would the Army want to kill us?"

"Government doesn't like its departments messing outside their areas. Espionage belongs to the D.S.A. and the C.I.A. and the F.B.I. They each have their slice of the pie, but the Army's got squat in the way of its own authorized shadow resources. Yup. All adds up to Army. All of Yates's tie-ins were groundpounder issue, and the Army's the only service flying attack choppers."

"D.S.A.'s got military staff, including Army." Didn't it make sense for a covert agency to be involved with undercover activities and just using Army resources? "Maybe they sponsored the run."

"Maybe," Markowitz said. "But you're forgetting one angle. If it was one of the spook shops, a shadowrun would be business as usual. There'd be no need to remove the tools."

Like a light turning on, Andy saw where Markowitz was coming from. "So you're thinking the Army hired your team for the run, and now they want to get rid of anyone who can connect them to the operation just to keep their slate clean."

"I don't like it, but that's the way it looks to me. Sammy's gone. Tonight they tried for the car. It should have been Kit and me in the car. A double-header for them. No runners means no way to connect them with their under-the-table work."

"That's a pretty cold plan."

"There are some cold fish in uniform. Ever hear of Newman's Grove?"

"No."

Markowitz nodded knowingly. "I didn't think so. They kept it very, very quiet. Likely you won't hear about it 'less you run into someone who was there."

"Like you?"

"Never said I was." Markowitz tossed the fragment onto the table. "Whoever sent the chopper knew about tonight's run."

Clearly Markowitz wanted to stay away from the topic of Newman's Grove now that he'd made his point. Andy obliged. "How would anyone know our route or timetable? We didn't lay one down."

"I got an idea that fits. Chichi Davis."

"The dwarf at the fuel stop?" Andy had thought the dwarf an okay guy. Clearly Markowitz knew something he didn't.

"Yup. The little bastard's ex-Army. He must have sold us out."

Could it be? Andy *had* picked up the Yellowjacket on radar just after they left Davis's place. Could there be something to Markowitz's paranoia?

"There's another thing that puzzles me," Markowitz said. "Cops should have responded to our little battlefield by now. This ain't exactly the Barrens."

He was right. They were close enough to the crash site that they'd have heard sirens in the still night air. Why hadn't they? Andy remembered the cordon around the Compensation Army camp down on The Mall, and the one he'd seen near the bridges at the Pentagon on his way to his meet with the fixer. It took a lot of people to man those barricades. With all the police involved in that, they'd be running shorthanded elsewhere. "Maybe they're busy."

"Exactly what I'm thinking. We need some input." Markowitz called out to the shopkeeper. "Hey, Johnny, flick on the screen and jack up some news for us."

The shop's vidscreen lit, flipped through a crazy quilt of images, and settled on the face of Shimmer Grace, the WFDC prime-time anchor. The station's frenetic "live" logo danced in a corner of the screen, which meant the Shimmer was up past her bedtime. Obviously something *was* going on.

Live feeds from cameras in several districts of the DeeCee sprawl were showing scenes of urban violence, or of police patrols in empty, trashed streets. Most of the shots from the Barrens were lit by fire. Shimmer kept up a heated commentary on the "terrible violence" and the efforts of the "beleaguered FedPols" to control matters. There were frequent repeats of a "threatening pirate broadcast," talking about action being taken by the Comp Army.

"Hey, Johnny, when did all this start?" Markowitz asked.

"Yesterday. FedPols put out a curfew request for south and central subdistricts about nine PM. Made it a crapper night. Bad as tonight."

A curfew request wasn't a legal requirement, more of a warning to good citizens to watch out for themselves and stay out of trouble by not staying out. It went a long way to explaining why they'd seen so few people on the streets and why the shop was so empty. As Markowitz had said, this wasn't exactly the Barrens. There were a lot of good citizens in this regional district.

Unlike the Arlington district. It had been different there once, but since the Blood Dust incident three years ago, property values had been declining in direct proportion to the increase in crime.

"Looks like we're going to have a little trouble getting home," Markowitz said.

"A *lot* of trouble." It was Kit. Bare legs and feet flashing beneath an urban camo poncho, she was heading for their table. The shop's door was still swinging closed. "There is no safety there. We have been compromised."

"You have any trouble? They see you?" Markowitz asked anxiously.

"No trouble. And while they did see me, they didn't know it." She seemed pleased.

"Good," Markowitz said. Andy felt like he'd been handed a riddle, but Markowitz asked another question before he could ponder it. "What did you see?"

Kit told them how three armed men had broken into Markowitz's office-apartment. They'd swept the place, obviously disappointed at finding no one. Although one had wanted to leave the doss alone and use it as a trap, another had insisted that they take what they could, arguing that Markowitz and company had flown and wouldn't be back. The third had agreed with the second. They took the telecom, the computers, the security system control box, and all the weapons, and went away. Kit had come to warn Markowitz rather than following the thieves.

Markowitz looked at Andy. "How do you feel about conspiracies now, kid?"

"You're converting me, but—" He was concerned about Kit. "We still don't know who they were. There are coincidences even when there are conspiracies."

"What about them, Kit? Any ideas?"

"They were gray men, Harry. Strange men. They were foreigners, but not."

"Don't go all mystical on me," Markowitz said. "Explain."

Kit shrugged. "Either an aura meshes with a place, or it doesn't. It's a question of comfort, familiarity, and rightness."

"I'd never heard that." Not that there was a lot about magic that Andy *had* heard. He hadn't much cared to—still didn't—but he wanted in on the conversation.

"The shadings are subtle, Andrew. Many magickers miss them."

"We all know you're good, Kit," Markowitz said. "What do you think this aura stuff meant?"

"I had the sense that they felt they were in foreign territory, but it was territory which ought not to be foreign, or so they believed. Their attitude wasn't personal, but came from their sense of belonging. It was a family vibration. The sort that suggests political affiliation."

"Like they came from another country?" Andy asked.

"Perhaps. I'm still not very good at understanding countries." Kit shrugged. "They were carrying Beretta 200STs."

"That's standard issue for S.I.A.," Markowitz said.

That was a curve ball for Andy. "You think they were Confederated spooks?"

"You been listening to the news out of Fredericksburg? This 'foreign territory that ought not to be' stuff sounds a lot like the CAS attitude to North Virginia," Markowitz said.

"Maybe they were carrying the Berettas because they wanted to *look* like CAS spooks," Andy suggested.

"Kit wouldn't be wrong about the attitude," Markowitz said firmly, but without explanation. "Seems like we've got two sets of hounds on our tails. I'd say we need a place to lie low."

"What about Shamgar, Rags, and Beatty?" Kit asked.

"They're all smart enough to look out for themselves," Markowitz said. "But we better try to get in touch anyway. Looks like it just might be a good time to crawl into the shadows and pull them in after us for a while."

>>>>>WFDC FEED COVERAGE
  —[06:12:11/8-24-55]
REPORTER: TAYLOR WEINGARTNER [WEIN-324]
UPLINK SITE: GOVERNMENT ZONE, FDC

Weingartner: "Violence continues to erupt in the Federal District this morning, as the night-long clash between Compensation Army marchers and the Federal Police continues into the day. Public transportation is at a standstill and all bridges over the rivers are closed as police struggle to control rioting in what is beginning to look like a war zone.

"When interviewed at a Government Zone command post and asked to explain the causes of the violence, Chief of Police Cynthia Locke had this to say: 'We didn't start this. My officers have shown reasonable restraint. I wish I could say the same for Randolph's Compers. The occupation of Metro Central went over the line. For weeks I've been getting requests from the regional commissioners to forcibly evict the Army. I should have listened.' "<<<<<

>>>>>LIVE FEED COVERAGE
 −[06:13:51/8-24-55]
REPORTER: SUZIE CHIANG [CHIA-704]
UPLINK SITE: ELGIN, IL

Chiang: "This is Suzie Chiang of WCHI, back in Elgin, Illinois. Our attempt to penetrate the so-called 'exclusion zone' have failed. We were turned back by armed and hostile federal troops while we attempted to enter the city.

"Chicago is isolated, cut off from the world by a mixture of federal, state, and corporate troops. Nothing is coming out of the city, but some things are going in: air drops of emergency food and medical supplies, but also flights of helicopter gunships. The official position is that this is a VITAS plague containment. But is it?

"Some of the troops cordoning the city are *not* wearing biosuits. Although we've been briefed by the highly-touted medical strike teams, we've still seen no field hospitals. In fact we've seen no signs of anyone with more than a summer cold. The Chicago barrier has few of the signs of a medical containment. 'A work in progress,' the military PR flaks say. But this reporter has to ask: what kind of plague can be fought with gunships?"<<<<<

16

Plan Baker was an insurgency defense plan, entailing elements of the Army taking over security for key locations in the Federal District, which they had done within an hour of General Trahn's order. Moving to their stations, the forces had encountered resistance from Compensation Army marchers along some of the routes; the detachment headed for the White House had received the brunt of the marchers' ire. But insults, jeers, and the occasional thrown debris or refuse weren't enough to stop the UCAS Army. All detachments moved into their positions and reported their perimeters secure before dusk. It had all gone very smoothly.

The hot summer night had started peacefully; then had come the pirate broadcast with the Consie woman speaking for the Compensation Army. Army? No one in the military called them that. They'd been styled "marchers" or "demonstrators" until last night, when the preferred term had become "rioters." The first fire had been reported within minutes of the pirate broadcast, at around 2200 hours. A staff sergeant, watching the news coverage on the rec hall vidscreen, had commented on how much the scenes reminded him of the Night of Rage. Many of those watching agreed with him.

That description had chilled Tom. The rioting wasn't *that* bad. It couldn't be—the Night of Rage had rocked the world, this violence was confined to the city. But that made little difference to someone looking death in the face as the mob closed in. He managed to get a call in to his grandfather, using the connections he'd sworn never to use, to warn his grandparents and sister to believe what they were hearing on the media and stay inside.

General Trahn held command of the Southeastern Military Region, from Pennsylvania and New Jersey to the Virginias, but with the crisis in Chicago, available forces were not great. Trahn had drawn nearly all his forces toward the Federal District, but even so deployment was light, too light to hold against any real assault. At least that was *not* what they were expected to have to do.

As thin as conventional forces were stretched, the unconventional assets such as Task Team Rocquette, Tom's Provisional SR Battalion, were attenuated beyond reason. Given their defensive mission and the unreliability of transport between their defended locations, Tom had split his assets as evenly as he could, but the penny-packet approach worried him. Each site was important enough to merit the special options Special Resources could provide, but detaching support to each of the defended sites left him with only two response teams, one lacking a mage.

Tom was bleary-eyed from a night of worrying when he arrived for the morning briefing. He didn't like his wakeup reports from his battalion, and he liked what he heard in the briefing even less. According to Colonel Jordan, things had gotten far worse overnight.

"As you can see from the display, ladies and gentlemen, rioting has now spread from the fringes of the Compensation Army camps and is affecting Arlington, Alexandria, and Rosslyn in the Arlington District as well as Foggy Bottom, Shaw, the Government Zone, and all southern neighborhoods in the Washington District. We all know, trouble breeds trouble, and this frag-up is no exception. Apparently unrelated rioting is also occurring in the Anacostia Barrens and the go-gangers known as the Halfies were overactive last night, raiding Capitol Heights and Seat Pleasant. Too much inspiration, I suppose.

"The Regional Commissioners are screaming bloody murder, and the FedPols are stretching, trying to cover. They're beyond their limits, ladies and gentlemen. Something is going to give, and soon.

"Corporate security forces continue to operate on a purely reactive basis. Currently only direct threats to their owners' vital property draw response. The suits seem to have realized that their previous unrestricted efforts were wringing them out, and have abandoned attempts to cover all bases in favor of assuring defensible perimeters for their primary business properties and enclaves. This has reduced the visible deterrent of disciplined, armed troops on the streets, and has probably contributed to the rioters' confidence. Like the politicians, the boss suits are screaming, only they're blaming us as well as the FedPols for failing to restore order."

"Not our job," someone said. "Bunch of drekheads."

"Thank you for the evaluation, Captain Black. I hadn't noticed," Jordan responded. "If you don't have any further insights, I'll continue.

"The rioters' numbers have decreased. More than ten thousand have left the city, but that still leaves approximately thirty thousand marchers. This remainder must be considered the most committed. We estimate at least half are armed and prepared to resist."

"Remember Grozny," grumbled another voice.

"We all remember that debacle, Captain Petrovsky. We have no intention of repeating it in our country. That does not mean we see the rioters as pushovers. We have confirmed that they're armed with military-grade weapons, including assault cannons and heavy machine guns. The source of these weapons remains unknown, but a foreign source of supply cannot be ruled out."

Meaning the Confederated States, Tom thought, leaving it to someone else to say it. Captain Black obliged him.

"We cannot rule out that source," Jordan said. "The rioters are also improving their armaments by *coup de main* and by their own industry. They've captured one Mobmaster and more than a dozen lighter SWAT vehicles from the FedPols. They've also set up a conversion shop in the old rail yards near National Airport and are improvising armored cars out of construction and cargo vehicles."

"No match for a tank." Captain Black again.

Or for a Steel Lynx configured for anti-armor work.

"Not everyone wears a tank, Captain," Jordan pointed out. "And are you sure you want your armor in the streets? We haven't seen the rioters use anti-armor weapons, but then they haven't had much cause. You volunteering to find out? Didn't think so.

"Now, as I was saying. Everything is not bleak. Our perimeters at the White House, the Congress complex, and the Pentagon-Fort Myer complex remain intact, having successfully repelled probes against them without loss. We have no indications that the rioters are preparing to further contest our control of those locations. The perimeters at Langley, National Airport, and Frederick Douglas Bridge Triangle have yet to be tested by the rioters, but the Triangle has been experiencing disorganized incursions on the south bank of the Anacostia. These do not appear to be a significant threat.

"At the moment, our greatest concern is maintaining the flow of information. Intel satellite downlinks are limited to twelve-hour incremental availability, hardly suitable for a situation as fluid as this. Having lost two reconnaissance aircraft to the rioters' triple A and another to hostile magical action, we are restricting aerial recon to observation drones. They too are taking a surprisingly heavy beating. SR reports that our field recon assets are down to nearly fifty percent operational."

"Fifty-two," Tom said, giving the exact figure. "But we've recovered three and should have one of those back on line momentarily and the other two in about five hours."

"It's still too few," Trahn said. "Reduce the overflights by half for now."

"It's a big city," Jordan said.

"And if we don't conserve the drones now, we could have a bigger problem later. For now, we know what we need to know."

A commo tech stuck his head through the baffle curtain. "General, Police Chief Locke is inbound and requesting permission to land. She wants to see you, sir."

"I was wondering what was keeping her. Bring her in." Trahn returned his attention to Jordan. "Jemal, what's goosed her?"

Jordan keyed the display, shifting it to a street map. "A significant change to the equation is that the rioters have moved underground. They've taken control of the following Metro stations: Metro Center, Gallery Place, Smithsonian, L'Enfant Plaza, Federal Triangle, Waterfront, and Rosslyn. The occupied stations include all the intersection stations serving the inner zones of the Federal District. Several trains have gone off-line, which resulted in a system-wide shutdown at 2107 hours last night. We believe the rioters have commandeered the trains and superimposed manual controls in order to make use of them as shuttle transportation.

"FedPol teams have erected barricades in the tunnels leading to Arlington Cemetery, Union Station, Capitol South, Howard University, and Rhode Island Avenue. An attempt to secure the Farragut North station resulted in a firefight. That station must be considered contested. The status on other inner stations is unknown. So far, all barricaded stations report no encounters with the rioters, but I believe the effort to reclaim Metro has pushed the FedPols beyond their limits."

Jordan detailed the other areas the rioters held, just finishing with the bridges when Police Chief Locke arrived.

"Everyone tell me you're the man to see," she said, striding up to General Trahn. Unlike yesterday's businessmen, Locke didn't seem to think she needed privacy. Her angry voice was loud enough for everyone in the TOC to hear. "I've got a fragging war on my hands. War is your business, General. How about some help?"

"I don't see what I can do for you, Chief Locke," Trahn pointed out calmly. "At least some of the rioters are citizens, which makes this a civil disturbance and not a war. My orders do not cover riot control. That is not my mission."

But it had been planned for, Tom knew. General Trahn wasn't the sort to overlook contingencies.

"Are you going to stand on the Emmitsburg Act? People are dying out there."

"People were dying in Emmitsburg, too. The Congress saw fit to enact legislation to prevent the military from taking action if a similar case arose again. We're not dealing with a single metatype here, but otherwise this situation is very like that one, Chief. Perhaps you can get Congress to rescind the act and make military intervention legal."

"Who's asking for intervention? I need information. I need support. Your people are already defending several locations. Why not a few more? If I didn't have so many officers tied down watching things, I could organize effective action. What about it?"

"Right now we're providing defensive perimeters for targets of genuine national and military concern. Simply holding our own, as it were. Your 'few more' locations would require us to step outside that purview. And if those locations are attacked?"

"You give the fraggers a bloody nose. Self-defense. No problem."

"I'm unconvinced Congress will find 'no problem' with our taking such a role. The honorable gentlemen have not shown themselves well disposed toward the military," Trahn said, expressing a sentiment with which Tom doubted anyone in the TOC would disagree.

Locke's face colored. "Drek! What the hell do you want?"

"A clear mandate," Trahn said simply.

"Martial law?"

"That would be a clear mandate," Trahn agreed. "However, it would require a Presidential order, perhaps stemming from an appeal by the Federal Capital Chief Commissioner."

Locke wasn't stupid. "And you want me to arrange it?"

Trahn gave her his poker face.

"Can you get me a line out of here?" Locke asked.

"Sergeant Clay, get Chief Locke a secure line to the Chief Commissioner's office."

Locke took up the commo headset. The boom mike concealed her lips as she spoke and the white noise generator blanked out her words, preventing them from escaping the microphone save through the secure line. When she finished, she handed back the headset and said, "Chief Commissioner Ericson is calling the President."

Trahn nodded. "Would you like some refreshment while

we wait? Colonel Jordan, assign an orderly to see to Chief Locke's needs."

Locke took only a cup of soykaf, which ended up cooling undrunk as she studied the tactical displays and asked questions Trahn told everyone to answer, "under standard security conditions, of course." Which meant no one told Locke anything more than they might tell any civilian official whose office was likely to be as leaky as a rowboat after a tussle with a machine gun. The real briefing was suspended as long as she was present. It wasn't long before a commo tech said, "General, it's the President."

"Your Chief Commissioner is a fast talker, Chief Locke," Trahn said. She smiled grimly at him, but said nothing. Trahn put on the headset and folded the microphone baffle out of the way. Nodding, he signaled the commo tech to open the line.

"This is General Trahn." A pause. "Good morning, Mr. President." The conversation went on for some time, with Trahn responding mostly with yes-sirs and that-is-corrects. Once he paused to order a datafeed sent to the White House with a synopsis of the tactical situation. Finally, Trahn spent a long time listening, after which he said, "Yes, Mr. President, I understand." A pause. "And good luck to you as well."

All eyes in the TOC were welded to the general as he put down the headset.

"Gentlemen and ladies, the President of the United Canadian and American States has ordered me to assist the civil authorities of the Federal Capital District in restoring order. This is not, I repeat, *not* a state under martial law. As the President has already declared one such emergency in the case of Chicago, he feels that such action here is not warranted at this time."

Tom caught Trahn's slight emphasis on "at this time," and saw Jordan nod at it. The intel officer was not the only one who suspected that martial law was coming. The President was only putting it off long enough to cover his butt.

Trahn turned to his J-3. "Colonel Lessem, is Plan Charley updated?"

"Current, sir."

"Then distribute it. Anyone with questions to be on-line in ten minutes. I expect roll-out in thirty minutes."

And roll they did. Task Force Lessem moved out of Fort

Belvoir, heading toward the central Government Zone from the south, while Task Force Kemper from Fort Meade came in from the north. Tom got all of his recon drones into the air, watching for developing trouble spots and surveying the progress of the task forces. He concentrated on Task Force Lessem since they were closer to the rioters. Even with Captain Black, in command of the task force's armor, keeping his tanks back and letting the infantry afoot secure travel lanes for him, they made good progress. Within three hours they'd swept through Alexandria in the Arlington District and put paid to the rioters' incipient armored force in a tenminute battle in the old rail yards. Black's caution was proven wise when the troops searched the workshops and uncovered a stash of shoulder-launched anti-armor missiles.

"Confederated issue," Tom observed.

"Could be contraband," Jordan reminded him. When Tom looked skeptical, he added, "But I doubt it. Let's hope Johnny Reb is satisfied with supplying arms and not men, because with Trahn concentrating on securing Washington, we don't have anything looking south."

The intel officer's admission disturbed Tom. He knew from the briefing that there was activity south of the border in Virginia. Ignoring that activity was not prudent, but limited resources meant limited options. Fortunately the operation was proceeding so well that the border shouldn't go unwatched for long.

Unfortunately, almost immediately after the successful action against the rail yard, Task Force Lessem ran into trouble. The force had successfully moved along Jefferson Davis Highway and through the shanty town that spilled off Gravelly Point and huddled around the southern anchors of the Potomac there. The helmeted and armored troopers moved like a plague of beetles, sweeping the streets clean wherever they passed. It wasn't an apropos metaphor given the outbreak of insectoid magical creatures in Chicago, but Tom couldn't help seeing the soldiers as he did. Maybe it was the Chicago situation that sparked the imagery for him.

But the Chicago bugs offered no quarter to the hapless people in their way. Here, humanitarian concerns applied. The task force's tanks and IFVs mounted blaring loudspeakers that called upon the marchers to disperse peaceably and urged them to respect lawful authority, promising no reprisals against rioters who surrendered themselves to military custody. Most of the shanty town's population simply turned out and watched, but the rioters holding the bridges remained firm behind their barricades. They were well armed and supported by a magicker, and Black's armor was effectively neutralized by the need to avoid serious damage to the bridges.

When the first tank rolled toward George Mason Bridge, intending to bulldoze away the rioters' barricades, it simply stopped on the entry ramp as a blanket of darkness rolled out to cover it. The spell dissipated almost immediately, but as troops confronted by unknown magics were wont to do, Black's command took no action. When the tank became visible again, it was turned around and backing toward the barricades. Presuming the vehicle was under hostile control, Black's other tanks opened fire and destroyed it.

"We need those bridges cleared," Trahn said, looking at Tom.

That meant Special Resources. "I'll take Team One, sir."

Trahn nodded. "Authorize a flight of Yellowjackets to support Team One, Jemal, but tell them to hang back until needed. We want to keep the provocation down. And warn Archie Lessem that the cavalry is on their way and that he shouldn't get too anxious about taking the bridge yet."

Team One had two armored vehicles, Tom's Ranger Tactical Command Vehicle and a Ranger Drone support vehicle. Neither the command car nor the DSV was rated for frontline combat, and they had no escort, which made going into a riot zone worrisome. In close urban confines, the front line was anywhere the hostiles happened to be holed up. Even a heavily armored panzer was vulnerable to an ambush under such conditions, and Team One didn't have the infantry support that tankers like Black insisted were necessary for employing tanks in urban environments. But they did have Furlann; the mage's astral vision was their protection against surprise. Furlann might not be able to stop an ambush, but she ought to be able to give them warning. In fact, Tom was counting on it.

His concerns proved unfounded as they rolled through the quiet streets without incident.

"What's it going to take to square away their mage?" Colonel Lessem asked when they arrived at his command post.

"Line of sight to the bridges is what I need," Furlann said, leaning into Tom's mike. "The overpass by the Pentagon should do."

"That was our mage," Tom said apologetically.

"Understood," Lessem said. "Your lead, Team One. Go where you will."

Tom told his driver to position the command car wherever Furlann wanted. He ordered the DSV to pull up within the safety of the Pentagon perimeter and put up an aerial drone; he wanted a picture of the local situation that wasn't subject to override by higher-ranking commanders. Once in position, Furlann propped herself in the TCV command cupola and went into trance. Tom surveyed the bridges via telelink with the drone. All three automotive spans were choked with abandoned cars and debris, and packed with people. The rail span was empty, and missing a ten-meter section. The rioters didn't have any need to defend that.

"I've got her," Furlann said, coming out of her astral recon. "Stupid pervert."

Tom didn't think Furlann's last comment was meant to be heard, but he had. "The magicker?"

Furlann began to fuss with her fetishes. "You can tell the colonel that he'll have a distraction momentarily."

As Tom passed the word, a fireball blossomed on the central automotive span. Flames engulfed the width of the roadway and licked at the nearby upriver span. Screams arose from the wounded, but those at the center of the conflagration never screamed—incinerated before they ever got a chance. The arcane holocaust consumed living and organic matter, but left untouched the concrete and asphalt of the bridge and the metals and plastics of the vehicles on it. It was an impressive display of thaumaturgic power.

"Gotcha, you stupid git," Furlann said with obvious satisfaction.

Tom sat stunned, as Colonel Lessem broadcast the order for his troops to advance on the bridges. Black's armor began to rumble forward as Furlann slid back into the command car's body and dropped into her couch with a tired sigh.

"What did you do?" Tom asked, for clearly she had been responsible for the devastation on the bridge. She had taken out the mage, or she wouldn't be so relaxed. But she'd taken out more than the mage.

"Fed their spookdancer a fireball through her focus,"

Furlann said matter-of-factly. "She wasn't fast enough to do anything about it. Her loss."

"You didn't have to do that. She was in the middle of all those people. We're under orders to minimize civilian casualties."

"Most of those scum were SINless, and if there were any citizens with them, they were stupid and were proving it by backing the wrong side. Better they're out of the gene pool."

"You still didn't have to—"

"You'd rather she pumped one at me and it grounded out in the middle of this nice cozy box?" Furlann snapped. "She was a fragging toxic shaman and she knew I was here. She didn't have your nicey-nice spare-the-cits compunctions. It wouldn't have been long before she tried the same stunt on me. I just made sure it wouldn't happen by feeding her more than she could handle."

"It was overkill."

"Overkill is the only sure kill." Furlann threw her head back and put an arm over her eyes. "Now if you don't mind, I'm going to take a nap. Van Dyne with the Pentagon team can keep watch."

She couldn't have dismissed him more thoroughly if she'd been a general. Tom climbed up into the vehicle commander's seat and leaned against the coaming. At the bridges, the troops were forcing their way across, making good on Colonel Lessem's orders to secure the crossing. Clumps of prisoners were being escorted back toward the Pentagon perimeter and the field command post straddling Army-Navy Drive, just below his position. They were a ragtag, unintimidating bunch, most looking as though they could use a good meal. They marched along dejectedly. Some few looked up at the command car and gave Tom the finger. One looked up and shouted.

"Tom? Tom Rocquette?"

Startled, Tom looked down at the dirty streetrat who knew his name. A soldier laid his hand on the kid's shoulder and looked to Tom, awaiting the nod to move the kid along.

"Don't you recognize me?" the kid shouted. "It's Andy, Andy Walker."

Andy? The kid did look like the picture Genifer had shown him. But . . . "Andy Walker's dead," Tom shouted down.

The kid started to protest and Furlann popped the turret

hatch. She snarled at Tom and gave Andy a sneering once-over. "You know, Walker, in my expert opinion, that git's alive. We mages know these sorts of things. And he *is* telling what he thinks is the truth. So why don't you two be good boys and take your reunion a bit further away from the vehicle so a girl can get her rest?"

Tom followed Furlann's suggestion, but not to please her. If this really was Andy, he wanted to know what was going on. He climbed out of the command car and signaled the soldier to bring the kid up the embankment.

"You better have a good story," he told the kid when they were face to face. "Starting with why everyone thinks you're dead."

"It's a long story." Andy looked down at the ground, kicking at it. "Look. We're not involved in the rioting. Honest. We got caught on the other side of town last night, okay? We were trying to get back across the bridge when the tanks showed up. I guess we just were in the wrong place at the wrong time."

"That's true enough." Andy avoided Tom's first question while raising more. "Why do you keep saying *we*?"

"I've got a couple of friends with me." Andy suddenly seemed to realize he was alone. "At least I did."

Deeper and deeper. Tom turned to the soldier. "Corporal, help this kid find his friends and bring them all back here." If Andy had accomplices, best Tom have them all in one place before they got scattered into whatever processing and detention Colonel Lessem had set up for prisoners.

In ten minutes the corporal brought the kid back, along with a middle-aged man in a rumpled, casual business suit. As they approached, Andy kept craning his head around as if he'd lost his mother at a mall. Tom heard the man whisper to Andy, "Don't worry about Kit, kid. She'll be okay."

"Who's Kit?" Tom asked, winning a glare from the man.

"The other friend of mine," Andy told him. "She was with us, trying to get home to Arlington. She must have got separated from us."

Could Furlann have been wrong? "Your home's not in Arlington."

"It is now," the man said. "The kid says you're his brother."

"Half-brother."

"Whatever. He's says you're an okay guy, which I'll buy

because I have to, but I don't think the answers you want ought to be tossed around out in the street. For the kid's sake."

"Just who are *you*?"

"Name's Markowitz." He fished out a business card and offered it. "I do investigations."

Tom took the card, but didn't bother to look at it. Anyone could print up cards. "Got an ID, Mister Markowitz?"

"Sure." He offered that and Tom took it as well. He walked back to the command car, disturbed Furlann's nap—which disturbed *him* not at all—and passed the credstick to his sergeant. "Run it through."

"We're not part of the Comp Army," Markowitz said. "We were just trying to get home like good citizens and hide out for the duration, when you stormtroopers came down on us like a drekload of bricks."

"You were on the bridge," Tom pointed out.

"Just trying to cross it," Markowitz said.

The sergeant leaned out of the command car. "Major, this man's wanted for questioning by military intelligence."

"What?" Markowitz sounded astonished. "On what grounds?"

The sergeant stone-faced Markowitz.

"I want to know, too," Tom said.

"Charges are unspecified, sir. Colonel Jordan is signaling that we bring him in. Any associates as well."

"Well, Mr. Markowitz, do you want to explain why military intelligence would have an interest in you?" Tom asked.

The man scowled at him.

"It's got to be a mistake," Andy said. The kid sounded scared. "Tom, you've got to help us. This is all a mistake. You're in the Army. You can help straighten things out."

Tom began to think he was detecting the distinct odor of shadow drek. Runners were close-knit, sometimes even family, and the not-dead Andy was counted as family by someone Tom counted as family. Could Genifer be involved in shadowrunning? He wouldn't have thought it, but these were strange times. And how was military intelligence involved in this? Genifer wasn't averse to pulling on their grandfather's old connections. Could something have motivated her to step over the line and abuse those connections, something that affected military security? Tom needed to know.

"I think that straightening out is just what this mess

needs. You two are going to climb aboard my car, and we're going to go see about doing that."

Grace: "We've got NewsNet MilSpecialist Worf Blitzer online with us now. Are you all ready to get the low-down on all those soldier types shooting up the city?" [*Query cam angle*]

[*Audience response: 96% positive*]

"All *right*! Say, Worf, what's the story. Who are all those guys in gray and black?"

Blitzer: "As you know, Grace, the Riot Command Center has yet to release an official roster of units involved in this suppression mission. Putting together our own roster hasn't been hard. With the Chicago crisis, there are less than two divisions of combat-ready units left in the area, and most of those are assigned to border posts in North Virginia. To start in the north, both of the remaining battalions of the 101st Air Insertion Division at Fort Meade have left Meade as the core of what is being called the Task Force Kemper. You were just showing shots of their MacAuliffe Infantry Fighting Vehicles moving down Route 95. Those MacAuliffes are effective armored vehicles."

Grace: "Armored vehicles? They have *tanks*?"

Blitzer: "No, just IFV's. Light armor. However, the army's southern force, Task Force Lessem, has the 131st Heavy Battalion, 100th Armored Division. They have tanks. Real heavy armor.

Grace: "Heavy armor? Like *panzers*?"

Blitzer: "Heavy armor can be panzers, but the line battalions of the 100th Armored are equipped with tracked M2B2s and Ranger IFVs. The division does have a company of LAV

armor—panzers—but that is currently detached for service
in Chicago. The use of tanks may be controversial, but perhaps more unusual is the deployment of Provisional Special
Resources Battalion 7711, a rag-tag conglomeration of tele-
operated and Thaumaturgic Corps units operating as Task
Force Rocquette. We know little more about them than their
name, but we do know that they were responsible for the fire
incident on the George Mason Bridge."<<<<<

17

When Andy had spotted Tom Rocquette sitting in the
armored vehicle up on the overpass, he'd been ready to try
anything to escape the soldiers. Sure, Tom was a soldier too,
but he was also Andy's half-brother. That had to count for
something, didn't it? Although Tom had never been exactly
warm toward Andy in the past, he hadn't been hostile either.
Andy was pretty sure Tom liked him.

Of course Andy had been just a kid then, and not a SIN-
less street scut whose cyberdeck had been confiscated by the
soldiers.

Andy hadn't really been sure what to expect when he
hailed Tom Rocquette, but he'd certainly hoped for a more
enthusiastic reception than he'd gotten. Though not outright
hostile like the other soldiers, Tom was cold and distant. He
seemed unconvinced that Andy was Andy, which was under-
standable. Bundled into Tom's armored vehicle and headed
for who knew where, Andy did his best to convince his half-
brother that he really was alive and not just an impostor by
talking about the times that they'd met.

Unfortunately Markowitz seemed to be trying to sabotage
his attempts to make Tom look on them favorably.

"Soldiers against the citizens," Markowitz said. "Quite a
show. Been watching Nazi training vids?"

The low light level inside the vehicle made it hard to read
Tom's expression as he asked tonelessly, "Nazi?"

"Yeah, you know, goose-step for the Reich, and grind those
heels on anyone in the way. Kick the lowlifes out of the way
of the master race. Get those annoying genetic undesirables

into camps where they can be taken care of properly. Is that where the marchers are going? To camps?"

"There haven't been any Nazis since '07," Tom said quietly. "Is history then among your investigations, Mr. Markowitz? You seem to have quite a knowledge of defunct political systems."

"Names change, but black hearts don't," Markowitz replied. "And why shouldn't I know history? More to the point, shouldn't you? Even more to the point, I know violence when I see it. Even were the motives pure, what those soldiers are doing out there is illegal."

"Not a historian but a lawyer. Is that it, Mr. Markowitz?"

"What is it with you and pigeonholes?" Markowitz asked. "Never mind. Doesn't matter. A man in my business has to know enough law to get by, and I do. For example, I know it's illegal to use UCAS military forces against citizenry."

Andy hadn't known that.

"Without a Presidential order," Tom said.

Andy hadn't known that either.

"You got one?" asked Markowitz.

Tom nodded. "It so happens we do."

"Lord save us, then. The Nazis aren't dead, and we have the singular honor of participating in the return of the purges. *Heil,* Steele."

"This is not a purge." Tom's voice sounded a little strained. "We're simply working to restore order and shut down the rioters."

"Rioters?" Markowitz repeated incredulously. "There aren't any rioters out there. There are just people trying to defend themselves from Locke's jack-booted stormtroopers. Or at least that was what they were doing until you and your armored henchmen showed up. Bang! Down comes the tool of manifest political will. Bang! Another fine SS hammer to bludgeon down the *Untermenschen.* How come you're looking so annoyed, Major? Your jackboots too tight?"

"That's out of line," Andy said. He hoped Tom would understand that everybody didn't think he was one of those bad guys Markowitz was talking about.

Markowitz turned on him. "What's out of line is what *his* people are doing," he said, pointing an accusative finger at Tom. "There are good people out there in the camps and they're dying because they dared to stand up for what was theirs, because some fat-cat politician has got better uses for the money. Those good people are dying because they stood up and asked for what had been promised them. All they want is just compensation."

"Good people?" Tom was heated now. "Good people don't ignite their neighborhoods, or anyone else's. Last night's fires drew the line, and the rioters crossed it."

"So you intend to douse the fires in blood. Very democratic."

"We intend to see that no more are set."

"How? By killing people? I expect that will work real well. Things get very quiet when everybody's dead. Very convenient solution, too. No witnesses."

"You're off base, Markowitz," Tom said.

"It's true, though," Andy told him. "I saw soldiers shoot people who were trying to surrender."

"No." Tom's voice wasn't very loud and Andy wasn't sure he'd heard him speak.

"Don't you think your brothers in camo are killers?" Markowitz asked.

Tom cleared his throat. "If anyone was killed, it was because they offered threatening resistance. Though I wouldn't expect someone with your left-handed view to understand it, Mr. Markowitz, I can assure you that the Army isn't full of indiscriminate killers."

"Oh, they're not being *indiscriminate*," Markowitz said. "I never said that. In fact, I noticed a definite preference among the soldiers for finding resistance among the metahumans. Why, to my certain knowledge, a simple surly glance proved threatening enough to your well-armed soldiers that they felt compelled to conduct the summary execution of at least two orks, a troll, and a dwarf woman with her baby."

"You must be mistaken," Tom said.

"Must I?"

Tom didn't answer. He just stared at the cabin wall.

"You're a puppet." Markowitz told him.

Turning slowly to look at him, Tom said, "You have a melodramatic bent, Mr. Markowitz."

"Comes of being a failed romantic, or so I'm told. Maybe that's why I still believe sometimes a man will stand up and do the right thing, even when his chummers are doing something else entirely. It's hard to buck the herd, but sometimes you have to. I know you know what I mean. Andy here told my you're an okay guy. Didn't you, Andy?"

"Yeah. I did tell him that, Tom."

"That's right. Listen, Major. You've got a chance here to show me that I've got you all wrong. The kid told you right: neither of us was involved in the rioting. Getting caught on the bridge was bad timing and worse luck, that's all. There's no significance to it. We really don't want to be involved in this mess. I'm sure you can understand that. So why don't you just drop us off and we can all forget we ever met?"

Tom shook his head, a half-smile on his face. "I seem to recall someone telling me there was no rioting. How does someone not get involved in something that isn't happening?"

"You just don't want to be an easy guy."

"I have orders, Mr. Markowitz. I have to carry them out."

"Yes, sir, Major Nazi."

"I think it's time for you to shut up, Mr. Markowitz," Tom said in a chill voice.

Andy thought about telling Markowitz he agreed, but didn't see how that would help. Fortunately he didn't have to; Markowitz got the hint. Andy was relieved. The tension was too high already. What had gotten into Markowitz? He was usually more placatory when dealing with people—at least with people other than Andy. Maybe he was worried about Kit; she was still out there somewhere. Had the soldiers picked her up as well? Andy hoped not, for her sake.

After riding in silence for a while, Tom suddenly heaved himself out of his seat, moved across the cabin, and slid into a tiny bucket in front of a stripped-down drone control station. Andy had seen similar set-ups in the tech bays at Telestrian, so he could tell what Tom was doing as he activated switches and entered commands. He was calling in a relay from a reconnaissance drone. When the picture brightened the screen, Andy saw that the drone was hovering above the continuing melee on the bridges. No one on the bridges or far shore was bothering it; they were all far too busy. At Tom's command, the drone focused closer on the interface between the soldiers in their gray and black camo uniforms and the motley riot of colors that was their opponents.

The insane violence of the confrontation was right there on the screen. Tom couldn't deny what they'd told him now.

The drone showed them soldiers shooting marchers. The drone's viewpoint was high and distant; it made it hard to tell if those being shot were dead or not, but they were surely injured. More often than not, the soldiers shot without provocation.

As Markowitz started to say something, Andy gave him a kick in the shins. Surprise silenced him. Tom never noticed, which was fine by Andy.

Tom toggled the console to communications mode.

"Colonel Lessem, this is Major Rocquette. I think we have a problem developing on the bridges."

Almost immediately the colonel's response came over the cabin's speakers. "What is it, Rocquette? The rioters got another mage?"

"No, sir. At least not to my knowledge. The problem, sir, is with our troops. General Trahn isn't going to be happy."

Lessem chuckled. "Not fast enough for the old man, eh? Well, you'll have to tell him that if he wants the job done faster, he'll have to send me some more troops. Either that or take the shackles off."

The colonel thought that the troops were being restrained? Andy couldn't believe it. Tom's silence suggested that he too was surprised by the colonel's response.

"Nazi stormtrooper tactics," Markowitz whispered.

Andy hoped Tom didn't hear.

Tom addressed the microphone. "Colonel, I respectfully suggest that you check the feed from drone Able-Charley-two-three. I think you will find that things are not progressing as smoothly as you believe."

"That so?" A pause. "You're running under orders to report to HQ with some prisoners, are you not?"

"Yes, sir."

"Then I suggest that you tend to your business."

The connection cut out.

Having seen the excessive violence with his own eyes, Tom could not deny what Markowitz alleged. The Army *was* using stormtrooper tactics. It didn't make sense to Tom. Just like Furlann's sledgehammer-against-a-fly approach on the bridge, this was an overreaction.

"You want to reconsider taking us in now?" Markowitz asked.

"No," Tom said. Other people disobeying orders didn't free him to do so. "You both have to go in."

Markowitz harrumphed. "I hope your *führer's* headquarters has the latest in torture racks. The old models are *so* uncomfortable."

"Torture?" Andy sounded scared.

"He's trying to scare you and browbeat me," Tom told him. "You're just going to be asked some questions. No one is going to torture anybody."

"Are you sure?" Andy asked.

"You have my personal assurance that there will be no torture," Tom said. It was an easy promise. The UCAS army wasn't like the Aztlanians.

"I am *so* relieved to hear that," Markowitz said.

Tom looked to Markowitz. "A private beating afterwards, citizen to citizen, is another matter."

"I'll consider it a date," Markowitz said. "Though if you're wrong, I expect to be allowed time to recover before we have our discussion."

"You'll need to be in top condition," Tom promised him.

Andy was looking back and forth between them as though he were watching two lunatics, which perhaps he was. Markowitz made Tom itchier than he'd been in a long time.

When the command car pulled into the vehicle park nearest General Trahn's TOC, Colonel Jordan stood waiting for them, flanked by a quartet of his white-gloved military police. Tom trooped Andy and Markowitz over to the colonel.

"Hello, Markowitz," Jordan said. "In trouble again, I see."

Markowitz nodded to him. "Apparently. The usual mistakes, I expect. How you doing, Jemal? How's the wife?"

There ensued some incredibly ordinary chitchat. Tom listened, amazed. Jordan turned to Tom and saluted. "Major, I relieve you of your prisoners."

Tom returned the salute.

"Report to the general at his van," Jordan said.

Furlann accompanied Tom as far as the TOC. She didn't say anything, which was fine; Tom didn't feel like talking to her. Her acerbic manner was entirely too like Markowitz's, and Markowitz had already rubbed him raw. Tom logged in and found himself a place to await the general's pleasure. Sitting and stewing about what he'd seen and heard, he didn't notice when Furlann disappeared, but she wasn't around when the general summoned Tom into his presence.

Once the military formalities were out of the way, Trahn invited Tom to sit.

"I understand you have a problem with the way this operation is being conducted," he said without preamble.

Colonel Lessem would have informed him about Tom's call. "No fault with command, sir, but the troops seem to be operating outside the mission's parameters."

"How outside? Response has been left to unit commanders. You seem to be questioning their judgment. Just what is your problem, Rocquette?"

Trahn shook his head sadly. "This is not a training exercise, or a mop-up after an outlaw policlub rally. There's a large and hostile mob out there, threatening the health and safety of the citizenry you are sworn to protect. It's our nation's capital that Randolph and his ungrateful followers have chosen to devastate. You can't think that half-measures are enough. Half-measures get you killed when the other guy is giving his all, and there is absolutely no reason to believe that the rioters are giving less than their all. Are you asking our soldiers to let themselves be walked over?"

"No, sir. That's not what I meant at all."

"You were at the briefing, Rocquette. You know that our troops are significantly outnumbered by the mob. We have to utilize all our advantages. One of those advantages is the unity of our command structure, Major. We cannot afford debate. It will weaken us, slow us, and divide us; and if that happens, good soldiers will die. Is that what you want?"

"No, sir. But people are already dying, General."

"People who have stepped outside the law."

"The law is supposed to protect people, even felons," Tom pointed out.

"You're living in the last century, Rocquette."

Was that so bad? There were some who called the end of the last century a golden age. "The laws of the land still apply."

"Some of those laws have been amended," the general reminded him. "Listen, son. I know you're intelligent. Surely you can see what's happening around us. Surely, you can sense the moral rot. We're groaning under the legacy of that bastard Howling Coyote and his disciples. This used to be the greatest country in the world. Now look at us. We've been cut off at the knees and beggared because we've accepted the yoke forced on us by the creatures of this new age. How can a man survive in this world?"

Trahn seemed to expect an answer. Unfortunately Tom was full of questions, not answers. Basically, he agreed with Trahn about the condition of the world, but he was unsure how such a philosophical position fit into the situation at hand. He also knew better than to contradict a general. He tried for a safe reply. "A man does what his honor will let him."

"And you think that our response to the rioters is something less than honorable?"

That had been one of Tom's concerns. "A fair fight is honorable. Militarily, those people out there are a rabble."

"I would prefer a fair fight, but that kind of honor died when the Sixth World was born. Men, real men, can't fight fair against magical things. The Dissolution Campaigns taught us that. No chance at all, not without using every weapon available, ignoring the niceties."

"Times have changed since then, General."

"They have, they have indeed. They've gotten worse. Look at Chicago—we're losing a city there. If we had a real army, I doubt we'd be having such problems. We could have squashed those bugs as soon as they waved their antennae above ground."

Tom didn't know the details of what was going on in Chicago, but he'd seen what was happening here in Washington. "But we're not dealing with bugs here, General. We're dealing with people."

"We *are* dealing with people," Trahn admitted. "People who've accepted the corruption of the Sixth World. People who've lain down and spread their legs for it. People who've sold out honest humans. People who've given up their right to fair and honorable treatment. If you have any doubt of that, you need look no further than the way they ignored our warnings before we moved against them. They were offered the opportunity to disperse peacefully and safely. They passed it up. Maybe they thought we were bluffing. Lord knows the government has bluffed often enough. But the time for bluff is over. It's time for action and men, *real* men, must heed the call. I was told that you were a man who understood those necessities, Rocquette. Was I told wrong?"

"I don't know exactly what you were told, General, but I've always been a good soldier."

"These are times that call for more than just good soldiers. These are times that cry out for leaders." Trahn's stare was penetrating. "There are those who speak highly of you, Rocquette. They say you're more than a good soldier. That you're a leader. A man who knows the right course when he sees it. Are they wrong?"

"I hope not, sir."

"So do I." Pointedly, Trahn glanced at the bank of monitors lining the van's wall. "Now, was there anything else?"

There was; but after everything Trahn had said, Tom wasn't sure he'd be wise to bring it up again.

"It's all right, Rocquette. You can speak your mind freely."

All right, then. "I'm afraid I'm still unclear on why we aren't using some of the less lethal methods available for riot control, General?"

"Stop right there. I know where you're going. Son, I know the authorized equipage as well as you. I also know some things you don't. The situation is dirt simple. For a variety of reasons, supplies have not been forthcoming, and we do not have access to our authorized non-lethal means. We have no recourse but to use the means at hand. If we had that stuff, don't you think we'd be using it?"

Tom nodded. He wanted to believe they'd use non-lethal means if they had them.

"All right then," Trahn said. "You'd better get back to doing your job. You won't disappoint me, will you, Major?"

"No, sir."

Trahn smiled paternally. "Just follow orders and you'll be fine," the general said and dismissed him.

Tom left the van wondering if the general's parting comment was what Nazi generals had told their stormtroopers.

>>>>>WFDC LIVE FEED
  —[08:07:33/8-25-55]
DEECEE AM MORNINGRIDE WITH JESS BOK [BOKX-345]

Bok: "Welcome back to DeeCee AM Morningride for another rush-free rush hour as all public transportation into the
District remains shut down and the ban continues in force on
personal vehicles on all main arteries and all bridges into the
central subregions. Remember, if you want the latest
datafeed updates on street closings, as well as FedPol and
military blockade locations, give us a call. SMALL CHARGE AP-
PLIES.

"As you might expect, last night's rumblings from local
politicians are working their way up the food chain. Morning statements from a random sample of public officials
show that our elected representatives are hopping mad. A
common opinion holds that the FedPols have failed, and that
the military intervention ordered by President Steele to bail
out the FedPols may be failing as well. There is growing
fear that the rioting will spread.

"Hey, partners, you think I'm kidding? Let me feed you a
sound bite just in from WFDC reporter Derry Dale down in
Fredericksburg, capital of North Virginia."

Dale: "Governor Jefferson, what's your take on the military intervention in the UCAS capital?"
Jefferson: "Derry, you know it's really not my place to
take a stand on this, but I have to say I'm concerned that the
UCAS forces are in over their heads. The situation is bad
and growing worse, and I'm not sure they can handle it. This
makes me extremely concerned for the safety of our citizens
in Arlington."
Dale: "Governor, did you just say '*our* citizens in
Arlington?' "
Jefferson: "Did I say Arlington? I meant North Virginia.

Isn't that what I said? In any case, the safety of our citizens remains my first concern."

Bok: "Kinda hits ya where ya live with warm fuzzies, don't it?"<<<<<

18

Colonel Jemal Jordan, who Markowitz whispered was General Trahn's intelligence officer, took custody of Andy and Markowitz. Tom went off, apparently bound to see Trahn. The woman with the Thaumaturgic Corps insignia on her long leather coat went with him, but the rest of the command car crew stayed with the vehicle. Andy saw them huddle together and start talking as he was led away.

The mage puzzled him. She'd stuck up for Andy when he'd first hailed Tom, but hadn't said a word since. It wasn't because she wasn't interested. He'd caught her watching them occasionally during the trip, while she was supposed to be asleep. Mages had their own agenda, everybody said so. Andy wondered what hers was. She frightened him a little, but he supposed that was mostly because he'd never met a mage before.

There was Kit, of course, but Andy had trouble thinking of her as a mage. She was too . . .

Well, this wasn't the time or place to be thinking about that.

They were taken to a building festooned with roof antennae. Inside, they walked down a flight of stairs, then along several featureless halls, emerging in a chamber filled with consoles and people working at them. Each of the stations was equipped with a privacy screen that restricted the computer's projections exclusively to the operator directly in front of it. No one looked up from the workstations as they entered, but the guards noticed. Steely eyes had fastened on them as soon as they appeared.

Two doors and three archways, all guarded, offered exit from the room. They went through the central archways and down another corridor. Andy was put into a room with no door save for the two guards on either side of the entrance.

Colonel Jordan took Markowitz further down the hall and
out of Andy's sight.

Andy felt even more alone than when he'd left Telestrian.
At least that had been a voluntary exile. He looked around.
No windows. The light came from a panel flush with the
ceiling, illuminating the dingy beige walls and ceiling and
the scuffed gray concrete floor. The room had a plain wood
table and four chairs, also plain wood. The chairs didn't look
comfortable. Andy paced.

An officer—a captain, Andy thought—came in. His name
tag said Stratton.

"Please have a seat," Captain Stratton said, taking one
himself.

The captain knew Andy's real name, which wasn't surprising, considering he'd shouted it to Tom. The captain's
questions told Andy that he knew much more than just
Andy's name. He knew that Andy was from Telestrian, and
had been involved in the Montjoy Project, and that his
"death" had been faked. The captain wanted to know if
Andy had helped Markowitz's Montjoy run from the inside,
and how long he'd been associated with Markowitz's
shadowrunners. Andy thought it would be a bad idea to answer those questions, and a worse idea to lie.

"I think I'd like to talk to a lawyer," he said.

"Is that so?" Captain Stratton smiled politely. "Would that
be a Telestrian lawyer to look after the interests of deceased
citizen Andrew Walker, who is beyond the need for legal
counsel? Or would it be a public defender to plead for the
nameless, SINless gutter trash sitting in front of me, who
doesn't have a legal leg to stand on and isn't entitled to a
public defender anyway?"

"Never mind."

"Very well. I hope you're beginning to see the value in
cooperating."

"I guess so," Andy said, but what he really was doing was
imagining the trouble he'd get into if he didn't cooperate.

"Good." The captain returned to his questions.

Andy answered Stratton this time, giving honest truth
when the question concerned something verifiable from his
Telestrian life. When the subject of the datasteal came up,
Andy glossed it, saying he'd been coerced and never admit-
ting to his part in helping Yates in the Matrix. He told

Stratton, again honestly, that he hadn't had any previous connection with Markowitz or any of his runners.

"So if you weren't involved, why did you run?" Stratton asked.

"I was scared." And that was chiptruth. Andy had faked his death for fear of being connected to the data theft, and he told the captain so. "It might not have been the smartest thing I ever did."

Stratton nodded as though he agreed. "Tell me what happened after that."

Andy told him about encountering Markowitz on the street and about the beating he'd received from the ork gang, which seemed to earn him some sympathy.

"So that was how you came to be in Markowitz's company?"

"Yeah. It was a coincidence. He helped me after I got beat up. I didn't know he was the guy who'd led the run against Telestrian. He's been trying to help me build a new life."

"Very kind of him," Stratton said in a way that said he didn't think kindness was at all involved. "And what sort of activities has Mr. Markowitz engaged in of late? Other than helping you, that is."

"I don't know."

"You weren't helping him in his business? Returning a favor for a favor, perhaps?"

Whatever Andy might have said next was interrupted as the mage stuck her head in. "Anything?" she asked.

"Mr. Walker and I are getting along just fine," Stratton said. He smiled agreeably at Andy.

The mage nodded. "Where's Jordan?"

"Down the hall, waiting for you," Stratton said.

The mage left. Captain Stratton had "a few more questions." Andy stuck to his story of Markowitz's help, spinning out a tale of the man's trying to find a doss and some work for Andy. Surprisingly, Stratton seemed satisfied with the tale.

"Don't go away," he told Andy as he left.

Being left alone wasn't so great. There wasn't anything to do in the room, so it didn't take Andy long to get bored. He started pacing again, and imagining how much trouble they were in. He was starting to wonder what had happened with Markowitz when the mage's voice drifted down the hall.

"Bring me my ritual bag from the car." Then slightly

louder, as if calling after someone already leaving on an errand. "And get the rats, too. The street rats, not the lab ones."

The ritual bag Andy more or less understood; mages needed tools to conduct much of their business. But the rats?

He understood the "what" of the request when a soldier hustled by the door bearing a stainless steel cage of live rats, but the "why" escaped him totally. Unless . . .

Unless they were intended for a sacrifice. No. The Army couldn't be involved in black magic, could it?

When Tom finally found where Jordan had squirreled him, Andy started babbling something about black magic. Tom told the kid to calm down and start over. There really wasn't much to his story, unless you knew Furlann. Not that Tom ever had more than suspicions about her magical ethics, but a mage with a Presidential pardon for magical crimes was not the sort of person the Church considered for their exorcism squads. The UCAS Thaumaturgic Corps was a lot less picky. The kid might actually be right.

"Where did they take Markowitz?" Tom asked.

"I don't know," Andy said. "They dumped me here and kept going. It can't be very far, if I could hear the mage ordering her sacrificial animals."

"All right, Andy. All right. Stay calm." Tom wasn't sure what to do. If Andy was right, some serious badness was going down, and busting it up would be the honorable thing to do. But if Andy was wrong, Tom might be the one who ended up busted. Still, he had to know. "I'm going to go check it out."

"I want to come too."

"Not bright." None of this was.

"And leaving me here *is*?" Andy pleaded. "Come on, Tom. You're the only friend I've got here, besides Markowitz. You can't leave me now. If they're using black magic on him, how long before they start in on me?"

Another witness might not hurt. "All right, but stick close to me."

"Not a prob."

There *was* a problem just outside, in the corridor. Two, actually. The guards would have orders to see that Andy didn't leave. But what if he were going deeper into the complex?

"I'm taking the prisoner to Colonel Jordan," Tom told the guards as he marched Andy through the arch.

The MPs exchanged a glance, but said nothing. An exchange of salutes and Tom and Andy were past them and headed down the corridor.

Tom had come prepared to cover his own hoop on this one, though this wasn't quite what he'd been expecting. As they walked he fished a small recorder out of the cargo pocket on his BDU pants, slid the switch to On and hooked it on his belt webbing, making sure it was visible. He'd used similar devices out in Denver when dealing with foreign nationals at prisoner-exchange sites and other sensitive meetings where the people back home needed to know exactly what had happened.

They passed another pair of guards and Tom repeated his half-truth. A little further on there was a door, closed. Tom put his ear to it and heard Furlann's voice. He recognized the language as Latin, but he couldn't catch more than a word or two. It was enough to support Andy's fears. Tom had dreaded finding out that Andy was right. Now it was looking as though he was.

Tom tested the door, confirming that it was unlocked. He rapped once and threw it open, striding into the room without waiting for a response. Furlann, bent over a censer, stopped her chanting and looked up. Colonel Jordan spun to face the door, revealing Markowitz, reclining in a chair that looked remarkably like a dentist's couch. He didn't move. Jordan's hand was on the butt of his sidearm, but he didn't draw it. That threat didn't halt Tom. What stopped him were the colored chalk lines on the concrete floor. He put an arm out to stop Andy, hard on his heels, from breaking the ritual circle.

"What's going on here, Colonel?" Tom asked, trying to make it sound like a justifiable demand for information.

Jordan glared at him, stifling a reply as his gaze took in the recorder at Tom's waist. The activity lights were visible; the colonel would know that the conversation not only was being recorded on the box, but was being transmitted to Tom's Ranger TCV to file a duplicate.

"We're interrogating a prisoner," Jordan said when he composed himself. "Not that it's any of your concern, Major."

"I brought this man in, Colonel. I feel responsible for him."

"What you're doing could be considered insubordinate," the colonel told him.

"Questionable orders must be questioned, sir."

"I gave you no questionable orders."

"You ordered me to surrender this man to you, sir. That was well within your authority. Subsequently, I learned that unorthodox methods were apparently to be used to interrogate him. I felt it necessary to confirm that this was not the case. Meaning no disrespect, sir. I came to do that. It appears that my concerns had some merit, sir."

Tom nodded to the ritual equipment Furlann was tending. He wasn't a mage, but his job required a working knowledge of theory as well as practice. What he saw hinted at the more dire aspects of magic. The eviscerated rat was the final touch. He had to swallow to get enough moisture in his throat to speak. "Do you understand the nature of Captain Furlann's equipment, Colonel?"

Jordan's eyes narrowed. His response was cool. "I do. I think, however, that you misunderstand the purpose of this arrangement."

"I disagree, sir." Tom made sure that the button lens of the recorder swept across Furlann's arrangements. "If you really do understand what Captain Furlann has set up, then you must also understand that the procedures you're preparing to employ are illegal, even for military intelligence pursuing security matters within the military. With regard to civilians, including hostile agents, such procedures are only allowable after showing due cause for the record during a national emergency, which has not yet been declared. Since martial law is not yet in force, civil liberties haven't been suspended," Tom pointed out.

"For the moment," Jordan replied.

"Which means that, for the moment, any prisoners, especially civilian prisoners, must be treated according to the law. And according to the law, a civilian is not bound to submit to your interrogation. Mr. Markowitz is therefore not required to answer any of your questions. Certainly not without his express permission, and probably not without a lawyer present."

"Do you want a lawyer, Mr. Markowitz?" Jordan asked.

Markowitz was grinning. "No, but given the chance to talk, I'll happily say that I want to go home."

Jordan smiled tightly. "Then get up and walk away. According to Major Rocquette here, you can—legally—do so. Show us."

Markowitz didn't move.

Tom had experience dealing with magic and knowledge of Furlann's skills. "Have Furlann drop her spells, Colonel. Arcane restraint is still compulsion."

Glowering, Jordan nodded to Furlann. A moment later, Markowitz was up out of the couch.

"We'll talk again, Mr. Markowitz," Jordan said.

Markowitz sighed, chafing at his arms. "I hope not, Jemal. I liked you better before you became Trahn's lapdog. Hope he's feeding you well, because you're going to need to be in good running condition to catch me."

"We're not worried about that," Furlann said, closing a small box and slipping it into a pocket of her coat. She whispered something to Jordan. He nodded.

"Since you aren't willing to cooperate in the best interests of your country, Mr. Markowitz, you are free to go."

"Do I get a safe conduct off the base?"

"That won't be necessary. Don't you trust me?"

"You have to ask?" Markowitz shrugged. "Having a pass wouldn't matter if you wanted to haul me back. Come on, kid. Let's get out of here."

"Just a minute," Jordan said as Tom turned for the door, herding Andy in front of him. "The self-named Andrew Walker is not a citizen. He is not free to go."

Andy gulped audibly.

"He gave his statement to Captain Stratton. Are you disputing it?" Tom asked.

"It has not yet been verified," Jordan said.

"The only reason he's here is because I brought him," Tom said. "I admit to family concerns because Andrew Walker is my half-brother. I also admit that I resent the treatment he's received."

"That's your prerogative. He's still wanted for questioning."

Jordan's callousness pickled Tom. "Is he? Why?"

"Because of his association with Markowitz."

That was what he'd hoped Jordan would say. "Is that so? Well, the bulletin on Mr. Markowitz stated specifically that anyone *associated* with him be brought in as well. Andy told Captain Stratton that he has nothing more than a chance acquaintance with Mr. Markowitz. His *association* with Mr. Markowitz is purely accidental."

"He was captured along with Markowitz on the bridge."

"If that's your case, you're going to have a very crowded interrogation room. There were a lot of people captured along with Mr. Markowitz. Are you saying they were all *associated* with him?"

"Don't be absurd, Rocquette." Jordan rubbed the side of his cheek with a finger. "You've made your point about Markowitz," he conceded. "Take him and get out of here. You've lost on Walker. He's staying here."

Andy grabbed Tom's arm. Tom didn't need the cue. "If Andrew Walker doesn't leave now, I intend to observe your interrogation."

"You're overstepping your duties," Jordan said.

"All my concerns regarding Mr. Markowitz obtain with regard to Andrew Walker. Therefore, I must insist that I remain. If I see or hear anything that goes beyond the bounds of standard procedure, I will file complaints with the Judge Advocate General."

"Don't push this too far, Rocquette," Jordan warned.

Tom figured he already had. What was a little further? "Also I expect that Mr. Markowitz will soon be making a call to the International Civil Liberties Union," Tom said, hoping the man would play along.

Jordan smiled. "If he does, that would confirm his association with Walker, justifying our need to interrogate the both of them."

"Not really," Markowitz said, taking his cue. "Call it a good deed. You know, helping out those in need with no friends to save them from evil, overbearing governments and militaries? It sounds like the act of a good, concerned citizen to me."

Furlann again whispered in Jordan's ear. Tom wondered how well enhancement would pick up her words on the recording. He *really* wanted to know what she was telling Jordan. It was probably a hopeless wish; if Furlann was saying incriminating things, she was too smart not to use some kind of distortion spell to shield herself from being recorded accurately. Enhancement wouldn't cut through that.

Whatever she said to Jordan made him amenable.

"Very well, Major Rocquette. I accept the validity of your concerns. Your objections have been noted, but as nothing has been done, no blame need be applied. Both Markowitz and Walker are free to go at this time. Their release is at your request. Let us all hope you have not compromised national security. I trust that you will see them safely off base and ensure that they do not get into further mischief."

The parting shot put a burden on Tom while covering Jordan's butt. Tom hoped he hadn't completely compromised his career. He didn't think that was likely, but only time would tell.

Jordan dismissed them. Holding and stroking one of the surviving rats, Furlann silently watched them leave. The mocking smile on her face left Tom wondering what he'd missed.

"Did you hear what he said?" Markowitz asked when they were out of the building. "For the *moment.* For the fragging *moment,* like civil liberties and constitutional rights were a temporary inconvenience. Which, to him and his masters, I suppose they are. They'll find their way. Yeah, that's got to be it! The scheme must already be in play. You watch—any minute now the politicians will be yelping for help to put down the rioting."

Tom had been listening to morning reports on his way over, and knew that the outcry was already underway. "And then what?"

"Trahn is going to make his suppression of the marchers very bloody," Markowitz predicted. "He's going to cut loose, given the chance."

"Why do you say that?" Tom wanted to know why this man, who had never spoken to Trahn, had gotten the same impression as Tom himself.

"Maybe he wants to pretend he's with the rest of the boys in Chicago. Maybe he just wants to play with his toys. I don't know." Markowitz shrugged. "But it's going to happen. Call it a hunch. That's what I call it when I can feel it in my bones and don't have the evidence to back it up. I have *very* reliable bones."

"You can't act on a hunch."

Markowitz gave him an evaluating stare. Tom expected another smart remark, but instead Markowitz said, "No, you can't, can you?"

Tom nodded. "You'll need evidence to back up your accusations. So get it, if you can. Until then, you're just wind trying to tear down a good man's reputation."

"And a smart man doesn't leave his butt hanging in the wind," Markowitz said, nodding back. "Maybe I misjudged you, Rocquette."

"I'm sure you did," Tom told him. As if it mattered.

A smart man didn't throw his lot in with a bunch of shady characters, even if one was a half-brother, as long as there were other options. What Tom had done for them was already above and beyond. Any debt he owed to his blood was paid. If this was the last he saw of either of these two, he would almost certainly be better off. So why was he considering doing more? Could he really be thinking that Markowitz's left-viewed paranoia might have a basis in reality?

Tom made sure the two of them made it to the base's boundaries. Fort Belvoir was far enough from the downtown troubles that the buses were running. Tom made sure they got on one of them, using his own credstick to pay the fare. Just before he boarded, Andy scribbled out an e-mail drop point and gave it to Tom, saying, "Let's keep in touch."

"Sure," Tom said with little enthusiasm. With any luck the kid would fall off the face of the earth. He'd already fragged up too much of Tom's life.

>>>>>WFDC FEED COVERAGE
 −[10:43:57/8-25-55]
REPORTER: DERRY DALE [DALE-365]
UPLINK SITE: FREDERICKSBURG, NORTH VIRGINIA

Dale: "Governor Saul Jefferson, Governor of North Virginia, addressed the General Assembly here this morning. After reporting on the continued turmoil in the Federal District of Columbia, he called for federal authorities to take what he called 'positive and effective steps' to restore order in the District. The governor's comments showed a much

higher level of dissatisfaction than that expressed by either
Governor Shales of Maryland or Governor Landowne of
West Virginia in similar addresses to their state legislatures.
Governor Jefferson concluded his remarks with this state-
ment:

" 'Violence is spilling out of the central Districts and into
the suburbs. President Steele has tossed a rock into the pond
and the ripples are spreading. And as with a thrown rock, the
thrower has no control after the rock has left his hand. The
UCAS Army is the rock, honorable ladies and gentlemen. It
is out of control, causing more violence than it stops. Once
again we are seeing a good example of why the federal government has no business trying to govern districts that belong under other jurisdictions. Take a good look at what we
are seeing to our north. When you do, I want each and every
one of you to stop and ask yourself, "Is this my country I'm
looking at?" You'll find the answer in your heart. I know
that I have.' " [*Standing ovation*]<<<<<

19

Seeing Andy and Markowitz away from the base didn't end
Tom's worries. The problem that had thrown the two of
them into his lap remained, and he remained disturbed by
the twin problem of what was happening on the bridges and
what *wasn't* being done about it. The Army was supposed to
have methods of dealing with riots, non-lethal methods. The
acknowledgment of the need for such methods had come out
of the civil disturbances during the early part of the century.
Early Special Resources units had field-tested devices and
techniques to deal with those kinds of problems, determining
what were suitable for addition to the Army's inventory and
doctrine. Tom had been trained in applying a wide array of
technological and magical operations to quell civil disorder
with minimal casualties. And he knew the troops had at least
received familiarity training with one or another anti-rioting
tech system.

So why wasn't that training being put to use? Why was
Trahn relying on the old brute-force methods? Trahn said it
was because the Army didn't have the equipment and sup-

plies for the tech solutions, and a check of the depots confirmed that nothing was available in local storage. The suppliers hadn't delivered. It came as no real surprise that the Army didn't have what they needed; it had been that way too often during Tom's time in service. The Army shouldn't have been shorted that way, but they had been. The politicians took no action. They never did.

Magic should have offered solutions, but Tom hadn't bothered bringing it up to Trahn. Neither Furlann nor any of the other available mages were rated for riot-control spellcraft. Supposedly all members of the Thaumaturgic Corps could adapt in the field, but Tom knew the reliability of magical field adaptations—which was to say that relying on the mages wasn't an option.

So what *could* be done?

As a Special Resources officer, Tom's job description was more widely and loosely defined than most military specialties. In some ways, he had even more latitude than military intelligence. His job was intended to cover the development of new technologies, both natural and arcane, and the employment of those technologies in both conventional and unconventional environments. Creativity and innovation were watchwords in SR units.

The situation in Washington wasn't conventional, by any stretch; neither was riot control the Army's conventional service. So was it a reach to believe that doing something about the mess downtown might fall to an SR officer? When the commanding officer wasn't asking for SR to provide an end run, it sure was. Whether a reach or not, such a justification might be enough, if the person needing justification had succeeded. The Army rarely asked anyone to justify success.

To Tom's mind, what was happening in the streets was what really needed justification.

The other thing that needed justification was his not doing anything he could think of to improve the situation. Unfortunately, the only angle he could figure to try was well outside of channels. Good soldiers didn't jump channels. Well, it wasn't as if he'd been a model soldier all day.

Using the commo unit in his command car, he patched into the local telecom network. "This is Major Rocquette from General Trahn's headquarters," he told the synthetic secretary who answered his call.

Without warning, the screen image dissolved, replaced

with a Telestrian Industries holding pattern. Pleasant music played behind a sultry feminine voice extolling the virtues of Telestrian Industries. In less than a minute the screen came back to a real image: a plush corporate office with a desk as big as Tom's command car. The executive behind the desk was the elf who'd come to speak with the general. To Tom's surprise, the ID feed from the pickup identified the elf as Stephen Osborne. Wasn't he the fragging *head* of Telestrian Industries East?

"Yes, Major Rocquette," the elf said. "What can I do for you?"

Tom was caught off-guard. He forgot his planned opening statement. He improvised. "I'd wanted to speak to someone about Telestrian's failure to perform its contractual obligations."

"Has something happened of which I am unaware?" Osborne asked. He sounded wary.

"I don't understand your question, Mr. Osborne."

"Just what is the purpose of this call, Major—Rocquette, was it?"

"Tom Rocquette, sir, in command of Provisional Special Resources Battalion 7711. We're showing an anomaly in our supply depots. The records do not show us receiving shipment on"—he transferred the slew of provision orders— "any of these equipment and supply orders."

"Telestrian always fulfills its obligations, Major. A moment, please, while I check." Osborne consulted a comp built into his desk. "You are correct. We have not supplied any of those items. There is a payment hold on those deliveries. I'm afraid the government has gotten too far in arrears on its bills."

What? "We're in the middle of an emergency! That equipment could save lives!"

"I'm aware of the situation," Osborne said coolly. "Perhaps if you would give me some details as to the interest in these supplies, I could be of more help."

It was Tom's turn to be cautious. "Let's just say the general is reviewing all options. We need that equipment, Mr. Osborne."

"Is the general available?"

"Not at the moment."

"I see. Well, I'm afraid I have no authority to turn over any equipment at this time."

"Why not? You're the head of the company, aren't you?"

"Telestrian Industries East," Osborne said. "While that makes me the senior Telestrian official in Washington, that does not give me carte blanche. Your supplies and equipment are cost-centered to Telestrian Industries, our parent, and the payment hold was placed by headquarters. That puts the matter out of my control. So you see, I haven't the authority to release any of what you're asking for."

Tom couldn't believe what he was hearing. "So you're saying that Telestrian, good corporate citizen that it is, is content to sit on that stuff while people die who wouldn't if you shipped what we need."

Osborne didn't look discomfited in the least. "I'm afraid I haven't been clear. Telestrian is very concerned about the situation in Washington. But like yourself, I am constrained by rules. While I am the head of Telestrian East and my corporation's senior official in this region, I do not have the authority to release any bindings placed by headquarters. Figuratively speaking, my hands are tied. Unless I hear otherwise from headquarters, none of that equipment will be released."

Tom was familiar with passing the buck. Osborne seemed to be a master of the technique, but maybe he'd handed Tom an opening. "You say you're very concerned about the situation in Washington?"

"Deeply concerned."

"And that you would do something about it if you could?"

"We are good corporate citizens, Major."

"Well, maybe you don't have to release the equipment for it to do some good."

Osborne gave him an appraising stare. "Just what are you suggesting, Major?"

"What I'm suggesting is this," Tom said, struggling to get it straight in his mind so his evolving scheme would sound workable. "During civil emergencies, corporate security forces can be deputized to aid properly constituted authorities. Right?"

"It's part of the standard extraterritoriality agreement."

"Well, suppose Telestrian security was deputized. And suppose Telestrian security was issued the equipment currently held in local Telestrian shipping depots. Telestrian security could employ that equipment—supported and protected by our forces, of course. The rioters would be met with overwhelming, but non-lethal, force. We could win this battle, and there would be no need to violate the delivery hold as long as the equipment remains in Telestrian hands."

"An intriguing twist of the rules, Major. Unfortunately, our security forces are rather busy attending to Telestrian properties. Your plan would require reducing our security below acceptable levels."

"If there were no rioting, you wouldn't need enhanced levels of security. The important thing is that the riots get quelled, isn't it? That way everyone will be safe."

"Telestrian is sympathetic, of course." Osborne looked more annoyed than sympathetic. "I will look into the possibility of implementing your idea. Give my regards to General Trahn."

The connection blanked.

Well, he'd taken his shot. Tom couldn't think of anything to do but see if the shell landed.

The guy who came out of the back office at Eskimo Nell's was the biggest norm Andy had ever seen. Some trolls were smaller. He lumbered toward them, his shaggy head nearly brushing the lowest of the ducting pipes that made up the industrial-chic decor of the bar. Markowitz put out his hand and the man engulfed it with one of his own.

"How ya doing, pal?" the giant asked in a voice surprisingly high for a man his size. "Something must be going south if you be dropping in on me. Heard your office got lifted."

"True," Markowitz admitted. "But I'm not out of business yet."

"Glad to hear it. Been touring the monuments?"

Markowitz gave him a quick rundown, concentrating on what they'd seen of the Compensation Army camps and the rioting. Andy got the feeling that none of it was news to the big man, until Markowitz outlined their encounter with Colonel Jordan.

"That Jemal," the big man said, shaking his head like a mother despairing of a child gone bad. "Comes of keeping the wrong company. Speaking of company . . ."

Markowitz picked up on the cue. "Charlie, this is the late Andy Walker. We need to get him fixed up with an ident, which with any luck he won't lose this time. We also need access to a deck and a telecom."

The giant scratched his beard, studying Andy with his cool gray eyes. He glanced sideways at Markowitz, who was going down his list of specs for the machines to which he wanted access. When Markowitz finally ran out of requirements, requests, and demands, the giant raised an eyebrow, "This Cruncher's kid?"

"My dad's name was Matthew Walker," Andy offered. It seemed a good idea not to cross this man or to lie to him. "Only his friends called him Cruncher."

The big man nodded his shaggy head at Markowitz. "Linda'll take care of you. Standard rates." He shuffled back into his office.

Linda was a perky blonde who led them through the bar, chattering about the latest news from the Government Zone and running through the spiel on the origins of Eskimo Nell's name. The patrons ignored them. She might have been a hostess taking them to their table; but she didn't take them to a table, she took them through a door and down a flight of stairs to an acoustic-tiled corridor lined with plain green doors. She opened one, reached in to flip on a light switch, and stepped back out of the way with her hand open. Markowitz passed her a credstick. Though she had a reader hanging from her waist, she pocketed the stick and left. Markowitz didn't say a word; he just put a hand to the small of Andy's back and urged him into the small room. It wasn't much more than a cell, with a bunk bed crammed hard up against a plastic table with mismatched plastic chairs. A crapper and a sink filled most of the little space left.

Andy was thinking about other things. As the door swung closed behind them, he whispered, "Was that *Mr. Crick*?"

Markowitz smiled. "The one and only. Heard of him?"

What Washington shadowrunner wannabe hadn't heard of Mr. Crick and Eskimo Nell's? Heck, he'd used it as a base of operations in his virtual shadowrunning games. The place was touted on the runner nets as one of the area's prime hangouts for those in the biz. Andy had checked out the clientele as they passed through the bar and dining area, noting with amazement the amount of chrome, leather, and artfully not-quite-concealed sidearms. Almost every person there had looked like a runner, with an aura around them that said they definitely were *not* wannabes. There was even an ork who'd looked a bit like Andy's virtual street samurai partner Buckhead. It was unbelievable. Most unbelievable of all was the fact that Andy was *here,* doing shadow business. Despite the fact that he'd met the Dodger in the cyberspace analog of Nell's, he hadn't entirely believed the physical place really was what it was rumored to be. But it was. And he was here. It was awesome!

But something about the place bothered him. Besides the smoke upstairs that had made him cough, of course. If *he* knew about the place, so did a lot of other people. He said as much to Markowitz.

"Ever hear of a Wild West place called Hole-in-the-Wall?" Markowitz asked.

"No," Andy replied.

"Place used as a hideout by nineteenth-century runners and other outlaws. Lots of people knew about it, at least in general, but the Law never busted it—because it was too much trouble. The payback wasn't worth it, and John Law don't like busting his hoop for nothing. Worse, he don't like getting his hoop busted for what he does.

"Well, they tried putting Mr. Crick out of business back in '44, just after Nell's opened. But John Law ran into a nest full of hornets he couldn't do anything about because as soon as he turned one way, he'd get his butt stung, and by the time he turned back, the bug was ghosted and gone. John Law don't like it when his life is uncomfortable. He learned his lesson and went back to his doughnuts and soykaf, looking the other way and letting life go on. Doesn't hurt that Mr. Crick buys the occasional dozen of doughnuts, either. This place is a hole in the wall of society, kid. Be thankful it's here for us to bolt through."

"I am."

"Good," Markowitz said absently, as he began to check out the machines sitting on a table in the center of the small room. All Andy had eyes for was the cyberdeck. It had a Fuchi Cyber-6 case, but whether it boasted the power and software Markowitz had specified remained to be checked out. Andy did that while Markowitz used the telecom.

The cyberdeck was fancier than anything Andy had ever used, far hairier than his deck that had been confiscated by the soldiers. The mods he'd been able to afford and hack together looked primitive next to this set-up, technomanced to an ultrakeen edge. The muscle of the utilities was impressive. And the master persona control program—what a hunk! "You could bust into Renraku or even Fuchi itself with this."

"Not on today's hit list, kid. Just do what we talked about and start working on those files."

It was a shame not to use this wiz hardware to go Matrix surfing, but Andy understood the necessity of taking care of business at home first. He jacked in and fed the data files down from his headware into the cyberdeck. Manipulating copies on the machine would protect the originals if something happened to the data while he was trying to crack them. As he dumped, he felt a relief as if he had gotten over a head cold and was finally able to breathe freely again. He knew that the space in his skull hadn't changed, but it felt like it nonetheless. The file icons glistened before his virtual eyes, offering him a choice between the files he'd taken himself from the Telestrian matrix, and copies of those recovered from what Yates had stuffed into Andy's headware. They were all armored in encryption and none offered any easier entry than any other. Picking one at random, he marshaled his cutter software and went at it, trying to break through the protective shells.

When Andy popped out for a break, he saw Markowitz slumped in his chair, staring at the blanked telecom over steepled fingers. He looked as though someone had clubbed his pet pooch.

"Whuzappening?" Andy asked.

"Beatty's dead."

Andy felt like drek for having such frivolous thoughts about Markowitz's expression. "How?"

"Same thing that almost happened to Shamgar. Guess it's an advert for cyberizing. Shamgar popped the two muscle boys who came after him. Those toughs are in Fairfax Hospital as John Does, but our chromed friend is still healthy. He plans to continue that way. Accordingly, he's leaving on a vacation, to visit a cousin out Seattle way."

The two orks had been muscle for Markowitz's run against Telestrian. Someone was targeting more than just Markowitz, which meant they were all in danger. "Any word from Kit?"

"Kit's okay, or at least she was two hours ago. I left a message for her to come here."

That was good, wasn't it? But two hours could be a long time, a lot could happen.

"Rags is okay, too," Markowitz said, reminding Andy that there was yet another member of the runner team. Andy felt bad again; he'd liked the troll, sort of. It didn't seem right to have forgotten him, even if he was worried about Kit. "He was already on vacation, and left town before the drek hit. I've sent him word to stay clear till this blows over."

"So we're on our own?"

Markowitz nodded. "That's the bad news."

The three of them—assuming Kit made it back—against the Confed intelligence network. Bad news, indeed. "Is there any *good* news?"

"Depends on how you look at it. Way I figure it, if they only sent two after Shamgar, the bad guys don't really have the goods on us. They may have names and numbers, but they don't have specs. If they did, they'd have piled more muscle on Shamgar. All of which means we can still surprise them. At least, we could if we knew who to surprise."

"*That's* the good news?"

"You take what you can get in this business." Markowitz shrugged. "Speaking of getting. You get anything we can use out of that data?"

He hadn't; that was why he'd jacked out for a while. "The decoder is still working. It's good, but whoever locked up that data was good too."

Markowitz slammed his fist against the table. "Damn, I hate having nothing but smoke to work with! What are the fragging connections?"

"Do we even know that everything's connected?"

"You're kidding, right?"

"Well, no, actually."

"Look, kid. As complicated as some of these shadow scams are, it's actually simpler when there are connections. Random events do happen, but counting on them for explanations will get you dead, like Beatty. If I'd caught on sooner, he might not be. There was more than one reason for the drek to come down on our heads on the delivery, just like there was more than one reason for Sammy Locksley to get whacked. It's not like none of us have made any enemies. But there *was* a connection. If I'd seen it sooner . . ."

Andy didn't see how Markowitz could blame himself for what had happened to Beatty or the other rigger. "How could you have known?"

"Does it matter? It's plain now. Beatty went down just

about the same time they hit Shamgar. Same time my place got trashed. It was a coordinated op. Sammy was just their first shot. We've got bad boys on our tails."

"Too bad we don't know who. We might be able to make a deal."

"Sometimes you can deal, but you've got to have something to deal with. We're still sucking smoke."

"Yeah." It was pretty scary. Virtual runs had been so much cleaner. So much safer. Andy decided he didn't like having people trying to kill him. "We don't even know who's after us."

"We've got angles, we just need to sight along them. Given what Kit told us about the guys who did my office, I'd say we're looking at a Confederated undercover squad. Marine Ferrets, or maybe vanilla S.I.A. Numbers are right for a Ferret team, but the style's a little more like the spooks."

"A combined operation?" Andy suggested.

"They've got the same bosses, more or less, but working *together*? As likely as cats and dogs hunting dinner together." Markowitz shook his head dismissively, then stopped suddenly and looked thoughtful. "But you know, you may have the seed of something there. The timing on the strikes was real tight. A little *too* tight for either one, though, especially for an outcountry op."

"But if they're the ones who got Sammy Locksley, why didn't they go for the whole team then?"

"Good question." Markowitz frowned. "There must be shadow connections. Telestrian must have some kind of interest in this—beyond the usual proprietary concern about stolen data."

Making such an assumption about Telestrian seemed a little paranoid to Andy. "How do you figure that?"

"I don't. It's one of my hunches, okay? Humor me a little and massage those files with 'CAS' and 'Confederated' as hunt codes. Try 'Richmond' and 'Atlanta,' too."

Hunt codes offered the decoder software points of reference against which to match possible data combinations. Enough of the right kind of codes could offer the leverage necessary to unravel an encryption. It had always seemed odd to Andy that you needed to know what something was about to find out what something was about, but using hunt codes could cut decryption times to fractions of what they would otherwise be.

Andy tried them and when he saw that Markowitz's suggestions seemed to be working, he dropped out of full Matrix interface into a user interface that let him have a fuller awareness of his meat environment. He pointed at data scrolling across the cyberdeck's screen. It was one of the Montjoy files Yates had grabbed. "Look. Here and here. These are credit transfers, but they go through a lot of unnecessary steps, like someone is trying to launder the money. If you follow them back, it looks like a lot of the funding for the Montjoy project has been coming from CAS contracts."

"Yeah, I see. Maybe that's why the Army wanted a look-see."

Another file held a contract with an unspecified "contractor" for the Montjoy cybernetic control system. The contract had a clause requiring confidentiality under the threat of substantial financial forfeiture. "The Confeds wouldn't like having their secrets stolen, but with Telestrian's promises of exclusivity blown, the corp stood to lose a lot of money. So maybe it wasn't the Army after you guys, or even the Confeds. It might have been Telestrian. Doesn't it make sense that they'd want to whack anybody who stole Montjoy from them?"

Markowitz shook his head. "Data steals happen all the time. You don't geek everybody who dips you and hikes off with your wallet. Hell, even the Azzies aren't *that* kill-crazy. Business is business, and those failure-of-confidentiality clauses usually can't be enforced anyway. Not the compromised corp's fault, don't you know. Has to be that way or there isn't any business."

"So you still think the Army were the ones after us?"

"After me and the team," Markowitz corrected.

"What about the orks who beat me up? *Someone* sent them after me. Someone's after me, too." Andy rattled the bracelet Markowitz had put on him before their run in the Concordia. "You thought it was just a cover to get you to trust me."

"You were beat up too badly for that," Markowitz said.

"That's not what you—"

"I *know* what I said," snapped Markowitz. "That kind of ganger hit isn't an unusual corp response to a runaway who knows too much. Sometimes they want to scare the runaway back into the fold, sometimes they just want to close the account book. Since you were 'dead,' it was probably the latter. If the beating was a direct connect to this other stuff, they would have hit me at the same time."

Markowitz seemed very sure about that. "Maybe you were next, and the soldiers scared them away."

"Street orks and Confed hit teams working together? I don't think so. Somebody at Telestrian wanted you gone, that's all."

"If that's what you thought all along, why did you put this explosive on me." Andy held up the arm with the bracelet.

"There isn't any explosive."

"But you said—"

"I know what I said. It's not going to hurt you, okay? Just forget about it."

"But—"

Markowitz grabbed his arm and ripped off the bracelet. Andy winced, but nothing happened. No boom. Markowitz threw the bracelet on the floor.

"There. See? No explosive." Markowitz sighed. "Get your brain in gear, kid. We've got other more important problems."

Andy stared at the bracelet. No explosive?

"The Army did have my name on their pickup list," Markowitz mused. "But that don't add up."

Andy didn't see why not. "You convinced me they came after us with the Yellowjacket. If you're right about simpler conspiracies, they must be the ones who hit your office, and got Beatty and Sammy, and went after Shamgar."

"You're forgetting what Kit told us about them being foreigners, but not."

"I'm getting confused."

"No drek, kid. It's a confusing situation."

"Wait a minute. If the Army wanted you dead, why did Colonel Jordan let you go? If they knew about the datasteal, they had reason to hold you. Tom's argument about questioning you wouldn't apply."

"Yeah, I noticed that right off. The run against Telestrian has gotten us tangled in a lot more than the Montjoy Project."

"Like what?"

"Do I look like Sherlock Holmes? I haven't got it scanned yet. Let's take another look at your decodes. There's still some files we haven't got unlocked."

Andy pulled down the latest. They had more fragments,

but the pieces still didn't add up to anything that made much sense.

"Add another couple of hunt codes," Markowitz said.

"I'm pushing my active memory as it is."

"So pull down some floating memory and reallocate. Mr. Crick will front the resources. Just do it."

"Okay." Andy did it. It wasn't his cred that was burning here. "What codes?"

"'North Virginia' and 'Fredericksburg.'" Markowitz nodded solemnly as the decoder chuckled to itself while the machine worked through with the new input. "That string. Try 'Jefferson' on it," Markowitz suggested.

Like the other words Markowitz suggested, Jefferson was a name long associated with Virginia, but Andy didn't see a connection. All Virginia, but why? How was it going to help? He tapped it in.

The decoder digested the new instruction and spit out a new, improved possibility almost immediately. Thirty percent of the file was still unknown, mostly financials, but the best fit to the hunt-code possibilities had ninety-percent confidence for the text portions of the files. That meant there were hundreds of pages of theoretically decoded information, ready to read and try to make sense of. Andy dumped a copy to the telecom for Markowitz and jacked in to do his own search. Eventually a joggling of his meat body intruded on his cruising. He slid back and popped the jack.

Kit, looking no worse for her travails, had joined them in their little refuge. Andy was glad to see her safe. He was also glad to see food on the table: a plate of salad and cheese wedges and a bowl of fried, breaded somethings surrounded by bowls of dipping sauces. His stomach growled.

"Eat, then we'll talk," Markowitz said, talking around a mouthful of cheese. He didn't wait, though. He filled Kit in on his speculations while he stuffed his face. Nibbling on one of the breaded dippers, she listened with a rapt expression on her face.

"Some of these are blackmail files," Markowitz concluded. "Nice careful notes of credit transfers and a fine selection of 'gifts' to Governor Jefferson from supporters. Normal graft, till you look a little deeper. It seems that all of his most generous supporters except one—our good friends at Telestrian—have their home addresses in the Confederated States; suggesting that the honorable Mr. Jefferson is in the southerners' pockets, which explains a lot of his recent posturing."

"But why is Telestrian holding that information on Jefferson?" Kit asked.

"Yeah." The connection evaded Andy too. "It's not like it's a patriotic thing. They're not based in the Confederated States. Their home is in Tir Tairngire. What's in it for them?"

"Money." Markowitz shrugged. "It's the usual answer when you're dealing with a corp. Elves aren't any different than norms when it comes to a desire for the almighty nuyen."

Andy was still a little lost. "So both Telestrian and the Confeds are linked to Governor Jefferson, and Telestrian and the Confeds are in bed together on Montjoy. What's the connection between a bought politician and a new cybernetic control system?"

"I'm still working on that, but there's got to be some kind of convergent interest."

"Because you don't want to believe in coincidence."

"Right."

"So where does the Army fit into this?"

"I'm still working on that, too. But it was their damn Yellowjacket that was trying to fry our tails. I'm sure of that."

"Right," Andy said, just a little skeptically.

"I had a friend check out the wreck," Markowitz said defensively. "It *was* Army, and not stolen. It's currently listed as lost in an accidental crash during a training exercise on the day of the attack. The only surprise about the thing is that they didn't blame the wreck on the Comp Army. That would have been an easy fix, considering the situation at the time."

"We've got to tell Tom about this," Andy said.

"Tell him what? We haven't *got* anything."

"We've got the blackmail files on the governor, and his connection to the Confeds. We've got the connection between Telestrian and the Confeds. He said he needed evidence."

"Nothing we've got has anything to do with General Trahn or with the rioting. What does he care about Jefferson or Telestrian? He can't use it. But if we contact Rocquette, we'll be touching the military net and it will give Jemal a chance to track us down. That boy likes to hold a grudge. Besides, what makes you think Rocquette sticking up for us was anything more than a good-cop, bad-cop routine?"

"But the connections to Telestrian might be important," Andy said, not understanding why Markowitz was balking. "Whoever put the watch on my personnel file in the Telestrian matrix had his agent set to report to a UCAS delivery address, a military address."

Markowitz looked up sharply. "What's that?"

"Didn't I tell you I found that out?"

"No. Anything else you didn't tell me? Like whose address it is?"

"I don't know who."

"So you really got nothing but more smoke."

"It's *got* to mean *something*! Doesn't it prove the Army is involved? That could mean that Trahn was involved. He could be working with the Confeds."

"Trahn? General UCAS-Over-All? I don't think so. To do what?"

"I don't *know*!"

"Let it lie for now, kid. We've got some thinking to do before we jump, and we've been running on near-empty for too long. I recommend some sack time. It's what I'm planning on."

Markowitz suited his actions to his words by scraping his chair back, getting up, and tossing himself back down on the lower bunk of the bed. It didn't take but a few minutes before he was snoring.

Andy glowered at him. He didn't want to let it lie. Believing that Tom had acted out of good will because he and Andy were related, gave Andy something to hang on to. He wanted to do something to help Tom back. He decided to tell Tom despite Markowitz's misgivings. He'd let Tom decide whether the information was useful.

He had to go in person. Markowitz was wrong about Tom, but he was right about one thing: Andy couldn't use the Matrix to transfer this stuff, cutting into the MilNet was too dangerous.

"You can't go alone," Kit said.

Andy started. How had she known what he was thinking? She was a mage, but mages weren't supposed to be able to read minds.

"I could see it in your eyes," she said. "You have very expressive eyes."

"This is my problem. I can't drag you into it."

"Why not? A romp would be fun. Certainly more fun than sitting around here. Let's go."

>>>>>WFDC LIVE FEED
 —[21:06:22/8-25-55]
REPORTER: TAYLOR WEINGARTNER [WEIN-324]
UPLINK SITE: GOVERNMENT ZONE, FDC

Weingartner: "Fires light the skies of the Federal District tonight, stretching a long day of violence into the night. Sporadic outbursts of conflict continue throughout the Government Zone and surrounding areas. The police and military are struggling without apparent effect to stem what appears to be a rising tide of insurrection. Standing beside me here, deep inside a Compensation Army-held area, is Christian Randolph, leader of the Comp Army, with his first public statement in days."

Randolph: "When I and my fellow marchers for justice were dubbed the Compensation Army, I had no idea we would come to this day, a day when we were, by virtue of our common cause and our shared bloodshed, a real army. *The* real Army, for if anyone can lay claim to be the true Army of these united states, it is we. *We* are the ones standing up for the rights of the people. *We* are the ones standing against the lies and the hypocrisy of the entrenched, self-serving politicians and the uniformed lackeys. *We* are the ones fighting for freedom from tyranny and oppression."

Weingartner: "Mr. Randolph, what you're—"

Unidentified soldier: "General Randolph."

Weingartner: "Excuse me, General Randolph. What you're saying is a far cry from your peaceful message of only a week ago."

Randolph: "A week ago peace *was* possible. Now, that

option has been stolen from us, *ripped* from our hands by the oppressive fascists who have infiltrated the nation's government and its military. We came seeking justice and now we find that we must *seize* it with our own hands. What has begun here in Washington is only the start. They can disperse us. They can even *kill* us. But *we* will not die. *We* are the people, and *we* are the future!" [*signal interrupt*]<<<<<

20

"Gotcha," Specialist Wallis crowed. The transmitted image from his GM-Nissan Swatter attack drone showed a lot of smoke and dust below. Frantic figures darted for cover. One brave soul wearing a Consie beret stood her ground and fired up at the drone. She passed out of the image area as the drone banked away.

"That'll shut the fragger up for a while," Wallis gloated. "Too bad we didn't have orders to do him."

"Him and all his damn blue-topped Consies," agreed someone else on the commo line.

Another voice, added, "I hear they're roasting and eating FedPols down in the Metro tunnels."

"Heh. That ain't nothing," Wallis drawled. "You hear what the blue bonnets are doing to guys they capture? The cut their balls off, roast 'em, and feed 'em to the guys. I seen the fires. The fraggers use spells that keep the guys from dying, but don't block the pain. It's a Satanic rite thing. All them Compers are Satan worshi—"

Disgusted, Tom killed the channel. He'd heard the stories. Anyone with a brain would know they were sheer fabrications. They had to be. There were no reports of the Compers actually managing to take any prisoners; all of the Army's casualties were accounted for. But the troops kept repeating the stories to each other, believing them, and it didn't seem as if any officer other than Tom was trying to shut the rumors down. Even he couldn't do it all the time. Who had the energy for that nonsense after ten hours without let-up on the streets?

Who did the troops think they were talking about? Tom had heard the same atrocities attributed to the Sioux Special

Forces Wildcats and the entire Pueblo Council army back in Denver. This stuff was just as much drek. Tom couldn't understand it. It wasn't some foreign enemy out there on the streets. It was just UCAS people, a lot of them citizens, and most of them not even fighting back. Sure the Compers had armed troops and were resisting, but who had pushed them to it?

Tom looked at the prisoners Lieutenant Hanley's squad was herding in. Street people most of them, and mostly orks, though there was a full range of metatypes including a scruffy elf in old U.S. Army fatigues. That last was a Comper for sure. The old fatigues and BDUs were the closest thing the Compers had to a uniform, not counting the blue berets of the Consie faction. But were the rest of these people Compers, or just unfortunates who'd gotten in the way of Hanley's house-to-house sweep? Who could tell?

"Where do you want this lot, Major?" Hanley asked.

"Put them with the rest, Lieutenant. We still haven't got enough trucks to take them out to the camps yet."

"Very good, sir."

Hanley was a good man, and proving better for this particular job than his commander, Captain Lee. Tom was ashamed of the thought, but he couldn't help thinking that maybe it wasn't all bad that Lee had caught one from a sniper.

"Major, I've got Task HQ on line," Sergeant Jackson shouted from the command car. The sergeant had a tendency to forget to use the tac channel when he got excited.

"Patch it over," Tom called back.

The line was bad—the Compers seemed to have jamming equipment that was fouling commo—but Tom recognized Colonel Lessem's voice. The task force commander talked faster than any other officer on the commo net.

"Captain Black's got trouble," Lessem said. "The Compers are leaning on him hard. He reports a full company worth of Consies with heavy weapons, including assault cannons and anti-armor rockets."

The Consies were undoubtedly the best armed Compers, but Black's report sounded more like overactive imagination than observation. "Fischer's drones were in support." Tom knew; he himself had pulled them off defense on the Langley perimeter to support Black's team just two hours ago.

"Both down," Lessem reported. "You need to move your team to his support. Now."

"I'm waiting on transport for a couple of dozen prisoners, sir. I can't move until they're taken care of."

"Good point. We can't afford to have them loose again. Take care of them and then get yourself over to Dupont Circle and bail out Black's butt."

"Just what do you mean, Colonel?"

"Apply your team to relieve Black's anxiety. I don't care how you do it, understand? Have Furlann fry the fraggers, or winkle them out with the drones, or send in the grunts. You've got Lee's company, that should be more than enough. Just do it."

Was Lessem being deliberately obtuse? "I meant what do you want me to do about the prisoners, sir?"

"I told you to take care of them," Lessem snapped. "You know what I mean."

Tom wanted him to be very, very clear. "I can't say that I do."

There was the soft hissing of static. The hesitation told Tom that Lessem understood the situation as well as he did.

"It's very simple, Major. You're in a hot zone and they are hostiles preventing you from doing your duty. You've been tasked with eliminating all active opposition. Are you telling me you will not follow your orders?"

Tom knew what he had to do, but it scared the drek out of him, even if he wasn't going to go all the way with it. Not if didn't have to. The consequences were more than he was ready to deal with. "I can't do what you're asking, sir. I hereby formally protest being ordered to kill prisoners, and request that you withdraw your orders."

Lessem responded without hesitation. "You do not have any prisoners. You have active hostiles in your area. Eliminate them."

"We do have prisoners, sir. The people we're holding have surrendered under the expectation of fair treatment as promised by the Geneva, Bern, and Santiago Conventions. By the Conventions of War they are prisoners and due proper consideration as such."

For a long moment there was only the hiss of an open line. "I'd heard that you're a regular barracks-room lawyer."

Not the phrase Tom would have chosen, but he knew an illegal order when given one. He also knew his career was over if Lessem didn't back down. Hell, it was probably over even if Lessem *did* back down. They both knew what had happened, and Lessem wouldn't forget that Tom could bring it up again.

Tom was doing the right thing, but that didn't make it easier. All his life he'd set his sights on a military career. He'd just crossed a line that could break a career. Since he was the junior officer involved, the career broken would likely be his, despite the fact he was in the right.

Right or not, the colonel was done talking to him.

"Stay where you are," Lessem said, and cut the connection.

Tom went back to the command car and stood leaning against its side. The Ranger TCV felt solid, immovable. He wished he felt the same about the figurative ground beneath his feet. There'd be another call soon. Ten minutes later, Furlann stuck her head out of the command car. "The general wants to talk to you," she said, taking off her own headset and offering it to Tom.

Not the open frequency. No surprise there. Tom doffed his helmet and snugged the headset into place. "Major Rocquette."

"Major, are you having trouble doing your job?" Trahn sounded calm, as if Tom might be having difficulty getting a computer program up at an office workstation.

"I cannot obey illegal orders, sir. It's my sworn duty to protest and oppose them."

"Who's side are you on, Rocquette?"

His grandfather's suspicions of evolving factions in the service came back to him. "It's not a question of sides, sir."

"That's where you're wrong, son. It's always a question of sides. You will report to my headquarters. As of now you are relieved of command. Captain Lee will take your place."

"Captain Lee has been taken to the aid station," Tom told him. "Medics say he may not make it."

"Then find the next senior officer in your neighborhood and put him on the line."

Maybe Lee wasn't such a bad idea. "That would be Captain Furlann."

"Fine. I prefer someone who understands duty."

Ignoring the slight, Tom handed the headset back to Furlann. "Your problem now, Ice Heart."

She smiled coldly, as befitted her nickname. "What can I

do for you, General?" she said into the mike. Tom didn't hear the rest, because she ducked back into the command car. That wasn't his place now; he'd been relieved.

When Furlann finished getting her marching orders from Trahn, she came out of the Ranger, trailed by Jackson.

"Sergeant Jackson, escort the major to the trucks," she ordered. "He's leaving for HQ. I'm in charge here now. General Trahn's orders."

"Yes, ma'am," Jackson said without hesitation.

The sergeant took Tom back to the truck park where they'd been trying to collect enough transportation for the prisoners. There were only three vehicles, too few for the dozens of people they'd rounded up, but any one of which was more than enough to carry Tom to perdition. Just one problem—there was no driver.

"It's all right, Jackson." There was no point in running away. He'd been taught that you took the consequences of your actions. He'd done what had to be done, and now . . . "I won't be going anywhere until the driver shows up."

"Just the same, Major, I'd better wait."

To keep your own butt covered, eh? Tom understood that. He couldn't blame Jackson, couldn't blame him at all. Drek, he'd have been better off if he'd kept thinking like Sergeant Jackson. The prisoners back there were all strangers. What did he owe any of them?

"If you're going to be a good soldier, you'd better call Furlann and tell her she needs to arrange for a driver."

"I will, sir."

But not just yet?

The sound of machine gun fire echoed off the buildings around the truck park. Jackson looked back toward the command car. He ran his tongue along his lower lip, shaking his head slowly. Tom closed his eyes, wishing he could close his ears as well.

What good had his protest done? He hadn't saved anyone. All he'd done was frag himself.

Andy watched as the spotter drone swooped past on its circuit. He waited until he was sure its pickups weren't oriented in their direction before giving the okay to run across the street to the barricades the Compers had set around the entrance to the Rosslyn Metro station. Andy hoped none of the Compers were trigger-happy, because although they didn't look like soldiers, they weren't Compers either.

None of the men and women on the barricade opened fire. Neither did the drone turn back to see what was happening.

"Good timing," Cinqueda said when they were safely inside the Comper perimeter. They were the first words the street samurai had said to Andy since she'd simply walked out of the darkness as he and Kit neared the military cordon around the Rosslyn city center. Kit had smiled and greeted the woman by name, but there'd been no introductions. There had been no time because, as Kit pointed out, the patrols were tightening the noose and the three of them had very little time to get through before the opportunity was gone. The tall, silent samurai made Andy nervous, but since Kit seemed to trust her, Andy did too.

As Kit had known Cinqueda, so did she know the two Compers who were apparently in command of the occupied Metro station: a slim scarecrow of a black man wearing a ragged "Native Washingtonian" tee-shirt under his US Army field jacket, and a bug-eyed ork who, unlike his co-commander found the weather too hot for even one layer above the waist, let alone two. The ork wore a blue Consie beret and scowled at the newcomers. The norm, however, seemed quite happy to see Kit.

"Say and hey, little fox," he said. "You looking good. Been missing Jimmy D?"

"No more than I ever do," Kit said, "which is to say not at all."

"She's as smart as you said, Jimmy," the ork told his crestfallen partner.

"What would you know about smart, you old tusker," Jimmy said. "Everybody knows orks don't got no brains."

"Excuse him, Ms. Kit. He's been diagnosed with projectaphilia. He's always seeing his own condition in other people."

Andy had never heard of projectaphilia, but Kit's giggle said it was a joke. Jimmy D's mock expression of disgust was part of the joke. Andy guessed that things couldn't be all that bad if the Compers still had their sense of humor.

The ork's expression became serious. "All joking aside, Ms. Kit, you made it just in time. We've got a train almost ready to roll. Might be the last one. Been two days since we had rail power and the batteries are just about shot. It might be a one-way trip unless you're willing to walk back through the tunnel."

"Might be a one-way trip anyway," Jimmy D said just as seriously. "We been getting word that the sojer boys be working themselves up to come down hard on our heads. Might be no station to come back to, in an hour or two."

"All goes well, we won't need a ride back," Kit said.

"Or if it goes bad," Cinqueda added.

There were nervous smiles all around.

"All right, then. You and your friends is welcome to a ride on the People's Free Underground Express."

So saying, the ork led them down the long, long escalator into the bowels of the Rosslyn station. The platform was a weird cross between an emergency medical station and a flophouse. The air was thick with the stink of blood, vomit, garbage, human waste, and too many unwashed bodies. People lay everywhere, most sporting one or more bandages and many moaning or crying in pain. Topside had been hot, but down below where it should have been cooler, the large number of people canceled the natural underground chill— and then some. Even Kit, who had stayed so bouncy throughout the hot summer night, seemed to be finally starting to wilt. No surprise there. Rosslyn station was, for all practical purposes, a cesspit.

They boarded the one-car train. It was less crowded than the station platform, but it still stank. There were only a dozen others in the car, including the dwarf woman at the controls in front. It seemed that not very many people were interested in heading into the city. As the doors were cranked closed by Compers already aboard, Andy asked Kit, "How did you get them to agree to this?"

"Favors," she said and refused to discuss the matter further. Andy didn't want to know what kind of favors; Jimmy D's reaction to Kit was too fresh in his mind.

When they reached their destination at Farragut West station, Andy wasn't sure they hadn't gotten turned around in the tunnel. The station was every bit as reeking and crammed as Rosslyn. After a moment, he noticed a difference and wished he hadn't. There were more wounded and dead here.

Andy didn't wait for Kit to suggest getting out of there. If not for all the bodies in the way, he'd have bolted for the exit. As it was, he stepped on several people in his haste, leaving a wake of shouts and curses. He didn't stop. The climb up the dead escalator was tough, especially with so little oxygen in the air, but Andy made it gladly. Emerging, he found the harsh, fouled summer air of the city seemed delightfully clear.

Kit and Cinqueda weren't far behind. They hadn't talked on the ride or in the station, and they didn't talk now. Kit indicated their direction, and Cinqueda took the lead, shepherding them through a stop-and-start route that somehow slipped them through any cordon the Army was keeping around the station. Andy saw soldiers from time to time, but none of them ever seemed to see the runners sliding through the shadows.

Once the station's barricades were a couple of blocks behind them, Kit took the lead. As Andy understood the plan, she was using some subtle magical art to locate Tom. Every so often she would pause, tilt her head up as though sniffing at the air. Most times she would nod and go on, but twice she made them change direction. Andy didn't know if it was because Tom was moving or because Kit was finding them a path that avoided the roving groups of rioting Compers and the reaction teams of soldiers or FedPols. Occasionally the sullen clouds overhead were illuminated by a sudden flash of light or the roving beam of a spotlight. He heard gunshots, screams, explosions, and sirens, but they never came upon any of the sources of the sounds.

"Very near," Kit said as they crept into the broad intersection of Rhode Island Avenue and Seventh Street. Someone had abandoned three hulking military trucks there.

"At hand," Cinqueda said.

Andy saw the direction in which she stared and squinted. The trucks weren't abandoned. Two soldiers stood near them. One wasn't wearing a helmet. A flash of light in the sky lit them. Yes, the one without a helmet was Tom!

The helmeted soldier had his head down and was talking. "Captain Furlann, this is Jackson. We don't got no driver down here. You wanna get somebody down to the truck park, Ma'am, so I can get back to work?" He was quiet for a moment, then said to Tom. "She says the driver's on his way, Major."

If Tom was waiting for a driver, he would be leaving soon. "That other guy's a problem," Andy said. "We need to talk to Tom alone."

"Subtle or fast?" Cinqueda asked.

"I don't know how much time we've got," Andy said.

"Good answer," Cinqueda said, and she was gone.

"I wish we had time to warn your brother," Kit said. "He may mistake Cinqueda's actions, and that would be unfortunate."

"Why? What's she going to do?" Andy asked.

"Questions better asked before now," Kit said. "Wait. Watch."

It wasn't long. Andy saw Cinqueda, a blur coming at the soldier from behind. The soldier didn't know she was there until she touched him, and by then it was too late; Cinqueda had him disarmed and bent like a bow. One of her arms was around his throat, the chrome-nailed fingers of that hand caressing his hair. Her other hand held his weapon. His helmet spun lazily on the pavement. For a moment Andy didn't understand why she'd stopped her assault, then he saw that Tom had pulled his pistol and was pointing it at Cinqueda's head. At that range, he was unlikely to miss. Tom's voice was deadly cold as he spoke.

"He goes down and you follow him, samurai."

"Test of speed, soldier?" Cinqueda asked. She smiled, tight-lipped. "You'll both lose."

"No!" Andy shouted, bounding to his feet and racing forward. His shout drew everyone's attention to him. Better that than somebody getting killed. He skidded to a stop a few steps from the frozen tableau, panting, "Nobody has to get hurt."

"This augment with you?" Tom asked.

"Yeah. Sort of." It wasn't like Andy was actually in charge or anything. However, Tom seemed to think so.

"Tell her to let Jackson go. Easy and slow."

Andy nodded, but he decided a request was more suitable than an order. "Cinqueda, would you let the soldier go?"

She responded with a slight shrug of her shoulder and a blur of motion. No longer held, the soldier stumbled forward. Tom shifted aim, but Cinqueda laid a hand against the barrel of his pistol. She was well out his line of fire.

"Told you," she said.

Slowly Tom holstered his pistol. "You okay, Jackson?"

The soldier rubbed his neck, replying hoarsely, "Been worse."

Kit walked up to Tom and looked up at him. "You were under guard."

"That's right. Would you be the missing Kit?"

"Not missing, but Kit, yes."

Tom turned to the soldier. "What happens now, Jackson?"

"Some things it's better not to see, Major. I figure your driver's arrived, so if it's all right with you, I'll be getting back to my post."

"It's all right, Jackson. Thanks."

"Null persp, Major."

"Good luck, Jackson. Keep watching your hoop."

"Always do, Major." Jackson gave Cinqueda a brief nod before stooping to scoop up his helmet. Slapping it on his head, he turned and walked away.

"What was that all about?" Andy asked.

"You don't want to know," Tom said. The bleak look in his eyes confirmed it.

"We cannot stay here," Kit said. "Others will come."

Cinqueda raised an eyebrow and faded back into the darkness as Tom said, "If this is a rescue attempt, I won't be going with you."

"We didn't know you needed to be rescued," Andy said.

"I don't," Tom said gruffly. "What *are* you doing here?"

"I had some information to give you. I thought you might be able to use it."

"Information about what?"

"Telestrian and the Confeds." Andy jacked into the viewer he'd brought and downloaded the incriminating files for Tom to read.

"So Telestrian is working with the Confeds, and the governor of North Virginia's involved as well. A few things are starting to make sense." Tom told them about Telestrian's hold-up on the supplies and equipment that could have made the confrontation with the Comp Army far less deadly.

Tom's news made thing fall into place for Andy. "Everything Telestrian has done has jacked up the tension, hasn't it?"

"Looks that way," Tom agreed. "And by denying the Army its supplies, they've helped make the inevitable confrontation with the Comp Army a bloody one. Net result: the UCAS government looks bad, right at a time when anti-UCAS sentiment is running high in North Virginia. It all puts Jefferson in position to claim his state's better off with the Confederated States."

"He's said as much on the news," Cinqueda offered. She'd rejoined them without Andy noticing her return. No one else even seemed to notice she'd left. "He'll be inviting CAS troops in next."

Tom snapped her a look that suggested to Andy she'd hit close to the mark.

"Border crossing means war, yes?" Kit said.

"Confeds don't want a war any more than we do," Tom said.

"But with the trouble up in Chicago, they might think this was a good time to make a grab," Cinqueda countered. "They've always claimed North Virginia and the regions south of the Potomac were theirs, anyway. If they were squatting on the territory, they could stake a legal claim that would be messy to dispute."

"Chicago or no Chicago, we'll fight if they try it," Tom said. "And while we're beating each other's brains out, the Azzies make their own grab at Texas while the Confeds' backs are turned. The Azzie claim there goes back even further than the Confed claim to old Virginia."

"Steele hasn't got the balls for a fight," Cinqueda said. "Especially not with North Virginia saying it wants to go South."

Tom looked as though he were afraid she might be right. "I just wish I knew Trahn's connection to all this," he said. "I know he's being friendly with the corps. He met with Osborne from Telestrian Industries East just as all this was blowing up. He can't be working with the Confeds. He's got nothing to gain from losing North Virginia."

"What if he wants a war?" Andy asked. "If the Confeds send troops and there's a war, he'd get a chance to be a hero."

"He's already a hero, and a war wouldn't do any good. He knows that probably better than anyone," Tom said.

"But you said he's involved with Telestrian," Andy said.

"Involved, yes, but I can't picture him mixed up with a plot to split off North Virginia and hand it to the Confederated States. To haul the rest of Virginia back into the Union—that I'd believe."

"But he's not *innocent*," Andy insisted.

"No," Tom said sadly. "Not innocent."

"Well, there you have it," Andy said. "Whatever Trahn's up to, right now everybody but us thinks everything's just happening naturally. Nobody knows that the Confeds are pushing it. Nobody knows what Trahn's game is. But *we* know there's shadow work afoot. If we expose everybody, people will wake up." Andy thought that exposing a Confed conspiracy would be great. *They* would be heroes.

"Don't be absurd," Tom said. "Who are you going to bring this stuff to, who won't bury it?"

"He's right," Cinqueda said. "Too many parties would get burned, and if it's one thing folks in this town are good at, it's covering their hoops."

Andy couldn't believe the situation was hopeless. Somebody had to be honest enough, and uninvolved enough, and still have something to gain. "Who's in a position to do something?" Suddenly he knew who. "Let's take it to the President."

"Only one problem," Tom said. "Any idea *how* you're going to take this story to him?"

"You're a military officer, Tom. You could—"

"Get nowhere near him. Not now. You won't be able to get near him, either."

Andy was unwilling to give up. "What if we go straight to the public? Tell everyone. If everything is out in the open, there'd be no way to hide what's been done. No faction will be able to bury the truth. Something will *have* to be done."

"How are you going to do that?" Tom asked.

"I don't know," Andy admitted.

"But Harry would," Kit said.

"Who?" Tom asked.

"Markowitz!" Andy grinned. "Kit's right. He would know."

All they needed to do was get back to Arlington, and it turned out that Tom had an idea about that.

>>>>>NEWSBLIPS FEED
  -[22:12:03/8-25-55]
ACCESS CHARGE APPLIED

Welcome to NEWSBlips, your instant information service. Please tap any blip and receive additional informative blips that you need to know. Access charge will be applied. Have a nice day!

BLIP
   Government troops are obstructing fire-fighting efforts in riot-torn Washington. "It's for their own safety."—General Nathan Trahn, Commander, SE Military District

BLIP
   General Trahn a liar. "The feds are using the rioting as an excuse to burn out those who support the right and proper destiny of Northern Virginia."—Teresa Lee, Fairfax Regional Commissioner

BLIP
   Corporate representatives expressed concern that their assets are at risk and that the federal government seems unable to provide protection. "We must look to other resources."—Stephen Osborne, Allied Council of Concerned Corporations.

BLIP
   President urged to declare martial law in Washington. "May as well. The Army's running things anyway."—Senator Gorkakov (Dem-MN)

BLIP
   Genocide in progress. "The government is orchestrating the so-called crises in Washington and Chicago as a cover

for a pogrom against metahumans."—Spokesman for International Civil Liberties Union.

BLI—*FUZZZZZZ*
There is no North Virginia, only Virginia! Read your maps! Vivat the Old Dominion! *FUZZZZZZ*

BLIP
NEWSBlips apologizes for the interruption. No access charge has been applied for the previous item. Normal charges apply for additional informative blips that you need to know.<<<<<

21

Tom suggested they take one of the trucks since it was faster than walking. Andy pointed out that it wasn't their truck. Tom, to Andy's surprise, said he could drive.

"I thought you couldn't help," Andy said.

"You're headed across the Potomac, right? Past the riot cordons?"

"Yeah."

"So am I," Tom said. "Since my driver hasn't shown up, I may as well drive myself, and since I'm going that way anyway . . ."

"We might as well go with you." Andy looked at Cinqueda and Kit. "But we don't exactly look like we belong in an Army truck."

"Except as prisoners," Cinqueda said. "And one major doesn't look like much of a guard detail."

"I can fix that. There is a trick I can pull, so long as I don't have to move," Kit said. She snatched Tom's helmet from where it hung on his belt and plopped it on Andy's head. "We shall be soldiers."

In an eyeblink she changed. Andy shook his head and blinked again, for Kit had been replaced by a burly black soldier—who giggled just like Kit.

"Look at yourself," the soldier said with Kit's voice.

He looked down. His hands were coarser and his clothes had become a gray and black camouflaged uniform. A web belt festooned with pouches cinched his waist. Andy looked at the others. Tom was still Tom and Cinqueda was still herself.

"I can do little for her, since she has surrendered so much of herself. She can be our prisoner."

Kit's illusion faded as they climbed aboard the truck, but she renewed it once they were aboard. Tom opened the panel between the cab and the back of the truck so they could communicate. Thus Andy heard Tom tell the guards at each checkpoint that they encountered, "Prisoner to go to Belvoir."

To Andy's relief, the scheme worked.

They had crossed the river and were somewhere in Arlington when Tom pulled the truck off the road and around behind a shopping complex. It was darker back there than it should have been, a lone, unbroken spot casting a pool of light at the far end of the building. The overcast sky offered only the reflection of the urban sprawl and the ember glow of the fires across the river by way of illumination. Andy could barely see his own shadow as he leapt from the truck. He almost walked into Tom as he came around the truck's side. Cinqueda's sudden, restraining hand on his shoulder was all that prevented a collision.

"I think it's best I leave you here," Tom said, addressing Kit and Cinqueda. He seemed to be making a point of not looking at Andy. "You should be able to get to Markowitz without trouble from here. This side of the building is dark, but there's a convenience store open around the other side. There are telecoms. Okay?"

"Be fine," Cinqueda said.

Andy was worried about what Tom was going to do next. "Won't bringing us out here get you in trouble? I mean, you lied about taking Cinqueda in as a prisoner."

"I wasn't lying," Tom said.

Andy was confused. "But Cinqueda's not a prisoner."

"I wasn't talking about her."

"You thinking about taking me in again?"

"No."

Tom's attitude was baffling. "I don't understand."

"I don't expect you do. I've got to get going."

Andy offered the helmet. Tom took it with a tight smile and turned away to climb back into the truck. The engine revved and the vehicle lurched away. Dull red taillights glowered at Andy like a petulant demon until their light was overwhelmed as the truck splashed across the pooled light from the building's lone spot. The truck turned the corner and was gone.

Andy felt like a kid as Cinqueda and Kit led him through the abyssal darkness. It was darker here than in the city proper. Though he was nearly blind here, they seemed to have no trouble at all. He wished he had the implants he'd been scheduled to receive before leaving Telestrian, or even just the military helmet with its augmentation visor. He didn't like feeling so helpless, and Cinqueda's cold chrome touch chilled him. Kit's guiding touch, on the other hand, was warm, and not exactly motherly either. Andy contrived to stay nearer to her than to the other woman.

When they reached the telecoms, Cinqueda complained but did produce a credstick when neither Andy nor Kit had any. Once the system was open, Andy used a trick he'd read about on the nets to jigger the box's calling code so it would misdirect any trace. They contacted Markowitz, who was, fortunately, still at Nell's. He didn't like being woken, or so he said. He didn't sound sleepy when he demanded to speak to Kit, nor was he slow in cutting Andy off when Andy tried to explain the situation.

"Not on the line. It isn't safe," Markowitz said, proving it by telling them where they were calling from. "Kit, head for the place where we first met Yates. I'll join you there."

Andy didn't know where Markowitz was talking about, but Kit did. It turned out to be an all-night Denny's in the decaying sub-sprawl near the big Beltway-95 South interchange. Markowitz was waiting for them. Eagerly, Andy told him about Tom connecting General Trahn to Telestrian.

"It's not evidence, kid, but it's a link. The important part is that the public will buy it, and the bad public relations may be enough to get the goons off our backs. Corps get real shy when there's a spotlight on what they do, especially when they're messing with governments."

"I thought they didn't worry about governments anymore."

"Sure they do, but it's mostly a PR thing. If they *really* had no use for governments, do you think we'd still have any?"

Andy wasn't sure. It wasn't something he'd thought about while still safe in Telestrian's womb. He put the thought away for the moment. "Kit said you'd have an idea how we could get the information out."

"I know some people."

"Cheese?" Cinqueda asked, but she wasn't offering any.

Andy thought that a little strange, but shadowrunning lore said that street samurai were all a little strange. Hoping to be polite, he said, "No, thanks."

Kit giggled.

"Cheese is a pirate," Cinqueda said.

"What good is a software thief for this?" Andy asked.

"A pirate *newsman*," Markowitz said. "He runs ITRU Independent News. He's got satellite uplink to the broadcast birds and pretty good cut-ins on the cable nets. He's our best bet for getting the word out. Cheese likes blasting the government and has a thing for dissing the Confeds; claims it's in his blood. He'll like this one."

Kit looked unsure. "Do you think he still remembers the last time you asked him to put something on the nets?"

"I'm sure he's forgotten all about that," Markowitz said unconvincingly.

"Bring money," Cinqueda advised. "Just in case."

The ITRU station was a GM-Nissan Metrohauler extended panel van. It wasn't a new one. Small patches of different colors were so overwhelmed by large swaths of rust red anticorrosion paint that it was impossible to tell what the original color scheme might have been. Twin parabolic antennae on the roof and the crude, hand-painted ITRU logo on the sides were all that showed the truck to be more than a derelict waiting to be scrapped. The blood-shot-eyed youth who answered Markowitz's pounding on the rear door was dressed as if whoever had painted the van was his fashion coordinator. The kid—he didn't look like he could be older than thirteen—had an ITRU logo on his ball cap above the legend "tech eng."

"Whatchu want?"

"We need to talk to Cheese," Markowitz said.

"Hey, I knows you, man. Cheese no wanna see you."

"I don't care." Markowitz caught the door, keeping the kid from slamming it. "You tell him I'm here."

"You leggo de door, man."

"You go tell Cheese."

The kid left the door in Markowitz's possession and disappeared into the red-lit interior. Markowitz followed him, saying, "Come on."

Andy looked to Kit for confirmation, but she was already on her way up the truck's short ladder. By the time Andy boarded, Markowitz had threaded his way through the machinery crammed into the truck and was confronting a short, overweight black man whom Andy might have mistaken for a dwarf if his shoulders had been wider and his beard fuller. The man was nearly snarling at Markowitz and showing strong-looking, amber teeth nearly the color of cheddar cheese. His ITRU cap had the legend "The Big." He had to be Cheese. Kid Tech Eng had disappeared into the darkened depths of the van.

Cheese's voice was a hoarse grating, more appropriate for an urban brawl casualty than for an independent newsman, but that voice had volume. Whatever had gone down before still bothered him, and the shouting match between him and Markowitz was spectacular, if short on details. Kit intervened, flattering both men and calming them down some. She gave most of her attention to Cheese, who did chill some, but it was the credstick that Markowitz finally produced that finally did the trick.

Cheese slotted the stick into a Commercial model desktop reader whose case had obviously been tampered with. He seemed satisfied with the reading. "Dis scam, she is real, hey? Really real?"

"Everything we dug up looks good," Markowitz said.

"Dat what you says de last time," Cheese said, squinting at him.

Andy was tired of the continuing suspicion. "Yeah? Well, I don't know what happened before, but this time it *is* real. This is important and we've got to let people know about it."

Cheese's bright eyes turned to Andy. They ran him up and down, then lingered on his datajack. The newsman absently caressed his own jack as he evaluated Andy. His lips split into a broad grin, gleaming with his yellowed teeth. "Hey, man, like you really real pos-ee-teeve! Like dey says, dis she eez conviction. Maybe I do goes wit dis story after all."

"I think you should," Kit said softly.

"De lady, she knows, hey?" Cheese spun in his chair, fingers flying across buttons and dancing across the control keyboard. Without any apparent shift in rhythm, he tossed a datacord to Andy. "Watsay you makes de data dump? De Cheese, he tickles her up and sees if she sing. We gots us a good tune, we takes to de airs." Louder. "Heyzee, Mouse, puts us a movin' and finds us a line to de sats."

"Wilco," a feminine voice replied from somewhere up front.

Andy squinted in that direction and thought he made out a couch with a figure reclining on it. A rigger? The truck lurched into forward motion; the figure did not move. Definitely a rigger.

He was curious to see the interface she was using, but he had a job to do. He jacked and shifted the digest of the data they'd uncovered from his headware to Cheese's board. Cheese split his attention between reading Andy's dump and performing a host of technical manipulations to set up satellite-dish alignments, frequency matches, and cut-ins for slipping through encryption sheaths on the cable bounces.

"Cheese?" It was the rigger. "We got—"

"No times, no times. We is taking to the airs." Music filled the interior, backing an angelic choir that sang about the coming of the ITRU Truthcast. Cheese spoke into his microphone, astounding Andy. The man's voice changed utterly. His street dialect vanished, the wheeze disappeared, and from his throat came a cultured, deep, reverberating voice that might have come a Shakespearean actor's.

If he could speak like that, why had he talked to them in such annoying tones? Kit noticed Andy's perplexity.

"He has a voice modulator," she said.

He'd guessed that. "Why doesn't he talk that way all the time?"

"Bad hardware," Cinqueda said. "Rasps the vocal cords after a while. Gonna shred them one day if he—"

Cinqueda's head swiveled toward the door.

There was a bang outside. A loud pop. The truck canted and a squeal arose from beneath them. Everyone except Cinqueda went tumbling. Machinery, tools, power cells, and computers slid from their precarious perches in showers of sparks and splintering crashes. The truck's red interior lights failed. The front of the truck hit something. The rear slued around, trying to bypass the nose, but it too slammed into something. The engine coughed and died. Save for a chorus of fading malfunction alerts, the truck was silent.

Andy tried to extricate himself from the pile of stuff that

had landed bruisingly on him. Nearby, Cinqueda crouched low. In her left hand she held a big, wide-bladed knife Andy hadn't known she was carrying. The ribbed blade lay along her forearm. Her head tilted minutely, as if she were trying to locate a sound.

"Four in contact with the vehicle," she whispered.

"No magic active," came Kit's voice from out of the darkness.

"Helmet coms," Cinqueda said. "They're going to—"

The truck's back blew away in a blinding flash.

When Andy could see again, there were four men in rubble-dot urban camouflage jumpsuits standing at the back of the truck. Visored helmets hid their faces. No insignia were visible on anything they wore. Each man held a dull black Steyr automatic weapon.

"Walker." The speaker turned his head slightly toward one of the others. "You're buying the beer, Joe."

Andy felt a chill dance down his spine as the man looked back at him.

"Weedeater Osborne'll be pleased to know he was right. He'll be even more pleased to know that a disloyal little fragger like you is no longer anyone to worry about."

Cinqueda shifted. Muzzles came up. Andy tried to throw himself through the truck's floor as the gunfire erupted.

Andy's idea, to go public with the information concerning the conspiracy, was just about the only way Tom could see to pour some sanity on the fires of craziness that were consuming Washington. Having that chance had made it easy deciding to commandeer one of the trucks and take Andy and his friends out of the riot-control zone. Tom didn't go with them to meet with Markowitz, though. That wasn't his place. He still had orders to report to General Trahn. So what if he was a little late? What was the commander going to do, cashier him? He'd be doing that anyway.

The drive gave him some time to think about what had happened. He'd done what he had to do, and all that was left was following through. If Gramps was right, and there was a cabal within the senior command, Tom was fragged. Maybe he was fragged even if there wasn't; no one had successfully challenged an illegal order since the Vasquez incident, back before the breakup of the United States. He hadn't thought much about that until now. It used to be that a soldier was expected to know the difference between right and wrong, and to stand up for the right. Now? Well, many people over the years had told Tom that a lot more than borders had changed when the old U.S. of A. went down. He hadn't believed it. Now, Tom was probably about to learn just how hollow some of the Constitution's words had become.

A convoy of a dozen McAuliffe air-transportable IFVs rumbled past him, headed toward the central districts. They'd be teaching some lessons soon. Tom wondered if his lesson was going to be any less harsh.

But he had his honor to consider.

He passed the horse farm and the entrance to the southbound bypass for through traffic on Route 1. Not much further. He slowed as he approached the Fort Belvoir gate, pulling the truck to a stop in front of the guard post. The soldier who came out to meet him was a private, a young female ork looking too perky to have been in uniform long. She'd have her own lessons to learn.

"Major Rocquette to report to General Trahn," Tom said, handing over his ID tag.

The squaddie slotted the tag into her pack. Her brow furrowed as the screen lit up. It would be whispering instructions into her helmet speaker. She looked confused. "What happened to your guard, Major?"

"He never showed up. I got tired of waiting. You going to let me in or not?"

The guard took a step back and shifted her weapon to a slightly more aggressive position. She didn't point it at Tom, though, not quite. "I'm afraid I have to ask you to get out of the truck, Major."

Tom didn't switch off the truck. To do so would have meant dropping his hand from the guard's line of sight. He didn't want to push this kid, who was clearly nervous. Tom exited the cab, slowly. The kid was just doing her job.

She was scared; he could tell that by the wide, wide pupils. Not every day she was told to take an officer under guard, he expected. He tried to make it easier on her by not appearing to be threatening.

"What's your name, squaddie?"

"I'm not supposed to talk to you, sir."

"Drek, squaddie, you can tell the *enemy* your name."

She took time to think that over. Orks grew up early, but

they didn't often grow up smart. Hell, if she were smart, she wouldn't be in uniform. As he knew, the Army was tough enough on male orks; he'd done his share of making it so. But now that he was facing the muscle of the behemoth, he felt an unfamiliar sympathy for her. Finally, she said, "Booker, sir. Harriet Booker."

"Do yourself a favor, Harriet, and get out of the Army. Find yourself another job."

The concept clearly disturbed her. "I'm not supposed to talk to you, sir," she repeated.

He let it go.

They waited in silence. The MPs who showed up wore the shoulder flashes of the 3412th Military Police Battalion. Jordan's boys. They weren't supposed to be part of base security. Having them come to take him into custody, instead of Belvoir's regular white gloves, meant that Trahn was keeping the affair in the immediate family. Tom's hopes of publicity for his personal problem dropped to nothing.

And it was too late to run.

Without formally placing him under arrest, they relieved him of his sidearm—so much for military courtesy—took him to the building where Jordan had held Andy and Markowitz. He didn't think it a coincidence that they brought him to the same room where Furlann had been intending to violate Markowitz's rights and person. The rats and the thaumaturgic equipment were gone—the latter being Furlann's own and not to be parted from her—but the false dentist's chair was still there. This time Tom saw that it was equipped with restraining straps. Jordan must have been busy elsewhere; the room was untenanted. The MPs closed the door on Tom, and he heard the lock snap home.

He waited, wondering how Andy and Markowitz and their crazy crew of shadow folks were doing. Now that he'd had time to sit and think, he could see just how quixotic a quest the kid and his friends had undertaken. He had to admire them a little. Whatever else they were, they were brave. But how much good would they do? How much good *could* they do?

Unfortunately, it was likely to be too little; for some, it was already certainly too late.

Time passed.

He heard footfalls in the hall. Jordan? No, just a sentry making rounds, stopping to chat with the door guard. By the familiarity of their exchanged greetings, they were old friends.

"You hear that Steele's on base?" the sentry asked.

"No drek?" said the guard.

Tom didn't believe it either.

"Yeah, no drek," the sentry said earnestly. "Half the freqs are full of chatter. You got your helmet swapped to music again?"

"Beats listening to nuthin'. You'd do it too, if'n you could figure how," the guard said defensively.

"It's a guard's duty to be alert."

"Save the drek for the sarge." Bullshit was fine, but the guard remained interested in the rumor. "What's Steele doing here? I thought he was hiding in the White House basement till it was all over."

Tom imagined the sentry's shrug. "Must have finally decided things were too hot in his back yard. I hear he's scampering out to Camp David and leaving us behind to clean up his mess. That's why he's down at the TOC talking to Trahn. The man's on his way to less troubled climes and wants to make sure the head garbage man gets the cleanup underway. The man doesn't like bailing out of his fine, fancy home. Doesn't look good, with nominating conventions less than a year away. This town's got a memory. Well, jelly-spined Steele won't have all that long to wait, from what I hear," the sentry said.

The guard was hooked. "Why's that?"

Tom wanted to know too.

"Trahn's got the push against the Metro stations set for midnight. Once we've got the entrances, the engineers are going to pump down gas. That'll take the fight out the Compers."

"Gas is illegal."

"I expect Trahn's clearing that little impediment out of the way with Steele even as we speak."

They talked some more, but the sentry never said a word about a pirate broadcast exposing the Confed connection or implicating Trahn in anything. Clearly Markowitz hadn't come through. Andy's plan had been flawed, but it had seemed to have a chance. But that thought recalled Andy's other earlier suggestion, one that Tom had put down as foolish. He'd said they ought to take their story to the

President—and now here was Tom, less than a hundred meters from the President.

How could he just sit around and let things happen?

A locked door and a guard, was the answer.

It was a lousy answer and he wanted a better. He looked around the room, hoping for inspiration. He found it in the interrogation chair. A bit more searching and he found a sharp way, one that, with a bit of effort, put the necessary tool in his hand. Jordan's boys should have been more careful about cleaning this place out. Tom swung the liberated restraining strap, gauging the weight of the buckle that swung at its end. It would do.

He went to the door.

"Guard," he called out. "I need to talk to Colonel Jordan. I've got something important to tell him."

It wasn't a new trick; but some tricks couldn't be ignored—simply because they might not be tricks.

"It can wait," the guard said.

"No, it can't." He checked his watch. "It's after 2300. The Colonel will have your balls on a platter if he doesn't hear what I've got to say before the hour's out. *I* won't mind if he does, but *you* might."

Jordan's boys had people scared enough to not drop drek without permission. It followed that Jordan ought to have the same effect on the boys themselves. Paranoia begins at home.

"Step away from the door, Major."

Tom smiled. He *had* pushed the right button. He stepped away as told, waiting tensely as the guard ran his key card through the slot.

"All right, Major. Now you open the door and keep backing away as you do." The guard had both hands on his weapon and kept it leveled in a business-like fashion.

Tom started to follow the guard's orders, but before the door was fully open, he whipped out the strap through the widening crack. The guard reacted, bringing his weapon up to block the sudden threat, as Tom had hoped. While the weight wrapped its trailing strap around the guard's weapon, Tom flung the door the rest of the way open and launched a kick into the man's unprotected belly. The guard went down, doubled over and whooshing air. That kind of strike had inevitable consequences and Tom was on the guard before he finished vomiting. Tom waited till the man had blown what he was blowing before putting pressure on the right points. He didn't want him to choke to death.

An empty corridor would be less suspicious than one soldier looting the body of another. Tom dragged the guard into the room and shut the door, but only after making sure the lock wouldn't reseal. He relieved the guard of his white helmet and Sam Browne belt, the MP brassard as well, and the sidearm. He left the gloves. He'd never liked the damned things. He didn't take the rifle either; Military Police majors didn't carry rifles.

As he put on his stolen goods, he realized he was breaking the rules now. So be it. The situation had forced him to it, and he couldn't see another way to do what needed to be done. He wouldn't get near the TOC without some sort of disguise; he'd seen the way the others on base had reacted to Jordan's white-pawed dogs. If pretending to be one would help him bluff his way into the TOC, he intended to do so. Afterwards, he'd take whatever punishment a court martial prescribed; justice was justice. But justice wasn't what those poor fraggers out on the streets were getting.

As a last touch, Tom took the guard's utility knife and sliced the unit patch from the MP's uniform. Using cement from the MP's emergency kit, Tom slapped the patch onto his own left shoulder. It was sloppy and wouldn't pass inspection, but he wasn't expecting to undergo inspection. Reversing his rank tabs from their dull black field side to on-base brassy, he was ready.

Though it made him uncomfortable to see it happen, his pretense opened doors for him and passed him by guard station after guard station without question. The rank tabs got him past questions that the white helmet and belt didn't, and the 3412th patch got him past what his major's leaves didn't.

As he reached the edge of the tarp covering the TOC, Trahn and the President were just getting up from their seats in the heart of the command center. Secret Service guards took their cue from the white-gloved Military Police, and didn't question Tom as he entered. As Tom crossed the inner white-sound privacy barrier, Trahn and the President shook hands, as if sealing a deal. Trahn was talking.

"I'm glad you've finally come around, Mr. President. There just isn't any other viable alternative."

This was it. Now or never. Tom raised his hand to point at Trahn, to accuse him before the President.

>>>>>NEWSNET FEED COVERA****STATIC****
  -[23:17:02/8-25-55]

LIVE ITRU BROADCAST TRUTHCAST

"This is independent TRU Broadcast Truthcast bringing you the news that's too true for NewsNet. Uncovered for you tonight: the great covert Confed land grab. Listen and learn!

"For years, deckers from the Confederated American States have been working subtle propaganda within our databases. Just what sort of propaganda? Call up an atlas with a map of North America, and take a look at the border between CAS and UCAS. Look to the eastern part. Odds are you'll find the boundary marked along the Potomac more than a few miles north of reality. Seekers of the truth, this fiction will *become* reality if the minions of southern domination have their way!

"Independent TRU has learned tonight of a Confed conspiracy to rip North Virginia and the South Potomac regions of the Federal District, out of the UCAS. Without knowing it, you've been soaking for weeks in the preliminary steps and rhetoric, getting marinated for tonight's burning fires. You've been prepped and primed, cozened and misled and taken along the path. Such *fools* mortals be! Awake, awake! Damnation awaits those who let others dictate their lives! I tell you *true*, seekers!

"Damnation, too, for those who *aid* the evil aggressors. Who? You know them. By their acts they show themselves. They are all around you. *Look* to the politicians. *Look* to the corporations. And, yea, I tell you, with great sadness in my heart and no little shame, to look also to those sworn to defend us, for the *military* walks hand in hand with those who wish to take what is ours. Let your eyes be opened, seekers, as Independent TRU names names and\|"
****static****<<<<<

22

The runners were caught in the tumbled truck, forced to take
what cover they could against the fire from the soldiers
who'd ambushed them. Markowitz started shooting back; so
did someone else from deeper inside the truck. Andy kept
his head low. Being nearer to the back of the truck, he was
in danger of being shot by both sides if he moved.

There wasn't much he could do but cower. He didn't have
a gun, not even his replica Narcoject. He'd lost that to the
ork gang and, with the press of events, he hadn't gotten
around to replacing it with anything more useful. Even if
he'd had a gun, he wouldn't have known how to do more
than point it, pull the trigger, and then hope he hit something. It was not like he'd had firearms training; he'd never
needed it.

He wasn't the only one not shooting at the soldiers.
Cinqueda crouched behind the barrier of ITRU's tumbled
physical assets. Head bent down, she looked as though she
were mediating. Or praying. One of her hands was stretched
above her head, the tips of the fingers protruding just above
the top of the barrier, almost as though she were reaching
out in supplication to beings above.

Andy noted a small black tube no more than two centimeters long between her index and central fingers. A thin wire

ran from the cylinder into an open port on her wrist. He'd read about such things. She was using a tiny camera to view the scene without exposing herself. The pickup must be transmitting an image of the scene at the truck's rear directly to her optics. Andy wondered if the transmission filled her vision, or if the pickup's image was inset within a normal eye view. Whichever way it worked, he wished he had one so he could see what was going on.

In a motion as smooth as quicksilver flowing across steel, Cinqueda uncoiled. Her arm snapped forward and her big knife flew. Then she dropped back behind the cover, resuming her crouch. She might never have moved. It had happened so quickly Andy wondered if he'd only imagined her moving, but her weapon definitely was gone. Someone outside the truck screamed. Andy risked a glance and saw one of the soldiers stumbling back, the hilt of the knife protruding from his chest. Ballistic cloth was good against bullets, but not much protection against low-velocity edged weapons.

A bullet hummed past Andy's head and he ducked back under cover. When he opened his eyes, Cinqueda was looking at him. "Not your party, kid. Stay down."

Good advice. He nodded.

"Grenade coming," she commented casually. "Hold fire, Marksman."

She sprang up, over the barrier. Her hand blurred, reaching out and meeting something arcing into the truck. It was as neat a move as you might see in a zero-G handball match. The object, the grenade, reversed its course. Cinqueda did not; she landed, crouched, by the ruin of the truck's back door.

Outside the truck, the soldiers were reacting to the sudden change in the situation and ducking for cover. Faster than Andy could have. They must have enhanced reflexes to move so quickly. All Andy could do was watch.

Cinqueda moved even faster than the soldiers. Instead of leaping to the ground, she reached up and grabbed the edge of the truck's roof. More graceful than a gymnast, she swung herself up, wrapped her stomach around the edge of the roof, and with a shove, disappeared from sight.

The grenade exploded with a flash and a bang. Smoke billowed on the street. Andy caught a whiff of acrid smoke that made his nose burn and his eyes sting.

"We're too cramped in here. Get out while we've got cover," Markowitz ordered. "The smoke won't last long."

Something white and furry and about the size of a small dog shot past Andy and out the back of the truck. Andy went, too, when Markowitz crawled forward and gave him a shove. He landed badly and fell, his ankle sending shrieks of pain through his leg. Rolling over, clutching his leg, he felt something wet and warm under him. Blood. He'd come up against the soldier who'd gone down from Cinqueda's knife throw. The man's visor was half open and Andy could hear him gasping. The stench of vomit was overpowering. Andy retched himself.

"Negative capture option," groaned the wounded soldier. "Execute."

"Shit," Markowitz said. He sprang back to the truck. "Everyone out! Everyone out of the truck!"

He disappeared briefly inside, coming back with Cheese in tow, urging him to move. Wailing wordlessly, the newsman resisted when Markowitz tried to shove him out of the truck. Markowitz holstered his pistol and gripped Cheese with both hands. Swinging the overweight newsman like an Olympian heaving the hammer, Markowitz flung him from the back of the truck.

"Incoming!" Cinqueda shouted.

Markowitz dived after the newsman.

Something flashed at the corner of Andy's vision, headed for the truck. Instinctively, he hugged the ground and covered his head. The explosion washed heat and burning, stinging fragments over him as it lifted him and tossed him, rolling, down the street.

Andy lay on his back, staring at the overcast sky. New smoke was rising to smudge the heavens. Ears roaring, he tried to ask what had happened, but he could barely hear his own voice. Markowitz, rising shakily beside him, obviously hadn't heard him speak. Andy looked back at what was left of the truck. It was a burning, ragged heap.

A new motion caught Andy's dazed attention. One of the soldiers was running away. The man cut into an alley. Andy thought he'd escaped, but he came right back out, moving faster than he had going in. Andy caught a glimpse of something big and gray, with sharp glittering teeth and glowing red eyes, bounding after the soldier. But whatever it was stayed at the alley mouth as the soldier dashed back onto the street.

Markowitz rose to his knees, drew a bead, and drilled the soldier before he'd gotten ten meters down the street. A ragged figure capered out of the shadows and kicked the fallen soldier. Markowitz swung his aim to the alley, but instead of firing, he lowered his weapon. "SpellMan?"

The little shaman approached. His eyebrows wiggled as he wrinkled his nose several time in rapid succession. "On the mark, Marksman."

Cinqueda reappeared. "Got the missile man," she said, tossing down the Steyr she'd obviously acquired from one of the soldiers. Fire from the burning truck reflected on her chrome eyes. "Threat situation is now negative."

That was when Andy realized there was no more gunfire. He looked around and breathed a sigh of relief when he saw that Kit had made it out. She was examining Markowitz, frowning at the small wounds he'd acquired and showing no concern for Andy, sitting on the ground and hugging his ankle. Cheese knelt in the middle of the street, staring at the smoking wreck of his truck. Tears rolled down his cheeks, tracking runnels in the dirt and soot caked onto them, but he made no sound. Of the rigger Mouse and Kid Tech Eng, there was no sign. Four figures in urban camouflage lay sprawled at various points around him. None moved, not even the one whom Cinqueda had spitted with her knife; he lay still as she plucked the blade free and wiped it on his uniform.

"Who were these guys?" Andy asked, watching Markowitz wander from body to body, examining them. "Those weren't Army uniforms. The camo pattern is wrong."

"Strangers in their own land," Kit said enigmatically.

"I've got a pretty good idea." Cinqueda stooped over the man she'd killed with her knife. Her chrome fingernails flashed as she slashed at the corpse's shoulder. His uniform sleeve fell away, revealing a bare shoulder upon which was tattooed the Stars-and-Bars.

"Confed Marine Ferrets." Markowitz had the expression of someone who'd just tasted something unpleasant. "God, I hate it when I'm right, sometimes."

"We all hate it when you're right sometimes," Cinqueda

said. "If you knew the opposition's ID, you should have told me. I've got a brother in the Ferrets."

Remembering the way she'd torn into the marines, all anonymous in their helmets and uniforms, Andy was appalled. "He's not one . . ."

"Of these? No." Cinqueda turned her chrome stare on Kit. "I should have been told."

Kit looked away sheepishly. Her voice was tiny. "I would have told you if your brother was among them."

"You'll get the bill," Cinqueda said and turned her back on them.

She walked away into the night from which she'd come. No one protested or moved to stop her. Markowitz stripped another belt from a corpse and fell to examining it. SpellMan grabbed the one Markowitz dropped and looked furtively around to see if anyone was watching him belt it on under his jacket. When his eyes met Andy's, he gave a toothy grin, but didn't let go of the belt. Andy looked away. He'd looted bodies in his virtual shadowruns, but this was different. It was—he didn't know—disrespectful somehow.

"Can these guys really be Confed marines?" Andy asked. "They recognized me, and were talking about Osborne when they busted in. The marines don't work for Telestrian."

"What's to wonder?" Markowitz said without looking up from his search. "We already knew Telestrian was playing cozy with the Confeds and playing rough with us. Someone had to get these guys and their equipment across the border, and it's easier for a multinational to put transport across a border than it is for a foreign military." Markowitz tossed away the web belt whose pouches he'd been examining. "Too bad we don't have one of them left to wring the details from. We might have been better off if Cinqueda's brother *was* here."

"No," Kit said. She didn't elaborate.

Markowitz was right; there were too many unanswered questions. "How'd they know where we were?"

"You didn't watch the walls! They have eyes, they have ears, but not all of them belong to the bad guys. Lucky you!" SpellMan grinned. "They heard, I heard. They came, I came. Lucky you!"

"I understand that you followed them, but how did they know where we were?"

"The old haunts are the good haunts, but not all times are

good. The Ferrets hunted Marksman. They hunted the Marksman's old places and left their tiny techno spies behind. Too many to watch, too many. So they sit and wait, I sit and watch. They listened, hearing about your plan to broadcast. They told a suit, and the suit told them to be ready. 'Watch,' the suit said. 'Watch for Walker. If he is there, bring me his head.' When you talked, the suit told them where to find you. The Ferrets are spread all about, and their closest ran to the hunt. I whispered to the City and went where they went, but faster. I prepared. Then, much heroics. The rest, as they say, is docudrama." SpellMan preened, picking specks of dust from his filthy jacket.

"The suit was Osborne?" Andy had to know.

"No names, just a theme. Happy music. 'We're stepping out and making our place,' " SpellMan sang.

Andy's throat was dry. He knew that song. He'd sung it. *The Adventure of the Future*. "Telestrian Cyberdyne." And they'd ordered his death. To them, he had no part in the future.

"Not news," Markowitz pointed out.

Any last thoughts that Telestrian might be innocently implicated in the terrible events of the last few days were dead. He'd wanted to believe their involvement was a mistake, that they'd been duped by the Confed government. But dupes didn't offer their services so freely, and dupes didn't ask for the killing of those who'd been their own just for being involved. He'd never thought the corporation perfect, but he'd thought it was basically good, or at least committed to caring for its own. But he'd been one of its own and the corporation had sent men to summarily kill him.

A heavy truck in Army drab rumbled across the intersection a block down.

Andy felt Kit's hand on his arm. He looked down and saw her staring at where the truck had passed. "What is it?"

"Danger for your blood."

The MPs and Secret Service men fell all over themselves grabbing Tom. He didn't struggle as they grappled him, hoping they'd realize he wasn't hostile. That didn't save him from having his arms twisted painfully behind him. The jurisdictional dispute ended once he was restrained, both security teams uniting in dragging him out of the TOC.

"Halt! Let him be," Trahn ordered. "Major Rocquette, what's this all about?"

Trahn hadn't been fooled for an instant by Tom's disguise. But if he knew who Tom was, why was he willing to let him speak? It didn't matter—this was probably the only chance he'd get. "I came to speak with you, Mr. President. It's important."

Steele looked Tom over and turned to Trahn. "What's this all about, General?"

"Let's hear what he has to say, Mr. President. If it's important, the source doesn't matter much, does it?" Trahn looked at Tom with cold black eyes. "Just what is it that you have to tell the President, Major Rocquette?"

"It's a matter of national security," Tom told him. He started pouring out in detail what Andy had learned about the CAS bribes to Governor Jefferson, the connection between Telestrian and CAS, and how Confed agents had operated to eliminate the runners who'd uncovered the information. Given where he was, he felt free to point out that military intelligence had uncovered significant amounts of Confed weaponry among the Compers. He suggested that the uprising by the Comp Army could very well have been instigated by Confed activists, pointing out how the insurrection seemed to be fueling separatist sentiment in North Virginia. Although he stopped short of naming Trahn, he suggested that the UCAS military was feeding the separatist fires by the harsh response that encouraged the Compers to keep fighting. Reminding everyone of the CAS forces gathering near the Virginia-North Virginia border, he returned to the political angle. He hoped that Steele, who hadn't shown much military acumen, could at least understand the dangers arising from that quarter.

"In the light of the recent North Virginia state legislation, and the governor's statements and increasingly strong pro-independence stand, I think the evidence suggests we're not seeing representative government at work here, but rather the furtherance of personal and self-serving concerns. Whatever interests are at work here, they're edging us close to a conflict we do not need and, I hope to God, do not want. We are close to the two-hundredth anniversary of the Civil War; we don't need another."

Tom felt winded when he stopped, amazed that no one had interrupted him. Amid the buzz of conversation that followed his conclusion, Steel turned to one on his aides, a small, dark man with triple datajacks studding his temple, and said, "North Virginia is a one-term governorship, isn't it?"

"Yes, sir."

"So Jefferson is out when?"

"Election this November, sir. Inauguration of successor in January."

"So that means . . ." Steele looked thoughtful for a moment. "You know, I don't recall hearing his name coming up much among the Democrats."

"Rumor puts him out of favor with the party, sir." The aide put an odd emphasis on rumor, suggesting that he meant some other source he was unwilling to name in the present, more-or-less public company.

Steele seemed to accept the aide's statement far more readily than Tom's information. "So he won't be taking the success track following Hahn or Wilkie to Congress. Our Mr. Jefferson could very well be a hungry man."

"Or an embittered one," said a blonde aide in a trim Sarmani suit. "Or an ambitious one. I expect he'd be eligible to govern a reunited Virginia, and Virginia has always been fond of heroes as candidates. Any of these motivations could make the man amenable to blandishments from outside sources."

Steele nodded. "If what Major Rocquette alleges is true, this situation is very serious."

Thank you, Mr. President, for stating the obvious.

The President turned to Trahn. "What about our military being involved in this plot? Is it true?"

"Mr. President, I will state here and now, and at any venue you care to name, that neither myself nor my staff is in any way involved in selling any part of this country to anyone. None of us joined the military for any reason other than that we are patriots.

"Personally, I've no truck with traitors who would sell out their country, even a small part of it, Mr. President," Trahn said with conviction. "I can have troops on Governor Jefferson's doorstep in fifteen minutes, if you order it. It might be best if we had Governor Jefferson where he could answer some questions."

Was Trahn being honest, or just throwing a confederate to the wolves? The former seemed more likely. If Jefferson were to answer questions, he would surely provide the names of his co-conspirators; it was the way of traitors to want to take others down with them when they fell. But if Trahn wasn't part of the conspiracy, just what *was* his connection with Telestrian?

Trahn was still talking. "We may be overreacting, however. Major Rocquette's allegations seem to be only speculation and innuendo. He hasn't presented any hard evidence."

Everyone looked at Tom. "I had a reader with pertinent files," he said. "It was confiscated by Colonel Jordan's MPs when I was . . . detained."

"We have no reader, nor any record of a reader," Jordan said without waiting to be asked. He turned and tapped at his console. The screen changed to an arrest report: Tom's. "See for yourself, Mr. President. The records show that only a side-arm and webbing gear were confiscated from Major Rocquette when he was, as he says, detained. Oh, and of course the truck he commandeered without orders and drove here."

"I was reporting as ordered," Tom said.

"And you have given your report," Trahn said before Tom could say more. "You have given the President more than enough to think about, Major. And since he's got a lot of important decisions to make as soon as his staff corroborates your accusations, I suggest we get back to our jobs and leave him to his."

"An excellent suggestion, General," said the blonde presidential aide. "The President is indeed pressed for time."

The aide launched into orders to the presidential staff to prepare to relocate. Trahn gave his own orders and the TOC blossomed with sudden, bustling activity.

Tom realized what had been done. The issue of his detention and what lay behind it had been shunted aside. He was out of the spotlight, forgotten. But not by everyone. Jordan appeared at his side and ordered the MPs to take him to the general's van. Tom was hustled away.

Fifteen minutes later Trahn joined him. "At ease, Rocquette."

Tom most certainly wasn't, but he tried to appear so. Trahn slumped into the worn, leather-covered chair that was the one luxury appointment in the caravan-office.

"I'm disappointed in you, Major. Your impulses were good, but I'm sorry your judgment didn't match. You were misled into believing I had a part in this conspiracy. You should have checked your facts. If you'd come to me, perhaps I could have set you straight without involving those civilians. Some of the President's staff are not sympathetic to the military, and I'm afraid you've fed their paranoid fantasies about us. And you've embarrassed yourself. It didn't have to be this way. I hope you've learned something by this."

Trahn didn't mention the order to kill the prisoners. "Oh, I have, sir."

"Good. You should have known I wouldn't have been involved in any plot to weaken the Union."

But he *was* involved in other things. "I didn't really believe that of you, sir."

Trahn offered a sympathetic smile. "Misunderstandings can occur quite easily, as I am sure you would agree. We've all had our share of misunderstandings recently."

Were they coming to the matter of the illegal orders now? Tom intended to make sure they did. He was tired of misunderstandings. "Like with the prisoners?"

"By your own evidence, they were likely insurrectionists." There was controlled anger in Trahn's voice, but curiously, Tom didn't feel it was directed at him. "Whatever they were doesn't matter right now. We've got a job to do. We can overcome misunderstandings when we've got a job to do, can't we, Major?"

"Sometimes, General."

"This had better be one of those times," Trahn said in a voice that brooked no disagreement. "If you're correct about the conspiracy, this rioting is an intolerable threat to our country and it must be put down with all alacrity so that we can turn our attention to other matters. We need every soldier we can get on the streets, doing his job. So I'm sending you back out there. It will give you a chance to work off your aggressions. I'm offering you another chance, a chance to prove you're a team player. Do you want to take it?"

Tom swallowed, thinking hard. This wasn't going the way he'd expected. But the general, involved or not, had a point: if the Confed-inspired riots weren't put down, the country was in trouble. If Tom was locked up in the stockade, there wouldn't be *anything* he could do about it. "I've always considered myself a team player, sir. But I've always needed to know the score as well. I think I'm up to speed now, sir, having seen the scorecard. I want to be on the winning team, sir."

"Very good. You're going back to Furlann's team, but not in command. You'll be under her orders until this blows over. I'd rather not deal with the mess of a formal rank reduction, even a temporary one, so I don't want you making trouble for her. You understand?"

Combat in the streets would offer plenty of opportunities for Tom to be taken out of the general's hair. Tom understood all right; he understood that his death would simplify the general's problems. "Yes, sir. I understand."

Trahn rose from his seat and walked to the ramp. "Jemal, arrange transportation for Major Rocquette. He's going back to work."

>>>>>WFDC LIVE FEED
—[23:29:22/8-25-55]
REPORTER: DERRY DALE [DALE-365]
UPLINK SITE: FREDERICKSBURG, NORTH VIRGINIA

Dale: "This is Derry Dale coming to you live from the Statehouse press room in Fredericksburg, where I've just been informed that there's been another delay. As you know, Governor Jefferson scheduled an unprecedented emergency press conference this evening, but he has yet to make an appearance. Speculation is rife among those gathered here. Many think the governor will be addressing the rumor that Confederated States troops are massing on the border. But one thing everyone here agrees on is that the state press secretary's preliminary teaser about the governor making an important announcement is without a doubt true.

"I've just been promised by the Statehouse official that the governor will be arriving shortly. Wait a minute, wait a minute—I believe we have confirmation. We're going to cut now to Jane Kateway of local WFRD at the Governor's estate. [*Inset screen added*] Jane, I understand you have word the governor is on his way."

Kateway: "That's right, Derry. Just moments ago a sleek,

swing-motor Orion aircraft lifted off from the grounds of the governor's mansion. We've been told that Governor Jefferson is aboard and headed for the Statehouse. In fact, if you look out the window, you should be able to see the running lights of his aircraft approaching."

Dale: "I'll take a look. I don't see any—Wait, wait. Yes, those are running lights. The aircraft is—Ohmigod!

[*Image shift, full screen: smoke cloud in night sky, trailing to ground; fire erupts beyond treeline*]

Dale [*offscreen*]: "No, no. It couldn't be. It—it is? No. I don't believe it." [*Pause.*] "I'm told that it's the governor's aircraft. We have no word on what's happened. Stay tuned to WFDC. We'll be staying on the feed as we investigate."

[*On screen: fire spreads to the trees*]<<<<<

23

Fire skipped along Wilson Boulevard, marking the death ripping from the Consie machine gun as it hosed down the street. Tom and the others huddled in the lee of the team's command car were sheltered, but they could hear the patter of the tracer and anti-personnel rounds and the frustrated scream of the interspersed penetrator rounds as they spanged off the Ranger's armor. In close where the penetrators hadn't bled off as much of their energy, the car's armor wouldn't be enough to shrug the rounds aside. But the vehicle was better off than the grunts. Even out here, the penetrator rounds still had more than enough punch to blow through the infantry-issue torso armor Tom was wearing.

"Rocquette, you go with Hanley and take command of the second squad. Listen up. I want both of your squads to advance across the Wilson School grounds, pinning down the hostiles from the front." Captain Furlann indicated the path she'd chosen on the mapboard. "I want you moving on them hard and keeping them very busy."

"The open approach is suicide," Tom told Furlann. He hadn't had time to assess the situation, but at first glance it looked really bad. It wasn't in his long-term interests to talk back to her; but if he didn't, he might not have any long-term interests.

"He's right," Hanley agreed. "Ground's too open. Most of this bunch are blue berets, and they shoot straight. The Consies have been trouble every time we've run into them, and those others didn't have any heavy stuff."

Furlann wasn't buying. "All this bunch has is that machine gun and enough charms to keep me from doing more than annoy them. If they had any *really* heavy stuff, they'd be punching their way out instead of letting us bottle them up."

Hanley looked down at the ground. "We're still too short to assault them. We saved Captain Black's butt, maybe he'd like to return the favor."

"Not an option," Furlann said. "The armor's still busy on the other side of the river. Besides, we're the ones in the butt-saving business. That's what being a fire brigade is all about. That's why we're here in Rosslyn dealing with this particular knot of resistance. We're plugging a hole that command wants plugged. You think we'd be here if they had a better option? You got any *real* ideas, Mister, I want to hear them."

Furlann snapped off the mapboard, forestalling Tom's effort to find another option. "We haven't got time to fool around," she said, picking up and slinging the captured Steyr autorifle she'd adopted to add to her image as a combat commander. "Get your people moving. Fischer's bringing up drones from the Fort Myer perimeter to get them in on the hostiles' left flank and he's only got time for a couple of passes. If the Consies aren't pinned, his attack won't do half the job we need."

The drones should have been making the frontal attack. Tom said as much.

"You got a problem with your orders, Mister?" Furlann asked.

He did, but he understood what she was asking. Her orders were not illegal, just stupid. If he failed to make a good attempt to follow them, he could be found guilty of refusing to obey an order, dereliction, and a few other choice things.

"Well?"

"We'll go forward," he told her. But he'd be looking all the way for some out.

"Move," Furlann snapped.

They moved. Out of earshot of Furlann, he and Hanley had a chat. It had been a long time since Tom had been on the

ground, so he ceded tactical control to the groundpounder—
after making it clear they ought to take a more circuitous
route to the target. Hanley agreed; he had no more interest
than Tom did in losing people unnecessarily. As they moved
toward their jumping-off point, Tom discovered that it really
had been a long time. He wasn't used to the weight of the
combat armor and lagged behind. The squaddies didn't wait
for him when Hanley called for a sprint.

Tom hustled after them, losing ground as the troops cut
through the residential blocks and worked their way toward
the Key Street approach that would shield them from the
Consie fire for most of the route. Then his foot caught
against something, nearly causing him to stumble. No, not
against—something had grabbed his ankle. He looked down.
Nothing there. The squad was still moving forward, oblivious to his delay and making their best time. They had their
own butts to worry about.

He started after them. Something snatched at his arm, half
spinning him around. It felt like a hand, but there was no
one there. Another invisible hand wrenched his weapon
away.

A long list of unpleasant possibilities flashed through his
brain. One thing was certain, this wasn't anything he was
equipped to fight.

He tried to back away. Hard grips closed on his arms,
forcing him to stand still. It might have been a troll holding
him, if trolls were invisible. He wasn't going anywhere. His
unseen captor tugged him around.

Furlann walked down the street toward him, her long hair
drifting in the eddies of thaumaturgic power that crackled
and eddied around her.

"The manual calls the spell Magic Fingers or some such
nonsense, and treats it quite trivially," she said, "but as with
most spells, a strong will can improve the physical manifestation quite dramatically. I've a strong grip, wouldn't you
say?"

She didn't give him a chance to answer. "Most users feel
themselves confined by the spell, finding their effects constrained to a double-handed manipulation. Never having
much like for constraints, I've done a little work. Just tinkering, but effective."

The captured Steyr autorifle unslung itself from her shoulder and moved to float in the air before Tom's face, muzzle

directed between his eyes. "I find that a third hand improves the effectiveness of the spell quite a bit more than half. What do you think?"

He thought she was playing with him, enjoying having him at her mercy, of which there was none. "Do it and be done, bitch," he told her.

"Don't take it personally, Rocquette. This is bigger than you know. Like a good set of ritual protections, it's all layers on layers, but you messed where you shouldn't have. I thought you were smarter than that."

She hadn't said it yet, but he was sure she was going to kill him. Tom had suspected that Trahn had sent him out here to get himself killed honorably, but apparently the general didn't trust Tom to do the job right. He'd enlisted Furlann's aid.

Furtive motion in the shadows behind Furlann caught his eye. Help, or more trouble? There were people slipping from house to house, much as the troops had done, but by their silhouettes, they weren't soldiers. Tom's helmet augmentation opened the shadows for him, revealing Andy, Markowitz, and Kit running toward him and Furlann. His mind put the three of them into nineteenth-century horse cavalry uniforms. As they drew near, they slowed, making their approach more stealthy. Suddenly Tom was not so anxious for Furlann to get on with things.

"You can't get away with this," he stalled. If he could keep her talking . . .

"Of course I can. Invisible hands leave invisible fingerprints, and there won't be anyone looking for them around here anyway. Not that it matters. You'll be just another casualty on a long list. Nobody will think twice about finding you shot with a Confed weapon. Why, in some quarters, it may even confirm your status as a patriot."

"So I'm just going to be another unfortunate soldier who got killed in the line of duty."

"I'd have thought you'd appreciate such an epitaph."

"As epitaphs go, it's not bad, but I'd rather go without one for a while."

Furlann chuckled. "No doubt you expect your friends to arrange that. Oh yes, I know they've arrived."

The newcomers abandoned stealth at her comment. Markowitz took up a firing stance and leveled his weapon at her.

"Let him go," he ordered. "Or you're history."

"Let him go?" Furlann glanced casually over her shoulder. "I don't think so."

"She's dangerous, Harry," Kit said.

"Very," Furlann agreed.

"Got a cure for that," Markowitz said, He fired his weapon. He missed; he fired again. And missed again. "What the frag?"

"She's distorting our vision," Kit said. "I can't seem to get a grip on her spell."

"Tom's dead if you don't," Andy said, voicing Tom's own conclusion.

"You're meddling where you don't belong again, Marksman." Furlann gestured at him. With a curse, he flung his pistol away. It landed with a clatter, began to glow red, and exploded as the ammo cooked off. Furlann laughed. "You won't find me as easy to escape as that Yellowjacket."

"Furlann!"

Tom was tugged around as Furlann shifted to face the new voice. The Steyr went too, its muzzle and unblinking eye staring at him.

The new speaker was Cinqueda, the street samurai. Once again she'd appeared out of nowhere. She stood half crouched, one hand extended before her, the other cocked back and holding a heavy-bladed knife ready to throw. Such a weapon wouldn't throw worth spit for an ordinary person, but he didn't doubt that the augmented Cinqueda had the strength for it.

"Hoi, Cinq. How's the biz?" Furlann didn't sound like she felt threatened at all.

"Fine, no thanks to you," Cinqueda replied. "Don't make this go the hard way."

Cinqueda's knife was ready to throw. Tom had seen the street samurai move and knew that Furlann's best speed-up spell couldn't match the samurai's jacked-up reflexes. Cinqueda could launch her strike before the mage could do a thing. But would the samurai's optics compensate for the displacer spell that had foiled Markowitz? Furlann didn't seem to think so, because she didn't release her hold on Tom. The gun still hovered before his face.

"You wouldn't do it, Cinq," Furlann said. "We had too fine a time together. You remember, don't you? I know I do."

Cinqueda didn't move, not even a muscle twitch. "I remember that you always bet the wrong horse. Think hard on this one, Lanny. I never miss at this range. It's your choice."

"It's true I've never seen you miss, but then you never threw against my displacer."

"Is it as good as Black Mary Thomas's displacer?"

"Almost." Furlann said it with pride. Black Mary Thomas must have been a hellacious mage.

"Too bad for you, Lanny," Cinqueda said emotionlessly. "Black Mary's wasn't good enough."

Tom felt a tremor in the invisible hands that gripped him.

"You're bluffing," Furlann said.

Cinqueda's expression didn't waver. "Like I said, your choice."

The rifle pointed at Tom *did* waver. It quivered, as the trigger slowly drew back. Tom lost interest in the confrontation between the samurai and the mage. The weapon's dark, lidless eye became all-absorbing.

He knew he wasn't fast enough to dodge a bullet, but he couldn't just stand still. At the very least he could go down fighting. He threw himself against the invisible, restraining hands, fully expecting it to be the last thing he did.

Metal clanked against hardened plastic. The echoes of that sound were swallowed in the coughing burp from the Steyr. Irate bees buzzed him. Fire burned across his shoulder. A hot needle pierced his ear. Something the size of a Clydesdale kicked his forehead, shattering his vision into darkness. He fell.

Andy had been afraid Furlann had taken over Cinqueda's actions when he saw the street samurai throw her knife at Tom. Kit had said that the Army mage was dangerous.

But Cinqueda had thrown, not at Tom, but at the rifle menacing him. Though the samurai's throw was good, her blade failed to knock the muzzle far enough out of line. When Furlann triggered the rifle, the burst of slugs caught Tom. He went down in a splatter of blood and a spray of plastic shards from his shattered helmet.

Cinqueda had Furlann by the throat before Tom's body hit the ground.

"We need her to talk," Markowitz shouted.

Andy thought he needn't have bothered. If Cinqueda had

intended to kill the mage, Furlann would have been dead before Markowitz got his words out.

It was Tom they needed to worry about. Kit ran with Andy to see if there was anything to be done for his brother. Despite the blood all over his hair and face, Tom still breathed.

"The helmet saved his life," Kit said. "The other wounds are superficial."

She searched through Tom's belt pouches until she found a first aid kit. "Hold his head," she said, and went to work cleaning and bandaging Tom's wounds. She sang softly, too softly for him to catch the words. Andy hoped he was hearing a healing spell; Tom looked terrible. Feeling a little queasy at all the blood, he looked elsewhere.

Markowitz had taken Furlann's pistol from her and was holding it trained on the mage while Cinqueda tied her hands behind her back. Cinq was making sure to restrict Furlann's fingers as well as her wrists. That done, she gagged Furlann. Andy guessed that the samurai had some experience in securing mages. It was supposed to be impossible for a mage to cast a spell without being able to speak or make hand gestures. Andy hoped it was true.

When Cinqueda came near to retrieve her knife, Andy asked, "Why'd you come back?"

"I never left. Job wasn't done."

"You let us think you had," Kit said, looking up from her work on bandaging Tom.

"Served you right. You should have told me about the Ferrets. I *should* have left, though." Her chromed eyes tracked to Furlann. "It would have saved me some more . . . trouble."

"I'm glad you didn't," Tom said weakly. "This time I *did* need the rescue. Thanks."

"Make your thank-yous in negotiable credit and I'll believe you're sincere," Cinqueda told him.

"Don't try to sound so mercenary," Kit said. "It doesn't become you."

"I am a mercenary. Don't forget it. I won't when I send you your bill." Cinqueda looked away. "Vehicle approaching."

A few seconds later Andy heard it too.

"It's a Ranger," Tom said. He must have recognized the

engine noise. "Must be the task force command car. Help me up."

As the Ranger armored car bulled through the fence surrounding the back yard they had all violated, its turreted chain gun swiveled to point at them. A helmeted soldier watched them from the turret. Andy had no doubt the man's finger was on the trigger. With Furlann tied and gagged, and Tom all bloody, the little group probably didn't look friendly to the soldier.

"Jackson," Tom called out, waving weakly.

"Major?" The soldier sounded a little surprised. "What's going on?"

"Call back Hanley and his men."

Jackson's eyes wavered between Tom and Furlann till Tom told him what Furlann had tried to do. Jackson didn't like what he heard and made no effort to hide it.

"I've got a micro-grenade we could feed her," Jackson called out.

"Forget her for now," Tom told him. "Stop Hanley and the troops before they kill themselves following her stupid orders."

The sergeant disappeared inside the Ranger. A minute later, the command car's rear ramp dropped open. Jackson emerged with word that he'd gotten to Hanley in time.

"Why'd she do it, Major?" Jackson asked.

"Good question, Jackson. Just one of many." He turned to Furlann. "If you're willing to talk, we can take the gag off."

"But one word of a spell and you get popped," Markowitz added.

Furlann nodded understanding. As soon as the gag came off, she croaked a plea for water, complaining of the taste in her mouth. Andy had a bad taste in his mouth too, but his was figurative and had a lot to do with her.

"You've got a lot to tell us," Tom said to her.

"Maybe," Furlann said. "I'd like to be assured of certain considerations if I do."

"You're already getting more than you deserve," Andy said.

"Kid's right," Markowitz agreed. "You're alive. Talk if you want to stay that way."

"You've all called me a 'murderer.' You'll be one as well if you carry out your threat, Marksman." Furlann smirked at him. "Not your style."

"Nobody will think twice about finding you shot with a Confed weapon," Tom said.

Furlann's eyes snapped to him and her demeanor lost a little of its arrogance.

"Why?" Tom asked.

Furlann sighed. "Rocquette, you're a lot like the mess you tried to lay before the President. Too much trouble. Too many connections. Too many loose ends. Your problem with Lessem was bad enough, but all the other stuff just—well, let's just say that circumstances made it very expedient for you to be put out of the way. Disappearing would do as well. Think about it. You could save yourself a lot of trouble. Drek, you might just plain *save* yourself if you decide to go that route."

"You following Trahn's direct orders, or did the word go through Jordan?" Markowitz asked.

Furlann glowered at him silently.

Jackson looked near to boiling over. "That stuff the news pirate reported is true then! The fragging brass are in it with the Confeds. Trahn, too. God, who'd have thought it? Did that fragging Confed sympathizer hand you the Steyr himself? Tell you to have a good hunt? I ought to—"

"Easy, Sergeant," Tom said warningly, and Jackson subsided.

Furlann looked toward the fallen Steyr autorifle.

"Don't try it," Kit warned.

"Put it in the fridge, sister. All I was going to do was say, take a look at it. It's real Confed issue, and we really did take it from the Consies. Some of them are Ferrets, you know. Your Confed connection is real, and it's a serious problem that you're not helping. But it don't link this mess to Trahn. The Army's not taking the rap on that one."

"Don't think we can make the blame stick?" Andy asked.

"I know you can't, because neither Trahn nor anyone connected to him has got squat to do with the Confeds," Furlann said. "Except that we've been had, like the rest of the rubes. So you want to make trouble? Go ahead. Help the Confeds."

Markowitz wasn't convinced. "Why should we believe you?"

"Don't. I don't give drek if you do." Furlann brightened a little. "On the other hand, go ahead and try to blame Trahn and the Army. Do it and you'll be shown so wrong that nobody will believe you about anything else. Yeah, go ahead. I like the strategy."

"If Trahn's not involved, why was he colluding with Osborne?" Tom asked.

Furlann snorted. "I told him from the get-go that the weedeater was a double-dealing bastard, but he thought he had enough juice to keep Osborne toeing the line. Looked chill for a while. It'd still *look* good if you hadn't blown open Telestrian's hook-up with the Confeds. *Some* good you did, though hearing it must have slotted off the general to hell and gone. Double-dealing weedeater!"

"You didn't answer my question," Tom said.

"You *are* determined to frag it up, aren't you? Oh the hell with it! Everything's falling apart anyway." Furlann's tone lost its belligerent edge. "Let's talk protection."

"For *you*?" Markowitz asked incredulously.

"You want me to talk. I want protection. It's a simple equation. Even simple enough for you, Marksman."

"You want to live, you talk," he shot back. "A simpler equation. Even simple enough for you, Furlann."

She ignored him and looked at Tom. "Deal or no?"

"Talk first," Tom told her. "We'll see."

"Drek, it's not like you've got authority to do anything useful anyway." She looked down at the ground. She seemed finished with talking.

"You might want to change your bet, Lanny," Cinqueda said.

After a moment, Furlann said softly, "Maybe I do."

She looked up and her eyes swept across all of them, but ended on Tom. "You're an honest guy, Rocquette. You'll deal fair."

"Fairer than you have," Andy said.

Tom looked at Andy with a funny expression on his face, but he schooled it before turning back to Furlann. "Tell us what Trahn's got going."

Furlann blew out an explosive sigh. "Okay. Trahn's got an agenda, but it's got nothing to do with the Confeds, unless it's to kick their butts a few years down the line. He's not happy with the way the politicos have gutted the military. He's right to feel that way, of course, but he sees things as somewhat worse than they are; he thinks the politicos have brought us to the brink of destruction by internal anarchy and external enemies, and he's been planning for years to do something about it.

"Lately, he's been looking for a demonstration. When the Compers came to town and Steele didn't do a damn thing, Trahn thought he saw an opportunity. Having it come up in his own military district made him very happy. Back in July he had Osborne get the hold put on the riot-control supplies, and made sure that what was in inventory got used up or surplused. He knew that sooner or later the pot would boil over. When the situation in Chicago blew up, he knew the time had come. He had Jemal stoke up the fire a little by putting agents among the Compers to encourage them to violence. You see, he figured that once things got out of hand, which he was sure they would, he would resolve the situation with prompt action by the Army."

"Using the proper riot gear would have made the action quicker and cleaner," Tom said.

"But that wouldn't let him show that the Army had been slighted." Furlann shrugged. "Would have left a lot of the metagene junk alive, too. The general's a two-for-one kind of guy when he can get things to work out right."

"So he declared open season on orks and other metahumans," Markowitz suggested amicably. "To clean out the trash, as it were."

"That's right," Furlann said. Then she noticed the chill in the group watching her. "Hey, what's the problem? We're all humans here. We can't let the orks and the other metagene drek keep fouling the gene pool, can we?"

Fouling the gene pool. Orks. Metagene drek. Andy's father had been an ork. A Changed ork rather than a born one, but an ork nevertheless. So if there were ork genes, Andy had them too. How long before people like Furlann and Trahn decided that just having genes made you metatrash, no matter what you looked like?

"You're talking genocide," he said.

"Always a popular hobby with fascists," Markowitz said. "Tell me, Furlann, ever think that magical ability was metagenetic?"

"That's different."

Markowitz smiled an evil smile. "You sure your chummer Trahn feels that way? The Jews weren't the only ones providing fuel for the Nazi furnaces."

Andy liked the disquieted expression those words brought to Furlann's face.

Tom wasn't distracted by the race angle. "Why now? Considering what's happening in Chicago, the country has enough trouble."

"Considering what's happening in Chicago, it was the perfect time," Furlann said. "Trahn has got a thing for what he calls 'the great days, when it meant something to be a soldier in this country.' With most of the armed forces busy in Chicago, we're running short-handed everywhere. Trahn's always said that the UCAS military, as currently constituted, is insufficient for the country's needs. Pulling troops from the border to deal with the riots went a long way to demonstrating his point."

Andy thought such a view ignored an important point. "He thought he could pull troops from the border even with North Virginia talking secession?"

"All that secessionist drek looked like a lot of hot air and politico nonsense," Furlann said. "Nobody really thought they'd go through with it. They couldn't make the shift without Confed support, and nobody thought they really had any support from Atlanta." Furlann shrugged. "Can't be right about everything."

Tom shook his head sadly. "Trahn was willing to bet the nation's peace just to improve the lot of the UCAS military?"

Furlann replied, "Hey, the Army's his life. You ought to understand that."

"I understand where he came from—it's where he's headed that I have the problems with," Tom said.

"We've got to get the word out," Markowitz said.

"Your broadcast didn't work," Tom pointed out.

"Maybe we sent the wrong message to the wrong people," Andy said. "The Ranger's got MilNet connections, right?"

"Yeah," Tom said. "A Fuchi 5000 clone, but it's only configured for standard access. Any general posting will run through headquarters and censors."

"Good enough. With that deck and a few codes, I ought to be able to cut us in wherever we want to go. We can dump everything we've found out on MilNet. If everyone else thinks like Sergeant Jackson, we can get the action against the Compers shut down within the hour."

"Nobody's going to like hearing about this," Jackson agreed.

Tom showed Andy where to jack in and arranged a dump on the Ranger TCV's capabilities. It only took Andy a moment to find the unit's standard net-access codes. Everyone crowded into the command car to watch him work. He set up a slaved transmit using the Ranger's radio to run simultaneously with his excursion into the MilNet. Working with the whole group watching was like being on display; but as soon as he'd done what was needed to let them follow along, he forgot about the watchers. He whirled through the electron sky, wearing a shape that was government issue, drab and plain, but he felt like Paul Revere giving the alarm to Concord and Lexington, or maybe Cary Justus waking the Houston garrison before the Azzie troops stormed the perimeter. It was a hero's turn he was doing, spreading the word.

Taking what Furlann had told them and running with it, Andy informed the soldiers about Trahn's fabricated emergency with the Compers and his intention to make the confrontation as bloody as possible simply as a means to a political end. He didn't say a lot about the Confed threat—thinking that a straightforward connective chain would work better to convince the people that Trahn was leading them the wrong way—but he did emphasize the danger of leaving the border unguarded while troops battled the Compers. He had no compunction about telling every node he met about the illegal orders Tom had received and the attempted murder that had been his reward for trying to do his duty and refusing to go along—it was only because Tom requested it that he didn't mention Furlann by name, simply referring to her as the "failed assassin" who revealed much of the plot.

Something exploded overhead, blasting Andy back to meat awareness. The shock wave rocked the command car.

Jackson dropped back into the cabin from his turret seat. "Cut it off! Cut off the broadcast! We just had a beam rider dumped on us. Somebody's getting desperate."

Andy killed the transmitter. *Somebody* clearly had not liked what they had to say.

"Driver, roll us out of here," Tom ordered.

Andy was happy to hear that order. He'd played enough games of *Gulf Victories* to know what happened to electronic sources that broadcast for too long. They would catch a missile that could track the emissions to their source, a beam rider like the one the sergeant had just destroyed with the Ranger's chain gun. Even with the computer aid, Jackson had gotten lucky. They'd all gotten lucky. Anti-missile fire didn't have high kill probabilities; most likely the sergeant wouldn't hit the next one.

The receiver, however, wouldn't attract attention. Andy listened to what was on the air. He didn't like what he heard.

"Hey, MilNet source is calling us Confed infiltrators. They're saying that everything we put out is disinformation. That it's all spurious. They're telling everybody to ignore us."

"What did you expect?" Furlann asked.

"What kind of response are they getting?" Tom asked.

"A lot of confirms," Andy said dejectedly. He'd hoped they'd get at least some Army units to believe and stop the unnecessary slaughter. Clearly, he'd been too optimistic. "We've got to try something else."

"This isn't something we can stop in the streets," Markowitz said. "It would be like fighting the Hydra. Too many heads, and they all keep growing back."

"But there's one head that can't grow back," Tom said grimly.

>>>>>NEWSNET FEED COVERA − \|****STATIC****
− [23:53:50/8-25-55]

LIVE IEYE "ON YOU" BROADCAST

"We are the watchers, you loyal and true believers. On the beat, on the spot, on the money!

"This is it, chummers, your eyes and jacks are getting the dump live. That greasy pall of smoke is all that's left of ITRU Independent News. It was a hard military strike. No doubt about it. Sources at the government's Riot Command Center are denying any military involvement in the attack. Chiptruth, they say.

[*Scene: Burning broadcast truck; ITRU logo melting in the blazing fire*]

"Chiptruth? Not fragging likely!

"You want chiptruth? We ain't the guv'mint. We ain't the Man. We ain't the liars. We'll give you chiptruth. Just open them peepers. See the truth burning before your eyes.

"Now listen to what TRU was saying before . . ."<<<<<

>>>>>MILNET: BELVOIR COMMAND CENTER FEED
BROADBAND DISTRIBUTION: ALL NODES

Infiltrators have captured an Army access system and penetrated the MilNet. Deckers are responding. Stand by for transmission of necessary lockout codes to cancel transmissions from compromised stations. Ignore all transmissions from these sources. They are false.
—Col. J. Jordan, Belvoir Intel
    AuthConfCode 2874-876-25540-7676587-D9B23JJ<<<<<

>>>>>NEWSBLIPS FEED
    —[23:59:50/8-25-55]
ACCESS CHARGE APPLIED

Welcome to NEWSBlips . . .
    BLIP
Aircraft shot from sky. North Virginia Governor's presence on doomed aircraft unconfirmed.
    BLIP
President leaves for Chicago Crisis conference at Camp David. "The situation requires it," says President Steele of midnight flight.<<<<<

24

Tom directed the command car to "a less prominent position," then he and Sergeant Jackson collected the driver and disembarked. "Keep it tight" was his parting remark. Markowitz closed the ramp behind them.

"He's abandoning you," Furlann said almost as soon as they were gone.

"Nobody asked you," Markowitz said.

"Maybe someone should have. You needn't all go down with him. I can—"

"Shut up!" Markowitz ordered.

He ensured compliance by gagging Furlann again, more effectively than Cinqueda had. He used a mage muzzle he'd gotten from one of the Ranger's storage lockers. The muzzle was a complicated bag thing with lots of straps, and a flat plate that Markowitz forced into Furlann's mouth. She stared death at him until he tugged the bag over her head and cut off her vision. The only thing left to be seen of her face was her nose, poking through a hole in the hood—so she wouldn't suffocate, Andy supposed.

When Markowitz pulled out the mage muzzle, Cinqueda moved up into the command car's turret. "I'll keep watch," she said. Given that she'd apparently had some sort of relationship with Furlann in the past, Andy wondered if *not watching* was more what she had in mind.

Andy was a little miffed that she'd preempted the turret slot. He'd been thinking about crawling up there himself, to watch for Tom's return. Not that he doubted Tom would return. It was just that . . .

He needn't have worried. Within ten minutes, Cinqueda dropped back into the cabin and opened the ramp. Tom and the car's crew were back, and they'd brought an infantry lieutenant with them. Outside Andy could see more soldiers starting to board a handful of trucks that had shown up. The Ranger's driver squirmed past him on his way through the cabin and into his compartment. In seconds he had the command car under way.

"This is Hanley. He and his troops are okay," Tom said by

way of introduction. He made no effort to tell Hanley who they were. He did take note of the muzzled Furlann. "She try something?"

"Got tired of looking at her face," Markowitz said.

"She tried to convince us you weren't coming back," Andy said.

"Viper," opined Sergeant Jackson. "She's everything the major told you and more, Lieutenant."

Hanley looked to Tom. "These people part of your plan, Major?"

"Good question," Markowitz said. "Just what *is* your plan, Rocquette?"

"I'm going to do what I should have done before, and drag Trahn out into the open. His ends-over-means approach has gone too far."

"This wouldn't be personal, would it?" Markowitz asked.

"Damn straight." A who-the-hell-are-you-to-ask expression flashed across Tom's face. He chased it away with a shrug. "But it's more than that. If we can get *his* agenda shut down, maybe we can get serious about dealing with the Confeds before the country starts burning at both ends."

"Here," Cinqueda said, offering Tom a chip-holder. "You might need this."

"What is it?" he asked.

"A read-only, tamper-striped recording of Furlann's song," Cinqueda said. "In case she decides to change her tune later."

Tom took it and offered it to Hanley, who took it in turn, squeezed past Markowitz to seat himself at a console, and started to review the recording.

Andy could understand why Hanley would want to see the recording and confirm whatever Tom had told him. They had a dragon by the tail here; convincing yourself that you were doing right was important. Andy was convinced that Tom was doing what needed to be done, but somehow walking into the dragon's lair didn't seem like the right solution. "I still think we could have convinced a lot of people if we'd been able to finish getting the word out. That missile they tossed at us showed somebody else thought so, too."

"Nobody wants to take a chance on another missile," Markowitz said.

Andy wasn't sure that Markowitz was speaking for everyone, but no one in the command car contradicted him. Andy still thought they might take another chance at cutting into MilNet or find another independent news pirate or do *something* other than walk into the dragon's den, but no one seemed interested in his ideas.

"How are you planning to get past base security?" Markowitz asked Tom.

"I'll figure something out. We'll fight our way in if we have to. You don't have to worry. We'll drop you off well before that's a problem."

"No you don't. I've got some scores of my own to settle," Markowitz said.

"You'll need magical support," Kit added. "Illusion opens many gates that force cannot breach."

"And I've got a lot of the evidence," Andy said, tapping his datajack. If Kit was ready to go in, *he* wasn't going to be left out.

The closest anyone came to counting him- or herself out was Cinqueda. "I'm in, too, if I get an extra bump. Considering that we're way beyond what I agreed to. We're looking at an extra—"

"Not a dime," Markowitz said.

"Harry," Kit said softly. "We may need her help, and there won't be time to call her."

Markowitz looked pained. "Okay, okay. Extra for extra, mercenary extortionist."

Cinqueda smiled.

"When it's over," Markowitz added.

While they quibbled, Andy had been thinking over the situation. "Tom, what if we send out your confrontation with Trahn live? If he doesn't know he's on the air, he might say things he ought not. He won't be able to deny anything he says if there are a gazillion witnesses."

"Good in theory," Tom said. "How are you planning to do it?"

Andy was pleased Tom assumed he'd been thinking ahead. He had, and was eager to prove it. "This is a Ranger Tactical Command Vehicle for a Special Resources unit, right? So it's outfitted as a back-up control center for drone warfare. That means lots of transmitters, receivers, and circuits, all operating through an interface that has rigger access circuitry. There ought to be a ton of spares to service the drones as well."

"She only carries a quarter-ton," Sergeant Jackson said.

"I was speaking figuratively." Andy got his brain back on track. "I know rigs inside out, and I can patch together a system to let us secretly remote-view anything you can see. Video will be a lot more convincing than a simple audio feed."

"You're right about the video, but it won't work," Markowitz said. "Trahn can't help noticing if Rocquette's lugging a drone's camera. Those lenses aren't micro-sized."

"Cinqueda's got one that will work." Andy had watched her use it in the ITRU truck. He hoped she wouldn't mind him volunteering it.

"Resolution's low," she said, but that was the only objection she raised.

"So we'll run an enhancer program on the datastream." It was a trivial problem, under the circumstances. "We won't be doing aerial recon work. It'll be good enough. Once we get the signal, well, we've got broadcast equipment, right?"

"There's still the same problem with the signal out," Markowitz said. "There are more beam riders where the first one came from. They sent one, they won't hesitate to do it again."

Andy had that figured, too. The whole plan was risky in other ways, but not on that score. "Trahn's not crazy enough to have his own headquarters bombed, is he?"

"Probably," Markowitz said.

"Don't be ridiculous," Tom said. "Why, Andy?"

"I figure we'll be there in his headquarters anyway, so why not use his equipment? Serve him right."

"How are you planning to get access?" Tom asked.

Clearly he wasn't going to let a detail slip by unexamined. Andy was impressed. He'd known Tom was smart, but he hadn't realized he was so detail-oriented. Unfortunately, Tom had spotted a weak point in Andy's scheme. "Well, we still have the unit's codes to get us into MilNet."

"They'll lock out those codes. Probably did it already," Tom said.

That was what Andy had feared. "So I'll go around them. I've had access and seen the protection scheme. I know what I'm doing." Andy hoped he wasn't blowing smoke.

"Get to work on it. If you can convince me you can do the tech, we'll try it. Otherwise . . ." Tom didn't offer an alternative, but the clouded expression on his face said he'd thought of several and didn't like any of them. "Let's just hope your scheme's viable."

Andy got to work. It wasn't easy in the moving command car, but he managed. The chips running Cinqueda's pickup were designed for direct, hard-wired feed, but Andy was able to bypass them and link the optical circuits into a transmitter array, at the cost of some autofocus capacity. It was really short-range, but he was able to get it working by adding a booster transmitter to catch, amplify, and pass on what the pickup picked up. That was good; it meant Tom wouldn't have to trail any betraying wires. But it also meant somebody would have to be nearby with the booster, and somebody else would have to ride herd on the focus. His test showed that the system worked.

"We're ready," Andy announced, hoping he was right.

"Good," Tom said. "That's the Fort Belvoir gate ahead."

Tom remained aboard the Ranger, standing in the commander's hatch while Hanley talked with the guards at the base's gate and presented their "orders." Supposedly Kit was doing something to magically disguise Tom, but they'd all agreed not to rely on her spell. Kit's strength was stretched blurring the unit patches of Hanley and his men just in case word had gotten out that Task Force Furlann, now once again Task Force Rocquette, had gone rogue. Kit's illusions didn't stretch to the runners and the captive mage hiding in the cabin, so there was added incentive for Tom to stay put. He tried to look serene and above it all, while hoping his rank pips would sufficiently intimidate the squaddies at the gate that they wouldn't dare look inside the command car.

Returning from the gatehouse with a smile on his face, Hanley climbed aboard the Ranger. He tossed the chipholder with their "orders" to Tom. "The kid's gimmick worked. Computer says we're supposed to be here."

Andy's voice drifted up from within. Obviously he'd been listening. "I told you it would be fine. All it took was—"

"Spare us," Markowitz said, cutting him off.

Task Force Rocquette rolled through the gate.

There were few troops on base; Belvoir's standard complement, and the others called in for the emergency, were busy in the heart of the city. The base was relying on the gate guards, the perimeter network of rigger-controlled sensors and defense drones, and a single reaction company of

Jordan's MPs for defense. By coming through the gate, they had crossed the defended perimeter. Tom knew where the re-action force was bivouacked and selected a route to avoid them as his Ranger and the trucks carrying Hanley's men rumbled toward the Tactical Operations Center. Only the immediate defenses of the TOC remained to be overcome.

As per current doctrine, the Center had been sited outside rather than inside a building. The advantages of a hardened site were traded for less obvious ones: a more mobile mindset, easier dispersal to take advantage of that mindset, and better accommodations to the TOC's magical defenses, not the least of which was the elimination of the static-like blocks to astral lines of sight produced by buildings. Being outside didn't mean the TOC was undefended. Far from it.

The base itself was the first line of defense—already breached by TF Rocquette; Andy's technomancy with their "orders" made them acceptable to the TOC's computerized defenses. Magical wardings were the second line. The basic wards were simple and configured to sound the alert should anyone other than a soldier approach, which meant they would detect Andy and the other runners. They had their way through that barrier as well.

Furlann, the architect of the magical defenses, had been on the streets when Tom last confronted Trahn; she'd not had a chance to rekey the magical defenses. As the former Special Resources commander, Tom knew the disarm codes to lower most of them. He used those codes to open the way for his people. Though he couldn't turn them off, he knew about the remaining, more sophisticated magical traps. He armed Kit with that knowledge, and she proved more than capable of neutralizing them. The third and last line of the TOC's defenses was people; sentries and the Center's staff itself. They were soldiers all. It was the part that worried Tom the most.

The driver halted the Ranger. Tom checked his console. This was the designated stop. Why was he fretting? Their move against the TOC was all going very smoothly. And why shouldn't it? Who would think they'd be crazy enough to try something like this?

Tom gathered everyone around as they disembarked the vehicles. He went over the plan, ending with, "I want to be sure everyone understands that we go easy in there. Most of the troops in the TOC probably don't know what we know about Trahn and his scheme. The troops and desk jockeys aren't the enemy. They're just doing their jobs. Minimal rough stuff. Right?"

Nods and "Yessirs," from all around.

"All right. Let's get on with it. Hanley, give the sweep squad a two-minute lead, then start moving people to their jump-off points."

Tom led Sergeant Jackson, Kit, and a squad of Hanley's troopers. Under cover of a silence spell from Kit, they moved like ghosts through the woods ringing the Center. The first sentry never heard them coming. When he realized he had a dozen weapons pointed at him, he surrendered his weapon. Jackson bound the man's hands and sent him back to be detained at the trucks. The next sentry tried to shout an alarm, but his voice, just like every other sound he made, was swallowed by Kit's spell. Jackson and one of the troopers clubbed him down. None of the other sentries gave them any trouble.

When Tom and the squad had completed the circuit, the infantrymen following them were spread out in a circle surrounding the clearing in which the TOC had been set up. It lay just beyond the edge of the trees. Tom realized he was looking at it from the place where Trahn had met with Osborne; he could just see the console where he'd been working.

The vans, command cars, and trailers of the TOC's outer perimeter were parked face out, ready for instant departure. Or they would have been, had the state of readiness been higher. None of the vehicles had their engines running and all the driver's compartments that Tom could see were closed and empty. Camouflage nets and thin shock-fiber mesh were strung to limit the number of passageways into the center of the circle. During his circuit, Tom had seen that all but one entrance had been closed up. A reaction to his previous appearance? It didn't matter. For their purpose, this arrangement was actually better.

Tom told Kit to initiate the wider area silence spell under cover of which they would approach. Leaving Cinqueda behind to guard the little Asian mage, Tom passed the signal to advance. They had to move quickly to reach the TOC before the workers in the center realized something was amiss.

Tom, Hanley, and Jackson led Furlann toward the entrance, weapons ready but held with muzzles skyward as if guarding a prisoner. As Tom had anticipated, the sight of a mage-muzzled woman wearing a Thaumaturgic Corps coat riveted the guards' attention. The Military Policemen failed to see Hanley's men closing in around the perimeter.

At three meters from the entrance, Tom dropped the pretense and pointed his weapon at the guards. Hanley and Jackson did likewise. There were six guards and only the three of them, but their weapons were aimed and the guards' were not. Jordan's white-gloves weren't stupid, and none of them wanted to be the first to die. They dropped their weapons and raised their hands. Tom could see that they were disappointed when there was no clatter from the falling weapons. Motioning the MPs aside, Tom moved to the perimeter control box and deactivated the shock nets. He pointed his weapon at the sky, the signal for Kit to drop the spell. It had done its work; they'd reached the TOC without an alarm.

Markowitz and Andy raced across the open space as Tom, flanked by Hanley and Jackson, entered the center. A few techs looked up in shock at the sight of men with leveled weapons, but most remained unaware for the moment—jacked-in techs didn't notice much that happened around them. For the moment, those living in the Matrix could be ignored. As Hanley's men began to enter the TOC, Tom gave the order to surrender.

"Nobody moves or does anything foolish, and nobody gets hurt," he told them. "We're not Confeds."

Faced with almost sixty armed grunts with ready weapons, none of the staff or techs chose to be heroes. Several of the officers looked as though they were thinking about it.

"All we want to do is get some things cleared up with General Trahn," Tom said, hoping the itchy-looking officers would give him the chance.

Markowitz's arrival with the bound and gagged Furlann in tow seemed to do more to cow them than the weapons or anything Tom had said. Under the glare of hostile eyes, a squad of Hanley's men moved through the TOC, forcibly dumping techies from the Matrix by jacking them out. When the TOC was secure, Tom directed Andy to the main ops console. Andy scurried to the seat and jacked in.

They'd done it!

Or had they? Trahn wasn't present; neither was Jordan or Lessem. Tom hadn't really expected to catch Lessem. He'd hoped for Jordan, but could live with the disappointment as long as they got Trahn. But the general was nowhere to be seen. "Where's Trahn?"

When no one volunteered the information, Tom repeated his question, this time directing it specifically to the senior officer present, a colonel named Addison.

"We want to speak to the general, Colonel Addison. You *will* tell us where he is."

"Go to hell," Addison snarled. "Anyone who talks to these men will—" Addison shut up with a whuff as Jackson jabbed the butt of his weapon into the colonel's stomach.

The sergeant finished for him. "—will, if he's very lucky, not be up on the same charges of attempted murder the general's facing."

The sergeant's attempt at intimidation didn't work. No one spoke.

Markowitz whispered in Tom's ear. "He's got to be nearby or they wouldn't be so closed-mouthed. If he was far away, they'd be gloating about it."

Tom had reached the same conclusion. The general's personal van was closed; he'd only seen Trahn close it up when he went in to sleep. Addison was still curled on the ground, puking, so Tom asked another officer.

"All right, Major Ridley, your turn. The general's in his van, isn't he?"

"No," Ridley said, but his eyes flickered to the van, belying his words.

"By himself?" Tom asked.

"He's not in there," Ridley insisted.

"Sounds like Major Ridley here's an accessory after the fact," Markowitz said.

"We just want the general to answer some questions," Tom said.

"Are the charges true?" Ridley asked.

"I'm the one he tried to have killed," Tom said.

Ridley searched Tom's face and made a decision. "The general wanted to rest before the assault on the Comper-held Metro stations began at 2400 hours."

Tom hadn't known about that operation. The Center's clock said that jump-off time was only minutes away. If the general didn't issue the orders, the assault would hang fire. Maybe this mad ploy had a chance to do some good. If all was in place . . .

Andy gave a thumbs-up, signaling that he'd successfully taken control of the MilNet access for Trahn's command. Tom nodded affirmation. His mouth was dry as he activated the direct line to General Trahn's van.

"General, you asked to be called when the next phase of the operation was ready to begin."

The general's response was quick, but puzzled. "Rocquette?"

The ramp descended and Trahn emerged from his van. He stood at the top of the ramp and took in the situation with a glance, surveying the scene as calmly and coolly as if he were in charge. His icy glare made more than one of Hanley's grunts flinch. Tom knew how they felt. Despite everything that had happened, it felt wrong to be holding weapons trained on a general, especially one as decorated and revered as Nathan Trahn.

Trahn scowled. "I could have you shot for this, Rocquette."

"You already tried that once, General. It didn't work. Furlann told us everything. Your power play's over."

"You're the one making a power play," Trahn said without missing a beat. "I don't know what your game is, Rocquette, but neither you nor anyone foolish enough to go along with you will profit from it."

"We know what's going on, General," Hanley said as he brought Furlann forward. The lieutenant unstrapped the muzzle and pulled off the hood so Trahn would have no doubt about who'd informed on him. He shoved Furlann forward. The mage stumbled and landed in a heap at the general's feet.

At Tom's signal, Andy initiated the prepared data feed and brought it up onto all of the TOC's monitors. The recording started with Tom recounting Colonel Lessem's orders and Tom's refusal to go along, and was followed by Cinqueda's record of Furlann's story. With Furlann accusing him from all sides, Trahn remained unmoved.

"False accusations and a doctored tape of Captain Furlann," Trahn said. He helped the bound Furlann regain her feet.

"We can show otherwise," Tom told him.

Trahn shrugged. "Coerced lies, then. Look at the way you've brought Captain Furlann here. I'm sure she'll have a tale to tell when you're all hauled before a court martial."

"Some of us are civvies, General," Markowitz said.

"Criminal court will do for you. Treason is still a capital crime."

"Funny you should mention treason," Markowitz said. "Hey, kid, you get the hookup with the nets yet?"

"Open and pumping," Andy replied.

"Make sure you give them all the files. Let's let everyone see how the good general here engineered the riots for his own self-aggrandizement." Markowitz returned his attention to Trahn. "You threatened us with a trial, and that may yet come to pass; but you, General, are being tried now. By the public you've so recklessly endangered. This sorry scene is going out, along with all the data we've got, on a dump feed to the media *and* to MilNet."

"It's true, General," Furlann said. "Rocquette's got the goods on you." She took a step away from the general, as if to dissociate herself from him.

He ignored her, spearing Tom with his eyes. "You don't understand, do you? Don't bother to answer. It'll only be more lies. I'd ask you why, but there's no point. I can only assume that your heart is as warped as your father's body. You're just like him—no true soldier. You're just another symptom of the disease rotting our country from within."

"The only disease is in your mind," Tom said, sorry to believe that it was true.

"You're wrong, Rocquette. Very wrong. And what you're doing here is wrong. It will cost you dearly. The price for treason is high, and I'm going to see that you pay it in full."

This wasn't going as Tom had expected. Trahn was acting as though he were still in control.

"Tom?"

Andy's voice shook with uncertainty. Fearful of some unforeseen complication, Tom asked, "What is it?"

"There's a scrambled call coming in. It's Air Force One."

"Put it on monitor one," Trahn ordered.

The big screen switched from the outflow they'd arranged to a head-and-shoulders shot of a very distressed President Steele. Trahn drew himself to attention and faced the monitor. "What's going on, General? We're getting some very disturbing transmissions from your headquarters. The nets are buzzing."

"There's no need to be concerned, Mr. President."

Steele opened and shut his mouth, apparently aborting a

planned remark. His eyes widened. "No need? You keep talking like that and I'll be sure you *are* insane, as half the media hacks are already calling you."

"We're experiencing another attack by the Confed disinformation deckers," Trahn said. "It's being dealt with."

Tom had to wonder if the general believed what he was telling the President. Trahn *sounded* as though he believed it.

"General, we're talking about transmissions coming from your own headquarters. Security has been compromised. This does *not* look good, and I need answers for the questions I'm being asked. You're putting me in an awkward position, to say the least."

"As I said, Mr. President, the matter is being dealt with. For the moment, I need your support. The country needs your support. We need to continue with our program."

To Tom, the President looked distinctly uncomfortable. "A lot of people are telling me *you* are the problem, General."

"They don't understand the situation, Mr. President."

"Hell, Trahn! I'm not sure *I* understand the situation any more. This isn't working out the way you said it would."

"You must have faith, Mr. President."

Tom edged over to Andy's seat. "Is this going out too?"

"Every word."

"Does the President know?"

"I don't see how he wouldn't."

That put a different light on things. An awful lot of what Steel was saying sounded like butt-covering. Trahn was not as solidly backed as he might like to think.

President Steele squared his shoulders. "We've been blunt in the past, General, so I'm going to be blunt now. General Trahn, are you a traitor?"

"No, sir!" Trahn's voice rang with conviction.

What definition was Trahn using?

"And you didn't do what these people are claiming?" Steele asked.

Trahn sighed. "Can't you see what's going on?"

"*Make* me see, General," Steele said. "The seat is getting very warm beneath my butt."

"We're doing what needs to be done," Trahn began. He launched into an impassioned speech justifying what he'd done. Along the way, he admitted to just about everything

Tom and the runners had uncovered about the plan to use the Comp Army riot as a pretext to draw attention to the Army's "plight." According to Trahn, it was all for a good and necessary cause. The sacrifice was justified, to make the UCAS strong. "This is all about making you, and everyone, see the truth that needs to be seen, so that this country can return to the greatness we once knew."

"I've heard enough," the President said, stony-faced. "As Commander-in-Chief, I am ordering the immediate cessation of military operations in the Federal District. All military units will stand down, and all officers will report to their bases, pending a full investigation of this matter. The slaughter will stop."

As the President gave his orders, Trahn grew very still.

"It's out on MilNet," Andy crowed. "Along with Trahn's dismissal. Southeast Military District is now under the command of General Ravierez."

"I hope for your sake that your name will be cleared, General. But I must do what I must. I'm sure you understand that," Steele said. The Presidential channel went dark.

They'd done it. Tom felt a little stunned.

Trahn's expression was hard. In a barely audible voice, he said, "Now we see the real traitor."

Trahn spun, shouldering Furlann into the van interior as he slapped at the ramp control. The hydraulics whined as the pair disappeared into the van's cabin. Someone fired his weapon at the fleeing general, the shells spanging off the armored door as it slammed shut. Embarrassed, Tom realized *he* was the shooter. He lowered his weapon.

What did it matter? Trahn wasn't going anywhere. The TOC van didn't have a connector between the cabin and the driver's position, and there wasn't a driver anyway; Tom had made sure of that. Trahn wasn't going anywhere. Sooner or later he'd have to come out.

"All right, show's over. It's mop-up from here," Tom said. "Cut the media access."

But some of Trahn's officers still looked surly. Tom whispered to Hanley to watch them with special care. Then he turned his attention to making sure the TOC was receiving confirmations of the stand-down order from all units.

"Trahn's accessing the commo channels," Andy said.

"Show me," Tom ordered. It was not an unexpected move. Andy's fingers flew across the console. "Green screen is the commands he's giving. Blue screen is the feed from his transmitter. The yellow screen will detail whatever channels and accesses he tries to use."

Tom watched lines of computer code march by as Trahn identified himself to the TOC computer. When it accepted him, his face appeared on the blue-edged screen. Was he trying to send a call for help?

"Open MilNet access," Trahn's voice was calm again. "This is Trahn. Execute Plan Rational. Repeat, execute Plan Rational. Confirmation code follows."

Tom opened the direct line to the van. "What is Plan Rational, General?"

Trahn's face disappeared from the monitor; he'd sent his message and cut the connection. His voice continued over the direct-line speaker.

"The name is self-explanatory. Those of us who understand the insanity into which our country has slipped have put together a program to bring us back to the right course, the rational course."

"A military junta?" It seemed to Tom that his grandfather had been right about secret cabals within the military.

"I'm sure some of the media's left-coast refugees will call it that. I won't deny that our core of concerned people was built within the military, but our coalition is not limited to those in current service, nor even those who've spent time in uniform. We have a broad base of support among those unwilling to be led like sheep to the slaughtering pens."

"A rose by anther name," Markowitz said. "It sounds un-American to me."

"This country's first president was a general," Trahn responded. "Its greatest presidents have all been military men or civilians wise enough to listen to military men. Having served is no bar to understanding the greater politics that drive the nation; rather, it is a distinct advantage. I hardly need point out that the citizen soldier is one of this country's proudest traditions."

"Your take on that is as warped as your views on other things," Markowitz said. "Your coup doesn't have a prayer."

"Already, trustworthy men are moving," Trahn said confidently. "The president has obliged us by being so accessible. By now his plane has been shot down, and there will be no survivors. Given the current problems, I'm sure the perpetrators were assassins from the Confederated States. A very imprudent move on their part. We could go to war over it. I will be telling them that shortly."

"So that means you will be taking over the government?" Tom asked.

"Only temporarily. This *is* a democracy. I'm sure the public will select a good man when the choices are made clear."

"And *I'm* sure you're not going to get the chance." Tom turned to Andy. "Patch my mike onto the secure channel and put the link onto his monitor."

When the channel opened, Tom addressed the worried man on the screen. "Mr. President, you *were* listening to the feed?"

"Major Rocquette, I was. It appears that whatever the truth of your earlier allegations, your precipitous action was justified. You've done your country a service today. I'm afraid the immediate reward is something of a burden, though. I would like you to take charge of the command center until General Ravierez arrives. Hold General Trahn in custody until then. If you can arrange for any of his confederates to be taken into custody, do so." Steele cleared his throat. "And, Major . . ."

"Yes, sir?"

"You have my personal thanks. It's good to know there are still loyal men like yourself in this country."

"Thank you, sir," Tom said politely. He hadn't done this for Steele.

When the conversation with the President was over, Tom told Trahn, "As you can see, the president remains alive. You've revealed your plot and gotten nowhere. Your confederates outside the TOC heard nothing, nada, not a word."

"*I* am controlling transmissions," Andy added archly. "No transmissions go out of this place without my say-so. That includes your access, General. You really should have read the responses from your access attempts; you would have seen that you weren't going anywhere."

"You're isolated and exposed, General. It's all over," Tom said, glad that it was.

"You're all fools if you think this will end it!" Trahn shouted. "I—"

The connection cut in a burst of static. Tom's eyes went to the general's van. Something had happened in there.

No one spoke; the consoles hummed to themselves in the hush that had come over the center. The message board beeped steadily, asking for attention to the calls lighting up its board.

The soft click of the ramp release sounded abnormally loud. The ramp of the general's van swung down, hitting ground with a crash. The rush of air displaced by the ramp's fall carried with it the stench of burnt plastic and the sweet odor of cooked pork. Chafing her wrists, Furlann strolled down the ramp.

"What the frag did you do?" Tom asked, appalled. He had a very good idea of the answer. Trahn was likely the only connection to tie her with the plot.

"You heard him," Furlann said. "His own words condemned him as a traitor, according to the laws of the land. Death is the reward for treason in time of war. Anyway, it was him or me."

"This ain't a war," Andy point out.

"Try downloading reality, kid," Furlann suggested to him.

Strange words, Tom thought, for someone twisting reality to suit her own needs.

>>>>>WFDC LIVE FEED
  –[08:00:01/8-30-55]
DEECEE AM MORNINGRIDE WITH JESS BOK [BOKX-345]

Bok: "Good morning, good morning, GOOD MORNING! So, how's it feel out there, all you Morningriders? You all happy to be back in the pack, doing the old bumper-to-bumper crawl in to work? Honk if you're happy!

"Sounds like there's a *lot* of happy people out there. Keep them pearlies showing, Morningriders. Chief Commissioner Ericson *promises* that Metro will be back in service by Monday at the latest. Let's hope so, we need to get these amateur commuters off the road and back on the rails where they belong. Just kidding, all you first-timers.

"Hey, friends. I know you're all headed for the old grind, but don't forget to open up a sidebar or slip on the old walkie-talkie-man at ten for Sherry Bentfield's *Our Town and Country.* Sherry has got a *nova*-hot guest today: none other than *the* hero of the hour, Captain Rita Furlann of the Thaumaturgic Corps. That's right! The lovely lady who saved all our behinds from old General Runaway Trahn will be telling you the *real* story behind the media blips, and yakking direct with *you* on the WFDC 'Commune With You' lines. Be there! Hey, I know *I'm* gonna be listening.

"Till then, keep your eyes out for blocked roads around pockets of unenlightened Compers. Even though the FedPols and Army are getting help from concerned corporate citizens like Telestrian Industries East and Saeder-Krupp, there are still holdouts out there who haven't gotten the message, or the PTTS gas. If you want to avoid those little trouble spots, give us a call for the latest datafeed updates. SMALL CHARGE APPLIES.

"Remember, we're in business to get you there.

"We'll cut over now to Johnny Willard, who's been promising us relief from this hot sticky for weeks. Johnny just told me that this time the weather imps are going to come through. Chiptruth, Morningriders. That's what he said. Hey, Johnny—"<<<<<

25

Tom killed the car's radio as he took the off ramp at Glebe Road. He was almost at his destination and, having gotten out of the traffic, didn't need the distraction. Besides, he was tired of listening to the propagandists working so very hard.

He had no trouble finding a spot in a parking lot behind the site. The building wasn't a courthouse, or even a police station or military installation, but it was where he was going to give his formal statements on the matters of the last two weeks. It looked like an ordinary office building, and maybe it was, most of the time; its identifying sign had been removed recently. Whatever it had been, today it was where the President's Special Commissioners were meeting. Tom had already spent days answering questions; today's exercise was a mere formality. They'd promised him that after today he could get on with his life.

He wasn't the only one scheduled to appear before the Commissioners. Another vehicle, an old, dark blue Toyota Epsilon four-door, pulled into the lot. Markowitz opened the driver's door.

"Good timing," he said.

Andy and Kit got out of the back. The car shifted noisily on its springs as the fourth passenger got out, a bulky ork in a trench coat and slouch hat as out of place in the sultry morning heat as a swimsuit on a battlefield. Chrome glinted from beneath the ork's brows. Tom had to take his eyes off the ork as Andy came bounding up to greet him like a long-lost brother. Which, in a way, he was.

"Nice uniform," Andy said. "But you really ought to buff up the other decorations to go with the new one."

Tom looked down at the Presidential Citation star. Andy was right; it didn't look as though it belonged. Tom didn't mind. The disparity between the old and the new suited him. After all, Furlann had a star just like his, gotten in the same ceremony when Steele had pinned this one on Tom's chest. So much for the Citation being a badge of honor. He put it out of his mind.

"What's with the ork? Where's Cinqueda?"

"She was add-on," Markowitz said. "Shamgar's a regular. Say hello, Shamgar."

Shamgar glowered without a word. Once Tom would have taken such insolence as a personal affront, or ignored it as unimportant. Today he saw that the ork's attitude was directed at Markowitz and the situation. Tom could understand that and sympathized with it, but he found it odd sympathizing with an ork. But the ork hadn't been a part of what had brought them here as the other street samurai had. "What about Cinqueda's statement?"

"She believes she's already made it," Kit said.

Cinqueda hadn't talked to the Commissioners at all. If she wanted to let her recording stand for itself and not back it up, it was her call. He'd respect her choice. She'd more than earned that respect.

As they entered the building, Markowitz said, "You hear the latest? Christian Randolph was drugged by Confed insurrectionists. They took over his Compensation Army as part of a plan to stir up trouble in Washington and terrify the populace into looking south for salvation. The Confeds wanted to use the government's failure to quell the riots as an excuse to nab North Virginia and the sub-Potomac region of the Federal District—for the safety of the people, don't you know. Randolph had the poor fortune to become their puppet. The drugs induced megalomania and drove him over the edge. That's where all that wild rhetoric he was spouting near the end came from, and it's why he did that no-one-takes-me-alive immolation at the Block. Very sad story. He was an honest man, if somewhat naïve."

Tom wondered about that. "Is it true?"

"Who knows? It's raised a lot of sympathy for the Compers. The legitimate Compers, that is. Congress has decided to settle on the compensation claims that brought Randolph and his marchers to Washington in the first place. Ten cents on the dollar."

"Doesn't seem just to me," Andy said.

What was justice?

The collusion between Telestrian and the Confeds was being buried, in the light of the corporation's decision to arm its security forces with a full suite of non-lethal and low-lethality riot control gear and to put those forces at the government's disposal for stopping the violence. How could one fault such civic-mindedness and public spirit, especially when it prompted other corporations to do the same? The influx of manpower alone would have been enough to quell the rioters. It was the help that Tom had sought from them and been refused. Now it washed away their sins. Justice!

While they sat in an office, awaiting the Commissions' pleasure, he asked, "Any new word on Governor Jefferson?"

"Yeah," Markowitz said. "You want what's going to go out on NewsNet, or the truth?"

Tom sighed. "I suppose it was too much to hope for, that there would be only one story."

"Much too much to hope for," Markowitz agreed. "Officially, Jefferson's dead. Actually, he wasn't aboard the Orion when it went down. He'd gotten word from a source in Trahn's headquarters that his venture in revising geography wasn't going to be allowed to go to completion. He knew he was playing in the rough boys' league and decided to find a rock and crawl under it."

"So where is he? Atlanta?"

"Don't know." Markowitz shrugged. "If he ran south, he's stupider than I thought. The Confeds don't like spending money without return, and *Mr.* Jefferson ain't worth anything compared to Governor Jefferson."

The Commissioners interviewed Tom last. When he came out he was surprised to find the others still present.

"What do you do now?" Markowitz asked.

"Short term? Have lunch." Tom was hungry and it was well past lunch time.

"Okay. We'll buy," Markowitz said. "But actually, I was thinking somewhat longer term."

Longer? Tom wanted to see his grandparents. Talk to his grandfather. "Finish my leave."

"So you're thinking you're going to stay in?" Andy asked.

Actually, Tom *hadn't* thought about it. It hadn't *occurred* to him to think about it. The Army had been his life for so long that he just didn't think about living any other way.

"It won't be easy," Markowitz said.

"And what we just went through *was*?"

"Not the same at all. Trahn has friends, who won't like what you've done."

"Right now, Trahn hasn't got a friend in the country. Nobody was his buddy, nobody talked to him, nobody hung with him, nobody shared his politics, nobody knew he was going to do what he did, and most of all, nobody ever heard of Plan Rational. It looks like all of Trahn's rational friends were too rational for him. They cut their losses and dumped him as soon as it was obvious he was going down."

"Like Captain Furlann?" Andy asked.

"Very much like that," Tom agreed sourly.

"They're not going to change their stripes over this," Markowitz said. "Taking Trahn down bought you enemies."

"Maybe so." But was that so bad? His grandfather had told him that a man was measured by his enemies, not his friends. If Tom had made enemies of people who believed what Trahn had believed, that was okay. Justice of a sort, even.

Andy pulled Markowitz aside as soon as he could. "I think you ought to drop it."

"Why? I'm just getting started."

"Tom's made his decision. He believes he has a place. I don't want you to take that from him."

"It was your idea to try to get him to go freelance."

"So I was wrong. Some people aren't made for the streets."

"Oh?" Markowitz sounded suspicious. "Are we talking about him or you?"

"Him."

"So you're not going back to Telestrian, now that you've been cleared in the run against the Montjoy project? Isn't that why you traded the Jefferson files back to them?"

Andy hadn't known Markowitz knew about that. He might know the fact, but he needn't know the reason. "Go back? I don't think so! So what if they cleared my name? Andy Walker is still officially dead."

"Doesn't take much computer power to fix that. They can give you another identity if you ask."

"Oh, they'd give me another identity, but I doubt it'd be one I'd like. From what I picked up on the Shadowland net, Osborne's a vindictive guy. If I go back, my identity will be mud. I could end up really dead. Hey, I got their number.

"Right now, I see opportunities in other places. For example, Marksman, your team doesn't have a decker *or* a rigger, and I do both. You need me."

Markowitz took some more convincing, but in the end he agreed. And why not? After all, Andy was a shadowrunner.

Caimbeul was late.

Though I wasn't surprised, I was annoyed. It wasn't as though I were looking forward to seeing him, but if you drop in on someone with "important" news, you'd bloody well better be on time.

I'd made tea with all the things Caimbeul liked. Scones, of course, with lemon curd. Those ridiculous little sandwiches with the crusts cut off, slices of cake, tarts. He had a sweet tooth. But now the sandwiches had gone hard and the cake was stale.

I'd switched from tea to sherry, then to scotch. And still no Caimbeul.

Finally, six hours after he'd said he'd arrive, I heard the crunch of tires across my gravel.

I waited until I saw him emerge alone from the car before opening the door. Even though I had security sensors, you can't be too cautious.

"Prompt as usual, I see," I said.

"Ah, Aina, still charming as ever," he replied. "No 'how are you? Why are you late?' You wound me."

I snorted.

"Please, spare me the usual dancing," I said. "It's cold out here. Come inside."

I turned and went into the house. Behind me I could hear him getting his bag and shutting the doors to the car.

"Lock the door and switch the system back on," I called over my shoulder.

He muttered something under his breath, but oddly enough he did as I asked. I went into the great room where I'd started a fire earlier that evening. Sometime between the sherry and the scotch.

"Did you leave that woman at home?" I asked.

"Yes," he said as he shrugged off his coat and tossed it on the couch. He flipped down into one of the wing chairs in front of the fire. I handed him a snifter of brandy and poured myself another scotch.

"I'm surprised. I'd've thought you'd bring her along to iron your shirts. Or something."

"Or something?" he asked. Coy, that one.

"Whatever it is you do with girls young enough to be your great-great-great-great-great-great-great-great-great-great-great-great-great-great-great-great-great-great-great—"

He held up his hands. "I get the picture."

"Oh, please, I don't want to hear about your peculiarities in that area."

"Do you care?" he asked. "What goes on between us is none of your business."

I turned away from him, stung by his remarks. Of course his life wasn't my concern. It hadn't been for centuries. But old habits die hard.

The silence stretched out between us. Once I enjoyed them. But now it felt awkward and tense. I longed for things to be as they once had, but it was far too late for that. As usual.

"I had a terrible time getting through UK customs," he said at last.

"Were you carrying anything?" I asked as I turned and walked toward him. He gestured for me to sit across from him as though this were his house and not mine.

"No."

"Made any enemies in the UK lately?"

He smiled then. I was glad he wasn't wearing his makeup. That awful mask he'd adopted out of some perverse sense of humor. Wicked Caimbeul.

We chatted then about meaningless things. Things to distract us from the free-floating tensions of a failed romance and too many years of history.

The fire had begun to die down and we were both a little muzzy.

"So," I said. But it came out more like "show." "Why all the mystery about your visit?"

Part of me, foolishly, hoped that his surprise had to do with the sudden realization that he'd been momentarily insane all those years ago when he'd left me.

"I beat them," he said, his voice dropping into a slightly drunken, conspiratorial tone. "You've been saying that NAN would bring them back with all that blood magic. And you were right, Aina."

I felt a cold finger touch my heart. Suddenly the alcohol warmth fled and I was wide-awake sober.

"What are you saying?" I tried to keep my voice from shaking, but I failed. He didn't notice, though.

"They tried to get back, but I stopped them," he said. "Ah, well, I did have some help. A group of shadowrunners I enlisted. We went and played our little games on the metaplanes. God, it was fantastic. I haven't felt so alive since—I don't know when. Can you imagine it? Just my wits against them.

"Oh, there was some business with them recently in Maui, but that was easy enough to handle."

He gave a pleased laugh. Full and rich. I hadn't heard that tone in his voice in so long I'd almost forgotten he could sound that way. Had it been anything else to bring this joy about I would have been delighted, but all I wanted to do was shake him. Hard. Laughing and enjoying this ... this catastrophe.

It was just like him to think he'd finished them off. What hubris. What ego.

"... And then I told them the story about Thayla," he was saying. "And I sent them on a quest to find her voice."

"Did it work?"

"Of course it did," he said, indignantly. "What do you take me for? A dilettante? I know we've had our disagreements, but even you can see what a feat this is."

"What I see is that your ego is out of bounds again. In your endless fascination with being involved in the machinations behind things, you've missed the point. As usual."

"You're jealous," he said.

"What?"

"You're jealous."

"Of what?" I was baffled at this sudden turn in the conversation.

"Of me. Of my power. You couldn't stand it when I surpassed your abilities."

"Don't be asinine."

"Oh, do you deny it?" he asked. He had a competitive, smirky expression on his face that I wanted to slap off.

"I won't even dignify that with an answer. The things

which you pursue, Caimbeul, are vainglorious and, ultimately, irrelevant."

"That's something else you do," he said. "You always call me Caimbeul. I haven't been called by that name in three hundred years."

"Very well, Harlequin," I said. "But this is all beside the point. The point is you think the Horrors have returned and that you have beaten them single handedly, don't you? Or at least once. I have no idea what actually happened in Maui because you always leave things out when it's not all about you."

He gave me an annoyed look.

"Very well, Aina," he said sullenly. "There was a group of kahunas using blood magic on Haleakala. They managed to open a portal—some of the Enemy even managed to get through. But they were stopped in time. They were sent back into the void.

"See, nothing to worry about."

"Let's see. First, you encounter them on the metaplanes. You manage to 'defeat' them there. Next, some of them manage to breach this plane. And you think they've been dealt with?

"Well, I've been having dreams lately and I think you're wrong. I think you failed."

He laughed.

"Aina has a dream and we're all supposed to tremble in our boots. Is that it?"

"I had forgotten this charming side to your personality, Caimbeul. I've been right before."

"And you've been wrong."

"Not often."

He didn't have an answer for that.

"I thought you would be thrilled at this news," he said at last. "You're the only one who still understands what it was like. Back then. During the Scourge."

I shrugged. "There's always Alachia," I said. "And Ehran. Oh, but I forgot about your tiff with him. Surely they remember."

"Alachia sees it differently than we do. She always has. And Ehran isn't worth a pimple on a troll's butt. As for the others—"

"Don't hold back, Caimbeul, how do you really feel?"

After giving me a nasty look, he went and refilled his glass.

"Bring me some water," I said.

In a moment, he placed a tumbler in my hand and settled himself opposite me again. Another long silence played out between us. The water was cool and washed the strong taste of the whiskey out of my mouth.

"Tell me what happened," I said at last. "The first time."

He didn't answer me for a moment. Then he spoke.

"They were constructing a bridge, of sorts, using the energy spike from the Ghost Dance as a locator. They are as foul as I remembered, Aina. No, perhaps worse, for it has been so long since I'd seen them that they'd begun to blur in my memory.

"I had to test the runners to be sure they had what it took to stand against the Enemy. For the most part they succeeded. One fell during the trials, but they accomplished what I set them to do. They retrieved the Voice, but didn't make it back to the bridge before a man named Darke captured me. The bastard was working with the Enemy and had been following me across the metaplanes the whole time. And I'd thought I was tracking him.

"He was performing blood magic to corrupt the site. How many children were sacrificed I'll never know. But Thayla sang and the enemy fell back, and now we're safe."

I almost choked on my water.

"Wait a minute," I said. "That all ties up a little too neatly. Thayla may be able to keep them at bay, but who will protect her from people like Darke?"

"Oh, some of the runners stayed with her," he said casually.

"But you didn't volunteer for that duty," I said.

"Don't be ridiculous," he said. "I'm far too valuable to be tied to one spot like that. Besides, as long as she's there, they can't get through."

"Not there, at any rate," I said.

"And you're sure the creatures were driven back in Maui?"

"Of course," he said.

And how I wanted to believe him.

I stared into the fire. Long ago, according to our legends, Thayla's voice had driven the Horrors off. She had sacrificed herself for her people, like any great monarch would. Perhaps Caimbeul was right. Maybe he had accomplished it. Maybe he had driven them back. For now.

I relaxed a little. Maybe now there would be time to plan. To prepare. To warn those who needed to know.

The telecom beeped, startling me out of my thoughts.

"Who could be calling at this hour?" I wondered aloud.

"It might be for me," he said. "I left this number."

Oh, splendid, I thought. *Just what I need. Caimbeul's little friends with my restricted number.*

"Hello," I said into the old-fashioned videoless receiver I'd had installed in this room.

There was a long pause, then a loud burst of static. I jerked back, dropping the receiver onto the floor.

"Aiña," I heard. The sound filled the room. An impossibility. And, oh sweet mother, I knew that voice.

"Aiña," it said. "I have come back. I have come for you." Then the line went dead.

"What was that?" Caimbeul demanded.

The room was cold. Colder than the dead of winter. Colder than the grave. For I knew from long experience that there were things worse than death.

"That," I said, my voice shaking, "was the past come back to haunt us, Harlequin. You didn't stop them from coming through on Maui, my dear. One of them is here. Now. And he's coming for me."

BEFORE THERE WAS A SIXTH WORLD THERE WAS A FOURTH.

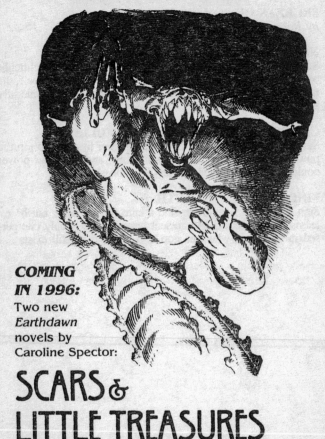

COMING IN 1996: Two new *Earthdawn* novels by Caroline Spector:

SCARS & LITTLE TREASURES

· The prequels to her incredible 1995 *Shadowrun* novel *Worlds Without End*.
· Read about Aina's first encounters with the Horror Ysrthgrathe in the Fourth World.

Don't forget to read the explosive trilogy which launched the Shadowrun universe!

SECRETS OF POWER TRILOGY
by Robert N. Charrette

NEVER DEAL WITH A DRAGON
Sam Verner must find his missing sister and flee the clutches of the Renraku conglomerate. But to extract himself, he must seek the help of a dragon—and dragons don't generally help people for free.

CHOOSE YOUR ENEMIES CAREFULLY
Sam must accept his destiny as a shaman in order to tap the power he needs, but what awaits him and his new power could be a secret even darker than the shadows.

FIND YOUR OWN TRUTH
Sam travels to Australia to find a cure for his sister, but he releases an unexpected and ancient terror. There is only one person in the world who can stop it. That is, if he still exists . . .

And don't miss these action packed titles

NOSFERATU
by Carl Sargent and Marc Gascoigne

Everywhere Elf Serrin Shamandar goes he feels evil eyes, *elven* eyes, watching him. He learns of a plan to wipe out humanity, and becomes desperate to confront the mastermind behind it, an enemy who has been waiting for more than three hundred years . . .

BURNING BRIGHT
by Tom Dowd

Kyle Teller is hired by the CEO of Truman Technologies to find his missing son. Finding the boy should be a cinch, except Kyle doesn't know what terrible parasitic power lurks and multiplies beneath the city of Chicago.

WHO HUNTS THE HUNTER
By Nyx Smith

From the distant forests of Maine comes the deadly weretiger, Striper. From the shadows of the South Bronx comes the dedicated shaman, Bandit. From the nightmare streets of Newark come Monk and Minx, seeking Life itself. The roles of predator and prey are turned around in a game more deadly than any of them expected.

HOUSE OF THE SUN
by Nigel Findley

Dirk Montgomery finds himself repaying an old debt in the Kingdom of Hawai'i. But he runs into a dark side of the tropical paradise and tries to stay ahead of the factions competing for control of the islands; the magacorps, the government, the rebels and yakuza. Plus dragons, elves, new friends . . . and old enemies.

COMING IN APRIL 1996
BLACK MADONNA
by Carl Sargent and Marc Gascoigne

Leo is a brilliant scientist and artist. He's also an immortal elf with the Real Truth, and he wants to tell the world. When he blackmails every major megacorp for money, people begin to take notice. Some of them just want answers. Some of them want him dead. But is the world ready for the Real Truth?

ABOUT THE AUTHOR

Robert N. Charrette has written over seven novels, selling more than half a million copies all over the world. The extraordinarily well-received and popular *SECRETS OF POWER TRILOGY: NEVER DEAL WITH A DRAGON, CHOOSE YOUR ENEMIES CAREFULLY* and *FIND YOUR OWN TRUTH* alone garnered sales of over 350,000. These books launched the Shadowrun® fictional line, following Sam Verner across the globe and telling the technomagical tales of his coming to grips with the new Awakened World in which *flesh* and *machine* commingle.

Charrette has also written several books for FASA's BattleTech® universe of awesome battle machines, including *WOLVES ON THE BORDER*, due to be re-released in the summer of 1996, and *HEIR TO THE DRAGON* slated for re-release in the fall of 1996.

He had a hand in creating the Shadowrun® game universe and spent his early career as a game designer, art director and commercial sculptor. Currently he is developing other settings for fictional exploration, including tales set in another realm of revenant magic as chronicled in *A PRINCE AMONG MEN, A KING BENEATH THE MOUNTAIN*, and *A KNIGHT AMONG KNAVES*, a trilogy published by Warner Books.

Charrette currently resides in Virginia with his wife, Elizabeth, who must suffer his constant complaints of insufficient time as he continues to crank out the novels as well as sculpt the occasional collector's miniature. He is active in a living medieval history group which reenacts English life in the late fourteenth century. He also keeps abreast of the latest developments in dinosaurian paleontology and pre-Tokugawa Japanese history—two of his favorite topics.

The Roc Frequent Readers Club

BUY TWO ROC BOOKS AND GET ONE SF/FANTASY NOVEL FREE!

Check the free title you wish to receive (subject to availability):

YOU'VE READ THE FICTION, NOW PLAY THE GAME!

S·E·C·O·N·D   E·D·I·T·I·O·N

WELCOME TO THE FUTURE.

Magic has returned to the world. Man now shares the earth with creatures of myth and legend. Dragons soar the skies. Elves, dwarves, trolls and orks walk the streets.

Play **Shadowrun** and **you'll** walk the streets of 2053. When the mega-corporations want something done but don't want to dirty their hands, it's a shadowrun they need, and they'll come to you. Officially you don't exist, but the demand for your services is high. You might be a decker, sliding through the visualized databases of giant corporations, spiriting away the only thing of real value—information. Perhaps you are a street samurai, an enforcer whose combat skills make you the ultimate urban predator. Or a magician wielding the magical energies that surround the Earth.

That's exactly the kind of firepower you'll need to make a shadowrun...

AVAILABLE AT FINE BOOKSTORES AND GAME STORES EVERYWHERE!

YOUR OPINION CAN MAKE A DIFFERENCE!

LET US KNOW WHAT *YOU* THINK.

Send this completed survey to us and enter a weekly drawing to win a special prize!

1.) Do you play any of the following role-playing games?
Shadowrun _____ Earthdawn _____ BattleTech _____

2.) Did you play any of the games before you read the novels?
Yes _____ No _____

3.) How many novels have you read in each of the following series?
Shadowrun _____ Earthdawn _____ BattleTech _____

4.) What other game novel lines do you read?
TSR _____ White Wolf _____ Other (Specify) _____

5.) Who is your favorite FASA author?
_____

6.) Which book did you take this survey from?
_____

7.) Where did you buy this book?
Bookstore _____ Game Store _____ Comic Store _____
FASA Mail Order _____ Other (Specify) _____

8.) Your opinion of the book (please print)
_____
_____
_____

Name _____ Age _____ Gender _____
Address _____
City _____ State _____ Country _____ Zip _____

Send this page or a photocopy of it to:
FASA Corporation
Editorial/Novels
1100 W. Cermak Suite B-305
Chicago, IL 60608